ORPHAN STREET

ORPHAN STREET

ANDRE LANGEVIN

Translated by Alan Brown

J. B. Lippincott Company
Philadelphia and New York

1

Ever so small and white, the handkerchief floats down to a square of marble within the great circle of light from the stained-glass window, and when the little girl's foot reaches out to touch it, it slips aside, pulled by some invisible string. The woman had been shaken by a strange kind of sob, like the muffled barking of a sleeping dog, and the hanky had slipped from her fingers. At the same moment the organ began to play softly, with the stops that produce effects of distant flutes, like those that puff out the cheeks of the cherubs painted on the vaulted ceiling.

He had barely had time to look up to where the music came from when the little girl, crying, held out her hand to the lady, also crying, and disappeared behind where he was, followed by other communicants in mourning, all with plaster-pale faces under their black veils. The hanky, after another little leap, comes to rest near the catafalque.

Maybe it's Balibou who's found him at last and is trying to get his attention! Then why doesn't it come this way? No, it can't be. Even Balibou hadn't been told. He's probably taken up residence in the big house and is going to wait for him there, dying of boredom and hunger, wasting his powers away by taking on a thousand different shapes in which nobody will recognize him, until he's no more than the shadow of the tree branch in moonlight over the empty bed. No one knows how Balibou can fly from one story to another without even pausing for a breath, faster than you can turn the pages of a book. Except Nicolas, of course, who heard the stories one night because they were in the last two beds in the long row, near the door, and Nicolas had been his friend for days, but then they'd quickly changed his place and made him sleep beside the "sailboat," the curtained cage where Pigfoot spied, and rattled her keys and chains, and kept her whip. Balibou had told Nicolas of the little black boy and his mother, the giant white panther, and how she would carry him gently in her mouth through a cactus jungle where no one could go without being ripped to shreds, with two banana trees at the centre of it, where apples, oranges, chocolate, and milk were also to be had; and the little green polar bear that its mother knew only by its smell, so that it sometimes went for weeks without eating because the wind changed and its smell was lost in the blue of the spruce trees; and the pigeon, too, that wrote messages in the sand with its beak, or the commander-in-chief of all the ants who had made his troops carry such big and heavy stones that they built a pyramid higher than a church and so steep no man could climb it and all the sand round about was the dust of corpses of those that had tried. But next day Nicolas had spent hours flat on his belly outside stuffing ants beneath a pebble, and then seemed to forget all about it. Anyway, it was months since he'd left the big house. And Balibou was now no more than the terrible, thin, ugly cat with the stumpy tail who would suddenly appear from somewhere outside, up on the wall, very pleased with himself for being so ferociously yellow, jumping around among the children just when they'd forgotten about him. The others only knew a cat called Balibou, for he got his name from the cat, but that was only a small part of Balibou, the part anybody can believe in with no explaining and no crushing of ants with pebbles.

Above, the pink angels of the church vault are staring at him, and from their blood-red lips emerges the distant twittering of flutes. Their bodies, naked and chubby, sustained by improbably short wings, float motionless in a blur of raspberry jam.

On the snow, at the hour when night falls and everything shrinks together with the crackle of a spark, long before supper: a stain the colour of cat pee, and there'll be no more Balibou.

Some men are coming down from the communion rail, faces of dust in their black armour, and then there's no one left in the wide aisle between him and the white speck of a hanky imprisoned in the great black shroud weeping tears of gold at its four corners. Why had the Blue Man deserted him so suddenly in this strange world outside, without a word, without a sign? He makes a dash for the handkerchief, and his fingers encounter an unknown softness, warm and cool at once, like water, smooth, but weightless. How he had kept on the look-out, from the sudden start of those events, until his eyes and ears hurt from the effort! Pigfoot grabbing the book from his hands and, never saying a word, taking him to the parlour where the two policemen were waiting with Saint Sabine, who merely murmured, raising her first finger: "You're leaving us to enter into life. Thank the little Jesus for giving you such a good uncle, and never forget what we have taught you here." She had given him a small brown paper parcel and, to his immense surprise, stooped to brush his forehead with her cold lips. As he was trembling all over, she added:

"There, there, you're a little man now. And luckier than the others, for you're going into a family."

With a small sigh of relief Saint Sabine had given him a little push toward the two men and turned her coif away. And there he was in the car, between his two guardians, outside the walls, devouring with his eyes those landscapes, distorted by unforeseen tears, that he had never seen; and there was life, suddenly offered to him, a great sea bearing him, wave after wave, into the unknown, all ties cut with his shut-in childhood and all those days so long he had thought they couldn't end, so endless at times that he thought the walls were growing faster than he could.

Shoo Balibou in the zoo like a flue in the glue of the pew. Balibouzoofluegluepew! Softly, the way you say a Hail Mary. Nothing. No string, not a twitch, not even an ant. A corner of hanky, slightly moist, on which the finger no longer slides.

In class he could always draw a picture of anything or fold an inkblot over and presto! cat pee jumped onto the screen ready for any adventure with the Blue Man or for any kind of dirty trick to get back at the crows who reigned over the children – an elephant with fins crushing the five-footed shark on the sea's floor or a sawstinged wasp slashing the bonds (in the belly of the walking tree) of the princess garotted by a thousand sleeping boa constrictors. Kneeling before the black cloth that weeps gold at its four corners he rolls the fine handkerchief in his right hand and suddenly forgets his frightful lion with the stumpy tail; for the faintly sweet perfume, faintly cool, that comes from the little white ball gives rise at the base of his stomach to the oddest sensation, more blurred and old than a faded, yellowed photo, so uncertain that he has time to hear the birds chatter in the presbytery garden before the choir bursts into song.

The birds, the trees and, somewhat less, the church (for he was never at a funeral before and he's almost the only child there and the church is too big) take him back to the other place, put him again within a horizon with four high walls.

For the first time the Blue Man had given an order without warning him. Even Pigfoot had known about it. His mortal enemy had been informed about this tremendous event: he was leaving the big house, for the first time, but forever. He hadn't even had time for a last look at those hundreds of faces that had always been part of his life, faces that most of the time suffocated him because there were so many of them, known and unpredictable, against which he had been obliged to struggle endlessly to maintain a vital distance, but which had been the world, his world. And he had felt the same kind of panic as when he arrived at the big house. How long ago that was, how many days of rain, of snow, of desert sun, of burning cold, in which he had somehow managed to grow up to be a little man that can be thrown out into life!

He was so little! A beginning of winter. An old lady had abandoned him in the very midst of a corridor as long as night. Suddenly all the lights came on, and they appeared, hundreds of them, in double file, all dressed in the same blue-striped shirts, the same overalls of coarse, colourless cotton, the same misshapen ankle boots that pounded and pounded on the naked floor worn low in the middle by so many feet. They were such big boys, their hair cropped short, their faces closed and hard. And the crows with rattles escorting them on both sides. He had covered his ears with his hands so the noise of the boots wouldn't shatter his skull, and had shrunk close to the wall to make himself even smaller, and when he got his breath again they were still filing past, as if they had turned at one end of the corridor and somehow come back from the other. How could even such a big house hold so many children, all the same, turned out by a machine that no one could stop? When he himself became a footstep among all the others he didn't notice the sound, but often at night in the dormitory, itself as long as the corridor, he would wake with a start as those hundreds of boots pounded and pounded on the roof and he could find no wall to shrink against.

He'd had no time to see a single last face, not even to say goodbye to the Chinese boy, the non-intelligent one to whom he'd just started telling stories two days before and who was so quiet he had to be told when it was finished, and then started looking for ants to eat.

Big Justin with the broken nose who'd tormented him so long, with kicks and blows and spittle in his face, pulling down his pants, throwing sand in his eyes, emptying the inkwell onto his scribblers, throwing his books in the mud, pissing in his soup, Justin, of whom everybody was afraid, perhaps even the crows, well, it was he who'd broken Justin's nose one day in a fit of rage, kicking his face with his heels, for he'd decided that day there was only one solution, to go at him if it killed him, and the Blue Man had told him it was now or never, and it was big Justin who got the broken nose, and bled, and had the blood wiped off by the crows. He never bullied anyone after that, and if he hadn't that break right in the middle of his nose, his face would look pretty good right now, for the face that's appearing on the black cloth, softened by gold dust and memory, is Justin's, smiling at him as if to say good-bye in the name of all the hundreds of boots shaped like cauliflowers, led by the crows with rattles. He feels so moved, he · thinks he'd gladly give a lump of wax to big Justin so that he could fix up his nose. Why wasn't Justin out in the world already? He'd always been bigger than "a little man," and even when Pigfoot slapped him maintained that his father was a priest in Jerusalem, and to prove it, said he had three humpless camels that drank nothing but holy water. No such father ever came to the visitor's parlour, and big Justin passed ferocious Sundays filled with chriss' and tabernack's which he hurled from his full height at the four corners of the yard, without fail, every time he heard a car on the other side of the wall. For that matter, the parlour shone so with cleanliness and solitude, with its ten black wicker chairs, its two brass spitoons, and its dead crucifix, that hardly anyone ever came there. But Justin would have liked very much to stop being beaten for telling the truth.

And then, in that parlour as cold as absence, they'd turned him over to two policemen, very tall, haughty, and deaf and dumb; and here he was crumpling a tiny perfumed handkerchief, with a smile that was only half a smile (because he felt disloyal) directed at good old Justin's face as it rose above the six great candles toward the winged babies watching his approach with gaping angel-mouths.

Not a sign from the Blue Man, not the least contact. This was to-

11

tal abandonment, and he couldn't understand it. As if he were putting him to the hardest test of his life by refusing all help, letting him find out by himself all the rules and traps and invisible trails, without even Balibou who knew all the tricks and understood what was up, seeing him totally with his sleepy cat's eyes and his knowledge of so many things that only go on in the dark, when children are asleep and the owls drink moon-milk to feed their young.

"You little bum, git out, and play outside!"

A man's hand digs fingers into his arm and shakes him roughly. He frees himself with a sideways jump and without a glance at the wheezing voice that makes good old Justin's face explode in the raspberry jam he goes to the sad lady who sobs like a sleeping dog, and holds out the soft, tiny handkerchief with its perfume more ancient than Balibou, older even than the first march-past of leaden children and their rattle-rhythm, older than the beginning of walls or the ball of snow swallowed so long ago in his mother's white forehead with its coldness of stone in the milky bubbling of satin.

He had had to slip between so many heavy pillared legs to reach her! – and climb over a strange piece of furniture covered on top with the skins of green cats to almost fall into the funny, high bed where her hair was so black in so much white.

And his hands and mouth couldn't believe the cold of the snow.

They'd pulled him down, scolding him softly in his ear, in his inability to believe:

"Aren't you ashamed? You've broken her rosary."

"Why is she sleeping in front of everybody!"

Before that there'd been a smell sometimes, not quite the handkerchief perfume, but something like it, the difference between the murmur of a voice and the softness of a hand.

Very pale, very beautiful under black veils, the lady and the crying girl don't look at him. They are far away, and alone. Suddenly embarrassed, he lays the handkerchief softly on the lady's joined hands, and thinks of his cauliflower-shaped boots marching down the long aisle, so noisily, on the marble tiles, that he almost feels like whistling to get his courage up. Once past the double row of stares, at the place where there's a wide desert space, he would like to run, but freezes on discovering half a dozen ghouls in black mounting guard around a small frame on wheels. He drops into a pew, and yawns for a long time as he tries in vain to rediscover, among the cherubs, big Justin's new wax nose.

"You're not going to hang around here all day!"

He'd barely gulped down his last bite of breakfast when Aunt Maria, her elbows on the table and not more than a foot away, her face, brick red and shiny, crushed out of shape between her hands, emerged from her long and silent contemplation with this embarrassing exclamation uttered in the nastiest tone. He, with his head over his plate, had just been thinking that she looked like Saint Tomato, the crows' cook, who had always been in a temper, exploding from one cooking pot to the next, except if you found her in the mid-afternoon when all her fires were out. Then she'd almost be nice to you, half asleep as she was, and she'd even play sometimes at letting them search for cookies in her ogress's apron, whereas Aunt Maria gets her temper up without even having to work, for it's Aunt Rose who does all the cooking, and Aunt Maria puffs a lot, and her breath smells of vinegar that's more vinegary than vinegar itself. So he'd looked her in the eye with a proud smile, Balibou-style, like the time the little black boy had succeeded in luring all the crows into the jungle and the white panther had gobbled them up, one after the other the whole night long, and then got so sick and vomited so hard she made waves in the cactus for at least half a mile around and next day all the crows were back in the refectory with long white panther hair in their coifs. It was a smile he'd never have dared to let Pigfoot see unless he had a clear getaway path, but Aunt Maria seems older and not so fast on her feet, and he doesn't really know her yet, even if he decided the first time he saw her (the night before) that she belonged to the class of "crow with a chair rung." But she hadn't seemed to take offence at his supercilious manner, and she'd added, in a voice that was no more and no less unpleasant than before:

"Go play outside. You're to come back when the Angelus rings."

And Aunt Rose, who has black hair and a pale face and a little wart on her nose that she puts yellow powder on, had put in her word between two licks of her dustcloth, in a gruff tone, but not as nastily as the other:

"That's right, go out for a run, manikin. Here, bring me back five pounds of sugar."

From the cupboard she'd brought a big, black money-box with golden lines painted on it like a frame, and had taken out two silver coins that she laid before him on a little square of paper.

"That's the ration coupon. He'll give you fifteen cents change."

Because it seemed understood that he knew already, he hadn't asked who would give him the sugar or the change. Aunt Rose had put the money-box back on the second shelf of the cupboard, and then, after looking at him for two seconds as if she were taking his measure, she had decided, going on tiptoe, to put it on the third shelf.

"We'll see if he takes after his father," Aunt Maria had spit out, rubbing the two coins between her thick fingers with their nails bitten to the quick, checking that there were just one, and another, and not a fraction more.

Because crows are bald, and he'd never given that a second thought (except in the case of Saint Agnes, but that was different), he'd been particularly fascinated ever since he awoke by women with heads of hair. The previous night when he'd arrived he'd been too intoxicated with the strangeness, too upset by the turn of events that had moved and shifted on their own, to be observant about anything, except for his uncle's apartment being strangely small, and the furniture too, compared with the image in his mind, as if it had all begun to disappear; and except for his uncle's being quite unlike the portrait the Blue Man had always drawn of him, but so far as his uncle was concerned, he'd decided to wait awhile, for that was all a little fuzzy and he didn't want to jump to conclusions; and finally, the fact that there aren't just two but three sisters, or rather aunts, including the youngest, or the least old, Eugénie, who had gone off this morning to her factory where it seemed she sewed shirt collars all day long. He hadn't asked, but he certainly wondered what you do with shirt collars all by themselves, like pantlegs with no pants.

In the other place he had dreamed almost every night about women's hair. It seemed to him, he didn't know why, that hair made the big difference – even more, that its lack constituted a kind of infirmity in the crows as compared with women who were mothers or girls or even aunts, so that somehow he couldn't quite manage to see his mother's head, but could invent it at will, especially at night, like everything that doesn't exist but could, things you never talk about, as you never talk about longing to be caressed, for that is all so vague and far away, too gentle to survive the dark, like the smoke filled with sunlight where the Blue Man was born, or like Saint Agnes, about whom he never knew if it was true for there are no words for that, and gestures, of course, can mean everything or nothing at all.

14

And he began to think that nothing, in the world outside, would ever be like the pictures he had freely invented in the other place, because, quite obviously, they were impossible here. Aunt Maria, with her white hair sprinkled with some pissy kind of cologne, and Aunt Rose, with her black feather duster of hair, were barely different from the bald crows. He'd have to choke back his pictures, and forget that they were his mother's sisters.

So far as the coins were concerned, he could have told them not to make such a fuss: he'd already had one like them, and he'd thrown it away in the courtyard and found it again a month later, nobody had picked it up, and you'd never say the same if it had been a marble. It was Nicolas who'd given it to him, because he was going home to his family at Christmas time, and he'd tried to tell him the man cut off at the neck was the king. King of the calves' heads! What kind of a king was that with no crown and no body? Balibou was always mixed up in money troubles, which probably came from the books, with all those thieves who were killers, and poor people and rich people, but that was money that shone like gold, and anyway when the ones that didn't get killed finally found the treasure chest on a little pebbly island they couldn't open it or it turned out to be empty, or contained nothing but a plan showing where to find the money that had turned into jewels, and Balibou could start running again, and even change sides just to see how it felt. It wasn't even as useful as medals, for medals weren't always the same, and you could put holes in them with a nail, or bend them between your teeth and it was fun finding names for them.

So what good was money, unless there were thieves or rich people? And he didn't know a soul who had ever seen one or the other.

He'd stuck the coins in his overall pocket and run out to play, and then into the church across from the house, for everybody was going in, and he didn't know where to go in the streets where every corner had four possible ways to run, leading heaven knows where. And even in the church they were sending him outside to play. Outside was far too big, and he'd have had to go *someplace* outside. When Pigfoot had sent them outside, it was to one place, and nowhere else. Here, outside was everywhere, but all the bits of it belonged to someone who was going to chase you.

What's more, the church bells keep ringing all the time. How is he to know when it's the Angelus? He'll have to keep an eye out for when the other children go home to their houses, all together.

He'll be very calm, observe everything carefully, act as if he weren't all alone, pretend to be an old hand at navigating all directions in every wind.

Since things started happening he's made out pretty well. How careful he's been to keep quiet in case his voice should drown out a signal, if one should come! He's made only two obvious mistakes.

The first was in the dingy office where the policemen took him first. For a second he had thought, because of the little man all in white who had funny sleeves like those of a cassock and a green celluloid visor over his eyes and made his guards sign some papers, that perhaps he could try for a contact, as he did with Nicolas when Nicolas met Balibou, and he'd answered for almost a whole week. That had been a new disguise.

"A flea in the bee on the sea."

Nicolas replied:

"Seas of bees in the fleas."

And the others hadn't understood a word, and Pigfoot got her toe caught in the thread, where her ball of yarn was rolling on the other side of the partition, where nothing at all was happening, but they knew, just the two of them, that something could have happened. And it was because nothing happened that Nicolas stopped giving the answer. Nicolas had become as stupid as the Chinese boy who instead of catching ants swallowed crumbs of earth.

"Eh? What do you mean by that, eh?"

The man with the sleeves had raised his visor and shown his yellow teeth. It wasn't a disguise. He was a man with sleeves and a visor, nothing special.

"You little bastard, I ask you how old you are and you give me some stuff about fleas!"

"Take it easy, pop," one of his guardian angels had said.

"They're all the same. Brought up like little animals. And then they come back three or four years later in handcuffs. Say you're sorry, you bad egg..."

"No, sir."

The same guardian angel had burst out laughing, had run a hand through the boy's hair, and said to the little man, whose visor was off, his white hair standing up like the ass-feathers on a chicken:

16

"He'll tell you he's sorry in four years' time, when he's murdered the dad he never had."

He'd jerked his head away from the guardian's hand, for the laughing had suddenly burned a tender place inside him.

The second mistake had stopped him cold. When they got to the apartment, while the policemen were talking to Aunt Rose, he had seen his uncle approaching, newspaper in hand, pipe in mouth, his eyes very blue behind his glasses, a friendly big head like Santa Claus, pink and white, his body smaller and rounder than he had imagined in a vague and distant memory, but still looking like the presents he'd sent every Christmas for the last two years. This was the Blue Man's first friend that he was seeing now with his own eyes, the first inhabitant of the secret universe where everything he missed was present in abundance, everything that was really life, that would be restored to him after a necessary time of privation. And he was a man, his mother's big brother.

So, for the first time, he threw himself into someone's arms.

"What the sam hill! What's all this about?" his uncle Napoléon had said in an irritated voice, retreating and throwing his arms up from the shock.

"A real savage! Just imagine!" Aunt Maria cried, rushing to him and holding him back by the shoulders.

"Now what kind of a way is that to come into a person's place?" his uncle had added, brushing furiously at the pipe ashes on his white shirt.

It had gone too far for any explanation, much less for a kiss. So he'd plunged back into his frozen lake, confronted with a doubt that he rejected with all his strength. Balibou, if you like, might be no more than a wretched old all-purpose cat, useful because time had been so immobile and only Balibou could get through the wall anytime he liked. But his uncle! – who he'd always been sure would come some day and take him away, with open arms, not a word said, for the looks they would exchange would tell all! Only his uncle knew how to find the Blue Man, who is not a cloud, not made of smoke, nor even the soundless voice he has always heard. Only his uncle knows that invisible face. Starting backward, as he had done, as if a dog had jumped at his throat, his uncle had created a deep chasm, and he had had to make himself very heavy so as not to tumble into it.

But everything had been so sudden, so fast, and the time during which he'd invented that meeting had been so long, that he knew he would have to wait some more, that stories have no sense if the people who are happy at the end become happy in the middle, and that even with Balibou, who he knows perfectly well always escapes in the end, he's been really worried at times, when he hadn't played the game for a long time and forgot that he was Balibou telling himself about Balibou. Whereas his uncle, who had his own story to tell, had every right to surprise him.

But then, everything was different. No more Justin, no more Chinese boy (who was the only one that could go in and out of class when he felt like it, for he wasn't very bright, and he was quieter when they let him come and go like a little dog), no more Nicolas, who was only his friend long enough for him to regret having told him too much, nor all the others, who always became unbearable because they always had the same faces, nor Pigfoot, who was so vicious that she made the smaller ones take the big ones' pants down on the pretext that they deserved a whipping whether or no; nor Saint Sabine, who everybody knew slept on a bed of nails, like a real saint, and had celestial visions so terrible that she couldn't walk for days and if you touched her at those times your fingers went right through her body, and every vision burned a hole in the walls of her room, where nobody had ever dared to enter; and no more rules, except go out and play between meals, and outside was the whole world, perhaps right to the ocean. So there's nothing to keep him in this church where he's really starting to get bored, and all he has to do is go out and go along a street and then another street, and look and listen, and all of that isn't books any more and even without Balibou there are things to be discovered everywhere, and because he's little and there are children in every house who must be playing outside he'll not be noticed and nobody will bother with him or speak to him. It's normal to be in the normal world, and he needn't hide in a corner like a frightened dog that sees a kick in every boot.

He opens his eyes and gets up to launch himself into the world, but just at that moment the ghouls, stiff as posts, more impressive than Saint Sabine pretending to be a statue, come toward him, pushing their cart with grey-gloved hands, followed by plaster faces veiled in black. He falls to his knees and, his head lowered, watches the slow procession filing past. The bell tolls slowly, slowly, seeming to vibrate for at least a minute long.

On her way past, the lady with the handkerchief lays a coin on his bench, without stopping, and without weeping. Other women

18

do the same, and even some of the men. The long strokes of the bell ring out over all these chopped-off king's heads disguised as nobodies. When the crowd has gone, he is still looking at the coins with surprise and a little shame. They took him for a beggar, or perhaps they had promised the dead man to give money to the first child they met.

He turns around finally toward the great door opened on a drape of sunlight crossed by the cries of birds. A brief hesitation, during which he looks to see if he is seen, and he scoops up the coins, keeps them in the hollow of his hand, and goes to play outside.

2

In the street there are cars filled with flowers and others filled with women, and men lingering, talking to each other, shaking hands, or lifting their hats to wipe their foreheads. Dogs, and women and children in ordinary bright colours are busy round about and everybody is talking loudly in the street and on the sidewalk. The sun is very hot and smells like a party. Farther along, on the same side as his uncle's house, four enormous horses, hitched to wagons loaded with big barrels, block off the street completely. What should he play at? Playing dead?

He drops on a step of the church and rattles the money in his cupped hands. All this activity is going to get under way and go somewhere. He'd love to go and see the horses close up. He's never seen such fine big horses, light bay with white beards on their legs, the balloons of their bellies swelling out under the tugs of their harness, clean and shining as if they just came from the shower. He's only been acquainted with one real horse, the gardener's, and it was thin and its hair came out in patches, and it farted all the time because it was sick, so that you didn't want to pat it, and you got tired of seeing it always pulling a garbage-cart with nothing clean on it. And it died one day, and the gardener too, and neither was replaced. Of course there'd been Balibou in his role of winged horse, no bigger than a fly in the giant's ear, or kicking holes in the wicked king of Arabia's flying carpet, the shadow of which was blinding the young prince, who was wandering ever deeper into the thirsty desert – but he didn't know how to get him back to earth as an ordinary horse, so that story hadn't lasted long.

Just as he's getting up to pass through the funeral and go to see the horses he receives a kick in the hands, and the coins fly in all directions, bouncing down the church steps to the black cars and the patent leather shoes of the stern-faced men wiping their brows.

"Little filcher! You've emptied the poor-box!"

He hasn't even time to turn when someone pins his arms behind his back and shouts into his ear, with a strange laugh. There's a kind of whispering, as if the voice were out of breath, and then when it gets a little air it goes up very high. He doesn't answer, but kicks furiously to get free, tries butting the chin with his head, but the other one is too tall and the twisting hurts his arms.

"Why don't you cry?" asks the shrill voice.

He looks around on all sides. Nobody's paying attention, and nobody's picking up the money.

"Guess who I am and I'll let you go."

He doesn't know why, but the breathless voice hurts him more than the hands digging into his shirt. A chilled voice, that shouldn't be allowed out, even in sunshine, it makes you want to run away, as a drooling dog does or certain smells in the humid dark of cellars.

Rolling with all his strength toward a lower step, he succeeds in freeing one hand, and he twists around on his stomach to bite the other hand still holding him.

"You little bastard!"

The voice flew up and perched there at once, almost crying.

"Why are you screaming?"

He watches the other lick the blood from his arm, and he's astonished. He'd never have thought such a voice could come from a man, that is, with a man's age, for he's lanky, all string and bones, with a pale face, heavy locks of hair falling on both sides of his brow, almost a girl's head, with green Balibou eyes. He's wearing a white cotton sweatshirt stained with strawberries, or maybe blood, and oversize pants that puff out like a skirt at his hips.

"Hey, Rat! Are you robbing kids these days? Come here till I pat your ears for you!"

His attacker is up with a catlike leap and holds out his hand to

22

him, looking with sun-crinkled eyes toward the big voice coming from behind.

"Come on, Eugène, we're just fooling around. What's wrong with that? Hey you, tell him, we were just tossing quarters."

The boy turns around and sees a policeman twirling his night-stick with one hand and jiggling the coins in the other.

"Don't get smart, Rat. I saw you. And where did he crawl out of, this one? Is this his dad's market money?"

The policeman seems so sure he can make the Rat crawl on all fours at will that he isn't even threatening, and doesn't come a step nearer.

"Come on, tell him we were seeing who could toss quarters the farthest, and they got mixed up in all those legs..."

"It's true, sir, and I was even winning."

Why should he want to help the Rat, big as he is, who jumped him from behind? Because he smells his fear of the police? Or because the Rat needs him to get out of this jam?

"I said come here, Rat."

He doesn't look mean, this policeman – certainly less so than the Rat, and it would be fun to blow the whistle that shines in the sun against his blue shirt or twirl his stick by its leather loop (only half as frightening as Pigfoot's long ruler which never made him give in), or even just chat with him, for he's good at kidding around, but he knows in his blood that policemen are on the same side as the crows, and in the other place the first law was sticking together, even when big Justin stuck a nail in his ass, and even when he'd had to deceive Saint Agnes, but that was another story.

Docile, the Rat goes down the steps toward the policeman, but dragging the boy along, almost begging him:

"Tell him it's your money."

"Did his father forget him in town?"

"No! He just got out from behind the walls himself, but they forgot to take off his uniform."

"I thought you'd cleared out of the neighbourhood for good. You were supposed to be in hospital at least ten years, Rat."

"Guess I have to wait for somebody to kick the bucket. No room. It's not that I don't like the mountains."

The Rat's hand is all moist inside, but he doesn't dare pull his own away because he doesn't want to seem to leave the Rat in the lurch. He seems more and more like a giant child. Taller than the policeman, he talks to him in a voice that pretends to be joking, putting his hand to his mouth repeatedly to wipe the spittle, and still leaving between himself and the cop the minimum distance for successful flight, like the kids in the other place with Pigfoot.

"Just don't try getting smart, eh Rat? You're free under surveillance as far as the sanatorium. Better not hang around, for we know how to take care of guys like you down at the station! You pissed on the old lady's flowers again yesterday. She called us in."

"Every time a cat goes by her goddam flowerpots she says it was me."

"She says she saw you."

"She can't see from me to you. And besides I've quit pissing. I'm sick."

"What do you mean the kid got out from behind the walls?"

He wasn't listening any more. The funeral was finally, slowly, getting under way, and the big blond horses were also coming closer, with a sound of clanking metal. Standing up on the wagons, the drivers, plump as the barrels, stretch out their arms with the reins, shouting. He can hardly hear the voice, scraping past the whistling of the Rat's breathing which vibrates right down to the boy's hand.

"It's Marcel's brother. He just got here yesterday from over there. He's with his uncle and the old maids."

Children are running in all directions in front of the rigs, and the horses are held in so tightly by the stretched reins that they shudder like a ground swell in their harness. The great white feet rise and fall without advancing.

He lets go the sweating hand, which he can't stand any more, and tries to run down to see the horses from closer up, but the policeman stops him, putting his baton in the way.

"Rat, why couldn't you go in the army or navy like everybody else? You're the only one left to play the big shot on the street here. They'd have had you good as new in a day or two in there. Now tell me, where did this money come from?"

"What do I know? He saved it up in jail, I suppose."

"I want to see the horses, I want to pat them."

He starts a rush at the nightstick. The cop scoops him up from the ground and suddenly his voice has a Sunday grandfather sound:

"OK, little guy. We'll let you have a look at the fine horses full of beer."

He sees that their tails are cropped, like Balibou's, and done up in great buns by the horses' shining cruppers. On the policeman's shoulder he's taller than their manes, and as he leans forward too far he falls with his face in the thick horsehair, getting a mouthful of it, his hands clutching at its strong-smelling dampness. The horse tosses its head and whinnies until he feels it in his chest.

"That's not where you take him for a drink!" shouts the driver.

Everybody down below bursts out laughing. The policeman straightens him up and sets him astride the horse, but his legs are too short and he tips over backwards.

"OK, that's enough circus tricks! Make a little room, there, I've got to get going. There's kids right under the wheels, for chrissakes!"

There, he's down on the street again, and the policeman pushes him gently toward the sidewalk.

"See? You've ridden a Molson horse!"

And he slips the coins in the wide pocket of the boy's overall bib and starts breaking up the crowd, still talking to them, from farther and farther.

"Now go play with kids your own age, if you don't want to end up like him. And as for you, Rat, if you don't take a change of air before a month is up, we'll put you back in the cooler at our place."

"You don't want me to knock a few patients off to make room for me?"

But the policeman is too far away now, and the street empties slowly, as the wagons disappear. A puddle of horse piss gleams in the sun, just in front of the church.

For a minute or two the Rat whirls in one hand a long silver-plated chain with a heavy plumb of lead at the end. He whistles, and very well, but often has to stop to wipe his lips.

The boy watches him, trying to imagine that Justin looks like him, but it doesn't work, for Justin is blond, in the first place, and anyway has broader shoulders than this one. It doesn't occur to him to ask the Rat why he kicked him, for he never has tried to find out why such things happened to him. Might as well ask why it rains or why there's no cake in the soup. He stares long at the Rat's funny-looking boots, winter boots, laced high, almost light yellow, and he feels too warm in his flannelette shirt that's been washed so often and worn by so many children that the blue stripes have melted into the white, which in turn is almost blue, and the mended elbows stick to him like scabs. As the Rat no longer pays any attention to him and seems not even to see him, he goes off toward his uncle's house.

"Hey! We can't split up this way. Come here and sit down, we're going to have a little chat."

He hesitates. It's not the policeman's warning that holds him back, but he needs to pee, and it bothers him somewhat that this big hypocrite should know things about him, as if he were going to catch some filthy disease. And right now he feels like wandering through the streets and having a look at everything.

"You know, Marcel told me to keep an eye on you."

"Why would he say that, when I don't even know you?"

"He and I were always friends. Next-door neighbours, what d'ya expect?"

"Did he tell you to kick me too?"

"Come on, that was just for fun. You don't expect me to say, 'Good day, sir, how do you do?' or, 'Hello, I'm the Rat!' "

"Well, some other day. I have to leave, I've got to go somewhere."

And he goes on toward the house, trying hard to remember neighbours from before, but all he can see is a victrola with a crank and thick phonograph records turning very fast, and something like a woman's voice that seems to sing through a flowing water tap or as if somebody were tickling her but she had to sing anyway.

"Hey! Little grump! You're not going to have it in for me like all the others, are you? Come on back, Pierrot."

That startles him. Nobody but his brother called him that, in his letters, and the two times he came to see him in the other place. His uncle and aunts haven't called him anything since he arrived. And then there's the Rat's funny imploring tone that holds him back despite himself. Like a big dog that was so old, or sick, that even a little tot wouldn't be afraid of him and would give him his last crust of bread. He turns back toward the Rat, who's whirling his chain faster and faster and pivoting on his yellow boots.

"How did you know that was my name?"

"You're Marcel's brother. The house right next door to yours, don't you remember? You were no bigger than this, and we used to play football together. And you were always looking for my little sister."

"Why was I looking for her?"

"Because she was your age, I guess."

Perhaps he remembers her. He's not sure whether she was the

one who was with him under the old blanket stretched like a tent from a post of the balcony. And he doesn't remember what he did with her to get punished, but he remembers clearly getting punished because of the little girl and the blanket. Who was it spanked him?

"Why would he ask you to do that?"

"Do what?"

"Keep an eye, like you said?"

"Because I'm the only one left. All the others have disappeared, mostly in the army."

"Why?"

"There's a war on, isn't there? They must have told you that much back there?"

"Sure. A war between the Catholics and the. . .English. Nicolas used to go into town sometimes, and he'd tell me all about it. He even said the Pope is winning."

The Rat drops his chain and bursts out with his breathless laugh.

"What a hell of a liar, your friend Nicolas! It's a war between all sorts of people, of every colour you can think of. They need room in the world from time to time, like in the hospital. And then they just hand out guns to everybody."

He's certainly not going to tell the Rat that the Blue Man is bigger than the Pope, and that he knows a lot more about the war than Nicolas, and especially more than the Rat, who isn't even in the army. But he promised to keep the secret, and he says no more. Except:

"I still have to pee."

The silver chain has started whirling again, so fast you'd think it was a motionless wheel.

"Let's go in the garden of the priest's house. There's a big tree with grape-vines."

"Why are the others all gone?"

"At the start, they wanted to earn some money, after the years when it took you a week to lay your hands on a measly quarter! But afterwards they came and took them away by force."

"Marcel isn't in the army. He's in the navy!"

"Yeah, but not the real navy with cannons and torpedoes."

"That's all you know! His navy's real enough to get him sunk twice. And he even froze both legs in the North Pole sea."

He had spoken up angrily. After all, he can't let the Rat get away

27

with everything. As if you could get hit with a real torpedo from a real submarine in the iceberg sea, and eat one biscuit a day with men taking turns holding a revolver over the biscuit box so they'd last long enough and to keep the others rowing so they wouldn't freeze above the legs, and not be in the real navy!

"Don't get mad, little grump! I give in, it's the real navy, where the ships blow up like firecrackers."

"And what about you?"

Pivoting around on his boots, whirling his chain, the Rat has moved away, and doesn't reply. As he turns, his long black locks fly above his head, then fall back over his eyes.

Not a man, not a child. Too late now. He'll never be a papa, nor a wagon driver, nor a policeman or an uncle, not even a soldier, let alone a sailor. And he's puffing as if he'd run the whole race already, as if he'd jumped past his age without going through it. He comes back now, flops down on a step and breathes heavily, paying no attention to the sweat running down his forehead and onto his hands.

"I saw you come here yesterday, with the police, in an ordinary car. I tell you, I can smell them coming all the way from St. Laurent."

"I asked you, what about you?"

"They got me once, but they'll never do it again. And I won't go to the hospital either."

"Why didn't you go away? That's what I mean."

"In the first place, I'm not good enough for their guns. My lungs...you've got to be healthy to go and get yourself killed. And besides, I was locked up for three years by those pigs, and by the way: you don't see them risking their necks either."

"Would you have gone if you could?"

"Are you nuts? Can you see me on the end of a gun killing guys I don't even know? When you come back, either it's feet first, or wearing a pretty medal instead of one leg."

"Aren't you brave?"

The Rat rolls onto his back and holds his ribs, laughing.

"It's not all that funny."

"Funniest thing I ever heard. You call that brave, selling your own death? You've got to be really poor, little guy, and have no imagination."

"Do you know any people that were killed?"

"Yeah, about a dozen, at least. And now they're going to fall like rain, for the big show is coming, just like high mass. Before, they were far away from each other. Now they're setting them up face to face, and no place behind to go for a walk. Ten years from now nobody will think about it. But those guys won't have been twenty for very long."

Now he's flicking his chain slowly along the stones, and it wiggles like a snake, and he laughs softly, about things he alone can see.

Under the old blanket, the boy remembers, it was so hot they'd started taking their clothes off, and the little girl was quite naked when somebody suddenly whipped the tent away. He's a little ashamed, for he's afraid the Rat might remember too. So he says, hurriedly:

"What are you sick with?"

"My lungs, I told you. Galloping consumption. Can't you hear it?"

"Why don't you want to go to the hospital?"

"Because it's like the war, either you don't come back at all, or you come back so thin you disappear in the wind on a street corner in wintertime."

"Aren't you afraid?"

The Rat's cat-green eyes bore into his, and for once his voice is deep as a man's, and the boy feels a chill from it even as he sits on the warm stones.

"My sister died of it. Your mother too, and a lot of chums that never saw twenty. I saw them die. So when you're certain, when you know, you're not scared. On the contrary, you're sure they'll let you run loose till it happens."

He jumps to his feet, undoes the chain from his belt and reaches the sidewalk. Pierrot follows him, and they walk together toward his uncle's house.

"What were you doing in church?"

"They told me to go and play outside."

"There it is, they always want you to go play outside, and then they wonder why you hang around the street. Come on, we're going to play. Run a little bit."

The Rat, in his own way, had managed to make him feel better, and he breathes almost as easily as if he were still in the other place, flat on his stomach in the dust, reading the Chinese boy a story he doesn't understand but finds so interesting he stops looking for ants.

"What's your real name?"

The Rat flicks his chain forward, as if he were going to throw it, but he doesn't let it go.

"My mother's the only one that calls me Gaston. But she's so scared of me she never talks to me at all."

"Gaston, why do they want you to go into hospital?"

"Go on, run a little bit, I tell you. It's not because of me, it's for other people, because it's catching. They shut you up, like a dog with rabies."

He thinks he could like the Rat, for Gaston only seems bad because they won't let him be sick and mind his business. To please him, Pierrot starts running backwards, smiling at him.

"Why do they call you Rat?"

"Don't know. Always did, even at school. Maybe because I was so skinny I could get through any hole."

"Don't you mind? It isn't a nice name."

"That's where you're wrong! That's the smartest animal there is. I'll explain it all...."

And without warning, leaning forward slightly, he flicks out with the chain which wraps itself around his legs, but without hurting. The Rat comes at once to set him free.

"Pretty tricky, eh? Come on, let's go for a piss. Then we'll go home."

3

You go in to the Rat's house by a funny kind of passage, like a big square hole cut in the house itself, dark and smelling of piss, and then there you are in broad daylight again, in a tiny field where there aren't any cows to eat the grass (which grows taller than a boy), but with daisies and little yellow flowers that fall when you touch them, and a path leading to a verandah with a rusty tin roof curved at the bottom like a slide. A dog barks loudly from somewhere in the grass.

"Shut up, Lucifer! Here's the palace, and the cow pasture. Goddam good soil, here!"

Sheets laid out to dry on top of the grass are covered with flies, and he hears bees everywhere. The dog was silenced at once.

"And a hell of a fine monument, as high as the Sun Life. Look!"

Gaston's long, white hand points to the sky, but what he's pointing at is not close by: great cages of steel whose legs are planted among the low houses and rise high, higher and higher, reaching out to two giant stone pillars, taller than the tallest church you could imagine, like an immense window standing there alone, with nothing around it.

"A giant's pantlegs," says Pierrot, laughing.

"Ha! I hope he's lost his ass," says Gaston admiringly. "Just think if he started to...turn on his tap. We'd all be in the river. Little yellow fish. A giant's pants! You do get ideas, don't you!"

He takes a long look at the bridge, as if he'd never seen it, and when he looks back at the boy he's not laughing.

"That's one bastard of a bridge, just the same."

"Are you sick?"

"No. Why, all of a sudden?"

"Your face changed."

"Now my face is changing! I wish I could change it. I'd show you faces to stand your hair on end."

"Balibou can change his face whenever he wants."

"Bali...what?"

"He's a cat. He's yellow."

"Then he's got a cat's face, that's all. The Rat doesn't like cats. It's war, and there are a lot of us rats."

"But when he changes his face he's not a cat any more."

"Not a horse!"

"Sometimes, but never a rat."

"Why not? He doesn't like cheese?"

"I don't know. A rat doesn't look nice."

"Do you want your ears boxed? You mean I don't look nice?"

"You're Gaston."

Barely showing above the grass, an old high-wheeled buggy raises its shafts to the sky. The Rat leaps to it with one bound, without touching the grass, and disappears completely.

"Gaston? Is that you, Gaston?"

The voice comes from the verandah at the end of the path, shriller than Gaston's, and much louder. He doesn't answer.

The boy moves into the grass to have a look at the tiny field, waiting for Gaston to give some sign of life. At the back, near a sagging plank wall, there's a big tree whose branches have all been cut. It looks like a post with leaves growing. On the other side, where the grass stops, he can make out a little empty space in front of another verandah, all painted white. He tries to move toward the buggy, but trips on a big piece of metal, and falls. The earth is wet beneath him. The daisy stalks and the plants with yellow flowers that fall are dripping with spittle. Perhaps the Rat hurt himself taking such a long leap into the buggy, or maybe he's choking. Pierrot gets up, but tries in vain to advance. There's scrap iron everywhere. He calls, first feebly, then louder, but his only answer is the dog, barking loudly again.

"Lucifer, shut up!"

And the dog is silent at once.

"I'm leaving. You're not a bit funny."

But Gaston's silhouette rises up in the buggy, higher than the shafts, as if borne by the long grass.

"Go around that way. There's a whole pile of old car parts here. A present from your brother."

"No, I'm going. It must be Angelus time."

"Come on, you've lots of time. Look, there you are, now you can go ahead."

When he gets to the buggy Gaston hoists him up with his long arms, and he understands why the other made his leap and why he wasn't hurt. It's full of inflated innertubes, and you think you're walking on balloons.

"Why do you call him Lucifer?"

"Because the devil sent him, and he thinks I'm the good Lord. When the weather's fine I spend hours here counting flies. It's good for my lungs. Just like out in the country."

He doesn't know why, but he'd like to hurry back to the street, to leave Gaston. Here, in his own home, he takes up too much room, his voice is no longer broken, he no longer gives that impression of a giant child that made you want not to hurt him.

"I want to go."

"What's wrong with you? You haven't seen anything yet. What about your old house, just beside mine?"

Now he's seen Gaston's he doesn't want to go in the other one. He thinks he remembers seeing Marcel tinkering with car engines. He even remembers the black car, high on its wheels, rounded behind, with a seat that opened up where the trunk should be, and little steps on either side for getting in it, and the smell of oil and wet rags when you shut the doors, and the window in front that opened when you pushed the bottom, the car that was always in their yard, that didn't go out very often or very far, and always made Marcel and...someone else...angry. And this car drives past all the houses he ever imagined, and over the flowers of gardens and even over the snow-white ducks in a lovely puddle, and it never has a driver for he knows that he doesn't remember the face because he doesn't want to remember.

"What's beer?"

"Eh? Beer? What makes you ask about that right now?"

"I don't know. Perhaps it was the horses."

"It's not far from here, almost on the river, it's made of water. Molson's..."

"It's not water, is it?"

"Mixed with happiness-piss. I only tried it once. I can't. Because of..."

"Of your lungs. What's happiness-piss?"

"That's what the rich people put in so the poor people will think they're happy and lose their heads when they drink it. You'd be surprised how poor, happy people can look sad and get mean! Don't ever touch the stuff."

"Then why do they make it?"

"I'll tell you that when you tell me why they make guns and cannons and bombs, and even factories, and why everybody has to work. Why me and not Sir Molson, or the priest, who drinks his wine."

"Oh, he doesn't take much. I know, I was an altar boy."

"Don't tell me you speak Latin!"

"Sure, or I couldn't be an altar boy."

"Do you believe in God?"

"Oh, I don't know. It's not so easy. I'd rather believe in... somebody else."

"Who's that?"

"Just somebody."

"Who?"

"You don't know him. I'm the only one."

"He does miracles, and goes on living forever?"

"Maybe. But I'm not talking about it."

"Why?"

"You have things you're the only one to think about."

"Yes, and if you knew what they were you'd stop believing in God or anybody else."

In a movement almost of rage he picks the boy up by the waist, tosses him up and lets him fall back on the innertubes.

"Hey, come on, I'm going to show you one of my evil thoughts."

"No, I want to go home."

Without replying, Gaston shoves him out of the buggy, takes his hand and leads him toward the other house. Where the weeds end there's a little square of lawn, and flowers of all colours along a white verandah. Above all, there is, lying on a canvas cot, a sleeping girl, almost naked, with an open book on her belly.

"She's a schoolteacher. Do I have good evil thoughts or don't I?"

The boy notices her hair particularly, blonde as the sun, curled and long enough to hang down below the cot.

"She lets on she's sleeping, for she likes me to look at her. What do you think of those thighs, eh? I'm a thigh man."

The boy pulls his hand roughly to go back to the path, but behind him he hears the Rat singing in a voice that is suddenly loud:

"Show your rear, teacher dear. . . . I'll give it a pat, or harder than that. . . . One and one are three and the rest's for me."

A door slams, and the Rat catches up with him, laughing with no sound but his breathing.

"You don't go showing yourself like that in this weather when there's a poor sick guy lying in the grass."

Pierrot can't bear the impression he has: of being tied to the other by a cord that he'll never let loose.

"Let me go home, Gaston, I'm tired."

"There's even a plough in this goddam hay someplace. My dad brought it to town with him. I guess he thought he could earn a living ploughing the streets. But he ran into a hell of a rock! Come and have a drink. It's too hot."

He pulls the boy toward the house. The dog, tied to the verandah, comes to lick his yellow boots. The Rat gets rid of him with a kick.

"I don't like dogs. But I have to have one at night to hear them coming."

"Who?"

"Those pigs that came and got me one night. It can't happen again."

He pauses, looks at the boy, one finger on his lips, and continues gravely:

"Because I've got a rifle. Always loaded. Always ready to spit."

An old woman, her wide, white apron touching the floor, opens the grilled door before they reach the verandah.

"You pretend to be rough because you grew up too fast. I knew somebody like you. Now he's got a broken nose and he doesn't try to scare people any more. I had a Pigfoot too, not so terrible as the ones you talked about."

"What! A Pigfoot? What for?"

"Well, she. . .it was my overseer, she hit us with a stick when our feet and hands were freezing in winter, and we had to show our underpants every night to see if they were dirty."

"Holy God! You were in jail! But they were brides of Christ! Imagine putting four-year-old kids in a place like that with those goddam madwomen! You've got to tell me about that."

"No."

That was final, no answer possible. Anyway the old woman was talking, with a trembling voice quite unlike the one that called a while ago.

35

"Gaston. My, oh my! Why didn't you answer? The dog barked and you made out you weren't there. Oh, me!"

"Stop snivelling, ma, and give us some lemonade. There's a thirst on."

The kitchen, lit only by a low window that looks out on the verandah, is cool and smells of cake. There are only two chairs, dark green, a long table higher at one end that the other and covered with a yellowed, cracked oilcloth, and a two-storey wood stove joined to the wall by a long, black stovepipe.

"Sure I'll get you some lemonade. My, oh my! What were you doing, hanging around outside in that heat! My! You ain't going to last long if you just please yourself all the time. Who's that one?"

"Marcel's little brother, just got out of jail yesterday. A real hard little nut."

"Oh my! Little Pierrot! He looks so much like his poor mother. How come I didn't know him right away!"

"He looks like his ma as much as I look like you, old girl. Why don't you want to tell me about that place, Pierrot?"

"Because there's nothing to tell. It was just a big house, that's all."

"I like that: 'The Big House!' As if he'd just come back from some dandy English college! At least wait till you get your jailhouse stripes off before you start telling fibs. You can't fool me, Marcel told me everything."

"He did not!"

"Why not?"

"Because I didn't tell him anything."

The old woman sets down two glasses all frosted from the cold lemonade. Gaston empties half of his at one swallow, then wipes his lips with the back of his hand.

"Oh my, Gaston, not so fast! You're going to block your stomach again. My, he does have a funny outfit on, the little fellow. My! Just like a little *habitant*."

"D'you think they put bows in their hair and give them white shirts and patent leather pumps! It's like a jail. All dressed the same, and everybody gets a number."

"I was not in jail! Why do you tell her that? And besides, at Christmas they put a big red bow right up here, and we looked like real little girls."

"I thought you weren't going to tell me about it."

The boy doesn't answer. Drinking slowly, he stares at Gaston's mother, who seems to love him so much that she cries all the time, and says, "My, oh my!" as if every word hurt her throat. Gaston puts his feet up on the oilcloth and looks at the ceiling, saying not a word.

"And where's he staying now?"

"At my uncle's place."

"Which one?"

"Well, I've only got one."

"Oh, my, you've got four or five on your father's side. Your mother's brothers, I don't know much about them, they didn't like your father and they never came around."

The Rat pounds the table with his fist and spills the boy's drink.

"God damn it, ma, you could use your head. Do you have to go and blab about his father?"

Her eyes and voice start crying again:

"But what did I say? My! Don't get angry like that, it's bad for you. Wait, Pierrot, I'll fill up your glass. He's very sick, you know."

"Just bugger off, will you? Jesus Christ, go watch the street through your venetian blinds. He's staying with his uncle Napoléon and the old maids. Napoléon's had schooling and he's not proud. He's got a good job down near the Place d'Armes."

"Are they going to keep him?"

"I don't know. Nobody told me."

"We don't know. OK now? Go do your spying at the other end of the house."

Maybe the Rat really is mean, talking like that to his old mother who loves him so much and cries a lot, maybe it's not just his sickness. There are really bad sons that are cursed by their fathers and struggle through a life of evil and poverty until they come back and ask to be forgiven and they make a feast for them. But a mother never curses her children. She cries and stays hidden behind the blinds because if she went out they'd see her eyes all red and all her troubles that she can't talk about, she'd be too ashamed. He'd like never to see the Rat again, for he's different from Big Justin or even Pigfoot. Kind of crazy. He's nice for a minute, more than nice, just like a big brother, and then it comes over him all at once: he has to hurt somebody. The boy hasn't known many dogs, but Gaston keeps making him think of a dog. It's not the dog's fault, he's made for biting. Same with Gaston. Maybe something suddenly hurts him too much and he doesn't want anybody to know. Pierrot tries to think of a way of going without being rude. When Gaston is thinking, silently, he continually wipes the saliva from his lips.

"Why do you wear winter boots when it's hot?"

The Rat looks at them in silence, turning them this way and that.

"Because they're as pretty on green as they are on white. And I always have cold feet. They're so far away. With these boots, I can go anywhere and nobody hears. Now yours, I'm not very proud of them. Got to do something about that."

"Yes," says the boy, pulling his cauliflower ankle boots back under the chair. His feet are hot in them.

The mother has disappeared. He listens to the flies buzzing in the doorway, then gets up, uncertainly, for Gaston is still looking at the ceiling. He wonders if he can go without saying anything.

"Don't you want to know what they locked me up for, those three years?"

If he says yes, he'll never get away. He says softly:

"No. We're friends now. I'll come back."

"Because the dirty Greek grocer who hardly speaks French said I told him to hand over the cash and pushed a revolver in his back."

"I don't want to know about it. It's your story, and you're my friend."

"A revolver! That goddam hunky, it was a piece of broomstick. He was too scared to look. And we sure picked the worst day. There wasn't ten bucks in the till. A real scandal."

He pounds the table again, wipes his lips, whistles and gets up. He's thinking up something new now. Pierrot pushes the door open.

"So long, Gaston."

But Gaston bursts out more wildly than ever:

"Ten years for armed robbery, do you hear that? It's written down in all their lousy papers, I'm a robber! Jesus Christ! We'd had nothing to eat for months but potato-peel soup. In winter! You can feed a disease that way, not a man. But they'd thought of everything, with their direct relief. Might as well go begging, like you in the church this morning."

"That's not true! I'd rather die than beg!"

"All right, where did you get all that money from?"

"It was people from the dead man's family put it on my bench. I don't know why. And anyway, you're not my friend. How do I get out?"

"That's better! A little devil just like your brother! He was in the cooler too, for..."

"And that's a lie, too. Why do you act like a rat? I like you, and I know you're not a robber."

"I didn't mean to say that. They found out they were wrong about him. The proof is, he's in the navy, and the American navy at that! You're too young to understand it or get mad about it. Come on, I'll show you the house next door."

"No, I don't remember it and I don't want to. With you I'd hate it, that's for sure."

Gaston puts a hand on his shoulder and leads him outside.

"All right, we'll forget about it. I just wanted you to know that before this god-damned war, which got everybody out of the hole, we had to live like dogs: take what we could get where we could get it. At least dogs don't get shot at. We saw guns everyplace we went. We crossed the country in freight trains, and in almost every village there were men with guns to keep us from getting off."

"Was Marcel with you?"

"Yeah, and another guy who's dead overseas with a bullet in his gut, because he got away from it all here."

"Where all did you go?"

"Right to where the country stops, at the far end, at the sea that looks over at China. They had us cutting down trees with straw bosses all around. When we had enough of that they called us communists."

"Communists?"

"A kind of religion, I don't even know what it is. Marcel thought there was something in it, it might be the answer. Come and see your house, for God's sake! You won't know it again anyway. It still smells like horse shit."

It was true about the trains. Marcel, the last time, when he brought him so many candies he'd had to give them away, for the sugar made him sick because he wasn't used to it, he'd told him you had to jump on when they slowed down for the bridges, and it was tricky because they padlocked some cars and two hobos – that's what he called them – got into a refrigerator car by mistake and couldn't get the door open again, and they'd found them frozen stiff like two sides of veal, and in the work camps near the other ocean they'd cut trees bigger than he'd ever see, and when they'd refused to work because it was too hard and they were barely paid enough to eat, the police came with dogs and rifles and wouldn't let them leave, for they didn't want them to scare the people in the fine houses in the city. And now when he gets off his ship he has lots of money because he can't spend it at sea. And the Russians pulled all his teeth and gave him new ones for nothing, after the time he rowed for two weeks in the North Pole sea.

So the Rat really is a man, and it's his sickness that changed him, and you have to remember that, when you look at him and see that he doesn't behave, or when he's mean just for nothing. They should just try to keep him from doing harm to himself, and the police should let him alone, for he hasn't a very good life ahead of him. Pierrot takes his moist hand, and says:

"Sure I'd like to see it, I want to remember your sister that I went looking for the whole time."

Gaston begins to cough, for a long time, but as if it stopped in his mouth, and his hand gets more damp.

"It's this. . .damn. . .smell," he says, as if he had hiccups. "It's going to rain. Always rains when Dominion Rubber sends it blowing over right in your face. Look at that god-damn chimney puking out burnt rubber!"

Suddenly Gaston pulls his hand away, goes three paces into the weeds and doubles over to spit. When he comes back there's a little more red on his white cotton sweatshirt.

"Oh, Gaston! Why don't you stay in the house!"

She'd appeared without warning, her great white apron catching gobbets of spittle from the weeds. She claps him softly on the back. He rips off his sweater in a rage and throws it in the long grass.

"God damn, ma, how often do I have to tell you to keep me in clean sweaters? You let me go out again with this ketchup on me!"

"There's always clean ones in the drawer, you know very well."

"And if I was a pilot, and I had to change parachutes every day, eh? I suppose you'd put them in the drawer!"

He manages to burst out laughing, and lies down full length on the path breathing heavily.

"You'd think the grass stops the rubber. It smells good down here. Must be why toads never cough."

"Oh, my! It's still damp from the night. Don't be childish, Gaston. I'll bring you another sweater."

When he breathes, his rib cage rises with a noise like newspaper in the wind.

"My little sister, she was seven. Didn't take three weeks and she melted away like a candle! Molson's, now, they make a nice blue smoke, all it does is make you a bit itchy. Over there, on the other side of the bridge, it's worse. You'd wonder what they use to make linoleum."

He gets up, goes to meet his mother, grabs the sweatshirt from her and pulls it on, drags the boy toward the dark and humid entry passage.

"You were out in the country, weren't you? Was it Montfort?"

"I don't know. It's far away. Yes, it's far away in the country. . . .Up there, in the dormitory, you could see little mountains."

"That's where I should go, you know? I think the brides of Christ would like my looks. Just get a load of me!"

"You'd be too tall for the walls."

"Walls, for God's sake! Do they think you're going to take to the woods?...Hey, here we are!"

Along the sidewalk are plain boards held more or less straight by stakes, and behind them a little courtyard filled with flowerpots of every size, and behind that again a tiny house built of stones cut like the pieces of a Chinese puzzle. At street level there is only one paned window crossed by a straight wooden staircase. There's another window like it on the other side, and yet another, higher up, looking like a miniature dog-house. The house is prolonged by a kind of wooden shed or stable where the sunlight gilds a mass of horse litter. Here there is no door, and no glass in the windows filled with buzzing flies and bees. A tall tree seems to grow out of the roof.

Squinting, clenching his teeth, he tries to rediscover this picture in his head, diving as deep as he can, but there is a great, white void between the snowy cold of his mother's forehead and the twilight march-past of the hundreds of boots in the endless corridor, as if scores of pages had been ripped out. In this yard, with its invasion of flowerpots, he can't even recall the car, though it was like an enormous black duck. But he finds the house pretty, in its abandoned state, and he'd like to hear children playing there. What he doesn't understand, is how he remembered with such precision, though enlarged in scale, the details of his uncle's house.

Leaning on the boards, all smiles, Gaston waits patiently for his reaction.

"How does a child die?"

A cloud passes over the Rat's green eyes. He takes a minute to push a few flowerpots back with care and sit down on the gravel before replying.

"I don't know. Same as grown-ups. Same as everything alive, even flowers. Why?"

In his search for distant pictures one has appeared that he has never seen, but was always there.

"You mean my little sister? Don't think about it. What can you do?"

Gaston is disappointed at his reaction to the house, and lets him know it.

"It's run down, I know, but I like it. Even the priest says it's one of the oldest houses in town, built in the Indian days. Imagine, in those days it wasn't even in the city. That's why they call this the Quebec suburb. We were on the road to Quebec. Things you ought to know, eh?"

"It wasn't your little sister. I was thinking of my little brother."

"You didn't even know him."

"I know. But I just remembered somebody told me one day the baby was dead in his crib in the place they leave babies with no parents. A crib, that's Christmas, and it's a baby that's dead and just born. I could never understand that life makes babies for nothing. You can't imagine anything meaner than that. It's a nice house, Gaston, but I don't remember a thing about it. It's as if you told me it was the house of some uncle I don't know."

The Rat takes his hand, and pretends to need help getting up.

"Well, little guy, did we go out to play or not? No use thinking about things you don't understand. Maybe you'll remember inside. If there was even any furniture...."

He takes him inside the house, which smells of damp and cat piss. The plaster is falling, and he can see through holes from one room to another. Downstairs nothing is left but a blackened kitchen sink hanging by a pipe, and upstairs, a bathtub filled with earth. The rooms are so small he can't even imagine beds or chests of drawers or a family in them. Gaston tries to console him:

"It's only normal. Do I remember what the hell I looked like when I was four? Come on, let's go up on the roof."

"Were you born in the country?"

"God, a person never knows what you're going to ask next. You're a funny one with your questions."

"You told me your father brought his plough to work the streets."

The Rat had pushed up on a little trapdoor in the ceiling, clambered into the opening and held his hands down for Pierrot. Now they're up behind the little window that's like a dog-house. Gaston climbs out on the roof at once, for he can't even stand bent over in the attic.

"Don't let go of me. With those boots you'd slide down the tin. I've got rubber soles."

He lifts him by his waist and installs him, safely seated, on the peak of the gable.

"I can see your buggy...and the teacher. She's put on a dress redder than a flower. And your whole street of lamp posts that doesn't even reach the country. Just city, all the time, everywhere...."

The Rat, his boots well anchored on the roof's edge, his face even with Pierrot's breathing into his face, holds him firmly by the waist. He says:

"See those two churches over there? Well, your place is just in front of the first one. Can you find your way?"

"Of course I can! I left little marks all the way when I was coming with you. You don't think I'd trust you!"

Gaston lets go of the boy and pretends he's going back in the window.

"OK. The Rat says good-day to you. You don't trust me, eh?"

"I'm not scared. I've climbed lots of walls."

He turns to look behind, but Gaston is describing again.

"The big red caboose, there, that's Molson's. And the other one, closer by, that's the rubber plant. Beside Molson's, that's Campbell Park. The kids that play there come back as black as tar from the trains down below."

"You didn't answer. Are you from the country?"

"What do you care?"

"If you'd stayed there you wouldn't be sick."

"It's not much more fun, dying of nothing to do in Saint-Blah-Blah. Half a day to get to the neighbour's house, by horse. That makes a lot of silence, and if the neighbour lady's ugly you can always go and eat stones."

He wipes his hand slowly across his eyes, and Pierrot can hear in his mouth the rustling paper of his breath.

"Now! The film continues on this side. Look, your giant's pants. Isn't that a hell of a pair of galluses on them?"

The gigantic window, which from below seemed all alone in the

43

landscape, is followed by others with their feet in the water, and above them the bridge is upside-down, with a hole for the water to go through as it looks at the sky. A great green Meccano toy, and when it was finished they couldn't get it right side up.

"Those aren't galluses, they're stairways with no landings, for there aren't any houses. Do you come from the other side of the bridge?"

"Don't remember. Could be, for my father when he finally realized there was nothing to plough in the city, he climbed up on the bridge again."

"Are you crazy? Let's go down."

It's as if Gaston can see nothing and doesn't know where he is. He's standing alone on the roof, not holding the window, one hand over his eyes. His voice grows mean again, the hiss of an angry cat.

"Never get dizzy. It's not that. Your giant's pants, and. . . .We came to town at the worst time. Suddenly there was no work for anybody. They called it the crash. That's how it was. We're going down, monkey."

"Why did you start off talking about the pants?"

"Good lord, can't you stop asking questions and picking at every word?"

"If you talk to yourself I'll understand."

"All right. The pants, they belong to my father. One night the old boy tried to drink Molson's dry, and somehow he managed to climb up those stairs of yours. He didn't know there were no landings, and he fell down. That's the giant's pantaloons. Now get down before I drop you in the chimney."

They descend to the yard without a word. The Rat starts his chain whirling and suddenly begins flicking it at the flowerpots, hard and accurately. He breaks five or six and knocks over a dozen others. Pierrot picks up the chain and hurls it at his feet with all his strength, but it's much heavier than he had thought.

"You need some practice, you little devil. I'll have to show you how."

"No, I don't want to learn any of your rat tricks. Why did you throw it at my flowers?"

"They're not your flowers and it's not your house. They belong to the old woman that lives under the bridge. She brings them here every morning for the sun and gets them again at night. She must be crazy. There's not even any smell to them."

"That's even worse. What did she ever do to you?"

"Plenty. In the first place, she's so old she'll never die. And she has nothing to do down there under the bridge and she always spent her time watching us, your brother and me and your father, and she works for the police, not for money, just out of pure meanness. That's why I'm not crazy about flowers."

"Why did she watch Marcel and my father?"

"And she calls me Rat."

"What about what you said, you thought it was the smartest animal of all!"

"From her and the cops I won't take that name. As if I hadn't the right to crawl out of sewer holes. As if the rats hadn't saved the world!"

"Saved the world? How?"

"They keep all the filthy diseases underground, and let people think they're clean. But the rats can't clean out their rotten brains. Why did you go and talk about pantaloons and the country!"

"Why did she watch my brother too, and..."

"I've had enough of your stupid questions. Because she hates men. There now! Are you satisfied?"

And he heads back toward his own entry passage after giving a kick to the flowerpots, his yellow boots as ferocious as Balibou's paws.

The boy runs to catch up.

"Are you still mad? Well, don't be. Thanks for showing me the house. Maybe I'll remember. There was always a car in the yard, eh?"

Gaston looks up at the sky, his hair, as long as a girl's, hanging to his shoulders, and his voice barely reaches Pierrot.

"See? I knew you didn't want to tell me you remembered. Sure. A model T, and all the parts are rusting in my lovely garden."

"You know, I like you, Gaston. I'll tell Marcel you looked after me. That stuff you do, it's just because your friends have left, and you're all alone and it's boring."

"Boring? For me? I've no time for that, I'm in a hurry. I have more friends than I need: all the young bums in the neighbourhood, the new ones – they've no experience."

"What's a bum?"

"All the kids that grew up in the street because people told them go play outside. Hey, there's the old bitch with her watering cans."

Still near the bridge, a little old woman comes toward them,

45

slowly pushing a red cart mounted on bicycle wheels and full of pots of water.

"I don't like to hear her scream. Now, scram."

He runs the chain through the boy's hair, gently.

"You're too good, little guy. Green as a new cabbage. They'll get you too. I expect the Angelus has rung in all the churches in town by now. Your old maids won't be happy."

"Are we friends?"

"Almost brothers. A week around here and you won't be the same. Son of a bitch of a life."

Pierrot knows he's too little to help him, that nobody's going to understand that he's butting against a stone wall. It's not the first time he's realized that mostly you can't do anything but go away, but he never thought this about anyone as big as the Rat. And he wonders why things are never easy, and why it's not like in books where everything ends up fine.

"Well, so long, Gaston."

And he goes on his way, following the endless corridor of La-gauchetière Street, treeless, lined with poles, and so loud under his boots that he starts to drag his feet.

He doesn't turn around when Gaston shouts:

"I'm always around the streets, for my lungs. You can find me."

This time the chain hurts him very much, on the shinbone of his right leg.

He bends down and unwinds it slowly, then looks at Gaston, twenty feet away, whistling, leaning on a wall, and throws the chain in a bundle toward him. The coins the policeman had slipped in the front pocket of his overalls roll in the street, toward Gaston and the red cart standing almost in front of the board wall.

"So long, Rat," he says, in a voice that chokes a little.

And he doesn't drag his feet as he goes, so as not to seem to have a sore leg.

He's been playing outside, too long.

4

It's aunt Rose who opens the door for him, and she lights into him at once, her voice held low.

"Now that's a fine way to start off, my little man. Your uncle's been at his lunch half an hour already. And he wanted us to wait for you!"

"There weren't any church bells where I was. I didn't know."

"And where were you the whole time?"

"Oh, just playing."

He follows her into the kitchen where his uncle and Aunt Maria, sitting straight in their chairs, watch his arrival.

"By whillikins, that was a long mass!" says his uncle, getting back to his food.

"Did you buy the sugar?" Aunt Maria asks.

"That's right, what about the sugar?" demands Aunt Rose. It's her turn now.

Aunt Maria goes on: "And what about the money? The Rat took it from you, didn't he? What were you doing with that thief? Where did you go with him? I saw you from the balcony. You went in the church and then you were talking with that mental case."

"Come on, let him sit down," interrupts his uncle without looking up from his plate.

But Aunt Maria, who isn't eating, won't be deterred.

"Where's the money? Out with it! Oh, you're your father's son

47

all right. Sitting on one of the Molson horses, too! Everybody laughing at you. A real little wild animal, straight from the woods, never seen anything in his life! Did you ask the policeman to put you up there?"

"Why didn't you buy the sugar?" asks Aunt Rose, her voice a little quieter.

And Aunt Maria goes on, "I don't know why your uncle took you in. He's forgotten everything. And for all the luck he had with your brother. . . ." Aunt Maria is even redder in the face than this morning, and the vinegar smell on her breath is stronger.

"Leave the boy alone. You can go into all that when I'm gone."

His uncle's voice is louder, but his head is still bent over his plate.

"Here, tuck your napkin in your collar and eat," murmurs Aunt Rose, as she puts a steaming slice of meat on his plate.

But he's staring at his uncle, astonished by the pink jowls that tremble when he chews.

An educated man, but not proud, the Rat had said. He wears thick, heavy glasses which don't seem to help much, for he eats close to his plate, stretching his thick neck ludicrously out of its stiff collar.

Aunt Maria has been talking, but Pierrot didn't hear. He doesn't even know who she was talking to. Finally he says – to get her off his back once and for all –

"Why were you watching me? I thought you sent me out so you wouldn't have to see me."

"And saucy into the bargain! Just like his bum of a brother. Bad blood."

"Your aunt Maria's very sick," his uncle said, wiping his mouth and looking out the window. "You must be nice to her."

Aunt Rose finally sits down and eats something, but Aunt Maria, her cheek jammed into her palm, not even a cup sitting in front of her, stares at him balefully as if she were going to leap at him as soon as his uncle turned his back.

"If you stay here we're going to have to start buying clothes, and waste our money just the way we did with his brother Marcel. Didn't you learn your lesson, Nap? He's got the same surly look."

This time it's Aunt Rose who comes to the rescue.

"Oh, come, he's only a child. He's only eight, Maria, don't drag out all that business."

"Marcel is not a bum. He's a sailor. He even has. . .he has medals.

Did you ever see a bum with medals?"

"Holy Virgin! Medals! I suppose you've seen them?"

"No but he told me. That's just as good."

"And what about the sugar?"

"I forgot."

"And the money?"

"I had it here in my pocket. I bent over playing and it fell out. It's not my fault."

"That's a lie. You had it in your other pocket with your handkerchief."

He remembers. Now he has her trapped. He pulls out the hankie first and finds the two coins, sure enough, at the bottom. He puts them on the table in front of her, slamming them down as hard as he can.

"Little thief! Just like your brother, and only eight! Trying to tell us you lost it! Aren't you ashamed?"

"No. It's there, isn't it? I thought I lost it, that's all."

"Why, we're going to have to keep an eye on you the whole time. Unbelievable!"

"It's his first day, Maria. And the money's there. Just wait a bit before you judge and make comparisons. You must buy him some new things as soon as you can so he looks a little less like an orphan. What's more he doesn't know his way from here to the corner. You could tend to him a bit, take him to the park at least...."

It was at the window his uncle had said all that, as if he were intimidated by Pierrot, or as if he didn't know how to look at a child. But Aunt Maria doesn't give up so easily.

"I suppose you don't care if he runs around with the Rat?"

"You didn't need to let him out alone! And that'll do now!"

From his vest pocket he pulls a big gold watch and adds, without even looking at it:

"I'm late. Get my tea."

Pierrot at once locates in his head a picture in which the big round watch is shining and, just beside that picture, another from the past, quite clear and detailed, of a black box, with a window you can open, and you see in the back a little man, one leg in the air, his elbows bent, frozen in a racing pose, and when you turn a tiny crank he starts running, as fast as you make him go. The box, he's quite sure, is in the big bottom drawer of the buffet in the dining room, in the corner nearest the kitchen.

"How long have you been working in your store?"

"Your uncle doesn't work, he's a manager. Secretary-treasurer, he is," replies Aunt Maria at once. She still holds him in the anger of her blue, bloodshot eyes.

His uncle puts the watch back in his pocket. He takes time to clear his throat thoroughly before answering:

"More than thirty years."

"Why do people have to work?"

"Because...because food doesn't grow on your plate, and an honest man doesn't sit around doing nothing."

"Can't people do something that isn't work, like growing flowers or catching fish?"

"Gardeners work, and fishermen work, for heaven's sakes!"

"For money?"

"Whillikins! They have to eat, too!"

"You have to work to eat?"

"What on earth did they teach you there? I hope you learned to count, at least!"

"And why are there rich people? They can't eat a million's worth. What do they do with the rest?"

"It's not just food. There's all the rest, houses, clothes, furniture and...children."

"You don't see what I mean. I mean, why are there really rich people and really poor people?"

"Because rich people work hard and save their money."

"That's not true. In books the rich people make other people work and they go off in boats or go to parties."

Aunt Maria slaps his arm.

"Now you ask your uncle's pardon. You don't say 'It's not true,' to your uncle. Did you hear that? He's a regular communist."

"Why did you hurt me? You don't work, you can't tell me the answer. I just want to know. Look, why are there kings and ...hunchbacks? Why?"

"Your aunt worked for years. Now she's not well, I told you that. We can talk about these things when you've been to school."

His uncle pours a little tea in his saucer and drinks from it loudly.

"She's old, that's different. And being sick..."

"My lord, Nap, if you keep him around here long I'm going to have to go to hospital. Who can put up with talk like that?" moans Aunt Maria, finally getting up. She disappears into the dining-room rubbing her eyes.

"Why are there babies sick enough to die, and boys too, who couldn't work if they wanted to?"

His uncle chokes into his tea-filled saucer.

"You're making your uncle cough with your silly questions, and you hurt Aunt Maria's feelings. Now you go and ask her pardon."

Aunt Rose doesn't raise her voice, but he feels that he's made her angry, and his uncle too. Yet he doesn't see why such ordinary questions should make grown-ups mad. It was just the same in the other place, but the crows don't like children because there are too many of them and they haven't time to answer, and it's always little Jesus when they do answer, and he knows everything and you're supposed to listen to him in your heart, but Pierrot's never heard him, not even when he spoke as close as possible to the baby dead in the crib. But his uncle is educated, and not proud, and there's nobody around, and he's got time, even if he is drinking his tea.

"I won't ask her pardon, for she doesn't like me and she doesn't even know me, and she doesn't like Marcel, and she wishes I'd stayed where I was. And I wish I had too."

And he decides not to talk any more.

His uncle is drinking out of his cup now and rolling the mouthfuls around inside. Aunt Rose is stacking the dirty dishes. There's silence, but he's so used to that, it does him good, and he digs his fists in his eyes to keep from seeing.

The Chinese boy, who isn't really Chinese, just that he was born before his head was ready or his eyes were up in the right place, and he's not even yellow – he used to ask questions nobody could answer. Why couldn't he eat ants through his toes so he wouldn't have to look for them with his eyes, and maybe they'd have a different taste from one toe to the next? Why weren't there doors in windows and windows in doors? Why didn't snow grow like grass, and why didn't grass melt when he squeezed it in his hand? Why didn't rain go through his skin? Why were there no princesses with just one eye and why was Balibou naked and had the right to piss where he pleased? And even, why didn't Pigfoot have a little baby for him to play with? Pierrot would give him any old answer, never getting impatient, and the Chinese boy was always satisfied. And when he jumped at you and dug his fingers in your eyes, you knew it was because he was the Chinese boy and you hadn't been on your guard. Would that boy ever have time to grow up and go to an office or a factory every day? Perhaps after all the world outside was no more than thousands of walls in all directions, where you thought you could go as far as you wanted, or farther, until things got different, but they were always the same, like a grilled gate on a beautiful park where there was everything you could imagine, but the grille moves back as you move toward it and you can never get in, and the grille is there just to let you guess all the impossible things that are possible. Or that the beautiful park is nowhere, only in your head, but how do you explain why you can make such terrific things in your head, so easily, without ever having seen them, and hear words that people never say, and cure babies, and slice the rich up into little bits so that everybody can have a little, and grow trees that you can eat, just by taking some, without working, so you'd have time to listen and answer or find out when you don't know. He wouldn't have minded staying on in the other place, for a long time, if he'd been sure that in the world it was so different, and full of things that couldn't happen inside the wall.

Take Balibou, for example, he'd always known that he was real and not real at the same time, nothing but stories, but then the stories were real because he told them, and even drew them. So there must be a way for things that weren't real to be a little bit real, even if it was just playing at putting in the real world the things that were always real in your head. It was hard, because there were so many kinds of people, so different, and too old, and some of them had grown impossible themselves and were so scared of changing they'd rather just stay angry. Even if the Blue Man appeared and gave them the keys of all the doors in the world they wouldn't budge. Like the ants. Once he'd tried to help the Chinese boy, knocking down all their piles of sand with a stick, and putting some molasses two feet away, in clear sight on a naked rock. Well, what do you think! The ants spent the whole day building up their sand piles, even more than there were before. And not a one of them went to the molasses. And the Chinese boy ended up eating it with his fingers. That's why the streets are straight, with other streets, just as straight, crossing them at the same distance, because people always do the same things, and in the same place, and don't see the things they could imagine without even trying.

The uncle has finished his cup of tea. After wiping his mouth with great care, he sits with his hands joined on the white table cloth, as if he had forgotten about being late. Even Aunt Rose says:

"It's after one, Nap. Don't worry about the boy. I'll look after him. He may not be so bad."

Pierrot had taken his fists from his eyes and saw nothing but red for a moment. Now he sees his uncle, motionless, looking at the ceiling with sunlight filling his spectacles. Finally he speaks, with a voice so deep it seems to come from under the table.

"Oh, it's not the boy. They landed last night, and it's not like Dieppe this time, they're advancing. Thousands of ships and planes. The Germans never even saw them coming."

"It's near the end, then," says Aunt Rose with great respect.

"Oh, it'll be a long time yet, but the Americans' war machine, it's something fantastic. They can lose twice what the Germans have left and come up with twice or three times more. What they've manufactured in the last years, you have no idea!"

"We were saying the same thing. In Ninie's factory they've started making ordinary shirts again, just like before the war."

"It won't be so easy. Hitler most likely has kept some secret weapons for the end, worse than the V2's."

Aunt Rose leaves her pots and pans to come and sit opposite uncle Nap and digest the news. Her astonishment is loud:

"Well now! The invasion! Are our people there?"

"Of course. After all, they speak French."

His uncle gets up, takes a pair of scissors from the cupboard, and cleans his fingernails with one point.

"The boss is always at the radio. As if they were going to give some news of his son, the Colonel!"

Pierrot, who doesn't know anybody there, tries to imagine thousands of Gastons charging out of the dark, silver chains in their hands, wearing light yellow boots, whistling like sparrows in the morning, but he can only see one Gaston at a time. In his softest voice, he asks:

"The enemy, are they bad men?"

His uncle, having returned the scissors to the cupboard and dusted off his vest, glances uneasily at him:

"I suppose so."

"And the enemy's enemies?"

"Well, I'm late now."

And he goes off toward the bathroom. The boy shouts at his back:

"Are there bad fathers or brothers on one side?"

Aunt Rose pulls the tablecloth out from under his elbows.

"This isn't the time to bother your uncle with silly questions. It's no matter for children, this isn't."

Matter for children! They drag him out of the other place just before such a serious thing happens, without explaining anything to him, without even telling him what's going to happen to him! And the Blue Man has to go and disappear at a time like this! Now, that's not the same as Balibou, who can change in his head from one shape to another, from one bit of a story to another, and uses words the boy knows how to write, and has written, but always changes back into a yellow cat, ugly as sin and with a stump for a tail. The Blue Man, he's not sure. For a long time he thought he too came from a book, but could never recall which one, and he remembers all the books, from the very first one, which hadn't many pages and showed on the cover a boot with no laces that housed a poor family, right up to those with no pictures, just words, and he remembered those too and used them when he realized that he too could invent stories, for he'd just, in fact, invented one. Really, the Blue Man had no shape, just a kind of blue smoke so faint he could see through it, and no voice either, and no words, but he had always understood him, as if he spoke by looking (though of course he'd never seen his eyes) or just by being there, and only at night. Suddenly he'd be there, sometimes because he'd called him, sometimes not. And he'd be there for him alone, and in his blood – he didn't know how else to describe it – were the words he needed to help him accept being shut in, not inside the walls but in himself where nobody could touch him or see him, and that's why people always got their ideas about him from outside, and that's only the least important part; and words that helped him believe somebody loved him for what was inside, for what would allow him when he grew up not to be like the others but himself at last; words to assure him that everything that doesn't exist yet, because of the cold on his mother's forehead and the walls and the crows which prevent things from being as they were, all the things he dreams, because nobody can command his thoughts, and all that he doesn't know but needs to know, that all that is only a test which will likely last a long time but will still come to an end because the Blue Man, wherever he is – and he disappears sometimes for so long the boy begins to lose faith – will never forget, and will have looked after everything, and everything will be possible again.

But this has nothing to do with his uncle and aunts. In a way they're worse, for in the other place he was one in a crowd and could be nothing, that is he could be free from others watching him. Here he's always caught in a glance, even the Rat's, whom his brother had told to keep an eye on him. He can find only one explanation, the one his uncle just gave. Something so important was happening elsewhere that it was more important than Pierrot, and the Blue Man just couldn't come, and they'd known and grabbed the chance to move him as fast as they could and even the police had helped so it would be quicker and nobody would know. But he knows his uncle well, for it was his uncle that had somehow made himself unforgettable, and he's always suspected, without daring to say it for fear of breaking a spell forever, that there were very strong bonds between them. But he searches in vain for some kind of acknowledgement of the mystery from his uncle. It seems as if he too only looks at him from the outside. . .and, worse still, draws back when he tries to show him a little of what the Blue Man knows so well.

When the Rat made him go into the old house he felt, for the first time, a kind of dizzy suspicion that. . . .What if the Blue Man. . . .

He doesn't notice his uncle leaving, and when he opens his eyes he sees how the sun adds its own yellow to the powder Aunt Rose puts on the wart on her nose. She looks at him without anger, but rather with a kind of discouragement, or weariness.

"You still don't want to go and tell Aunt Maria you're sorry?"

"No."

"It's true she's very sick, you know. We have to be patient with her. She's just like that. She should even have been in hospital long ago."

"She's not sick, she's old and mean!"

Aunt Rose drums on the white metal table with the fingers of one hand and bites the nails of the other. She makes him think of a serving girl who doesn't know what to do when her work is finished.

"No, no, she just forgets you're a child, and she never liked boys."

"Why?"

"Oh, nobody knows things like that. Maybe because they're noisy, and you can't fuss with them the way you can with a girl. I must tell you while she's not here: you mustn't ever drink out of her glass, or use her knife, or lie in her bed."

"What would I do in her bed? I don't even want to go in her room. She doesn't smell good."

"I can tell you about the smell, too, one day, but there's no hurry. And in the bathroom I've put blue towels for you. Never use any others."

"You'd think I was going to get sick."

"Yes, it's catching. That's why she should be in hospital."

"Like the Rat? I mean, Gaston?"

"Yes, it's the same disease, and he's a thief as well. That's why you're not to talk to him."

"He's Marcel's only friend."

Aunt Rose gets up, sighing heavily.

"Come, I'll take you to the park. My god, we've all been brought up with that disease around us. Wait, I have to change my dress."

As soon as she's gone he dashes over to the dining-room buffet and opens the big drawer. It's there, in exactly the same place. He opens the little window, turns the crank and the little white figure on a black background begins to run, at first stopping often, until he gets the trick and can even make it go back or run in one place, as if the ground were moving.

A hand strikes his arm so hard that the box falls back into the open drawer.

"Have to put locks on all the drawers to keep you from nosing around!"

He doesn't even turn, but leans his head against the buffet doors, clenches his fists and tries not to breathe because of the ever stronger smell of rotten vinegar. With Pigfoot he could at least fight back, and say the worst things to her as he was being hit. He can't do a thing against Aunt Maria, for this is her house and she's sick. Suddenly, his head against the cold of the varnished wood, he sees again the parlour of the old stone house, a big green plush armchair, a thick phonograph record that turns too fast for the voice of the lady singing inside the flowing water tap, hears her voice begin to stretch and slide lower and lower until it dies in a last long burp because he pushed the handle too far. And he takes a man-sized slap right in the face, which makes his lip bleed. That was at home, a long time ago, and the man was...

He turns swiftly and blows as hard as he can in Aunt Maria's face, and she staggers back on her wobbly legs and has trouble standing even when she leans on the big table.

"Little sa...vage! I'll...train...you yet."

56

She crumples to the floor. He feels sick, and looks at her without moving.

He is set free by the arrival of Aunt Rose, in a dress with big flowers, a hat with flowers on her head and white lace gloves on her hands. She asks no questions, but helps Aunt Maria to her feet and pushes her toward her room muttering angrily:

"You're that way in broad daylight now, are you? And in front of the boy! Good lord, what are we going to do with you?"

While they're gone he goes to the piano and lets his hands run over the notes, wondering if the Chinese boy is waiting for him there, sitting quietly behind Pigfoot's little guardroom, for that's the only place there's any shade, or if he looks for him by showing the book to the others, rolling his little almond eyes that will likely never go up where they belong.

Aunt Rose comes back at once.

"Come along, I'm ready. You see how sick she is. Did she say something to you?"

"No, I didn't even hear her coming. Is it because she doesn't eat?"

"Maybe it is," she replies, as if she were asking herself the same question. "She'll sleep now, and then she'll be all right."

5

When she opens the door of the apartment there is a little girl sitting on the landing. He is so delighted to find her that he's embarrassed and unable to move.

And the girl! She jumps up at once and contemplates him without a smile. Her hair! He's never seen such hair, of a colour he'd never imagined: russet and golden at the same time, so fine that it waves in the light at her slightest movement, as if it were weightless, and falling far down her back. Her bare legs and arms and her face are very white, with little rust-coloured spots, and he drowns in the dark waters of her eyes. She has on a green dress with a wide, white collar. He decides that she's the most delicately lovely thing in the world, so precious that he could never put his hand in hers. And he can't move from the spot for fear she might dissolve in thin air.

Aunt Rose, already on the lower landing, shouts angrily at him:
"Will you come down out of there?"

But he remains paralysed by her honey-coloured eyes that stare at him with a look that is almost hard. For all his embarrassment he manages what he thinks is a smile, but it must be an ugly one, for the little girl sticks out her tongue, and goes on staring him down.

"Hello," he says finally, in a voice he doesn't know.

She crushes him with her silence.

"Get down here or we're not going to the park," Aunt Rose shouts in a rasping, impatient voice that puts him into a worse state of embarrassment.

He starts down, his feet like lead, he's forgotten how to walk in that pitiless gaze, and he turns his back on her at last after another smile that works no better than the first.

"If you're going to the park I'll go with you." She darts the words at him joyously, leaning over the railing. He trembles with emotion.

"Go to the park with your mother," says Aunt Rose roughly.

And she grabs him by the arms to drag him down the stairs.

"Why couldn't she come with us? What's it to you?"

A minute ago he was almost proud of her dress and her hat with the big flowers, but now he finds her ridiculous, looking like a crow dressed up as a city lady. But she doesn't answer, and drags him along at a marching gait, fiercely determined to bring him to his pleasures herself.

"What if her mother's out and she's all alone?"

"Alone? She's alone all right, and it's a sure thing her mother's out! Out all day and out all night!"

He hears the girl come down behind them, kicking her heels, and when he looks back she's on the lower landing, one leg raised, and a finger on her lips to tell him to be quiet. This simple gesture of complicity fills him with joy. The slightest sign exchanged with a stranger establishes a relationship. This he knows well, for in the other place, in the silence of the walls, he's often had to communicate with his comrades by signs alone, sometimes for months.

"Her mother is a bad woman. You mustn't speak to them. Not ever."

He can't even imagine what a bad woman is like, unless it might be Aunt Maria. How could anybody ever say it about a mother, and the mother of such a beautiful child? What happens to a child that nobody's allowed to talk to? Even big Justin, in the other days. . .he'd almost always forget that he was his enemy, and he'd speak to him, not always with insults. But the girl! You should almost have to ask her permission, it was such a pleasure to look at her, and he felt so clumsy and heavy when she was there.

"She's a real princess!" he said, with all his enthusiasm.

"A princess, is it! Poor little fool, it's time you got around a bit!"

His aunt's repressed laugh makes him furious. It was a real witch's laugh, with all the power to change the princess into a spotted toad. He begins to wonder if he's allowed to talk to anybody, or if it's the whole neighbourhood that's decided not to talk to his aunts. In the first place, why are they old maids? That's a disease that makes people nasty, he knows something about that.

As if no child wanted them for a mother. Like the crows, there was something lacking, they weren't quite women. It wasn't their hair. What could it be? Something you can't see, that's never talked about, something under their clothes, perhaps, that keeps them from having babies, and men, the real men, know about it. And that's why old maids don't like boys. As far as the crows were concerned, Justin maintained that they had no tits, and put little bags there which they took off at night when they went to bed. That's how he knew for sure, with proof, that Saint Agnes wasn't a crow, and they'd put her among them for revenge, to hide her away. Maybe old maids were the same way, but they found out too late to go in with the crows, or there was some other piece of woman they lacked. How could you know? They wore so many clothes, over and under, and none of the boys knew all that a woman has, for none of them said the same thing about it. Justin, whose father was a priest in Jerusalem, said, among other dirty things, that instead of a thing they only had hair between their legs. And that was why some people called it "camel's hair." And Justin was a damned liar, for he'd seen the statue of a saint all naked in one of the chaplain's books: Saint Venus, and you couldn't see hair or anything, even though she tried to hide herself with one hand. Old maids weren't made like the others, of that he was sure, and that's why they forbid him to talk to children and hated women who'd had babies. Maybe when he's seen some real mothers he'll understand, and all the things that bother him so much about his aunts won't matter then.

In the street he succeeds in freeing his arm, and walks on the edge of the sidewalk, as if he didn't know her. Every time they pass a grocer's, and the streets are full of them, tiny, all with the same Coca-cola or orangeade signs, she tells him the owner's name and what you can buy here and what you should buy there, according to whether things are better or cheaper. She shows him the neighbourhood, not just the corner stores but the houses of friends, and by keeping count he discovers that Aunt Eugénie has more lady friends than her sister, and that they're different ones; and she teaches him street names, and makes him repeat them, as if he couldn't read.

He barely listens to her anyway, for he keeps looking back, only when he can't help it any longer, but every ten steps or so just the same. The girl pays no more attention to him than the sparrows picking at the horse buns which men are gathering in two-wheeled garbage cans. She hops on one foot, then takes a jump, turning in the air, and lands on both feet, her legs a little apart, and then starts it all again. Twice he thought she'd given up, for she crossed the street to look long in the store windows; but then she went back to her lonely hopping game, keeping the same distance.

"Everybody knows us. I'll always know what you've been up to," Aunt Rose announces, as they reach the first street with streetcar tracks.

"What do you want me to do? Talk to myself because you won't let me talk to anybody?"

"You cross on the green light!" she screams, hauling him back by the braces of his overalls, as a streetcar comes rattling toward them.

Behind them, always at the same distance, the lonely child has bent double to trace signs in the dust with her finger, her hair falling down straight and touching the ground. A fountain of russet sunlight which his aunt brusquely banished by pushing him into the street.

"When there's a streetcar, you wait, because there could be a car behind it."

"Why didn't you leave me in the other place if you only want me not to talk?" he asks, with an anger he can no longer hold back.

And he searches in vain for words that could hurt. The ones he knows, you only say to men. He wants to run on Craig Street and back to Plessis, back to the haughty princess, and walk with her the whole day long. But she gives him no sign. Maybe the crows in all those years have succeeded in turning his face into a frightening mask, or marked him with a sign that only he cannot see.

Under her flowered hat, Aunt Rose has the ferocious face of one who will not be diverted from her path.

"You couldn't stay because of your age. Now you'd have to go to another place, with bigger boys."

"Another place?"

His voice chokes. So that was the only reason. He'd grown bigger, and there were other places! He's ashamed to have a shiver in his blood. What was the difference? Nothing here was like what he'd imagined it would be in that postponed future in which the Blue Man was to come and open the park gates for him, the gates of life, which can't be what he's known here since yesterday, for anyway it came too soon and too suddenly to be true.

"You're not so proud and rascally now, I see!"

Aunt Rose has her little triumph at the corner of the second street with tramways, just in front of the little park on the opposite side, all surrounded by a high iron fence, and much smaller than the battleground he was used to elsewhere.

"Why am I staying with you, anyhow?"

She has taken out of her purse the same two coins, which she holds out to him, and in spite of everything there's something in her voice like a little kindness which she refuses to show.

"Here, if you want to buy yourself some candies. But that's for a week."

She adds in a mysterious tone:

"We'll try once more. Because you're so much younger."

Then the old rasping voice is back.

"In the next place they'd teach you a trade. That would be much better."

As far as he can see, looking back, there's no princess. He looks at the playground where even the trees are fenced in, and where no more than eight or ten children, all younger than he, are running about in the dirty, yellow dust. On one side is the high red-brick wall of the Molson Brewery, and on the other a long building in grey stone, and behind, just nothing, as if there were a great hole dug in a straight line. He has no desire at all to go into this place that looks like an immense rabbit cage. He'd rather walk and walk all day, anywhere at all, without talking to anybody or even listening to the Rat and getting his chain thrown at his legs. He'd rather help the old woman water her flowers, or push the garbage carts full of horse buns.

Why did the russet princess disappear when she was so near the park? Maybe she was just hiding until his aunt disappeared.

With the same military stride his aunt makes him cross Notre Dame Street and goes straight up to a big, bald man sitting on an enormous barrel, his legs hanging down, a large silver whistle in one hand and a pipe in the other.

"He's just got here and doesn't know anybody. Mustn't let him out. I'll be back to get him at five."

"Good day, young sir!" says the attendant with a laughing voice in an expressionless face. "I'm here to keep the big ones out and the little ones in."

"Just for today, till he gets used to things," Aunt Rose orders in a more than usually bossy tone, as if she'd been running park attendants all her life.

The man with the whistle straightens up on his barrel. Nobody's going to step on his toes, which, by the way, are high above the ground, higher than Aunt Rose's belly.

"Look here! I'm not a baby-sitter. It's up to you to stay with him."

"I suppose you get paid to tan your skull. I said I'll be back at five."

She turns tail without even saying good-bye.

"Who the hell does she think she is? Not your mother, I hope?"

"My aunt. She's an old maid," he says haughtily.

"Well, that's one good thing! Come on in, then. We'll see about goin' out."

He goes straight to the emptiness at the back, and discovers, much farther down, a hole with no end either way, in which minuscule men play at making trains go ahead and back up. He leans with his two hands on the metal grille, and watches them with so much fascination that he forgets everything, even the one-legged princess who strikes fountains of russet sunlight from the sidewalk when she stoops.

6

"You like trains. I don't. They're dirty, and they go to war."

His nerves tingling, breathless, he's been glued to the iron grille for the last ten minutes, spending all his energy not to move a hair, especially not to turn away, his gaze plunging into the crater of trains which now move in a faint fog of green and gold in which he can't pick out details. Without really seeing her, or perhaps just a hint out of the corner of his left eye, he had known at once that she was there, two steps away, a leaf off the sun that the first breeze could scare away, mute and caged like himself.

The voice – not a child's, not a woman's either, dark and warm, with little shrill bursts, like glimmers of sun on the water.

She couldn't have been talking to anyone else, but he waits, for no words come, not a one, and he'd like her to go on, just to be sure, and not lose the feeling of melting inside, but enjoy longer this caressing warmth, but then he's never spoken to a little girl his age, didn't even think he'd want to, they'd always seemed to him, the few times he'd seen them from a distance, too wrapped up in the world of babies. And in stories girls had to be at least twenty before they could be important at all. Any younger than that and their mothers were still wiping their noses, or they pretended to be older by wearing high heels and paint on their faces and talking like magpies.

Not just because of her hair, but as soon as he saw her on the landing, he'd found her so different, so much alone in all her body, with gestures, looks, and a way of being all her own and that he'd never find again, that he immediately took her seriously, and even trembled a little before a thing that could exist only once, and for himself alone: even more than the soft, sweet pear Saint Agnes gave him, which he spent a whole afternoon eating, hidden away, and it was the best thing that had happened to him in the world, because he'd known all that time that it was a kind of miracle and he'd never eat another with equal joy.

"That's where they leave from."

Because she's pointing, he has no choice but to back off a little and look at her, to see which way she points. She doesn't smile, but seems to accept him as if he'd always been in her life.

"You mean the castle with the green towers?"

"Look at your hands, they're all black. That's train smoke."

She has an odd way of pronouncing, almost separating the syllables, word for word, not in phrases.

"It's not a castle, it's a big, big hall that smells bad, and it has doors all over where soldiers go through to get in the trains. They call it Viger Station. Are you from the country?"

He tries to get the black off his hands by rubbing them on the grilled railing, but he only succeeds in blackening his face as well, and he can't answer because he has an eye that's crying.

"Are you visiting the old ladies? Keep your eye open, I'll blow in it."

She blows hard, and he can't keep his eye open. In any case, it's in his nose she's blowing, and he doesn't dare say anything for he'd like her to go on.

"You always get cinders in your eyes here. I never come here. I wanted to get to know you because I'm bored."

Then why did she stick out her tongue at him? He should have known it was a game, and that it was Aunt Rose she was making fun of.

"You're too tall."

She pulls herself up by his shoulders, jumping to blow in his eye, but falls before she can reach it.

"Get on your knees, that'll be easier."

He doesn't have to be asked twice. She puts one arm around his head, props her legs and stomach against him and blows resolutely in his eye, holding the lid up with her finger. Her arm is so cool on his neck, and her belly so warm against his chest that he can't stand it long, pulls gently away and sits down in the brown dust.

"That's better. I can see you now."

"You must be dying of heat in that! You're dressed like the trainmen."

"My Aunt's going to buy me some new stuff tomorrow. This is the uniform."

"Take off your shirt. I'm going to sit beside you. Or do you want to go and see the station?"

He never took his shirt off there, not even in the hottest summer. It was against the rules. He certainly couldn't do it in front of her. So he stays frozen in silence, knowing quite well that she won't stay interested in a porcupine that rolls itself up in its own strangeness. At the other end of the playground he sees, under the eye of the man on the barrel, children in shorts, shirtless, running tirelessly after a red ball, and he can't remember ever having been so naturally a child of that age, that is, playing without having to look before and behind. He'll always have the marks of cords on his wrists and ankles to prevent him from being confident, the way you draw in air, without thinking about it.

"The trains can't go to the war. There have to be ships."

"I can't sit down beside you unless you take off your shirt."

Her little green dress with the white collar, and what's under it – which must be fine as the softest paper – are not, apparently, to be allowed to touch the yellow dust full of cinders. Even the Rat would have understood that. He takes off his shirt, his eyes lowered, and spreads it out beside him. His naked skin feels cold and hot at the same time, but he slips the braces of his overalls back up on his shoulders. She squats on it with her dress fanned out around her. Just let Aunt Rose try to throw out that prisoner's shirt!

"You don't believe me? Just come and see. Every day there are lines of soldiers waiting. Even my daddy left from there."

"Your daddy? What's that?"

"You know, my father! My name is Jane. My father doesn't speak anything but English. He's an aviator."

It takes some time for him to swallow these revelations, which made him sad. An *anglais*! And an aviator at that! It's as if she'd flown twenty feet away from him, and even his shirt wasn't clean enough for her. She could never be his friend.

"Mine's an aviator too," he said very quickly, without even thinking, so that she wouldn't get farther away.

"Is he a pilot or a bombardier? Mine's a pilot."

"Mine too," he said without a tremor.

And for good measure, and to get one ahead of her, he adds proudly:

"But mine went away in a plane. It was a flying fortress, too. And I have a brother who's a submarine captain."

She bursts out laughing.

"That's not true about the submarine, they're all German."

"So what?"

"Your father and mine would have to drop bombs on it."

"My brother's in the United States. And my uncle said the Americans have built three times what the Germans have, except for the V2's."

"What's a V2?"

"I don't know. It's a secret weapon."

"My mother's French, but my name is Jane anyway. When I took my father to the station I hadn't seen him for a long, long time. Since then he never came back."

"Mine either. Can you speak English?"

"Before we came here. . .let's see, a year, no, two years ago. We were in a house all by itself, on a mountain. Daddy hadn't been there for a long time, but everybody spoke English. Why do you say the trains don't go to the war?"

"The proof of that is, my brother commands a submarine. Because the ocean's there, and it's big, from Panama right to the North Pole."

"What's Panama?"

"I just told you, it's the other end of the ocean. He sent me a postcard. I'll show it to you."

"All right, where the trains stop there are ships. That doesn't change what I said. You thought I'd given up following, didn't you?"

"Oh, I knew you were hiding."

He has completely forgotten that he's taken his shirt off for the first time, and he talks to her as if he'd been talking to girls all his life, and if she were not so beautiful, if he didn't feel so happy in this green and gold froth that's not made for him, and if he weren't so afraid of slipping out of sight of her hazel eyes that surround him now with such a warming light, it would be just as if he were talking to a boy that was not too smart and didn't know any more than he did and believed everything you told him. But he knows that his own lies haven't made her less mysterious, and her daddy continues to bother him. The only difference between her and a boy — and it's the most serious thing that's ever happened to him until now — is that if anybody laid a hand on her, even his

68

aunt, he'd fight for her until he died, without hesitating a second. He's afraid only of her, though she's fragile as a sparrow, and of no other. In fact, he'll never be afraid of anybody again.

"Your uncle smiles at me when he's alone, but when he's with them he lets on he doesn't know me. Mama says they're crazy old maids, and you can't do a thing about it. And you, where do you come from?"

"From the chateau. Far away."

He didn't hesitate a moment, it was so fast it became true.

"And that's the uniform of the children in the chateau?"

"Because we were occupied by the enemy, the crows."

"And how did you get out?"

"The Blue Man sent two warriors to rescue me."

"To send you to those mean aunts. When they talk to me it's only to shout 'Get away!' And they say filthy things about Mama to everybody. Mama told me."

"That's only for now. When he comes back from the war he'll chase the crows and put flowers and trees and fountains everywhere. And all the children will do as they please, and they'll have horses and dogs and even a room if they want."

"Is the Blue Man your father, the flyer?"

"I don't know. I've never seen him."

"I saw mine for a whole day. And he was so handsome in his blue uniform, I can't understand why he left home. And kind, like I've never seen any other father. How many children are there in your chateau?"

"Hundreds. It's true, a pilot is a Blue Man."

"Sky blue. Can there be hundreds of children in one family?"

He'd rather talk about something else, because she has him into too many lies at once, and he's had no time to think, and isn't certain he has all the answers ready. Girls don't know enough about life to really trap you, but you mustn't stretch your luck too far.

"They're not even related to each other. They were all stolen."

"Stolen? Why would they steal children?"

"You see, they're. . .hostages! You see what I mean. The crows took the chance when their fathers were away at war."

"And before, weren't there any children in the chateau?"

"Sure, but that was different. They were children with no parents at all, and the Blue Man gave them his chateau."

"What are crows?"

"They're women without any hair, so they hide their heads with great wings and they can't have any babies, but it's for the same reason old maids can't."

"What's the reason?"

"Oh, I don't know that. It's a secret."

"If you never saw your father, nor the Blue Man, how do you know he's a pilot?"

"My brother told me."

"You've seen your brother?"

"Don't you believe anything I tell you? Of course I've seen my brother. He even sends me letters where the army cuts out parts with scissors, so nobody will know where his submarine is."

"And you dressed like that, every day? That's a sort of army, too."

"In a way. It was lucky we weren't girls, for girls...."

"In our school we all dress the same. And your crows are nothing but nuns, just like the ones in my school."

"It's not true! We weren't girls!"

He had shouted because two trains were whistling at the same time, down below, and because he was indignant. He goes down on all fours and with his finger draws a circle in the dust, with big square wings above, and in the middle a long beak with saw-teeth.

"You call that a nun?"

She goes on all fours as well to examine his drawing, which he can't see through her russet hair.

"I don't know what that can be. Mama said you'd come out of an orphanage."

"And what do you think an orphanage is, if you please?" he asks, with half dissembled anxiety.

"I don't know. A house where they put children with no parents. But you have a father, same as I do. I have a sister too, a big sister. But she's mean."

He doesn't like her having a sister, even a mean one. He thought he had her to himself, what with her father at war and her mother always out.

"How is she mean?"

"I don't know. She makes Mama cry. And she never stays home. Seventeen, she is. We don't even know what she does. My mother works making parachutes. She comes home late at night and my sister doesn't even help looking after me."

"Are you always alone?" he asks in a voice brimming with joy.

"Mostly, but grandmother comes sometimes."

"You won't be alone now. I'll be there."

She gets up, bursting with laughter, and he looks away so as not to see her little white pants, for she's shaking her dress out violently.

"What should I do with a boy like you? And what about your aunts? Anyway I have a good friend, Thérèse, and she often phones, and I have supper there every day, and they have a big family and I have lots of fun. She's to come and get me here."

And she goes over to the iron railing to watch the trains go by in the big hole. Her laugh hurt him, and even more this Thérèse and her big family and all the fun. An inspection during which he didn't have time to talk, and she turns him down with finality. She only wanted to get to know him, and she did it. Yes, girls are like that, butterflies that never stay in one place, and light only on their own shadows.

In the middle of the playground there's a raised stand with a pagoda roof, and a sign he manages to read: "LES CONCERTS CAMPBELL, tous les soirs à huit heures." On Notre Dame Street the streetcars never stop unless the light is red. Nobody gets on or off there, but there's always a Molson wagon to stop between the tram doors, and the sun shines on the swelling chocolate rumps of the horses.

He waits in vain for her to come back or call to him. Then he's afraid he won't be able to talk to her again before that Thérèse comes. He puts his shirt on above his overalls and goes to her.

"A big, white ship just went by, with two funnels."

Her beautiful, low voice brings him back from the dizziness that had almost seized him again, from the smells of the brewery, the rubber factory and the coal fumes from below.

"It was pulled by three train engines and it's going to stop in the station to take on soldiers," he says playfully.

"Very funny. You don't believe me? It's the first time you've been here and you don't believe you can see ships!"

He'd been very pleased with his idea of the ship in the railway station. Now he tries desperately to find another place for it and make her laugh. But she puts her little hand, faintly freckled with gold, through the grille to show him a place at the end of the long building that blocks their view on the other side of the crater.

"You see that little blue corner over there? Well, that's the river! You only see a little piece at a time, but if you wait you see the whole ship."

"It's so close, and we can't see it? What's the river like? Do you

71

have to go up on the bridge to see it?"

"I'm hungry. The french fries are here."

She knows it without even turning her head. Now he can smell the french fry wagon behind them. A rig of the same dirty yellow as the streetcars, with a box hanging under it, pulled by a horse with protruding ribs and hanging head, enters the park. She had left him suddenly and is already passing the bandstand when he decides to catch up with her. They reach the wagon together. He's astonished to see the Rat along with a fat man in a white apron stained with burnt oil. His astonishment turns to indignation when he hears the Rat speak to Jane in his dead voice:

"I was sure I'd find you here, little squirrel. I came just for you. It's my treat, and the vinegar too."

He holds out a paper cone so full that it's running with oil, and a few chips fall on her dress.

"Hey! Rat! Don't fill it so full! You can give me another one."

Gaston leans out of the rig and puts his two long hands in the russet of her neck to draw her to him.

"What do we give to the nice man?"

Not only does he kiss her, but she kisses him back, on the cheek.

"Now you eat and grow up. I can hardly wait to see you big enough to...."

And he gives a great slap in the back to the fat man, with a laugh that sounds like the hiss of the french fry wagon.

"Eh, lard-ass? She'll be a good piece, eh?"

Choking with anger, the boy puts his two coins in the window and says haughtily to the Rat:

"I'm buying for her. What are you doing here anyway, Rat?"

"Well! Pierrot's come to the park for a nice little playtime. My little *habitant* has found the little squirrel. It's true, you're neighbours. I'll tell you: I'm earning my potatoes, and getting some fresh air. Take back your quarter, we don't want it."

"You've no right to kiss her."

"You don't say! And why not?"

"Because you're the Rat, and you're sick. And you're not even related to her!"

Jane is greedily eating her french fries. It must be days since she put anything into her pretty beak. Too busy even to pretend interest in what's going on. The Rat is barely put out, and keeps laughing with a sound of hissing oil.

"Look at this little bastard! D'you think she belongs to you? You're not the one to stop me kissing the prettiest girl in the neighbourhood!"

For the first time the man with the silver whistle leaves his barrel and comes toward them.

"Jane, I don't want you to eat your chips if he gave them to you!"

He's almost disgusted at the way she's stuffing herself, her fingers all oily and great spots of grease on her nice dress. He is so angry that he doesn't notice the colour of her hair.

She talks with her mouth full, spitting a little. He can never forgive the Rat for making her into a girl like any other, without dignity when she eats, taking anything from anybody. He almost wishes she'd catch the Rat's disease.

Now the man from the barrel is scolding:

"Rat, I told you last time, if I saw you hanging around the park I'd have you put away. Now you're back as a potato vendor! Get out, and quicker than that!"

"Come on, you've got to give the oat-bag time to turn around. She never did know how to back up. You've got time to climb back on your barrel, Anselme."

His fallen angel watches him coming toward her and sucks gently at a chip, a glint of mockery in her untamed gaze. He rips the paper cone from her hands and hurls it at Gaston's face, and then, in a quiet voice, without looking at the lanky Rat who is breathing hard with a sound this time of torn rags, he says to the man in the white apron:

"I want something for the money I put there."

"I don't want any more. I'll never eat them again."

She puts her greasy hand in his and begs him with the most fragile of smiles:

"Don't be angry? I promise. I was just bored other times."

The man from the barrel blows like ten locomotives on his fine silver whistle. The high-ribbed horse with the hanging head turns slowly, and Gaston is still picking french fries out of his hair to throw at the boy.

"By Jesus, if you weren't Marcel's brother...."

But he ends his sentence outside the park. As the rig passes through the gate his long locks reappear.

"Hey! Little squirrel! Tell Isabelle I'll be around tonight...."

"Who's Isabelle?"

"Thérèse's big sister."

"Why is he going there?"

"I don't know. He's been picking her up for about a week now, with two other boys, younger. Mrs. Lafontaine doesn't like it, but Isabelle's like my sister, a bit. She says she's sorry for him, and there aren't any other boys in the neighbourhood."

He realizes that he hadn't noticed her hand in his, a thing he wouldn't have dared dream of five minutes earlier, and that he has no feelings about it, except that he doesn't like the grease. If she didn't have eyes like that, and hair, and that low voice with its water-glints that vibrate in his veins, if she didn't give the immediate impression of being so priceless and alone, she'd be nothing but a slob like anybody else, and he wouldn't want to go near her; she'd be someone he couldn't even begin to invent things about. But she doesn't know these things about herself, she doesn't realize, for she behaves like just anybody, doesn't even think about it, passes out of the picture he'd made so easily, forgetting who she is. Kissing the Rat to get chips! He still hasn't forgiven her. He takes her two hands with the tiny fingers and rubs them hard against his shirt.

"Aren't you ashamed to kiss a big bum like that with his mouth full of a dirty disease! Look at your nice dress, all greasy, and your hands too!"

She leaves him to it, a good girl now, her eyes a bit fearful, as if from now on she'd obey no one but him. His efforts succeed in smearing her with yellow earth mixed with coal dust.

"Come over to the fountain," she says, in a voice so humble that he's the one to be ashamed.

She takes him over to the little fountain, removes her white sandals sprinkled with black, and steps into the water under the spray that comes from the centre, just at her height. When she stoops over her dress is so wet that he sees clearly the outline of her buttocks.

"Come on in, it's great!"

The water darkens her russet locks which stick to her face like wet autumn leaves. He takes off his ankle boots which here, in broad daylight, sitting on the basin's edge, seem to have belonged to his grandfather's grandfather, and joins her under the cold shower that makes him forget everything else. She gathers water in the cup of her dress, then lifts it to splash his face, but he keeps his eyes wide open to see the pinkish-white of her thighs which, once again, have made her inaccessible, a tiny figure in the background of a beautiful picture in a book.

The fat man is standing on his barrel, whistling for all he's worth and making threatening gestures.

"They look like Chaplin's boots."

"Whose boots?"

"Don't you know him? A little man with your boots on, and a cane and a nice bowler hat that everybody bashes in. He's in the movies. We'll go together, you'll see, he's funny."

Her dress glued between her thighs, she shakes her head to get the water out, and then, suddenly, kisses him on the neck.

"That's cold, eh?"

She did it so quickly that it's not until afterwards that he shivers from the cold water on her lips.

In the distance, Anselme has quieted down on his barrel top, absorbed again in motionless contemplation of the world.

Pierrot puts his hands inside his boots, stretches out his arms and makes them walk in mid-air.

"I've been everywhere in these, from one wall to the other, right to the sky, but somebody cut the wings off them, and I was never at the movies, I never saw a ship and never saw a squirrel. Good old boots, they keep the same feet a long time, and now they're walking in the wide world for the first time."

"Thérèse's father's a shoemaker, and he's so funny. . . .He could fix them for you, make lovely soldier's boots out of them."

"What for? We're aviators, you and I! Can you climb trees, little squirrel?"

"There's a place where you can see the ships, you can even touch them. It's down behind the market. We'll go sometime. It's terrific, especially at night when they leave and all the lights are on."

"How do we dry off? On the fence?"

"We can lie down in the bandstand. Come with me."

She's already climbing the steep little stairway that leads under the pagoda roof, and lying down on the grey floor boards. It's dark and cool. Lying there, her hands clutched between her thighs to warm them, she is no more than a glint of tree green, a ray of sunlight falling through stained glass. He sits down beside her and watches her shiver.

"Are you cold?"

"Just nervous. Inside, I'm warm, warm. There's a band plays here every night. Mostly parents come."

"How old are you, Jane?"

He's not sure he pronounces it right, but the name pleases him.

"Ten. You?"

"You can't be!"

"Well, why not? I don't even know your name."

"Pierrot. You can't be ten because you're smaller than I am and they haven't even cut your hair yet."

"Pierrot is the moon's name. I don't want it cut. I'll be ten this winter, that's just the same. Do you want to ask my mother?"

"She's never there."

"She's there in the mornings, but she sleeps. Time is longer when she's asleep, for I can't talk to her. And there's often a gentleman with her."

"I don't want you to cut your hair either. I want you to stay ugly all your life. What gentleman?"

"I don't know. Not the same one. You have to have a man in the house at night. I suppose they're guards."

"Why did your father go away? I mean before."

"He was working in the States, and even in Africa."

"That's not true. Nobody works in Africa, for it's too hot and they'd have to kill lions or tigers all the time."

"Well, he must have been helping to kill lions. What about yours?"

"Mine?"

"You know, you never saw him!"

"That's not the same. My mother's dead; and then there were the crows."

He stops talking because he sees, in the farthest part of the crater, the first train whose cars all have windows, and he's trying to see if there are soldiers inside. But it's running too fast, and the sun makes a little bomb that explodes in every window. Why, if she had a mother, had her father not been with them all the time? There are old maids, and mothers by themselves, and fathers by themselves who go to war because they get money for it and they had none before, and that's why the Rat's father jumped off the bridge, and Jane never sees her mother because she's making para-chutes all night and sleeps in the daytime, and everybody's all shut up in themselves, like in the other place, like his uncle who's educated but doesn't like to be asked questions, and nobody loves anybody because you're not supposed to show it, and everybody thinks things that aren't nice about everybody else, such as, Jane's mother is a bad woman, and Marcel is a thief, and he himself, and the Rat, who takes it out on flowerpots. Things are a lot more com-plicated than he'd thought, and he hasn't yet found anything of what he'd thought of as normal – normal because different from the other place – except Jane, and even there he's not sure that she mightn't be just a beautiful shell, with another girl inside who doesn't know the difference between what's ugly and what's beautiful, and who could hurt, too, because she thinks more about pleasure than being friends, for that's the only thing that counts, and you'd give up your food for it without thinking twice, and everything that's unhappy when you're alone becomes happy when you're not. She's sitting curled up against him, and he's rubbing her arms gently, without realizing it, and when he does he finds her skin so soft and thin that he's confused and doesn't know how to stop.

"Do you know any children that have a mother and father at the same time? I haven't seen any yet."

"All children are like that. It's just because you're new here. Look at Thérèse and Isabelle! They've got a good mama, she's all sugar, and a papa so kind he's never tired, and he only thinks of them. Why don't you come and have supper with us?"

"Aunt Rose is coming to get me at five o'clock."

"Doesn't matter. Mama Pouf is a friend of theirs. She'll phone them and it'll be all right."

"Mama Pouf sounds funny but I like it."

"It's because she's so fat, and she's always on her feet, and she says 'pouf!' before she sits down, even when she hasn't time."

"So it's not a normal family."

"You've dropped from the moon, Pierrot, you don't know anything."

"I know more than you do. So much, the world will never be like what I know."

"Then all you know is stuff you dream. It's not the same."

She is all soft in his arms, and he has to lean on the railing to hold her up, especially because the sound of her voice in his own chest – like soft, warm milk – saps all his strength. He grasps her wrists to keep her from falling sideways, and discovers his own enormous hands.

"I know the Rat's going to die. That's not a dream."

"I think my father's not going to come back from the war, for I didn't know him well enough, and he's going to forget me in his plane."

"Your wrists – they're no bigger than three matchsticks. And I wanted to run away with you, forever, go around the world and see nothing but children like us until we're old, old! You couldn't go with hands as little as that."

"Why not? All women have littler hands."

"Not Aunt Maria or even Aunt Rose, and not the crows. Nobody but you. How could you manage to cross the precipice hand over hand on a rope?"

"You'd take me on your shoulders."

"Then we'll have to wait. I'm not big enough yet."

"No! Tell me right now! How would we go?"

In the crater now a train is passing that has nothing but wheels, and on the wheels, hidden under a great canvas, are enormous motionless frogs with long tubes in their mouths. He'd like to ask her what they are, but he's supposed to know everything.

"Well, we'd go down into the hole where the trains are. You see, you'd have to hang onto a big rope and slide down there."

"We could go around by Molson's. It's not nearly as high."

"If you know how to go I don't need to tell you any more. What's the use? And when you go around the world you mustn't ever take the easiest way, for that would be like playing in the street, with water to drink and restaurants for eating. I think we'd better not go. It's never any good taking girls along, for there's nobody to tell stories to afterwards. It would be just like never going away. Girls are supposed to wait and knit."

"What'll we do when we get into the train-hole?"

She stretches out her legs and lays her head on his knees to hear better. To keep the russet stream from ever running elsewhere, he quickly begins the tour of the world.

"We'll go into the little car at the back, the one that has a chimney, and no padlock, and isn't a refrigerator."

"That's the caboose, the kitchen. It's the only one where somebody's always there."

"There now, you see? It can't be done. With you, we'd never get away, for you know everything, and you'd talk all the time and we'd get caught."

"All I meant was, if there's nobody in it, the caboose is the best car, the very best one."

"At the start, Balibou would be nothing but the yellow cat with the stumpy tail that he usually is."

He waits, certain she's going to ask who Balibou is, but she doesn't open her mouth, except for a second, to show him her pretty white teeth and the tip of a raspberry tongue.

"Balibou has shown us the train, for it's leaving at night, and nobody comes to eat at night. But we eat, oh yes, for the next day... Well, the train drives all night, for it doesn't stop before a hundred miles, and it goes toward the North Pole, but that's a lot farther, you can't even say how far, and it goes through the great forest that's before the Indian country and where so many trains go through there aren't any more wolves, only white trappers and they can't catch anything but fish and. . .and red squirrels that are so bad and stupid they squeal all the time and they're easy to find. But an hour before sunrise, when you reach the land of the mountains and the Indians, Balibou changes into a railway engineer, and at the place where there are two directions, he unhooks our car and it goes rolling along alone for another whole day, far beyond Toronto and Chicago, the biggest Indian villages and. . ."

"My father wrote once from Chicago. It's in the States. And what makes the caboose go ahead?"

He thought she was asleep, and he was going to stop gradually, lowering his voice little by little, so that all he would have to do was look at her, but now he's obliged to be angry again.

"All right, it's stopped now. Are you satisfied? And it wasn't the same Chicago. And if you've been around the world already we don't have to start."

She puts her two cold hands behind his neck, raises her head a little, and he can't pretend to be angry any longer.

"And what happens at the end of the day?"

"It happens that the caboose rolls along because it has wheels and the rails go down valleys between mountains higher than the bridge – there, you silly goose! And what happens too is that there's a big hole like this one, in the middle of the forest, and there aren't any more rails because the Indians blew them up a long time ago to get rid of the whites, who are bad, and they're too lazy to go up the rivers in canoes like the Indians, and they invented guns because they can't see far and can't shoot arrows, for it's much harder. . .And there, in the hole, there are hundreds of trains that fell all over each other, for years and years, and they're full of skeletons, so old that when you touch them they fall in little heaps of white powder and you have to wade through the powder like snow. Ours is only a little caboose and we can roll right through this graveyard of trains, to a little clearing where there's nobody, but there are pretty wild flowers and a big sign that says in English: ANY WHITE MAN ENTERING HERE WILL BE SCALPED AND PUT TO ROT IN THE CAGE WITH THE CROWS."

"Why is it in English?"

"The Indians don't talk the same as we do. Anybody knows that."

"That means I could talk to them!"

"Indian English isn't the same. So Balibou changes into an enormous white wolf, with red eyes, and you run to my arms and cry that he's going to eat you because he thinks you're Red Riding Hood, and I say don't worry, because anybody knows Red Riding Hood was a lot smarter than you, and besides he's a white wolf and too proud to sleep in a grandmother's bed, and that it's only Balibou giving you the nicest wolf grin you ever saw, and you say to him, 'What big teeth you have, Grandmother!' and he laughs so hard his teeth get longer and you cry so loud when he tries to pat you with his big paw to show you he's only Balibou that thousands of Indians climb down the trees and hide behind them, waiting for night to fall, and..."

"I want to come back here. I don't want to go around the world, Pierrot, my hands are too little."

She sits up suddenly and shakes his shoulders, really crying now, but he's too far along to stop.

"...and that night, you see thousands of red eyes looking at your beautiful hair, and we hear them sharpen their knives, and Balibou has fun howling like a white wolf, for they howl louder than the others, and that's why the red eyes stay behind the trees."

"Pierrot, stop, stop. I'm going to have bad dreams."

"The caboose can't go back. Nobody has ever rolled backwards through the graveyard of the trains. We can't go back, Jane, not ever! We have to go on now, right around the world."

"I don't want to."

"I'll protect you."

"You said before you weren't big enough."

"I'm going to tell you a big secret, the main thing I know. Everywhere in the world there are more children than grown-ups. We're going to find them everywhere. And children are never bad. When they seem to be, it's because they're too unhappy. You just have to give them a little friendship, even if they speak English, pretending you're not giving anything, so they don't notice."

"That's not true. I knew some that pulled my hair and threw stones, and they even hit me. Sometimes boys bigger than you. And they called me Little Carrot, or Maudite Anglaise, and I swear it's true."

"But did you try talking to them? It's because they saw you were afraid. You mustn't be afraid, or they get mean. Like dogs."

"Aren't you ever scared?"

"I was, but not any more. One day I told myself it was better to be dead than afraid. And big Justin got his nose broken."

"But that's the same with grown-ups. If you can hit harder. You see, what you said isn't true."

"Look: when you saw me the first time you stuck your tongue out, right? And now you wouldn't do it any more."

"I'm not so sure. And anyway, that wasn't the same. It was because your aunts don't like me."

"You haven't travelled enough to understand. You'll see."

"I'll never travel again. But who's Balibou?"

"You'll know at the end of the trip."

She gets up, jumps around a little, her toes searching for a rhythm, then begins to dance, her arms dangling, striking the boards as if she had clickers on her shoes.

For the first time he wonders why there were no girls in the other place, and why he had always thought they were so insipid and bothersome that the best thing people could have done with him was leave him among boys.

"You're here! I thought you hadn't come. I was going home again."

A stout girl, taller than Pierrot, with dark hair and a face full of pimples, appears at the foot of the steps.

"That's Thérèse," Jane shouts, without interrupting her dance.

"They had me washing floors the whole day. On my knees. And watching me like hawks all the time! I don't think I can stand it. I just want to do one thing: sleep."

She flops down on the first step, and you can see she's really tired because the muscles of her face are moving all on their own and her knees are red and swollen.

"She's English. She doesn't know how to behave herself. Hello you, whoever you are."

He likes her right away, for she has a voice that will never hurt anybody, and even when she complains it's good humoured. Her bum is so big that she must have always known nobody was going to feel sorry for her.

"She got the crazy idea of working at the Miséricorde so she could buy dresses. You can see the yards of stuff she'll need."

"It's not true. It's because Mama hasn't time to sew, and I wanted to help out."

"What's the Miséricorde?"

The girls burst out laughing.

"He's too young to be told," says Jane, finally giving up her dance.

"It's a hospital where there are miles of corridors to scrub," says Thérèse with a smile that just keeps on going.

"And all they do is make babies without papas. And even their mothers don't keep them."

"Jane, there was one today told me she was only thirteen. Imagine!"

She sighs, louder and longer.

"This is Pierrot, my new neighbour, and now he's my only friend," Jane announces, holding her little lion head high.

"You mean the kid with the old maids?"

"What a way to talk! The hospital doesn't agree with you."

"They could at least give him something else to wear."

"He just got here. And anyway he's nice like that."

Jane has changed a little since her friend arrived, as if she had begun remembering things that he never knew, and taking him under her wing. He can't tell if she's making fun or if she's serious. He can't get used to seeing her change. Above all he's afraid she'll turn again into the greedy little girl he saw a while ago with the Rat. But then, two girls together can't be the same, and again he feels as clumsy as the Molson horses. To ease his awkwardness he says:

"I could help you with the floors. I'm used to corridors a mile long."

"Do you think the nuns are going to let you near those swollen bellies? Well, let's go. He's coming with us. I invited him."

"That's fine! It'll be a change from looking at you! Come, Pierrot, Mama'll be glad to see you. Jane's no surprise any more."

Thérèse has a voice as warm as the inside of fresh bread. She makes you hungry.

"Those corridors! If they don't give me a bike I'll throw the wet rag at their heads."

"And how will you get thin if they fire you?"

"Watching you eat the money for my new clothes."

Pierrot walks past the man on the barrel, very proud of his two lady-friends.

Anselme half takes the pipe from his mouth, to shout, but without much conviction:

"What about your aunt, peewee! What am I going to tell her?"

And Jane, in a voice suddenly very shrill, replies:

"If you can get down from your barrel, tell her you want to walk her home!"

7

"I want to go pee. Hello, Meeow! I'll be back."

"That's fine, mouse, but you don't have to tell your big news in front of gentlemen."

The same street as the Rat, but in the other direction, after another street with a beautiful name: de la Visitation. And the house is like that name. You go in, as you do at the Rat's place, by a passage under the windows, but inside there's a little garden, neat as can be, with trees that are just big blue flowers, a long cigar-coloured automobile shining in the sun, and, lying around everywhere, ducks, bears and even a neckless giraffe in brightly painted wood. Above all, there's Mama Pouf, floating on a canvas chair, surely the fattest, biggest woman he's ever seen, all soft, as if they hadn't blown her up tight, showing in plain daylight an incredible breast coloured with blue veins, not big enough, however, to hide a fat baby drinking noisily from it. Milk runs down on its little hand pressed deep in all that bounty.

"You look tired, my poor dear. What did they do to you today!"

He's angry at Jane for making her entry shouting about pee. The fact that she might have to, and especially that she should shout about it, shocks him as much as if an angel decided to blow its nose. But he's too overwhelmed by the spectacle to stay angry very long.

"This is Pierrot," says Thérèse. "That's Meeow. Two months, and he's still sucking like a kitten. Meeow, meeow, meeow...."

She kisses the child (and incidentally the breast) and all the sunlight in the garden trembles in Mama Pouf's milk, and Mama Pouf surrenders, motionless, to the sweetness of life.

"Pierrot? Where did you dig him up?"

Jane replies, pushing over a great, inert leg to get room on the chair.

"My new neighbour, and my friend. He's a handsome blond, eh?"

He had never thought about the colour of his hair, for nobody had ever mentioned it, and in the other place one mop was as good as another. Jane's expression embarrasses him more than the sight of the breast, and he begins to wonder how long he can survive in this feminine world that paralyses him so completely that he has the impression of violating by his very presence an intimacy from which boys should naturally be excluded.

"Why, he's a fine little man, to be sure, but he looks as if he'd just come from the hay market. What on earth were you playing at? Look at your dress, little mouse, you're still all wet!"

"We started round the world, together. Mmm! The lilacs smell good! You're going to give me a big bouquet."

"How could we say no to you, my princess? Round the world! And you're going to come back home every day, like that? It'll take you a long time."

Jane buries her face in the lower branches, and it looks like the sunlight on the sea he's never seen, and her powdered gold hair smells sweet and fresh, and he can't believe that all this exists for him, in a little garden hidden from everyone, a little lake of happiness where all the birds in the neighbourhood can come to bathe; but surely he should creep away without a sound, for he's not a girl, not a baby, not a bird, and it's quite clear he doesn't belong here. Yet he's glued to the spot, his eyes wide open, his nostrils dilated, on a little wooden bench where he sits afraid to move or speak.

Jane has managed to break off a branch and comes toward him turning it slowly under her nose, then gives it to him, and plops down beside him. He sniffs at it politely and lays it gently on his knees.

"I think I'm too fat to make milk any more. He drinks for a whole hour as if he hadn't started. So you're Adrien's son, Marcel's brother?"

"Yes, ma'am."

She somehow laughs without an inch of her body moving.

"Yes, ma'am! Now, isn't he well trained! Now, poor Meeow, you're going to finish that in the kitchen! I've got to make supper."

"You'd better call his aunt. She doesn't know he's here."

Leaning with one hand on the ground she manages to get her wide back upright, and the child and the breast descend a few inches. Then she slowly allows her swollen legs to drop over one side of the chair. Thérèse puts out a hand to help her, but she protests with the softest kind of anger:

"I'm not your grandmother, just give me time! You didn't answer me before. What did they have you doing today?"

"Scrubbing floors. It was easy."

"Scrubbing floors! On a day like today. And you thought you'd be playing with the babies! Serves you right! I don't want you ruining your health in a place like that. For five dollars, Mary and Joseph! We'll find you another job or you stay right here."

"Are you going to phone?"

"Phone? Oh yes. And I suppose it'll be that Maria answering. Full of beer and mean as a snake! Oh lord, I shouldn't, in front of the boy. But anyway he's going to eat with us. Let's have supper here outside. Two or three more days and there won't be any lilacs."

She's up at last, the baby never letting go, sucking as if he couldn't get enough. She now looks heavier, taller than any man, and he finds it terrible that she has to carry such a heavy body without any bones in it, just milk that keeps coming despite Meeow's tenacity. Once under way she has a swift and decisive pace. She disappears into the house.

Thérèse rubs her knees, smiling at him absent-mindedly, then begins clearing off a long wooden table littered with empty bottles, diapers, games, tools, newspapers, all the unimportant things that declare the existence of a family. He gets up to help, and of all the words he's read, one comes up in capital letters to the surface of his memory, a word he's never written or said, but it always made him think of the country, of a little village with cows and sheep around, a word in which he feels at home, as he does here: it's CHAUMIERE. And he sees for the first time that words like "thatched cottage" in books can come close to real life, even if it's not the same thing.

Jane, still sitting down, watches every move he makes, tapping her toe on the floor and singing softly, her eyes half closed in the slanting rays of the sun. The whole garden is nothing but flowers, sunlight, birds, green and russet colours, and smiles. He has everything stacked in his arms, bottles on top of newspapers and, under his nose, a diaper that he'd just as soon see elsewhere, but he can't make a move without risking the whole pile. Thérèse comes to his rescue, taking away the used diaper.

"Hey, lazybones! Do you think you're an English princess! You could help a little, too."

"All you had to do was ask me nicely."

And the squirrel skips over to him, taking from the pile a ball and a pair of scissors, delicately, with her slim fingertips. He puts the rest on the verandah and their two heads meet half-way down and he sees the sun take fire through her hair.

"Come and see the shoemaker's shop."

She gives him her hand and pulls him toward the end of the garden where there is a kind of shed painted light blue, with small windows decorated with flowerpots. A black ankle boot, almost a match for his own, decorates the wall above the door.

It's dark inside. It smells of glue, shoe dye, dust and school bags.

"Hello, Uncle dear!" Jane shouts into the long, narrow shop.

"Careful where you walk. I had a visitor this afternoon," replies a small, thin man busy at pounding nails into a lady's shoe held on a kind of anvil.

"There's a funny smell here," says Jane, sniffing before she goes any further.

"That was my visitor. She left her card."

"This is Pierrot. And this is Thérèse's father, a man who swallows nails all day. If you touch him you prick your finger."

He stops hammering, lays his hammer on the workbench, cups his hand before his mouth and spits out a dozen little square-headed nails.

"Well, I'll keep those for tomorrow. You still don't see who my visitor was?"

"A general, ordering ten thousand boots for the army."

"You're warm. It was old Eugène's cow, which I had to keep for half an hour. Don't go near the big door, for that's where the fear ran out of her."

"She came in here? It can't be true!"

"Not true? Do you want to touch it? We played the game all afternoon, from Visitation to Beaudry Street. The police came again to take his milk away. So we passed the cow from one neighbour to the next. She bawled so loud I had to open the big door. The smell of the leather made her so scared she said her prayers through the wrong end."

"Why do they want to take his cow?"

"Because it's not allowed in the city, and he has neighbours with good smellers. They had a truck. Finally they went away with the hay. We don't know how to feed her. Maybe you could take her on the church lawn. But she might go mad at your red hair."

This is an old game, for she starts running long before he has time to take after her with a great pair of scissors.

"Don't tell Mama Pouf. She might go get the cow and make her clean up. Well, Pierrot, have you no pride, running around with a carrot-head like that? And she speaks English, too, monsieur! Well, let's eat soup, come on!"

"Mama Pouf said we'd eat outside."

"Oh! I hope the wind doesn't turn, or they'll all know I work in cowhide."

When they arrive under the lilacs there are two boys sitting on the grass, a little smaller than Pierrot, dressed the same, with identical dark hair and identical faces, except that one is sponging a healthy black eye. And leaning on the verandah railing is a tall girl with hair as frizzled as a sheep's, red on her lips and fingernails, in a dress the same colour as the lilacs, a very thin girl, except for her chest, which threatens to burst the dress. She seems very proud of this fact, and is polishing her nails with superb detachment.

Thérèse, setting the table which is now covered by a white cloth, does the introductions.

"Isabelle. And the twins, Yves and Yvan. The whole family owes a black eye to your dirty Irish, Jane. Ten of them ganged up on our two and attacked them from behind, coming back from Lafontaine Park. A fine race!"

"Aha! Aha! There were ten of them, and they were all Irish, and they took you from behind? How many of them are left?" their father says mockingly.

Without rehearsal, the twins reply in one voice:

"You don't believe us, we knew you wouldn't."

"Last time you wiped them all out."

"I'm hungry," says one of the twins.

"Next time we'll ask them all to supper," says the other.

"And what about you, Thérèse, didn't you bring us back a baby?"

Thérèse hasn't time to answer for the door opens wide and Mama Pouf appears in all her majesty, holding a steaming soup-kettle at arm's length.

"Soup's on! Everybody's wiped their hands on their pants? You too, my old bootblack?"

Nobody replies, but they all sit down without hesitation, as if their names were on their plates. Jane sits beside Monsieur Lafontaine, pushing him over laughingly to make room for Pierrot, who's looking admiringly at Isabelle, especially at the way she wiggles her hips when she walks, and her breasts, which he imagines hard as marble. In a way he tries to pretend to know what he's doing here in this family, but it suddenly seems to him like a splendid photo, which you can't enter because it's only a picture. He makes himself as small as possible between the squirrel-mouse-carrot, who has swallowed them all long ago to make her nest here, and Thérèse, fat as a new loaf, but it's no use, their seats touch each other's, and even their arms, and he doesn't know how he's going to get down a single bite, pressed within so much tenderness.

"It was Aunt Rose that answered. Aunt Maria is sick, it seems," says Mama Pouf, beginning to serve the soup.

Just then an old white delivery truck, very rusty, emerges from the entry passage and with a rattle of scrap metal comes to a halt behind the long cigar-coloured car. A hefty young man, also black haired, a six-footer, comes and sits down at the end of the table, greeting the company with a little nod, but without saying a word.

"That's Gérard, my big brother. He's an electrician," Thérèse confides proudly to Pierrot.

"Will you take us to the port to see the ships?" Jane asks him.

"No, not tonight. I've ten minutes to eat, and enough work to last the whole evening."

"My lord! Where's it going to get you, working day and night? You'll end up with grey hairs and never looked at a girl."

He gets served first, and starts eating, without replying or looking at anyone.

"Mama, how do you expect to scare him with grey hair when you haven't a single one yourself?"

"Well, talk about seeing women, you see enough, Henri. What a trade, being a shoemaker! Always a woman's foot in your hands."

"Oh, get on with you. As if you didn't know they were all old twisted barnacles that want me to do miracles!"

"Isabelle makes bombs. Real ones, for killing."

Thérèse's admiration for her family is boundless.

The sun is declining slowly, toward the unknown city, and shadow has covered the length of the shop at the end of the garden. Once, in the other place, the crows had taken them for supper into a field, far outside the walls, and they'd all come back vomiting because something had gone rotten in the sun, and the crows had been furious as if the boys had been sick on purpose to spite them and prevent them from giving the children a treat. Through the years the evening meal had always been the most sinister time of the day, because that was the first one he'd eaten with the inmates, because the refectory was in the basement, because the day always ended in a weariness of heart that made them all ferocious, and he was sure nothing would happen until night when each one became his own solitude in the midst of collective loneliness, with all the time in the world to dream of those tomorrows which would end, all of them, in the same grey water where they washed their tin dishes.

Now he's eating with these people, and Jane and Thérèse surround him so thoroughly that he can't ignore them, but at the same time he's swimming in space, far enough to be able still to see them without being among them. And he remains outside the sounds and words that blur into a meaningless mumble. His own hands seem like strangers to him, in this group united by a whole network of memories they have lived out together, networks of words that evoke things he alone cannot know, or even cryptic references which they all understand at once. His own hands are somewhere else, and his words, some of which have meaning only for him, slip across the surface of beings and objects without touching or grasping them.

He eats everything that's set before him, answers words he hasn't heard, and everyone laughs, and the words, his own included, and the laughter, fall into a kind of abyss that separates them from their origin, and he feels such a weariness from reaching rescuing arms to them that he has to stop trying, and his joy has left him without leaving him really unhappy, for he's not used to joy and doesn't know how to keep it by him. And besides, the smell of burnt rubber falls like lead into the garden (now in twilight) and takes away his taste for food, and he's a little sick to his stomach, and can't wait to get up and run, run anywhere, all by himself, to escape from all the newness and find someone who'd barely talk, even if he knew lots of words, someone who'd never open his hands (for no one puts anything in them, ever), someone who never went farther than to lift ever so slightly the weight of time, in dreams only, to perceive the lights, far, very far away, and that would be enough for him, someone who is the person he knows best, he, the child with the Blue Man, a boy among four hundred others, who never, never had intruded into the feminine world.

"Pouf! Oh, no! I'd rather eat standing up, it's easier than getting out of this chair. Did you ever eat strawberries in that castle of yours?"

It was Meeow's cries, somewhere up there in his mother's arms, that had brought Pierrot back among them. The great breast dribbles with white in the half-golden shadow, and he hears the sound of robust sucking.

"Oh, yes! And raspberries and bananas and oranges and even...a pear!"

"It's a fine thing, dear boy, if what you remember is a castle and a pear. I'm starting to believe in that castle of yours."

And with her free hand Mama Pouf lifts a spoonful of strawberries up toward the sky, for her head is hidden behind her breast. Pierrot tries to eat with his left hand, because his right shoulder is flooded with a light so insubstantial that he had barely noticed its weight, and Jane is sleeping there, breathing deeply.

"Say, Gérard, were you able to find a generator?" his father asked.

"Hadn't time to look," replied the big, quiet electrician.

"Got to get the Buick turning over before Sunday. Weather like this..."

"Sure, sure. Last time we got it running we didn't even make it out of town. Three flats in half an hour."

Isabelle's voice isn't like her mother's, nor her sister's. It's hard and a little off key, as if she hadn't learned to play it properly. The smell of the factory has silenced the lilacs, but has not overcome the violently saccharine perfume that comes from Isabelle.

Gérard gets up and his big shadow falls over the table. A brief and sudden storm breaks out between him and his sister.

"Were you with the Rat on St. Laurent last night?"

"What's it to you? Is it against the law to go down to the Main?"

"With the Rat it is. Paul's coming from training camp tomorrow."

"And he's going right back. Why don't you mind your business, Gérard?"

"You're my sister, that's why. I know the easy way. I'll just happen to get him in front of my truck. He makes me sick, that guy."

"He never asked you to kiss him."

Helpless, Gérard is shaking with anger. He turns on his heel and disappears in the delivery truck, which goes swiftly into reverse with more racket than a locomotive, as if there had never been a darkened passageway with a sidewalk crossing it outside.

"One of these days he's going to run somebody down, that's for sure," the shoemaker said softly.

High up where it's suspended, the baby is sucking away for dear life.

"Empty already! My lord! Don't worry, Meeow, there's another one. Just take your time."

And another breast rises toward the sky.

"Pouf! There now, that's better. You know, Isabelle, he's right. Paul is a man, and he's rough. With the Rat you can only bring a lot of trouble on yourself."

"Nobody can live her life for her. If she makes a mistake she's the one who's going to pay."

The shoemaker hadn't raised his voice or threatened in any way, but the storm has passed, wiped out by the daylight of this obvious truth of his.

"You're only seventeen. You're only a girl. That's just it, I don't want her to have to pay. Pouf!"

This time she has descended on the canvas chair, and Meeow can be heard sucking closer, louder.

"And the war. When's that going to be over? It's like the Buick, we can't drive it till the war stops, for there aren't any parts. They're making bombs instead!"

"Good lord, Belle, what's the Buick got to do with it? Life is short, but it's long too, you'll see that one day."

She sighs, sigh after sigh, because of life, and flowers, and all the milk that may be drying up in her, and Belle with her hard breasts and her perfume stronger than burnt rubber.

"The Rat won't last the summer," Isabelle murmurs to herself, staring at an invisible star in the smoke-coloured sky.

And the Rat is there! He's just appeared out of the shadows of the passage, a dark, lanky figure, his behind raised high on a bicycle on which he cleverly navigates around the table and Mama Pouf's chair without grazing a single obstacle, to touch foot to earth before Isabelle and order her, barely out of breath:

"Come, my lovely! I've found a taxi."

She gets up, says a quick good-night to all, kisses her mother.

"Look at him, all dressed up!"

He has shoes on instead of the yellow boots, but he has the same baggy pants. The great novelty is an enormous tie and a jacket that's very wide at the shoulders and hangs, narrowing, half-way down his thighs. A glimpse of chain shines at his belt.

He dips his long fingers in a cream-bowl and pulls out strawberries at which he sucks ecstatically.

"Well, well! The squirrel's found her nest! In my little *habitant's* haycock."

And his pale, ghoulish hand hovers dangerously over the fading reddish fire in the hollow of the boy's shoulder. Pierrot pushes him off with a butt of his head against his forearm.

"What's the big idea! Does he think she's his for life?"

Then he whispers in Pierrot's ear, with his breath like rustling paper:

"Redheads always smell scorched. Touch and you're burned."

"My lord, Belle, you're not going out with that scarecrow! Just keep him away from Meeow! Is there a party in the graveyard?"

The Rat grabs Isabelle's hands and holds them high, beginning with knees as loose as if they were dislocated a strange sort of dance which his partner imitates. His eyes are staring, his long black locks over his eyes, and he whips her around behind him, grasps her again to throw her to the front and then, with a violent flick of his long arms, forces her to leap astride his chest, her legs wide apart. He leans back, staggering under her weight, straightens suddenly, lays her roughly on the ground and stands her up again, just like that! His shrill voice can barely wheeze through his heavy breathing.

"There, that's better than your tangos. Good exercise for you, Mama Pouf!"

"Poor boy, that's no kind of goings-on for you. You're going to tear your heart out, they'll take you home in a coffin!"

"Better get used to it, Ma. It's the new world. When the killers come back they'll be dancing that with tommy guns."

"Aren't you ashamed, Belle! Your dress is going to split wide open in front of everybody."

"I'm just a young girl that makes bombs. It's a new world, like he says."

One of the twins gets up and searches on the ground.

"We're sure goin' to find rat bones on the ground here tomorrow morning."

"This is going to be quite a summer, I can promise you that," Gaston announces in a sinister voice, as if he were going to blow up the whole neighbourhood.

And he hops on his bike, installs Isabelle on the crossbar and, like a black crow bent over its prey, disappears through the passage.

"His dog Lucifer has the right name. Our lilacs are going to wilt this night, just you watch. Poor devil, you'd think he had a date with Satan, and his behind was on fire already."

Along with the pity he feels for Gaston's illness, Pierrot feels the birth of a hatred nothing can appease, because the Rat had been Marcel's friend, had known Pierrot's father, and is now deliberately sullying something Pierrot can't name, but which seems more important to him than the worst of misfortunes. Even if he knows that Gaston can't look forward over a great stretch of time, he can not forgive him for blowing out every glimmer of light. On his shoulder the golden cloud has lost its colour, and he feels in his own breast the breathing sleep of Jane.

"Pouf! I do believe he's had enough. D'you want to put him to bed, Thérèse, and bring me a sweater? Drat it, now my other breast's running all by itself."

The shoemaker stands up suddenly, accidentally nudging Jane, to go to the other end of the garden where a tiny lady in a black veil is hurrying across.

"Don't run away on us, Madame Paiement. Come and have a coffee."

Pierrot doesn't hear the lady's reply, but Mama Pouf explains:

"She's been in black since they killed her boy at Dieppe. Her husband joined up to get revenge, and she's always alone behind her closed shutters. Oh, this war! It doesn't only mean a bit of extra money. There's suffering as well."

The woman sits down at the end of the bench, without raising her veil, and, straight as a ramrod, sips away at the coffee placed before her.

"Take your time, Madame Paiement, mass doesn't start for another quarter of an hour. You should have been out in that lovely sunshine."

"The lilacs are beautiful," she murmurs into her veil.

"Edouard'll be back soon, you'll see. They haven't stopped since D-Day. People are even scared of being out of work again."

"My son won't be back. I'll never even see his grave, for they don't know where he's buried."

"Why don't you open up your windows, at least," Mama Pouf insists.

"I wouldn't be able to see the votive light, and I'd be ashamed. I'm so glad the cat stays with him when I'm at church. Well, now, Meeow is such a quiet baby. I never hear him at all!"

"He's sucking away all the time, there's nothing else to hear."

"You're such a fine family. Edouard will be glad to get back."

She gets up, makes a hasty sign beneath her veil, and walks slowly toward the passage.

"Well, children, better think about bedtime and get home before dark. Bring them home, will you Henri?"

Pierrot is so strange to his uncle's apartment that he finds it funny to be sent there as if it were home. He could sleep in a different house every night now, or in this one for a whole week, and there would be no surprises. But he certainly doesn't want to be deprived of going home alone with Jane. The little woman in black had brought him back from a long dream-journey. At the beginning he had been more alone than ever in a dizzying great world full of streets leading nowhere, passed on like a parcel to aunts and an uncle who didn't know where to put him or even if they wanted to keep him, and then came that miraculous face that Jane had made, and that was the precious fruit of the day which he didn't want to share with anyone.

"I don't want him to come. It's only two blocks."

He'd been too vehement, almost shouting. Jane wakes with a start and squints up at him as if she didn't remember him, with a quick glint of panic that makes him want to laugh.

"I'm the bogey man, and I ate you because you went to sleep out of doors."

"Pour little mouse! She hates going home so much she always goes to sleep here. Sometimes she doesn't even remember walking from one house to the other. Well, if you're a little man, you walk her home. If Jane isn't afraid..."

"With him? Oh, no! He has a big white wolf called Balibou," his princess confides, having a hard time waking up despite valiant grimaces and twistings.

"Well! You do have dreams! Come and say good-night. And go around by Dorchester. It's better lit and there's more people because of the churches."

Jane is still dragging her feet, and has trouble reaching Mama Pouf's friendly cheek. When it's his turn to kiss Mama Pouf, he catches a strong smell of curdled milk.

"We'll expect you tomorrow, even if it rains."

She waves her soft hand, and smiles like a great moon.

The shoemaker sees them through the passage which by now is black as night. On the sidewalk he bends down to kiss Jane and says to her:

"Thanks for the cow."

"Why, Uncle?"

"For not saying anything."

"Oh! I forgot about it. I want to show her to Pierrot. Is she back in her yard?"

"Yes, but if Père Eugène isn't asleep he must be pretty nervous."

And he goes off down the treeless street where all the lampposts are lit for a celebration that must be elsewhere.

8

"Why does he keep a cow?"

"Because he sells the milk."

"Why does he sell milk from just one cow?"

"Because he's just one man."

She stops him before a passage that is much shorter than the others, but which seems closed by a black wall.

"It's in there. She's at the back, behind the fence, just like in the country. But I've never been in, at night."

"Come on, or I'll give you up to the Indians, they're sharpening their knives for they can see your hair shining in the dark."

"And Balibou will eat the cow."

"Even when he's a white wolf he eats cat food."

"What good is he, anyway?"

"Scaring mice."

He draws her through the wall of darkness into a courtyard that smells of manure. It's barely half as big as Mama Pouf's garden. They immediately encounter barbed wire, in front of an open shed with a very low roof, and because of the roof they hear the animal moving rather than seeing it.

"She's red."

"There's no such thing as a red cow."

"Have you seen lots of cows?"

"No, but so what?"

The cow, lying down, gets up on its knees and then to its feet, and the sound of its hoofs on the floor makes Jane shrink back.

"She makes too much noise. Let's go."

But as he doesn't move she's obliged to stay, her hand clutching his. The cow puts her head over the fence, chewing at a wisp of hay that hangs out the two sides of her mouth.

"It's funny, she chews the wrong way. Maybe she has no teeth. And she's brown, she's even kaka coloured. How can anybody believe what you say?"

"Come on, Pierrot, Old Eugène's going to be mad if he knows we woke her up."

"She wasn't asleep. Look at her fine big eyes. They're the same colour as yours."

Then, feeling that she's really afraid, he rubs his hand quickly over the stubble of the cow's head.

"There, I touched her. We can go now."

As they turn he sees, just ahead of them at the passage entry, a man draped in an old coat, with a torn straw hat on his head and, on his feet, ankle boots like Pierrot's, but without laces.

"Is that Père Eugène?"

"He's the wino," stammers Jane, trembling more in disgust than fear. "He does ugly things. Come quick, don't look."

At that moment the man opens his coat and calls to them, whining like a dog. Pierrot sees that he is naked, and the thing he holds out to them is so impossible, uglier than the ugliest sickness he could ever have imagined, that the boy is paralysed. Jane has already made for the sidewalk.

"Touch it, it's hurting me," begs the man, coming toward him.

Rage explodes inside him, blinder than the rage that hurled him at Justin after months of bullying, and his disgust drives his fingers into the gravel until his nails hurt, and he stones the apparition with all his strength, never pausing for breath, until it sinks in a wretched heap against the wall, and he goes on, blind to the blood that's beginning to flow, deaf to the animal whinings. And when his hands find nothing more to throw he goes at him with his boots, anywhere, at that soft body that crumples even more abjectly.

"Pig! Filthy pig!"

And he hits and kicks, hardly hearing Jane screaming in the street or the lowing of the cow or Père Eugène shouting out the window. Finally someone pulls him back by the shoulders and out to the sidewalk. He is trembling, and has trouble breathing through his clenched teeth. A voice speaks to him:

"Take it easy, my boy! You'll kill him. He's full of alcohol."

Jane runs her cool hand over his cheek, crying a little out of nervousness.

"Pierrot, you shouldn't have. He's harmless."

"I tell you, that's a real fighter you've found, little mouse. I won't have to see you home any more."

It's the shoemaker's voice. He's followed by the twins, laughing admiringly.

"We'll sign him up for the war against the Irish."

"He's worse than they are!"

Père Eugène arrives as well, with his pants pulled hastily on over his nightshirt.

"What am I supposed to do with that?"

"Let him sleep there. It won't kill him. If he's still sleeping it off tomorrow morning turn the cow loose on him. Will you get home, now, you two?"

The twins withdraw slowly, not in the least intimidated.

"I told you not to look. Everybody knows him around here. Boy, can you get mad!"

The shoemaker drives the twins back to their house front, then accompanies the others up Visitation to Dorchester. He gives Jane a kiss.

"Now, it's straight down there to home. And be polite to the ladies going to church."

And he gives Pierrot a good slap on the back:

"As for you, my little fighting cock, I'm going to teach you to pick on men your own size."

When they look back, two minutes later, the little man is still waving to them.

Pierrot's nerves are slowly calming down, but he could drink ten glasses of water at one gulp.

"I'd never have imagined a thing like that."

"He's a poor sick man, Pierrot. But I don't think he'll do it again. It's true you're not afraid of anything!"

Her admiration shocks him a little.

"That's nothing to do with being afraid. It's like. . .it's like when you get burned."

And they go on in silence to Plessis Street. He tries hard to forget what just happened, but his anger is still bubbling in the depths, against what he's not quite sure, but it reaches all the grown-ups he doesn't know, and life itself, which is no longer the prolongation of childhood dreams or the promise of marvels postponed but possible, but rather a spectacle that is presented pell-mell to children and everyone, and more than the smell of lilacs he retains the smell of curdled milk on Mama Pouf's dress, and he thinks, more than of Jane who is walking at his side, her hand in his, of the cat guarding the votive light that guards the photo of Madame Paiement's son, whose twenty years are more than dead, vanished who knows where, far on the other side of the ocean. And it's with a new gaze, almost suspicious, that he contemplates the little body of the russet fairy who gave him such joy by making a face at him.

"What happens next in the Indians' clearing?"

"You said you didn't want to stay."

"I do now. I know you're big enough to travel around the world."

"Very well. We go to sleep, because it's night-time."

"Not with those Indians sharpening their knives."

"See what a scaredy-cat you are. And besides, I was fooling myself just for fun. It was only the frogs sharpening their teeth on the rocks."

"Frogs don't have teeth."

"What's the use of going around the world with a know-it-all? Why shouldn't there be frogs with teeth in the world somewhere? Has anybody ever seen all the frogs in the world?"

"You're right, Pierrot. And I never even looked in a frog's mouth. But what about those red eyes looking at my hair in the dark?"

"Well, why should Indians have red eyes? Have you ever seen red eyes? I mean, red like paint."

"No, that's true."

"I'll tell you what it was. It was fire-flies, and they don't care about your hair any more than my boots. What do you think! There's lots of squirrels in the woods, nothing special about your hair!"

They've arrived at the house, newer and taller than the others. They live in the two apartments on the third floor, the top one. And now they'll always be living side by side, and they know each other. When they say "home" it will mean the same house, but not like Mama Pouf's, for between them are walls, and aunts and an uncle and her mother, whom he doesn't know.

"Why are you mad, Pierrot? It's not my fault."

They climb slowly, for they're tired, and need time to rediscover something between them, something lost.

"I'm not mad. It's nothing. Boy! A whole day!"

"You'll be more used to it tomorrow. It was all new."

Someone he can't see in the half-open doorway grabs Jane's hand and pulls her in. She manages to stretch out and give him a kiss on the cheek.

"Good-night."

She disappears and the door slams.

All the time he'd been at Mama Pouf's, he had savoured in advance this moment when the two of them would sit on the landing and talk for a long time, alone on the cold marble, until they went to sleep so they wouldn't know when someone came to separate them.

He rings his uncle's doorbell.

9

The rain falls gently, wrapping in drizzle the tall tapers of the poplars that rise above the walls of the old people's home across the alley, its shutters closed, their sombre green liquefied; Jane's apartment, beside him, has also grown vague, and even the school scribbler which becomes illegible in his damp hands, and the mist of his remembering, which is at once close by and then again as far away as the old stone house where nothing but a disconnected sink and a bathtub full of earth testify to days once his and now deprived by forgetfulness of all existence.

When he went out to sit on the back gallery he thought he heard the sound of a vacuum cleaner next door, but there's been no sign of life since, not a hint of a look between the slats of the shutters.

Back from shopping with Aunt Rose, he had wandered about the apartment awhile, but because he kept bumping into Aunt Maria he took refuge here with the little parcel tied with string which Saint Sabine had given back to him, announcing that he was a little man now, and life was wide open to him. Someone had opened the parcel and he found it on his uncle's bookcase, beside the couch where he sleeps, and it was with a kind of angry shame that he discovered the black scribbler which the crows had taken from him and he had thought destroyed. This scribbler, three postcards and two letters from Marcel – all that remains to him from hundreds of days lived in the herd, with rattles and rulers, inside the walls that took him in just before his memory was born.

The gallery, which makes a sudden right-angled turn to reach the covered stairs, steep and dark, where Jane's apartment opens, leading down to the alley, is so narrow that the rain comes in on the open scribbler on his knees. He's been reading it at random with some astonishment, for the words had imprisoned moments that were never as clear cut or isolated as his sentences. The rain comes in on his sweater as well and his new pants which disguise him as an ordinary boy, and he likes that, for he'll look as if he'd played in them at least once.

The whole afternoon had been spent buying these things, and Aunt Rose had got into a state, adding and subtracting, and saying over and over:

"However you look at it, manikin, you're wasting your uncle's money."

He escaped two or three times and wandered around among the racks and aisles. How could a store be so big, and display such quantities and kinds of clothing? In the other place they lined up once or twice a month at the linen room and were issued a shirt and overalls and socks, just by guessing sizes after a quick look, and they were never the same clothes you got, except in the long run you ended up getting a shirt you knew, and it had been patched again since last time, but you could recognize it by how worn it looked. They even called the linen room the "stores" but it held no surprises. But this afternoon he'd been stunned by an avalanche of novelty, even discouraged, then fed up with trying on pants after pants only to make Aunt Rose even more undecided. Finally he'd gone for a breath of fresh air outside, bored to death and dizzy from the crowd inside. When she found him she poked the end of her umbrella in his buttock.

"Little savage, have you no heart? Your uncle gives his good money and I waste a whole day and you're not even grateful, you take off like this! And we don't even know if we'll keep you..."

Finally she persuaded herself to buy a blue suit and Sunday shoes as well, and was even angrier afterwards. Because of the rain he'd had his first streetcar ride, and it wasn't much fun for it was stopped more often than it was running, and full of women smelling of sweat, and he'd had to stand up all the time and couldn't see out.

In his notebook he'd written stories about Balibou: a series of drawings like comic strips with a text underneath, but often it had no beginning or end or any relationship to the drawings, because there was one drawing he'd really liked and he repeated it with improvements while the story went on. He'd never succeeded in making Balibou the same shape twice, and the cat grew fat or thin at the most unexpected moments – especially his head – and his legs were never the same length.

But the notebook was for him really his only weakness in the other place, a thing so unnatural, so lacking in pride, so unmanly that it was almost a kind of cowardice. To write it, that is, for if it had all stayed in his head the secret would have been kept, all those moments when he was the only one to enjoy (without shame, for he could always erase a memory) a delight to which, in the eyes of others, he had no right.

It was the only time a living person had had its reflection in his mind without the difference between the two being so great that one grew unbelievable. But because of written words, read by others, and by that person above all, the living person had destroyed the reflection, and he was ashamed for days, guilty of the only fault a man can not forgive himself.

Saint Agnes! In the notebook she's only called the *princess*, but even Pigfoot had understood at once. Especially because he explained to himself in the notebook why Pigfoot got *her* name: when she wanted to slap a big boy she'd give him a kick on the shin to put him off balance and keep him from running away. It was no use knowing it, she almost always caught you by surprise.

The story barely exists as it's told in the notebook, for there were so many holes between the days, and the important things were left out, and what was there was so complicated that it would have been easier to read his mind, but nobody could do that, not even himself, tomorrow or even an hour later, with so many thoughts in a minute, and a thought isn't very exact and it's invisible, like drops, and no one of them alone *is* the water or knows the one that dropped before or after it.

So the beginning in the notebook made no sense: *It was in the red of my eyes that I first saw her white hand which was red too, and when she touched my forehead I felt nothing, as if she were going through it, but it was so soft that her fingers were like silk on my skin.*

It was because he had had measles and his eyes were so swollen in the dark room that the hand, though white, was red. And he had such a fever that his forehead, or rather his head, spread from wall to wall, and it was normal that the hand had to go through all that thickness before he could feel its gentleness.

"That part isn't so bad. That was his delirium," Saint Agnes had said when he was on trial. But she couldn't know (for she hadn't had the measles) that it really was like that, and that words, which never work in the way you expect, tell the truth even when they're strangely put together.

He'd started that way because that had been the first important moment, the sudden revelation, in the midst of his illness which wasn't really an illness because dozens of his comrades had caught it too, as a sort of collective punishment – the sudden revelation, not of the usual absence of hostility, but of a presence so naturally friendly that it became miraculously abnormal. A communication like those he dared not admit he hungered for in his most inadmissible dreams, in the form of a woman's living gesture.

Because going to the infirmary meant having a daily visit from Saint Sabine who described in harrowing detail the suffering of Christ or the martyrdom of a holy crow, and being always under the eye of the vestry-nun who was deaf and dumb but let out constant little raging barks, and because of course it meant staying in bed all day, he had succeeded in fooling Pigfoot longer than the others in her daily inspection, and when she finally caught him with his rash the others were already cured. So he went to the infirmary in terror. The first night and half the next day nothing had happened, for the fever had at once borne him into a red blur where he could hardly see. Then, instead of the vestry-nun, he'd discovered, for only a few seconds the first time, a young girl, pale and smiling, so ill-disguised as a crow that he'd wanted to laugh. Then, as she came back time after time, the apparition became precise, and she really was very young, pretty, smiling, with a little blonde curl that rebelled against her coif, and surprising movements of her hips when she walked. But she'd stayed on the shores of the red sea, still too troubled by fever, until that first contact of her cool hand. Certainly no one had touched him like that since he was in the cradle, and that white-red hand, soft and weightless, had in an instant sent him back through all the days of his life, to a limitless whiteness where nothing had a shape.

He had not dared move a hair for fear of frightening the hand away, and each time he came near after that he had closed his eyes and played dead. In the notebook, it came out:

106

*Hidden in the great chamber at the top of the abandoned tower, I
open my wound every morning with the point of my long sword,
which falls from my hands, for my blood has become scarce, so
that I may never be cured but always cared for by the mysterious
princess who dresses my gaping wound without ever soiling her
white hands. We have not yet exchanged a word, for I am afraid
she will recognize me as the enemy that I am and lose her honour.
But at times she sings so sweetly that I have to weep.*

But one morning she had shaken him roughly, laughing:

"Today we're going to have something to eat. Your fever's gone,
and so are your spots. And tomorrow, back to school."

He had been more shocked than if she had announced he was
going to die in a month's time. And at once he had forced the
knight to open his belly in three new places, telling him he was a
coward if he thought he could stay ill for long with a single
wound, and the princess told the knight, weeping without tears in
her great sadness, that she could not save him, and he must en-
trust his soul to God. But that didn't discourage in the least Saint
Agnes's hearty smile, nor delay a recovery that was progressing at
a gallop. So, to have the most of her, he got up and followed her
the whole day, talking a string of nonsense for the pure pleasure
of hearing her voice, which was always ready to play. She told him
she'd taught in a school for girls in the city before coming there,
and she'd never seen so many boys at once. That luckily the epi-
demic had given her time to get accustomed. That she could have
understood if children without parents had been naughtier than
other children, but that it wasn't so, you just had to give them a
little more. These innocent confidences had at once obliged him to
take her under his protection, and without a moment's hesitation
he had killed the knight in the tower through the agency of pitiless
blows inflicted by the princess's father, who, seeing her dishon-
oured, immediately had her shut up in the great house of crows.

*But, left for dead in the forest, the knight had gathered the
strength to drag himself to a woodcutter's cabin, where he was so
well nursed that two days later he set out to seek the princess, having heard of her sad fate from the woodcutter himself. When her
father learned of this he ordered her to be disguised as a crow so
that no one would ever recognize her. But I know her, and when I
grow up I will carry her off on a horse. In the meanwhile, we are
her servants, and watch over her.*

Next day he was back with the others, who told him that sister Saint Agnes would replace Pigfoot, who would replace sister Saint Sabine who hadn't recovered from her last vision and that's why nobody had seen her in the infirmary. The news had made him happy and anxious at the same time, for if the princess was replacing their overseer it meant that she was a real crow, only younger, and would grow ugly and never smile again.

That same evening she occupied the sailboat, in the dormitory, and she'd even let him sleep in the first bed, alongside, because he was "convalescing," a word he'd adopted at once and never allowed anyone to use in one of his stories. But her youth and all her smiles had not given her the needed authority, and an innocent racket had started as soon as the lights went out, simply because everyone was happy. She had been obliged to turn the lights on three or four times to beg them, almost crying at the end, to be good and go to sleep like the good children they were. Finally they had been good, one after the other, because they grew tired, and sleep had more authority than she had.

Jane must have gone to Mama Pouf's place before the rain started, without waiting for him. The wall across the way is still silent, enclosing its secrets. She'd been shut off from the world since last night. It couldn't have been her mother that dragged her so roughly into the apartment. That wouldn't be like a mother, and still less a grandmother. Maybe it had been one of the men who came to watch over them at night?

In the part of the alley that he can't see he hears the hoofs of a horse. Bored, he goes back to his notebook, as one goes back to reading on a rainy day.

The fancy handwriting, which he doesn't recognize, and which can't have been his own, with scattered printing and majestic capitals, disappears in the spray of the rain as if written in invisible ink. And old events blur and disappear as well, made meaningless by the number of hours he has chalked up in his life, and by his new pants and sweater and the itch to see his companion of yesterday. Yet the notebook is open at the passage that caused his greatest disgrace, when he became a ridiculous knight humiliated by the princess denying that she had ever offered her favours, and when, exulting in his first taste of feminine tenderness in this fenced-in world that forbade children to be children and women to be women, he'd had recourse to writing to embellish the fable.

She had left the night-light on behind the curtains of her cell, and for a long time he followed the shadow of her movements. Perhaps she'd taken off her coif and let down her blonde hair before putting out the lights, he could never be sure afterwards, but he was quite sure that she'd undressed in the dark. But in his scribbler he had written these infamous lines:

I wished to lower my eyes to obey the rules of honour, but so much beauty froze my gaze. Through the crack in the curtain I saw a head of long blonde hair like none in the kingdom. And – let my eyes never see the sun again – I saw a breast whiter than that of the chapel Virgin if you took the blue paint off, whiter, more round, and moving softly like a wounded dove. Then I became a man of honour and closed my eyes. I had the final proof that this was a princess condemned to life in the convent, the very one for whom my heart yearned.

Crushed with shame by the suffering nobility of Saint Sabine, whose bony martyr's fingers barely grazed the notebook, and above all by the chagrin and indignation of Saint Agnes herself, he had vainly tried to maintain that what he had written in his own words was merely adapted from some scene in a book he had read. Too many other passages in his scribbler identified the breast and the princess condemned to the nun's habit, and comparisons with the witch called Pigfoot turned up so regularly that no one could doubt his crime. Saint Agnes, blushing a little, speaking in a timid voice, tried to make excuses on the grounds of measles and delirium. Saint Sabine had rolled her eyes up toward the heavens, prayed for a brief moment, and then, after expressing (in a voice calculated to destroy all vestiges of taste for celestial canticles) her regret that this perverse child could not be expelled as there was nowhere else to send him, she had judged Saint Agnes innocent of that breast with the blue paint removed, and the author of those unchivalrous lines guilty of lying, and of the solitary sin, and of an offence against the purity of his comrades in leaving such filth within their reach, and had finally condemned him to spend three whole days on his knees, outside the house or inside, in the refectory and during recreation.

This had been before he had decided to settle his account with his personal enemy, and Big Justin had been jubilant for those three days, subjecting him without fear of reprisal to the most diabolical tortures. A few days later Pigfoot had announced with obvious satisfaction that Saint Agnes had been sent to a foreign mission, and her own reign had resumed without further interruption.

Something lovely and fragile had been ruined, and it had been his fault, and he had never again put in writing things that existed only in his head, and he had learned once and for all that there are thoughts that must never see the light of day.

Why had they given him back his notebook after so long? Had his uncle or his aunts read it? The rain is making a mush of the pages. He tears them meticulously and rolls them into little balls which he then throws down into the gutter from the end of the gallery.

The horse, dripping with muddy water, appears in the alley, pulling a low vehicle covered with a big rain-coloured canvas. Nobody is driving, and he stops of his own accord at the cabin-shaped cover at the bottom of the stairs. He has a long pouch under his muzzle, and to get at its contents drops his head as low as possible without being able to reach the ground. Then two men, soaked through, armed with enormous tongs, appear in turn, fumble under the canvas with their tongs, and drag out great blocks of ice which shine in the rain like plate glass. He hears them start up the stairs. One raps at Jane's door, the other comes toward him, pushes his chair away without a word, and deposits his two blocks on the doormat before he knocks.

Aunt Maria opens the door, and at the same moment Jane, pale in the drizzly light and strangely dressed in a light cotton robe that goes to her feet and makes her seem much taller, appears at the other end of the gallery, frantic as if she had only three seconds to save a hundred lives. She runs toward him (looking down to avoid the puddles, for she has cloth slippers on) then speaks very quickly, leaning on his shoulders with her weightless arms:

"I'm with grandmother. I just have a second while they're putting the ice in the icebox. Mama was in a fit yesterday because she was going to have to speak to your aunts, and she doesn't want to start that again, and nobody knows who you are, but you're certainly not a boy for me to play with. Just crazy!"

She kisses him quickly, her mouth smeared with rain.

"Jane, will you come in this minute!"

He hears a voice, but sees no one.

"She doesn't even let me open the blinds. I can just see you if I climb on a chair.

"Well, kiddies, if you don't let me past I'll pick you up with my big tongs."

"She's kissing you! You get in here this minute!"

Aunt Maria's voice is a lot louder and harder than the grand-mother's.

"Poor Pierrot! She's going to give you a spanking. You're very handsome now. You look thinner."

Aunt Maria grabs him by the sweater and pulls for all she's worth.

The squirrel puts her little wet mouth in his ear to breathe a se-cret that tickles as it's told:

"We'll have to see each other secretly now. Tomorrow, in the street or at..."

He will never hear the end because his aunt has succeeded in dragging him to the door and pushing him into his uncle's den.

"You've gone and got your new pants wet, on purpose. That's what I call just plain bad! And you're not to go on that porch! You'll go on the front balcony."

He stuffs his sweater, which she had pulled out, back in his pants, and looking her straight in the eye, states in a quiet but un-alterable voice:

"You're old and mean. I'm never going to like you."

She slaps him, but he doesn't flinch, going on in the same tone:

"I'll go where I like. And if you three don't like it I'll go away."

She draws back for a second slap but this time he's ready for her, and she connects with the bookshelf. Then she starts howling and chasing him around the apartment.

"Damned little savage! You'll end up in jail like the rest of your lot. The police will catch up with you."

"I'm not afraid of you or anything else."

He hadn't had to run very fast to put the length of the dining-room table between them. In any case, she quickly gives up and is reduced to glaring at him with impotent rage, rubbing her sore hand and puffing hard. There's even a trace of drool running from her mouth. He wonders anxiously if she's going to crumple up like the day before, and whether it's her sickness that smells of vinegar or the vinegar that makes her sick.

"...nobody knows who you are...you're certainly not a boy for me...." He doesn't just hear the phrases, he sees them written in huge red letters. And in his aunt's fishy eyes he sees the scream, "You'll end up in jail like..."

He's always known that he wouldn't find out who he was for a long time, and he's never known who other people were either, for you can only judge by their words, and words seem the same for everybody but don't even have the same meaning from one day to the next, depending on a smile or anger, or just a glassy look that is as silent as a rock.

In the other place it was easier. There were all the children who at least were on the same side, condemned to go through the same actions, wear the same clothes, keep the same distance; and that wiped out the greatest differences, even between the Chinese boy and Nicolas and Justin. And there were the crows, and they were all alike too, you knew where you were at because they were on the other side and played it that way. Nobody expected them to bring a box of chocolates, for example, and everyone knew none of the children would go and give Pigfoot a kiss. Anything like that would have threatened an order which took its very form from the fact that nothing like that ever did happen. Of course there was the pear Saint Agnes had given him secretly during the short time she was replacing Pigfoot, and long before his notebook was discovered, but precisely because of that pear he had always thought that even without the revelation of his lying fantasies the novice, too young and full of smiles, could not have stayed long among them, for she did not know the rules of the game and wouldn't have been able to choose sides one way or the other.

But here on the outside they'd always known who he was. He's not a boy for Jane, and he'll come to a bad end, just as the Rat isn't for Isabelle and she'll pay for it, just as the little redhead's mother is bad and you're not to talk to her, and just as uncle is good to buy him new clothes and not to know whether he'll keep him. His proper place is in houses made for boys like him, just like Marcel, who jumped over the wall one day and disappeared into the world, but now he's going to win the war, and he's turned into an American and that's why they have to give him lots of money. Of course there are Mama Pouf and the shoemaker who are like the things he'd imagined, but maybe that was because the weather was nice and the lilacs spread their smell over everything, or because Meeow had made him see everything through blue milk.

Luckily Aunt Maria has flopped on a chair. Now she's crying. Great tears run down her scarlet cheeks and splash on the table, in a surprising silence. He sits down too, at the other end of the table, and surveys her with perfect neutrality. Why does she cry if she's mean and likes no one? Why does a grown-up, who can do anything she wants, even hit children, have to cry? What kind of tears are these? She just has to put on her hat and go anywhere, in a streetcar or to a store or a movie.

"I can go outside if it'll make you stop crying."

"I forbid you to go out. And I am not crying. I'm unhappy."

"What's it like to be unhappy?"

She wipes off a tear with the back of her hand and looks at him without seeing him.

"Stop acting like a stupid man!"

"I mean, I could understand a baby being unhappy. Something hurts and he can't tell anybody. But what about you? You just hit me, I'm the one who should be crying."

"You're a man, and that means heartless."

He won't be put off by that kind of statement. But he never saw a crow crying. Maybe Pigfoot cried at night in secret in the sailboat, for she's no more crippled than an old maid, and she had to stand up to hundreds of children who just naturally hated her. But this aunt, crying in front of him, after slapping his face! Maybe if he asks her the questions over again, quietly, he'll find out something that will help him understand why outside isn't the same as he'd imagined and why people don't change but freeze like photos and always do the same things because those things go with the way the people always are.

"Is it because your hand hurts?"

"If I catch you you'll see if my hand hurts."

"Why are you always angry?"

"Leave me alone."

"Why don't you like anybody?"

She stretches her neck at him, as if she wanted to reach him with her eyes, then lets out a kind of stifled sob, stands up, gives him a last impotent glance and heads for her room, muttering:

"Little moron!"

"You were little once, weren't you, just like everybody. What were you like?"

But she goes off dragging her feet, for she'll always be Aunt Maria and she doesn't have to answer questions put by a child, and one who's going to end up in jail at that.

He'd never go so far as to ask her about that, for there are things that will never exist because he doesn't want to know about them.

He's very tempted to settle for a division between children and grown-ups. As for children, he has no doubt that they are a race to themselves, all alike but all capable of changing; and that by asking questions or punching them you can always succeed in finding

113

out who they are and imagine them playing different roles. Justin, for example: he has no trouble imagining him as a priest, like Justin's father, or a policeman or an iceman, or any old way. But his uncle, even if he lives with him for ten years, will always be a gentleman who goes to work, educated but not proud, and never answering questions. Aunt Rose will always cook and Aunt Eugénie will always cut out shirt collars and never pants or rugs. Papa Henri will always be a shoemaker. Even the Rat, who doesn't seem like a grown-up, will never change. True, the Rat is sick.

And what about Jane's mother, who makes parachutes, who gave her an *anglais* for a papa whom she's hardly ever seen, and who comes from the mountain where she was alone in the house? Yesterday he knew that Jane's mother couldn't be like the others, that something about her must be different and immediately noticeable, like Jane; but today he finds out that she's given him a tag he'll never get rid of: he wasn't a boy for Jane. That made her like the others, and the grandmother too, who wouldn't let Jane open the blinds. So there weren't just crows and old maids, there were mothers and grandmothers like them. What would a bad woman be, according to his aunts? Certainly not one that forbade her daughter to talk to other children, for that's what they did themselves. A mother that worked, and didn't stay with her child? Maybe. Maybe that's why she wasn't like Mama Pouf.

But Jane is a child, and a girl at that, and she's playing on his side. They're going to meet in secret. And she wasn't afraid to come and speak to him in front of her grandmother. But how will he know if she's waiting somewhere for him?

Because all these questions have no answers he leaves the dining-room, suddenly flooded with sunlight, and goes out on the front balcony at the other end of the living-room. On the other side of the street in the presbytery garden the dripping trees hold millions of crystals up to the sun. As far as one can see the streets are deserted, shining and clean. The eaves of the balcony are weeping as stupidly as Aunt Maria. The only living creature in sight is the priest, pacing up and down on the upstairs gallery of the presbytery, reading a book he seems to know by heart. On the neighbouring balcony, not a trace of red hair to be seen.

Running his hand along the edge of the eaves to get rid at once of all the big tears swelling in the sunlight, he realizes from a faint creaking of the living-room floor that he's been trapped, encircled. The blurred silhouette of his aunt is framed in the doorway, and between him and her there's only the width of the balcony.

To be sure, she's not very fast, but the distance is too narrow for her to miss every time. Without turning around, still playing with the tears, he warns her in a singsong:

"I'm not afraid...to jump down there."

"Come along. We have some shopping to do."

Her voice is almost friendly, and to his great surprise she has changed her dress, put on a hat, and even smells of some perfume that makes him want to cough.

"I know very well you'd jump, just to make a nuisance of yourself. You can expect anything of a man."

"You're not crying any more? You're not unhappy?"

"Be quiet and come along before the groceries close."

"Where's Aunt Rose?"

"She went to the hairdresser's."

"What's a hairdresser? Do they make the flowers grow on hats?"

He doesn't feel the least bit like going out with her and carrying the big black leather bag she's carrying. People will think she's his mother, or his grandmother, and he'll be more ashamed than he had been of his boots and overalls.

"I don't want to go. You don't need me."

"I'm asking you nicely."

"You didn't say please."

"You wouldn't make me cry again?"

"No, it's too ugly."

As if of its own accord, her right hand which is red and swollen begins to rise impatiently, but she succeeds in maintaining an almost amiable tone over the anger which is struggling inside her.

"I'll buy you an ice cream or a Coke."

He circles his aunt and starts rolling himself in the red velvet drapes that separate the parlour from the dining-room.

"I asked you never to do that, they cost a lot of money and you'll pull them down."

He can't understand why she needs him so badly, and he sees clearly that she's bursting with rage. To see how far he can go he repeats:

"How about saying please?"

"All right. I'm saying it. Now come."

He waits for her to reach the second landing before leaving the door, where he listens in vain. He has to hold back from ringing to see at least the grandmother's head stick out. Before starting down, he asks Aunt Maria very loudly:

"What is it you're sick with?"

She doesn't answer. He arrives in the entry as soon as she does.

"If you don't answer my questions I won't come with you."

She opens the door to the street and waits, her eye glinting fire.

"When we want answers we don't shout the questions for all the neighbours to hear."

She starts along Dorchester toward the other church. He follows her, a few steps behind, looking at her shoes, which are shapeless, and her legs, which are stained by big patches of blue, swollen like water blisters.

"Is it your legs? Is that why you fall down?"

She seems almost relieved.

"Yes, it's my legs. It's as if the blood couldn't get there."

"You're a liar. There's nothing catching about legs. Aunt Rose says not to touch your towels or your dishes."

He lets her get ahead, pretending not to know her. Then she turns around, and her white hair with dirty yellow streaks looks as if it had been buried for fifty years. He catches up with her.

"Why didn't you answer when I asked you what you were like when you were little?"

"I've forgotten."

"It's not true. You can't forget about being a child. Not even if you're a hundred."

"Why not, if you please?"

"Because that's the only time you're happy."

"And you're happy, are you?"

"Well, yes, it's a bit hard because grown-ups don't want you to be, they think it's rude or not polite or something. How were you then?"

"That was in the country. Far away from here. Near Quebec. I was a blonde, and I was sick already."

She stops dead and points to the other side of the street, to a little red brick house with a green roof, and a passageway going under it.

"Look, there it is."

"What?"

"Our house, of course. That's where your grandmother and grandfather lived when they came to the city. We've always lived around here."

"Did we come from the country too?"

116

Her voice grows angry again:

"Your bunch? I should say not. A poor lot, typical city folk. If we'd stayed in the country your mother would never have..."

She breaks off, and shoves open the door of a little grocery, ordering him to wait outside.

The street is suddenly full of life, as if someone had rung the recess bell: children running or playing marbles among the puddles, old ladies rocking in front of the houses, cars splashing them, and even the french-fries wagon where the fat man with the dirty apron is alone this time, half asleep and gazing at the bony rear of his horse.

"That's our famous nephew. A real little savage, afraid of everybody. Well, good-day, Madame Beauséjour..."

She points her finger at him to make sure there's no mistake. Out on the sidewalk again, she slips the brown paper package into her big leather shopping bag and holds it out to him.

"Take care, those are bottles."

"What about my ice cream?"

"We're not through yet. You'll get it after supper."

"Why don't you carry it?"

"Because you're the man."

"You mean the little savage."

"I didn't mean it that way. Just that you're not used to people."

He takes the bag because he feels sorry for her legs, and it makes him look as if he's doing something. He'd like her to finish the sentence about his mother, but he's afraid of destroying something. They've passed the second church by now.

"What's an old maid?"

She doesn't get angry, and answers as if it were quite obvious:

"Somebody who's not married, of course!"

"That's not what I mean. Why doesn't she get a husband?"

"Because our father died and we had to help the family."

"Would you have found a man if it hadn't been for that?"

"Maybe. I don't know."

"I know. All that isn't true. It's because you don't like men, and you don't like them because there's something wrong with you."

She stops dead again. Her hands are trembling on her handbag, which is black leather whitened by wear. He hastens to add, to calm her:

"It's like children being happy. That changes to being something that's wrong with you. That's why I asked you what you were like then."

117

But she'd only stopped because they'd arrived at another grocery. She tells him to wait. And comes right back with another brown paper bag, the same size as the first, which it follows into the shopping bag. He has to lift it a little to keep it from dragging, for it's too long at his arm's length.

She turns toward Lagauchetière Street and for a long time he lets her walk ahead. She turns back often to make sure he's following and tell him to be careful with the bottles. He'd like to push her with all his might and make her run, for they're getting close to Mama Pouf's place and he doesn't want to be seen. But she trudges on with the heavy stride that crushes down her shoes. Without looking, out of the corner of his eye, he sees one of the twins bouncing a ball against a wall of the entry passage, and he hurries on to catch up with his aunt who's now on her way home. For the third time she makes him wait in front of a grocery store at the corner of Plessis.

He puts down the bag, sits on the steps and looks at the superstructure of the bridge, which blocks the view down the street, far away, and seems so light under the slanting rays of the sun which even touches with gold the rows of poles planted on both sides of the narrow street and a few ruined trees.

He feels a tall shadow stopping less than a foot away, and looks back from the bridge to see the high yellow boots and the lump of lead swinging from the chain's end.

"I thought I knew that straw head, but the rest of it..."

The Rat gives two or three admiring whistles.

"Wow! Handsome as they come! A real family boy! The little redhead's going to like you now."

Pierrot rips at the chain with all his strength, but the Rat has strong wrists.

"Easy, Pierrot. That's not for kids. I'll give you a little tiny one if you behave."

He bends down and fumbles in the shopping bag, his long hands still holding the chain.

"Hey! Making the rounds with your drunken auntie, eh?"

"Mind your business, Rat. They're bottles, and her legs hurt."

"Yeah, beer bottles. She buys them in different stores so nobody knows how many. But people have caught on to how much she pours down her old legs."

"Why should she drink all that beer?"

"Just like everybody else. To piss away the poison in her head.

But the more they drink the more it turns to vinegar in the brains."

"So that's why she smells of...."

The Rat lets out a long rattle up where his mouth is, for he has to breathe that way at times, and waits till it's over before he speaks. The lead on the chain hangs motionless before Pierrot's eyes, at the yellow-boot level. His gaze climbs the chain to those two long girlish hands clenched at his chest, and up to the face whiter than plaster under the long black hair.

"Are you feeling bad, Rat?"

The breath of the Rat's laughter blows in his face, for he has crouched down suddenly and his pale green eyes stare straight into Pierrot's.

"Never felt better. Springtime. Girls growing everywhere with smiles enough to make you want to do nothing else."

"Nothing else but what, Rat?"

"Poor little bugger, I suppose you don't learn about life behind those walls. Well, it's...putting those smiles out, Pierrot."

"I don't like when you talk that way, I'm not sure I can be a friend of yours."

"I suppose your aunts told you I wasn't a friend of Marcel's...."

"No, I found out myself. You take it out on flowers, and you don't like girls."

"And you found that out all by yourself! I don't like girls?"

"No. You want to hurt them, and they let you because they're nice. Or else I don't understand. I don't like to see you with Isabelle."

"Or Jane."

The Rat's laugh comes again, crackling like fire through his chest.

"And you expect me to be scared, eh? There's a new cock in the neighbourhood, I'm not alone any longer?"

Pierrot looks behind him to see if his aunt is coming, but he can't even hear anyone talking inside.

"This is Pelletier's grocery. Don't forget it."

"I don't care about that. You order Isabelle and she does what you say. Yet she's proud enough."

"I may need you to remember that this is Pelletier's grocery. We can do things together, the two of us."

"No, Rat. At first I thought you could explain a lot of things to me that I don't understand, because you're not a real grown-up, but what I don't understand, it's even worse with you, a different kind of meanness."

"Listen, little buddy, I hear my streetcar coming. See you again. I won't let you make out all alone, you're too white."

"I like you anyway because of Marcel."

He has to shout because the narrow street is filled with the sound of a wagon and its galloping horses.

"Look at me. I just came from the doctor. That's it. Springtime. A hell of springtime. He wants to pump gas into my lungs, as if I was a tire. So I'm seeing the girls for the last time. It's going to be one hell of a show right to the end. I'll tell you that and no more."

The voice is so high pitched that it misses. The Rat shakes his shoulder roughly, his eyes blurred for an instant, then he's up and jumping on the back of the Molson wagon, which doesn't slow down.

Aunt Maria comes out at the same time.

"Hey, old lady, save yourself the trouble! We'll leave a barrel at the house!"

The great, fat horses drum with their iron shoes, making their own racket, the barrels bounce on each other, and the long shadow of the Rat on the back waves like a naked tree in the wind.

Aunt Maria has heard nothing, seen nothing.

"That's all. We're going home now."

"Why do you drink beer? You've got to help me, it's too heavy."

He doesn't know if she's looking daggers at him or if it's the blue in her eyes that's gone out, like old marbles worn from rolling, their inner beauties lost, their surface rough to the finger. She too has trouble breathing, but unlike the Rat, when she dilates her nostrils and the muscles of her neck strain, she makes no noise. The air can't get in, or it gets lost in the softened flesh. There are sweat drops on the hand that takes one handle of the shopping bag. He observes this without any feeling. She is as foreign to him and his life as the telephone poles or the word KIK in big red letters over the grocery door. She starts off again, slower now, without replying. He repeats, in his stubborn, neutral voice:

"Why do you drink beer? Gaston says you just poison yourself."

She mumbles something and her face gets a little redder.

"As if it wasn't enough being sick. Have to put up with you like a wild animal in the house, you only want to hurt a person."

"That's not an answer. Why don't you go to the hospital then?"

"Because I have a home and..."

She drops the bag but catches it with her leg as the bottles rattle. She jams her hat on her head, and he sees another great tear roll down, but it doesn't bother him for it seems to leave her eyes for no reason, like when you need to wipe your nose. She doesn't cry, she just leaks.

"If you want to know, it's what keeps me alive. It gives you strength. And now I don't want any more of your rough-neck questions. If I'd had anything to say they'd never have taken you out. Your uncle's too good."

"I don't know yet if he's good. He never says anything."

"I'm going to tell him everything."

"Well, then I'll find out."

"Little monster, who paid for your new pants?"

"I don't like new pants. They're my first pair, and they're not me."

He sits down on the curb and pays close attention to two dogs pretending to scare each other in the middle of the street.

"Come on, at least you can earn your supper."

He doesn't budge. She shrugs and goes off with the shopping bag, which she transports in front of her, between her legs. On the other side of the street, through a wide-open door, he sees a Chinaman with a wispy beard sitting on a low platform and sewing with long, slow gestures in the shadows. He crosses the street, goes into the shop, kneels in front of the platform, wondering how the man can see with so little light. After observing him for a long time he decides that the Chinese boy in the other place must have belonged to a different race, maybe Eskimo. The real Chinaman doesn't raise his eyes for one second, but goes on sewing rhythmically as if he were a mechanical doll.

Pierrot hears behind him a grumbling like that of the deaf-mute vestry-nun. It's another Chinese, younger and very fat, speaking to him, seemingly in ill humour, as he throws sheets into a cage. Pierrot turns and smiles at him, but the other goes on grumbling at him without looking. As he goes out of the shop, which smells damp and good, he waves his hand to see if the old man is not blind, and the latter, without looking up, his hand in the air at the end of his invisible thread, allows a vague smile to glimmer in his little eyes that are sewed together at the corners.

In the distance he sees his aunt stopped in front of the old people's home, the black bag on the sidewalk, fanning herself with her hat. He trots after her, a little sad that she should be old and sick and ugly, wondering, without really thinking about it, at what moment people had stopped loving her, and when it is that you stop being a child and start feeling like a hunchback and waiting to hurt people because you see that you're always going to be alone and nobody will change the way they think about you. When he catches up with her he says as gently as possible:

"I discovered a Chinaman who's condemned to sew all day on a plank. And he smiled."

He takes the bag in his two hands and raises it to carry on his back. She follows him without a word, her mouth open to help her breathe.

"If I told you I'd try everything to like you, would you like me?"

They're at the apartment entry. Aunt Maria starts slowly up the stairs without replying.

"If you don't answer, does that mean no?"

She stops on the first landing for a rest. She takes the bag from him.

"Go on up. All those questions of yours, they're pure meanness, just like your father."

He stops trying to understand. Once and for all he decides not to ask any more questions. Decides also that people, even in their own heads, see themselves the way others see them or perhaps see nothing at all except walls through which they don't want to leave or let anyone enter.

Maybe Jane, who has more experience, can explain it. But he's not even sure what she sees in her own head.

10

Aunt Rose has just gone out, ordering him to join her at church. He said yes at once so that she wouldn't wait for him, and rushed out to the green back porch. For a while he paces back and forth, looking down into the alley where there is no one to be seen. Then he leans over the balustrade and taps on the nearest shutter, which is opposite his uncle's den, but no one replies to his signal. Then he sits down on the canvas chair which is still soaking wet and imagines that Jane, imprisoned in her grandmother's arms, has managed somehow to smile at him through the slats of the shutter.

He's beginning to like Aunt Eugénie, the youngest, who barely sees him, but who gets it in the neck from Aunt Maria as soon as she appears, and can't put a word in. This is why Eugénie comes home as late as she can from the factory, leaves the table as soon as she can and goes off to the other church – Saint-Pierre – which, according to Aunt Maria, is where the snobbish ladies of the parish go, and the stuck-up young things who make shirt collars all day for two cents apiece. Eugénie, says Aunt Maria, thinks of nothing but eating, gulps her food down as if she were in a barn, can't hold her tongue and continually bothers Uncle Nap, who has worked so hard, with gossip that's only of interest to herself; she has no brains, and throws her money around as if Uncle Nap were going to give her an old-age pension. Eugénie never answers directly, speaking to Aunt Rose or asking Uncle Nap about what's new, and Nap, for his own peace and quiet no doubt, doesn't open his mouth more than twice during the meal.

"You're like cat and dog," Aunt Rose interjects sometimes between trips to the kitchen.

All this gives Pierrot a certain respite and lets him eat in peace without suffering Aunt Maria's baleful stare.

Tonight Eugénie went so far as to leave the table before dessert, protesting that she'd rather go and eat out every day.

"Oh yes, go on, hang around in public, at your age!"

"Good lord, Eugénie, you know she's sick. Try to be a little patient."

But she went to change in the room she shares with Aunt Rose, which opens on the kitchen, and when she came out she smelled of a thousand flowers.

"You smell like a trollop. Go on, run around, for all the good it'll do you."

At a safe distance, with one foot in the dining-room, Aunt Eugénie dared to throw her brick:

"The minute they saw you they never showed up again, that's for sure. And Napoléon, who stopped him from getting married?"

"Quiet, gee whillikins! Go outside and fight if you want to."

Then, with no transition, he announced:

"It's going to be over sooner than they thought. The Americans are racing ahead. Patton's doing a hundred miles a day. In the north, the Canadians have taken Falaise, and paid dearly for it. My boss doesn't even come to the office, he's so worried, but the Colonel lets him know how he's doing...."

"Will it be over this summer, Nap? It's too soon, there won't be work for the ones coming back."

Uncle Nap didn't answer, but went off to the bathroom, his English newspaper in his hand.

Pierrot had concluded that Patton, though he might be a great racer, wasn't much faster than a ship if all he could do was a hundred miles a day.

Aunt Maria, very calm, had gone off to church herself without saying a word to him, her glance almost gentle, as if she were relieved at the end of a difficult day. And he had helped Aunt Rose with the dishes.

Giving up, he leaves the porch to have a look from the front balcony, but stops in the dining-room, astonished to find his uncle, still in his vest and tie, his shirt-sleeves puffed out above his sleeve-holders, playing the piano by the light of the setting sun, which falls on a music book before him.

He leans forward to see the notes, his big white head close to the book, and his stubby fingers barely touch the keys. It's almost beautiful for a minute, then he stops, touches the notes with his first finger, plays four or five notes that don't satisfy him, then

124

plays them again several times, and begins again from the start, the part that was almost beautiful, and it stays that way a little longer this time, for he gets a few notes farther. Then he slides his large behind back a little, hoists up his pants and drinks a mouthful of yellow liquid from the glass on the piano. When this has been well rolled around in his mouth, he pulls up his cuffs, leans forward again with his nose in the music and begins all over.

The boy takes advantage of this to slip behind him and reach the balcony. The bells of the two churches are ringing together, and women in hats, some with their children, walk toward one or the other, greeting each other as they pass, speeding up as they pass the small groups of men taking the air in shirt-sleeves and braces. The street is almost as busy as on the morning of the funeral. He doesn't even look at the balcony next door, but goes back to the living-room.

In a halo of sunlight, a kind of Saint Joseph old enough to have had grandchildren and develop a pot belly, his uncle is now totally absorbed. He plays without stopping, wagging his head with the rhythm, quite violently at times, as if he were revealing a hidden man that exists when the aunts are out; and what he plays isn't like his usual self either: it's delicate as lace, tripping and skipping, with a movement of women's dresses when they were long and wide, music like that which Pierrot imagined when he read that the princess made her curtsy, blushing, at the prince's ball, or when the white lady, tormented by a fatal love, confided to the piano the last sighs of her languishing soul.

He has to shut his eyes to forget that this music is produced by his uncle's thick fingers, to forget the behind that takes up the whole width of the bench, and give himself up to the music and Jane who, for a second, takes over the room, occupying all its space with her reddish gold, her voice as liquid as rain, her raspberry lips cool against his neck or on his ear, her white, freckled skin, her laugh humble and proud at the same time. The music gives him totally to Jane, and he's glad of it; it lifts him out of the desert that was today, and he feels able to put up with anything in this house as long as Jane lives in it, even if he never sees her, because she came to him once, lonely like himself, and offered him her lively, unexpected joy by making a face at him, and because she lives in his mind without his having to shut all its windows to keep her in or ask if he has to wipe out everything else to make her possible.

If he ran away with the squirrel, not in a caboose, to be sure, but alone with her, anywhere, to see the world together, without grown-ups to bar the way, sleeping wherever they stopped, eating what they could find, and maybe going from one Mama Pouf to the next, and if they grew up together having fun with each other, they'd never have to play at being grown-ups even when they got older. In such a big city, where they knew no one ten blocks away, what could happen to them? They'd just be children, like the ones you see everywhere, and nobody could ask them who they were or where they were going, for they'd be Jane and Pierrot, a girl and boy playing, going for a walk, with a house in town somewhere, for they're there and don't cry but laugh the whole time. But what do they do about children alone in the streets at night? Maybe all they'd need is an abandoned house like the stone one under the bridge, the house in which he wasn't able to find his own beginnings.

He goes closer to his uncle, who empties his glass with a final swallow, and looks closely at the marks in the music book, which don't look like music at all but like funny numbers in another language.

"Didn't you go to church with your aunt?"

"Can you make music just looking at that?"

His uncle closes the piano lid, takes the music, hesitates a little as if he were going to explain, then puts it down again on the piano.

"Go play outside. You can come back in when your aunts come."

The sun is very red on his face, and he smells of iodine.

"It's beautiful. That's why I asked you if the music is in the book."

"Of course! I don't make it up."

"Who did, then?"

"Go and play. I'm not going to start teaching you music now."

"To make it up do you need a piano? You could do it, then."

"No, it's written in the book."

"You mean, it's like words. You play a note and write it down. Like dictation?"

His uncle gets up without answering, takes his empty glass and his newspaper which he had left on an armchair, and retires to his den.

Alone, Pierrot lifts the lid and plays a few notes, barely pressing down, first with one hand, then with two, but realizes quickly that this isn't music, as he has always realized that what doesn't happen doesn't happen. He never knew whether this was the gift of a few, like being very tall or walking on your hands like Justin, or if you had to learn it in a class. He goes after his uncle to the den, for he wants to know, and he's waited long enough to find out why his uncle is so unlike the Christmas presents he sent.

Sitting in the big armchair that hides the couch where he sleeps when he goes to his room just adjoining, where it smells of pipe all night for he leaves it in the ashtray under his nose, uncle Nap is reading his paper as if he were alone in the world.

"Why don't you want to explain the music to me? You've got time and we're all alone."

The blue eyes that appear above the paper are suddenly ill humoured, and the voice is rough:

"You still there? I'd like to be obeyed. You're too young for music, and it's nothing for you in any case."

"Why not? If I like it?"

"Because you'll never play. You're going to learn a trade."

"Can't you have a trade and music too? Why not?"

"Because you're a pest!"

And he gets up, waving the paper furiously.

"Out! Get out!"

As if to push him with the newspaper, he takes one step, then another, still shouting:

"Out! Get out!"

But as the boy doesn't move, and his uncle realizes that his paper is not a cane, he sits down again and tries to light his pipe, but he's puffing so hard the match goes out.

His uncle's anger hurts more than his aunts'. He really believed that his uncle, before the music business, was only pretending to be the plump, rounded gentleman, very busy, taciturn, opening his mouth for nothing but the war news, showing no affection, keeping him at a distance the better to hide a secret which would inevitably come out and transform Pierrot's life. Thus, from the beginning, he watched what he did, observed him with the same cold attention he always had for others, for nothing was sure between them and he had to be on his guard and not attribute to people what was not real, but search for the slightest sign that would give the game away. But his uncle was very strong, and revealed nothing, simulating a coldness that was almost hostile. To be sure, since coming out from behind the walls the Blue Man had disappeared in a whirl of smoke, leaving everything uncertain and improbable, leaving him in an emptiness in which incomprehensible things could happen; and yesterday, as he tore up the shame of his notebook he almost gave in to the idea that everything really existed as he saw it with his detached gaze, that is, in a cold and alien way that would never disappear, that he would always be alone facing people and things, that no one more powerful would ever hold out a hand, and that even the Blue Man existed somewhere between books and reality, between what Pierrot invented in order to feel protected, and cool daylight, which leaves nothing in the shadow, and perhaps, after all, does illuminate more than just appearances.

Until the music. For then he suddenly saw through his uncle, always stiff inside his role, another person who told him, by means of the piano, things too serious to be said otherwise, someone who was biding his time to change completely and make possible what everyone else pushed back with both hands into the prison of childhood, as if it were so dangerous the world would no longer be possible and nothing serious would get done, and nobody would know what to think or what to expect of others if it were allowed to flow naturally like air, this weakness that is typical of little innocents who think the world seems so big and people so indifferent only because there's another universe, a magic one, which can correct things as you go along, for each person individually. His most stupefying discovery has been that of his own oddity. Everyone else seems to accept that nothing can correct anything, especially those things that are at once the most serious and the easiest to correct, such as making people happy for no reason at all. Except Jane, perhaps ...

But there, his uncle's music is his first encounter with a secret language that shortens the distance between what everyone sees is possible and the impossible that everyone can feel is truer, and the music is more direct than books. For it doesn't go through your head but is understood by your whole body.

But once the piano lid is closed, his uncle can't talk any more but goes back to being the fat man preoccupied by creating emptiness around him.

This Pierrot can't accept without an explanation. He sits down on the couch behind his uncle, waits patiently until a couple of successful puffs have been made at the pipe, and starts again very calmly, determined to push it to the end:

"A shoemaker, like Monsieur Lafontaine – can't he play the piano? Why?"

His uncle takes silent refuge behind his newspaper screen.

"If you can make music you must be able to see that people who can't would like to know how. Why do you play the piano, anyway?"

"Leave me alone, dang it!"

"When you play you're not the same. There's somebody else inside you who never talks the way you're doing now. That's why you make music."

"You see? I don't need to give you an answer. Go play outside and let me read."

"But there isn't another man inside the shoemaker, because he's always kind. What trade do you want me to learn?"

"I don't know. They'll decide."

"Decide what?"

"What you can do."

"If I can do it I don't need to learn. Who's going to decide?"

"The people in the place you're going to."

"So I'm not staying here?"

"No. You can see there's no room, and your aunt is sick."

"I don't even know if I want to stay. I'm thinking about it."

At this, his uncle gets up, throwing his pipe into the ash tray so hard there are red cinders all over the table.

"Get up out of there and go play wherever you like, on the balcony, in the street, just..."

He doesn't let him finish.

"Yes, I can go now. I know you don't like being my uncle, and you'll never answer my questions seriously, and you don't care what happens to me."

His uncle goes back to his chair, his pipe, his newspaper, inside the big bubble that only bursts when he makes music.

Pierrot goes out on the porch, sees no light behind the closed shutters, comes back to the den, stands still in front of his uncle and announces coldly:

"I want to be a shoemaker. I won't need music and I'll never be like you."

"That's fine. Now go peddle your pots somewhere else."

He slams the porch door.

"And I'll never be so important that I won't answer children's questions!"

11

He saw her mother go out. A green car, its engine running, was waiting for her. The man at the wheel was at her side in a flash, put his arm around her waist and opened the other door for her. Away they went, without a glance at the balconies.

She was tall, thin, her hair a little lighter than Jane's, almost carrot red, in a pretty silk dress that shone in the sunlight, not at all as if she were going to work in a factory. But parachutes are so white and light, maybe they don't make them in factories with machines and chimneys but in big white halls where there are only fine ladies like her, wearing jewels (on the white skin of her neck he saw lovely red stones flashing) with long, delicate hands for sewing those great balloons full of wind.

He barely saw her, he was so busy taking in that elegance which he found intimidating, and he wondered if he'd ever dare speak to her; but he didn't like what the man did with her, putting his arm around as if she belonged to him, a bit like the Rat and Isabelle, and he wonders again how a guard or a chauffeur has the right to touch her like that; then he hears, from the neighbouring balcony, the small, warm voice that sends him so high in the sky that he breathes out the whole city in one puff.

"Did you see her? That's mama. And a gentleman I don't know."

He looks at her, stupidly. He's been turned back into the boy that had never met her, he's so delighted to find her sparkling with golden light, so graceful and smiling that he devours her with his eyes, unable to speak.

"Well! That's a funny face! Can't you talk? I'm going to be alone. The whole day, Pierrot!"

He'd like her to go on talking, never stop, not for what she says but for her voice alone, that music that sets every nerve trembling and is meant only for him. Finding her this way, with no warning, after so many long hours that he thought he might have invented

131

her as well, makes her so precious that his first word will make her burst like a soap bubble and he'll be there with his face splattered and only his aunts for company, buried in their perpetual winter. Stammering, his voice half stifled, like that of someone who has waited so long for a certain joy that he cries when it comes and nobody understands, he says:

"I'll come down right away. Let's go."

"You look nicer than I thought. Pierrot...I think I love you."

She leans out from the balcony, her foot off the floor, offering her tiny, laughing mouth, more berry than all the berries of the world.

"Don't go and believe everything I say, dummy! All night I saw an owl with big boots that kept him from flying. Where did you put them?"

And the raspberries part over little white squirrel-teeth. The deep water of her laugh: a cool hand on his burning chest.

Straddling the iron railing now, her pleated white dress up to her bottom, she announces across the street:

"Not one of them laughs when you tell them 'You're handsome and I love you.' They all get that stupid look. As if it was serious!"

She throws her other leg over and is quite outside the railing.

"Hey! Your hair's so stiff I'm going to call you Plush."

Her heels on the edge, her arms stretched out behind her holding the railing, and her whole body arched over the abyss, the white and russet bird, wildly amused, prepares for flight.

"I'll be a teddy bear if you like. Plush, I like that. But what are you doing! Are you crazy?"

He didn't react at first, it seemed so natural that she should have practised such acrobatics every day, but he's just noticed how deep the fall is beneath this little body dressed in white, suspended above street level, and her laugh is so near he expects to see her jump across.

"Never mind, come and kiss me anyway. Are you scared?"

"What if the iron gave way? Do you think you've got wings?"

"Aha! You're still in your big boots and you're scared to fly. And I'm the one that couldn't cross precipices on a rope! Plush is a scaredy! Oh, that's bad!"

He climbs over his own railing, notices that the edge is just the width of his foot, then grabs the railing and leans out, too violently, for his weight is no longer on his feet. He catches himself.

"Wrong! A bear could do better than that."

"What do my aunts say when they see you do this?"

"They faint for two hours and then they call the firemen to come and get them up. I think I'm going to have to call them for you too."

"It's too long, Jane, your arms will hurt."

"That's what you think! Here, take my hand."

And one of her hands lets go and flies toward him, just for a second. He pulls back and manages to get his balance by arching his body like hers. Between their lips there's just the distance of a kiss.

"See, you could do it. Stretch your legs."

"It's not my legs, it's my arms."

She nods violently and a russet froth caresses and blinds him.

Below, women are shouting and waving. A car has stopped and when the driver puts out his head to look he sees the world upside down. With a last effort of his knees he manages to stretch far enough to graze the raspberries which have never tasted so delicious. To help him a little she stuck out her tongue, and the feeling of this pink flash between his lips makes him dizzy, and his legs are a little wobbly when he pulls back, and he almost misses the railing when he hears Aunt Maria's rasping voice:

"You'd just like to fall and give us trouble, wouldn't you!"

He's back on the balcony, and replies quietly:

"Leave me alone. You almost pushed me."

But his aunt is too busy getting in a fury at Jane's faces.

"Little slut, get home with you! Go on, fall, that'd be a good lesson to your mother."

"See you downstairs?" says Jane, climbing back and showing her thighs pinker than a pear, and well-stretched silk panties.

"Children like you, they should be put away! Filthy, shameless thing! And the priest, he can see from his balcony! What's he waiting for, he should do something about the two of you. It's a scandal!"

Jane is dancing on her balcony, singing:

"Plush is scared of a bad old owl, smells like pee, smells like pee!"

Then she leans with her elbows on the railing and, while his aunt pushes him into the apartment with a rain of weak blows Jane is still making fun:

"I'd like you to meet Plush, the man of my life. Don't mess him up, he's too handsome. I'll be down and we'll take a world tour, my handsome Plush!"

Once in the living-room he makes for the front door, which he has time to open.

"What's all this racket about?" shouts Aunt Rose from the kitchen.

On the landing, he takes his time so as to cover Jane's descent, but Maria, her mouth too wide open, as if she couldn't breathe, stays in the doorway unable to utter a sound.

Jane comes out at last, still with the giggles.

"We've passed Chicago and Toronto. Whoo-whoo, the old owl! Plush, do they scalp owls too?"

"Come on, you've said enough silly things."

"Not silly. This is the game of the old owl and the little slut. You don't even know how to play."

His aunt has finally caught her breath enough to shout before she slams the door:

"Your uncle's coming, and he'll call the police. You won't laugh for long, you little gutter-snipe!"

They go down four at a time and they're in the street, together at last, free, with so many hours of sunlight ahead of them.

Far off, he sees the heavy silhouette of his uncle, umbrella under his arm and dark grey hat on his head, looking as always as if he were coming from a funeral. They cross Maisonneuve and head quite naturally for Mama Pouf's place. The Coca-Cola signs, the KIK and Black Horse signs have a holiday air under the steep, narrow outside stairways filled to the top with women and children, in a light, warm breeze you can almost touch, pocketed with smells of meals cooking away by themselves in the houses.

Her hair, held back by bobby pins above her ears, streams down onto her white dress, so light, of copper and sunlight, that he has to hold back from touching it to see if it's real.

"Do you know what mama said to me?"

"That she's going to have you put away."

"How did you know?"

"Because it's all you deserve, and people say that to all children."

"In a convent, she said. Where I'd only meet children of my own milieu. What's a milieu?"

"A place where there's no room for me, for she said I was no good for you."

"I'd learn music and a whole lot of things to make me a lady. I told her ladies were fat and I didn't want to be. And she laughed, with the man that was there, the one I don't like."

He'd like to talk to her about those men that come to guard them, and take the same liberties with her mother as if they were fathers, but he's afraid of putting his big foot in something too delicate for him.

"Your mother's beautiful, and better dressed than anybody. Parachutes are very special."

"You say funny things. Why are parachutes special?"

"Because of your mother. You can see she doesn't make shirt collars like Aunt Eugénie. She's dressed as if she made. . .well, movies!"

"You've never been to the movies."

"That doesn't matter. It's just the same."

"She doesn't make parachutes. She's a secretary, but I don't know what she does. And I think she doesn't go very often to the same place. Like the men, it's never the same number."

"Why's there a number?"

"I mean the phone number she writes down, to call if something happens."

"Maybe she's a spy. Spies change their number all the time to hide."

"Dummy, our number doesn't change. But she said we're going to move, too. Going back to where we were before. She's had enough of this part of town."

"She doesn't like us much. I can understand the aunts. But what about Mama Pouf?"

"That's vulgar, she says. You know. . .maybe I shouldn't say it. But why shouldn't I, to you? Sometimes I think I don't love my mother."

"That's just because the squirrel gets out of the wrong side of the bed sometimes."

"See, you don't take me seriously! No, it's as if I was a bother to her all the time, or it would be a lot easier if I wasn't there."

"I think it's just because grown-ups never have time. A child's going to live whether you fuss over it or not. And all the rest, if you don't watch it all the time it might disappear."

"What do you mean, the rest?"

"You know, everything besides the children."

"That's not true, look at Uncle Henri...."

"He's not the same. He's got a trade, and besides he'll never learn music."

"Oh, oh, you don't know a thing about it, my Uncle Henri can

135

play the piano, even if he says he never took lessons."

As they cross the street where the second church is, a car horn makes them jump and an old truck, very high on its wheels, like a kind of great cart disguised as a truck, stops in front of them on the wrong side of the street, and they see the Rat's raven-like face leaning out with a grin that splits right back to his ears, proud as if he were conductor of a streetcar.

"How about looking before you cross the street! D'you think I can stop a jalopy like this on a dime? It pulls like a Molson horse. Good thing I'm a muscle man."

And he stretches his long arm, thin as a broomstick, out the window, flexing it manfully.

"Got the big love, eh, you two? Don't say hello to your friends any more?"

"What are you doing up there, anyway? Is that the hospital ambulance? Are you going out to the country?"

The Rat opens the door by undoing the cord that holds it, then jumps to the street, pulling up his pants by the belt like a carter who's just unloaded his barrel.

"It's mine, little funny-man. I traded my bike for it, and they even gave me some cash into the bargain. You know, squirrel, from the driver's seat up there you shine like a spotlight from two miles away. A driver's got to stop, he can't see a thing. Got a kiss for the nice man?"

He leans down toward Jane who slaps his face as she turns away. Barely shaken, he straightens up, smiling.

"This isn't love, it's passion. Christ! Luckly little bastard, Pierrot. She's fallen for a few but never like that."

"I never fell for anybody," says Jane, furious.

"I know, neither did your ma. Well, it's lucky you've met a happy guy. We're going to Bonsecours market, come on. You can ride in the back. There's no rope to hang on with."

Two other young men emerge from the truck. One is tall and thin, with a narrow head and a face that slants back parallel to his nose, wearing army pants under a sloppy blue denim smock.

"This is Skiff," says the Rat. "He's so handy with the oars he never got his feet wet."

The second is a stocky yellow-haired boy licking an ice cream cone which is dripping down on the long raincoat that goes almost to his feet.

"This, as you can see, is Banana. We're in the trucking business, and I even repair frigidaires, like your dad."

"My father never fixed frigidaires."

"Big ones, my boy. Big ones, big as a factory. Are you satisfied?"

"It's not true. He's a...he's a pilot!"

"Always learning. OK, he was the Pope. Come on, get in or the cops'll be here."

He's blocking the street, and drivers are shouting and blowing their horns on all sides. The Rat doesn't get flustered, takes his time to help them up on the back, telling them to lean against the cab, then off he drives in a black cloud that smells of rotten oil, and screens the houses along the street, one after the other. When he changes gears it's as if the cab were going off alone leaving the truck behind. He twists around from time to time to see that they're still there, and makes faces like a happy child. In the back there are old tires, bits of chain, planks, and even chicken crates.

When he turns onto a street with streetcar tracks he makes a point of swerving back and forth on the rails to make them fall this way and that. Jane hangs on tight, digging her nails into his skin, shouting and laughing, but he hears nothing over the racket of the engine and the noise of the street. Then the Rat gets caught between a tram and the sidewalk and can't get up speed enough to pass before it stops and opens its doors. Beside the Rat, Skiff's head doesn't move, but Banana keeps looking back, his round face wreathed always in the same beatific smile.

At the stops he can finally hear what Jane is saying.

"It's like your railway car! We're going around the world, but this one doesn't need a graveyard. It's going to fall to pieces right here."

"Do you know those guys?"

"Never saw them. The Rat's always picking up somebody you don't know. He meets them at night."

"Did you always know him?"

"The Rat? You can't help seeing him, he's all over the place."

"What if we never went home?"

"Where could we go? I didn't bring anything to eat."

The racket interrupts again. Her reply disappoints him as much as the time she accepted the french fries from the Rat. He can't see why food is so important to her. He's never hungry, himself. She can't really play "running away" for she's too used to a house and her own things. Where would they get dresses? He can always find some old pants, too long or too small, but she – how could he imagine her in anything but these dresses made for her alone? And what if she got ugly or lost her teeth from not eating? He'd still love her, for she'd always be the same in his mind, and he'd do anything to find her food, but he'd feel guilty. He pulls her very close to him for fear she might get the slightest spot on her dress, and wishes the dirty old truck would stop somewhere soon.

At the next stop she confides:

"You're right, we could run away. The ships are just beside the market, but they leave at night. I'll show you. Then we'll walk home."

"Where do they go, these ships of yours?"

"I don't know. Far away."

The truck finally leaves the street with the tram tracks and starts around a square cluttered with horses and rigs and trucks as well, with tables made of planks covered with vegetables, dead chickens with no feathers, flowers, and bottles filled with different coloured liquids. The Rat has to halt frequently for people are wandering around as if it were a park. They even stop to talk in the middle of the street, but he makes his way through at last and parks beside an immense building in blackened stone, where there are as many stalls as stones and it smells of meat and wet hay.

"Have you ever been here?"

"Often. Mama Pouf buys her meat and vegetables here. The people come in from the country and it's supposed to be cheaper and taste better."

"So, you see, you'd have lots to eat."

She looks at him for a second, squinting a little, hurt.

"I can go without eating, don't worry, even for no reason. If you really want to we won't go back. You're supposed to get used to no food as long as you have water. But where would we sleep?"

"I'd like to see you go without eating! It's only in books that people don't eat, and mostly girls, when they're dying of love."

"Where would we take a bath? Boys don't think of anything because women look after them."

"There's water everywhere, and when there isn't, it rains. And in summer you can sleep anywhere."

"Do you think I'd be scared! The only thing is, I'm not quite sure yet that I don't love Mama."

"Same here, about my aunts. All of a sudden they could be good and nice for one week every month. Or sending us away turns out to be only a joke. Or a week from now you don't like me any more. We have to think of everything. Do we get down?"

"Plush, I told you it wasn't true what I said, about saying that to all the boys to see the stupid look on their face."

"That's why I never said it to you. Every time you tell a girl that she'll ask you for something to eat."

He gets down from the truck and holds up his hands to her, but without a look at those kind hands she jumps down alone.

As the Rat comes along she's just sticking her tongue out at Pierrot.

"Already! I knew if I stuck you in there together you'd come out enemies for life. A real love truck, this is."

"Why don't you ride in the back with Isabelle? Skiff could drive."

The Rat slaps his thighs and puffs with laughter that squeaks endlessly in his throat.

"Well, I'll tell you, I don't need the truck or Skiff around to shake her up. And she'd never make faces at me like this stuck-up little redhead."

Banana turns up, licking at another cone. His little round eyes cross as the white ball rises toward his mouth, and at the same time he lifts his old raincoat, long as a priest's frock, with one hand, as if to let the drippings reach a destination on his skin instead of inside it. Skiff has disappeared from the landscape.

"What a guy! A stinking temper, just like Marcel! And he minds grown-ups' business for them as if he could piss a whole foot and a half."

"Gaston, I'm telling you, don't talk that way in front of her."

The Rat brushes his long hand, white as death, across the boy's hair, and Pierrot forces himself not to flinch, so as not to hurt the Rat's feelings, but the slightest touch of that hand makes him bridle.

"You hear that, Banana? Don't do this, don't do that! See how these little snot-noses talk to us nowadays. No respect. As if his little carrot-headed *anglaise* hadn't heard a thing or two since she's done us the honour to live around here! Hey, Banana, tell him I'm the boss."

The tubby great blond obeys with his melting ice-cream smile:
"You're the boss, Rat."

Proudly, Gaston hoists up his oversize pants and looks up at the sky as if he had nothing more in common with the race of men.

"See, Pierrot? That's what authority is! I told you there was going to be one hell of a show, right to the end, and you'll see! When the rats crawl out of their holes nothing can stand up to them. I'm telling you, this is the season of the rat. Now then, come on, I've got a customer to see on the square. Skiff'll be along after. Coming, princess?"

"No. We're going to see the ships. You swear too much, and I don't like your fat blond."

Jane had put on her primmest air and her nastiest tone of voice, but nothing could discourage the Rat's good humour.

"Banana, a fat blond! Aren't you ashamed of picking on a guy that can't defend himself in the world?"

Banana smiles even more angelically, says not a word.

"Don't cry, Banana. Her turn will come, she'll get her comeuppance. By the way, you haven't seen Isabelle's famous soldier friend?"

She takes Pierrot's hand and pulls him toward the little church, sticking out her tongue at the Rat, but he catches up with them in one leap.

"OK, I'll be good. Come on, I want to show you something nice. A guitar."

She hesitates, and finally decides:

"I've seen them already, what do you think!"

"But you never heard me play."

Why does he want them around? He has his two friends and a truck. That's enough to keep him in fun all day. But suddenly Jane changes her mind and starts to follow him. The Rat is almost running, and the fat blond capers in his long raincoat.

"I know what. We can sleep in Mama Pouf's garden tonight. That way we can try it out."

She leaves him to admire a rabbit in a cage.

"Oh sure! That's the first place they'll look for us!"

"Look, he smells nice and his ears are pink inside. If they don't love us they won't go looking. And we can see how it is, sleeping outside."

"Mama Pouf won't like it. She's too kind to leave us outside."

"She's always busy feeding Meeow. She doesn't even know what's going on at her place."

"And your Uncle Henri?"

"He'll do anything I say."

"Even let you get cold?"

"Why don't you say it. You don't want me to love you. You make everything so complicated."

The Rat is standing in the back of a big glaring-red truck, almost new, behind the mountains of vegetables and flowers, talking to a man in overalls who's smoking a pipe and nodding from time to time. Banana's eating a carrot that has sand still clinging to it, and all its leaves on. The conversation goes on for a long time, and it seems the Rat has forgotten them, but he turns around quickly and points to them, and the man with the pipe looks at them, nodding. He waves to them to come over and helps them up into the truck.

"This is Siffleux," he says. "He's got more land than from here to the bridge, with a mountain on it, and a woods full of wolves."

"What's a *siffleux?*" asks Jane, who won't be intimidated by anyone.

The man looks at her, drawing on his pipe, his eyes expressionless.

The Rat is enjoying himself.

"It's like a big squirrel with more brains than you, and he digs tunnels underground. You see him here and *pssst!* – there he is behind you, quicker than the eye."

"You must mean a rat," says Jane with an innocent smile.

She gets a cloud of smoke in her face, and Gaston laughs his head off.

"That's what a *siffleux* is, Reddy!"

Then he takes them to the front of the rack and just when he's going to lift a big tarpaulin the man puts his foot on the Rat's long girlish hand, but without pressing.

"Get away from there. I'll get them for you."

The Rat is up in a flash, a nasty gleam in his eye for a second, but he manages a vague smile.

The man stoops down and, without raising the tarpaulin, pulls out a cardboard box which he pushes toward Jane. In the short time he is bent down, the Rat, above and behind him, flicks back a corner of the canvas and sees something all white and shining, like a refrigerator. When the man straightens up, the box in his hand, the Rat has already pulled back. He takes the box and holds it out to the boy:

"Pierrot, if you want to do me a big favour, bring this to Pelletier's grocery. You know the one?"

He looks at the box without taking it, for he has no desire to do him a favour. He wants to spend the rest of the day with Jane, and he doesn't like the looks of Siffleux.

141

"No. We're going down to see the ships, we told you."

"You can take it there at the end of the day. The truck'll be here till six."

The man piles some hay in front of the tarpaulin, then, going on tiptoe, takes from the top a black box which he handles with great care. Gaston exclaims with childish joy, his body taken with a kind of trembling:

"The guitar! You're a man of your word, Siffleux. Boy, that's a real treat!"

He quickly opens the box, which he's placed on the floor, and slowly caresses the varnished wood gleaming in the shadows.

"It's beautiful," says Jane, she too stroking with her small hand the wood that seems thin as leather.

The Rat plucks a string, his eyes rolling in reverence, and a low, full sound, reminiscent of Jane's voice when she speaks through a sigh, echoes inside the box of the truck. The Rat closes the case and says:

"OK, Pierrot? Monsier Pelletier's waiting for his parcel, and I have to run around all day in my old heap."

The boy consults Jane with a look, and she announces, her voice trembling a little:

"We can't promise. We might never be back."

"What, eloping at your age! Where do you think you're going? The police would have you by tonight."

Jane looks at him contemptuously:

"We won't say any more, but there are lots of ways of not being around some day. We'll see."

"Right, you go stow away on a boat, little mouse. Now, is it yes or no? What do you say, Pierrot? You can run away some other day. But not with a *bourgeoise*, I hope!"

"She said it. We'll see. If we're not back before six. . .What's in that box, anyway?"

"Cigarettes."

"Why does Monsieur Pelletier buy them here?"

"Well, this is the market. They're fresher here. Damn, I wish I didn't need Banana!"

"What?" says the blond smile.

"Shut up," says the Rat. "Where's Skiff?"

"Dunno."

"Well, we're leaving. I'm sure he's going to come for the box, aren't you Pierrot? And thanks for the guitar. Add it on."

Jane is down already and has snitched a strawberry that puts more gold in her hair and more red in her lips. Pierrot turns back before leaving. The Rat, his hands folded as if to protect something from the light, is passing a roll of bills to Siffleux, and it's so thick he has to take it in his two hands.

"We'll be back shortly for the deliveries. Don't forget the tires tomorrow. And a Buick '34 generator, could you find me one?"

"Mebbe," says the man with the pipe, with a tiny movement of his hand, his eyes cold as stones, looking far away, farther than the bridge.

"Let's go see what happened to Skiff."

They go back toward the old truck. The Rat, with the guitar case over his shoulder, seems about Big Justin's age, his happiness is so obvious in his whole body and especially in the fresh smile on his face. He gives Banana a great slap on the back, and Banana smiles a little more broadly, his raincoat carefully closed over the ice cream now drying on beneath it.

At the truck Gaston crouches suddenly, gathers them in his long arms, close to his chest with its sound of rustling paper, and under their eyes thrusts thumb and finger with a tiny space between.

"All that's left in my glass, kiddies, not a drop more! But Jesus it's good! Gas in the lungs, what an idea! The best springtime I've ever had. Almost makes you believe there's justice, *torrieu!*"

Jane frees herself adroitly, slipping under his arms.

"Let's go, Pierrot, he scares me. He's gone crazy."

She gives him her hand, all damp in his, and they retreat slowly toward the little church. They see Skiff coming back, his face sombre, his blue smock floating over his army pants.

"Look at him, he looks as if he'd just killed somebody," said Jane with more contempt than fear. "What are we doing, hanging around these big monkeys?"

"It's no go," Skiff announces. "You'll have to talk to him yourself. He wants some dough first."

"OK, I'll go. Hey, look at this little toy. The guitar! He brought it."

Skiff doesn't look, but shrugs impatiently.

"Listen, he's leaving in half an hour. You've got to go there."

"My sweeties, you're going to miss something. The greatest living guitarist..."

His voice lingers over the second last word, and he repeats it:

"Living, yeah!"

143

Then he turns barker, so that passers-by can hear:

"Ladies and gentlemen! you are ay-bout to hear something...!"

He jumps into the truck, sits down with a solid back rest, takes the guitar from its case with the elaborate care of an undertaker about his business, holds it under his nose and breathes in greedily.

Jane comes back toward the truck.

"He's got fingers that can make the devil dance. Let's wait."

"Oh, that smells of old countries! That's wood that comes from far away. Have a smell," he says to Jane, holding the guitar out toward her.

She sniffs from a distance, as if she were afraid of getting a noseful of mustard.

"It's almost the colour of your hair, little squirrel."

"It smells like cigars," says Jane.

The Rat plucks the strings in turn, twisting the small pegs at the end of the neck, then starts playing with so light a hand you can hardly hear him, and no passers-by approach. Then he looks up, his gaze lost in the blue sky, seeing no one, and little by little a vibration that comes more from the bones of his fingers than from the strings, a sweet, soft melody, takes form by bits and snatches, with long pauses, then he starts at the beginning and goes through without stopping, almost breaking at times as if to pause for breath, but catching up just in time, climbing, climbing, then dropping until you start to worry if he'll find his way up again, but he finds the very second where it would have turned to silence.

It's not the same music as Uncle Nap's. It comes from farther away and yet it's closer when you hear it, and it hurts a little, just enough not to make you really sad, and it's really this trembling on the edge of tears, this sensation of falling over and over again, without really falling, that makes you breathe along with the Rat, waiting for him, rising with him. When his uncle played, he knew the worst that could happen was that he'd close the music book. The Rat, reading nothing but the empty sky, puts his whole being into the vibration of the notes, and you stop asking if he's a grown-up or why his voice is high as a girl's, you're just afraid something might happen to him, that his fingers could be stilled.

People are standing around now, laughing and talking as they arrive, silent a second after. Even Skiff's flattened head seems transfigured, and Banana's smile has grown a little sad.

When he finally stops the conversations spring up again, but the people stay.

144

"Who taught you to play?" asks Jane, with unconcealed admiration.

Gaston points to his big ear.

"Nobody. Listening to records, for years. Anyway, music is a gift," he states gravely.

He starts again, a happy song this time, and he breaks its rhythm capriciously, so that you start out wanting to dance but you're afraid one foot might stay in the air, and he's playing louder now, sure of the solidity of wood and strings, beating time with his yellow boots a shade ahead of the guitar, for he knows when he's going to change direction, and he looks at his audience, laughing.

Everyone claps and asks him to go on.

"I'll teach you how, little squirrel, though I've never seen a redhead that could play. Now then, I'm going to sing for you this time because it's in English and I don't know what the words mean, but I know what the song means. It's the music that counts."

He clears his throat two or three times, pulls out a big, snow-white handkerchief, and blows his nose for a long time, but noiselessly.

"You'll have to excuse it," he says with false modesty. "It seems the great Caruso is dead. You are left with the Rat."

At first he plays without singing, a kind of distant gallop that soon comes closer, so loud now you'd swear he was beating the instrument with his open hand and was about to crash through it, then he slows down and begins to sing, with a voice that Pierrot has never heard from him, low, borne on such broken breathing that you feel his voice on the skin of your whole body, and the guitar beats a slower rhythm, but violent, and you can't understand a word, and he seems to know what he's saying, for his eyes are drowned in sombre green waters that draw him toward their depths, and he appears lost for ever, and he sings as if he were grinding pebbles, as if he were chewing at the world with his guitar, spitting it out in lumps, and then he's back with his distant gallop, then furiously close, then he sings again, angrily to the drum of his guitar, and the people actually start drumming with him, humming, and everyone feels his own vertigo at the verge of something no one understands, then he stops cold, as if he finally had crashed through the guitar.

For a long moment he stares at his public, then he leaps down from the truck, grabs a straw hat from a farmer, and passes it around, shouting:

"For the artist, ladies and gentlemen, for the artist who has so many children to feed!"

But most of them leave without looking at him, and only a few throw silver coins into the hat. He laughs the whole time and when it's over he takes the money from the hat and offers it to the boy.

"I know you don't like money. The other day the old lady with the flowerpots picked it all up crossing herself. But today it's the artist's fee. People have hearts of stone. Now, take this and buy something for Rusty, here, she hasn't eaten yet."

He blows into the guitar and places it back in its case, then takes Jane by her waist and sets her on the truck beside him. She kicks furiously to get down, but he holds her fast.

Pierrot holds the money between his cupped hands, rattles the coins and says to the Rat:

"Leave her alone. I'm going to turn around now. You give me a kick on the hands the way you did on the church steps that day."

"You monkey! We'll go and do that in front of the little church here if you like. But first I want to know what I was telling those people just now. What did the words mean, squirrel?"

"You don't say them right. But anyway you had to understand to sing it that way. It's crazy stuff, and it doesn't even make sense in English, you know very well."

"I understand *horse* and *black* and words like that, but not the rest. An *anglais* taught me the words when I was locked up, but he couldn't speak French. Just tell me what the words mean, I'll know what it's about even if you don't."

"All I know is, it's sad and somebody's going to die."

"I knew it," murmurs the Rat, with a kind of sinister enjoyment. "Now, I'll say the words and you explain them."

"We're going to see the ships. It's getting late."

"*I am running away from the night
On a black horse filled with death.*"

"You're scared of night, and you're getting away on a horse full of death. I told you it doesn't make sense."

"Doesn't make sense! What more do you want! A horse full of death. Oh, boy!"

He goes on:

"*I am my shadow at noon
And yet, the sun stains the grass with blood...*"

146

"You are your shadow at noon and...the sun makes blood marks on the grass. Your friend, there, he sang whatever came into his head."

"My shadow at noon! But the sun's setting already. So that's what it means. You can't understand it, I know...

Hoofs, hoofs stampeding toward the night..."

"The horse's feet running to the night."

"That's the chorus. Your words can't be right, for the music gallops there, and a stampede is more than running. That doesn't matter, I understand that part.

Death has nested in the belly of my horse
And a bullet is nested in my chest."

"Death made a nest in the horse's stomach...Rat, that's not very nice...."

The muscles of his arms, his neck, his face, are tensed and his eyes are as big as the whole of Jane.

"It's great, it's a killer! Go on!"

"And a bullet made a nest in my chest. Those are funny birds, Rat. You need the guitar with that stuff. The words all alone are nothing."

"Christ, English is a beautiful language! The right language for the last rites. Then there's the stampede part again and

I am riding a black wind
The prairie is galloping under black hoofs"

"You're driving a black wind and the plains are galloping under the horse's black feet."

"*I am riding out of the night*
But the night is in front
And the prairie grass at high noon
Is stained with blood from the sun."

"You're getting out of night but it's in front...and then it's the same: the prairie grass at noon has spots of blood from the sun. Hurry up, Rat, I want to see the ships."

"Night before and behind. I know it's better in English. Well, let's forget the chorus.

I am riding out of the night
But the night is swallowing, swallowing

147

And I will never know
What will be the running after noon."

Pierrot is angry at Jane for diminishing the sense by her interpretation and for rattling off her translation so as to get rid of the Rat, for he too has a strange feeling in his stomach from the words of the song, and he'd like to hear them again to the guitar, and he understands why Gaston is listening so avidly, so breathlessly. So he says:
"Be nice, Jane. I like the words too."
"What about us, aren't we going?"
"Right after, I promise."
"All right, then. You go out of the night again – and this isn't my fault now, you're the one who said it – but the night swallows and swallows and you don't know what the race is going to be in the afternoon."
"Why do you always say 'you'? In the song it's always 'I'."
"Because I'm talking to you. I'm not going to say I."
"Here are the last words:

"The prairie grass stampedes under black hoofs
And I am still and quiet
Riding a dead horse
Into the belly of the night."

Gaston pulls her still closer to his white face, his mouth and eyes wide open the better to absorb the last secret of the mystery, the last words that led to the final slap of the hand on the golden wood of the guitar and the sudden end of the song, like a cut. Jane too is tensed, but in her case it's readiness to jump from the truck and run away, but this time she says the words more slowly though she still won't give them any meaning:
"The grass of the prairie runs under the horse's black feet...And I don't move, I'm quiet, driving a dead horse into the night's stomach."
"My horse is dead," the Rat says simply, his eyes filled with green water, holding his right side, trying with his hand to stop a sudden aperture. A little green water grows dirty as it runs down like a tear in the bright sunlight.
"*Baptême!* That's going to be one hell of a springtime!"
Skiff and Banana are twiddling their thumbs, leaning on the truck, completely indifferent to the Rat and his mysteries.

148

"Come on, you guys, or we won't get anything done today."

Jane is already in Pierrot's arms, trembling a little, a little shaken by the words of the song, but glad to be freed of the Rat's famished gaze.

"I'm hungry, Plush," she says in a small voice.

"Thanks, beautiful. I don't think I'll play guitar any more. I'm past the age."

"You play well. The best I ever heard."

Jane says it from the bottom of her heart, with a half-smile that says she wants to eat.

"You're not a bad kid for an *anglaise.* I wanted to tell you, Pierrot, your uncle's store, where he works, it's just in front of the little church. Just in case you want to say hello to him before you jump the wall with her. But I'm not worried, she'll want to go for a pee and you'll have to come back. Well, good day my children! Us slaves have to work!"

He climbs into the cab, leans out to attach the cord that keeps the door shut, and takes off doing all he can to lay smoke over the entire neighbourhood. Banana and Skiff are beside him, as if they'd never left the cab.

12

"The Rat's crazy. He's going to get in trouble."

They're sitting on the sidewalk, at the end of the long market building, and she is eating french fries, pulling them one at a time with a toothpick from the paper cone, but she has so much vinegar on them that he smells Aunt Maria instead of his ice cream and he'd like to throw it away, but he's afraid she'd not eat any more and he's now convinced that a girl, unlike a boy, has to eat often, like a bird. The street is so narrow, between the high, sooty houses, that every truck that passes, and even every horse, raises a cloud of dust above them. Her white dress is already the colour of the street. And he's never seen so many flies, fat ones with green bellies, and all in a buzzing rage.

"Why do you say that? He's not crazy. It's just his lungs. I like him all right, except when he touches you."

She throws her cone and the few chips left in it in front of a horse tied to a post. The horse is looking at them with great, sad eyes. They can see the flies crawling on his ribs. At first he had kicked up at his own belly but now he's given up, resigned to his torture.

"Why doesn't he like potatoes?"

The animal had lowered his head to the paper, given it a push and gone back to the pose of a sad horse with no expectations.

"Because they've taken the green off the potatoes, see? And maybe the vinegar makes him think of bad things."

"I don't like you, Plush. Especially when you try to be funny."

At one gulp she empties half of her Coke bottle, and raises a delicate hand to her little mouth to smother the after-effects.

"I'll get you an ice cream."

"I'm not hungry. I threw some away, didn't you see?"

He goes anyway to fetch her an ice cream and when he comes back he's astonished once more by his joy at finding someone waiting for him on a sidewalk corner in the city, and a girl at that, who belongs to him – so sure is he that he will always be her protector.

She licks away conscientiously without speaking, for she has to be quick to keep it from running. Then she picks up her theme:

"The Rat is sort of electric, like a wire. I'm always afraid he'll go 'Crack!' in my face or fire will come out of his fingers."

"Did you see how he told us he only had this much left in his glass!"

"Crazy, isn't he? I don't like him, no. But he's interesting," she concludes in a high-heeled voice.

"I'd never have thought he'd play the guitar so well."

"I would. I told you before. It's his fingers. There's nobody like him, really. That's why you always wonder what he's going to do next."

"He might have been somebody big, if things had been different. I mean a great musician or I don't know what. It's not fair. I guess...fairness is for people that are born lucky."

She's finished her ice cream already, and slowly drinks what's left of her Coke, her little white temples wrinkled with thought.

"Fairness. That's a funny word...."

She rolls it in her mouth with a slug of Coke.

"Luck is easier, and it's real. Look, see that old guy with the crutches and holding out his hat? Why doesn't he have a car, if he can't walk?"

"Because he couldn't drive either, stupid!"

She gets up, shakes out her dress, which stays street colour, smooths out her hair with her hands and takes a step back, posing like a great lady:

"There! Am I beautiful?"

Pierrot hadn't time to stop her. She had bumped into the cripple who, seeing her in time, braced himself with his crutches against the shock. He rages at them just the same, and the boy tosses in his hat the change he has left and takes Jane's arm to go.

"No, you're not beautiful, and you can't even keep from walking on a cripple, you show-off."

"You got rid of your big boots and now you think you're great. And you wanted to run away with me, forever!"

In front of the little church she stops to read the yellow and red sign on the store that takes up the whole corner.

"ABDOULA & SIROIS, IMPORTERS, SPICES AND FRUITS," she deciphers slowly. "Is that your uncle's store? Is he an Arab?"

He laughs, reading the sign aloud in his turn.

"I'd never have thought it. I knew a camel called Abdoula, I mean a camel that was Balibou. My uncle's the secretary-I-don't-know-what. It's not his store."

"Do you want to go and say hello? I told you, when he's alone with me he's OK."

"I didn't go home for lunch. And Aunt Maria probably told him all kinds of stuff. And we had a fight yesterday because he wouldn't answer my questions. That was the real reason I decided to run away with an ugly girl."

"Are you scared of him?"

She pulls him across the street and goes from one dirty shop window to the next admiring the oddly-shaped big glass jars filled with seeds and powders of all colours.

"I want to go inside. Think of all the smells there must be in there! He can't scold you in front of me."

"Do you think I'm scared? Come on."

In the store they see first a long, dark room that smells of nothing but age and dust, and at the back, behind a counter as tall as themselves, lamps hanging from the ceiling down to just above the desks where men are working, bent over their papers. Jane goes toward the glass jars, but they are too far inside the show-windows for her to touch them. She sniffs loudly, pursing her mouth.

"It smells of nothing but pepper and mustard. You don't have to be an Arab to sell that. Where's your uncle?"

"I don't know. With the others, back there, I guess."

He is stunned by this dark establishment that seems to have sat in its own dust for a hundred years. The image he has of his uncle shrinks once more. What's an educated man doing in a place like this? And why would the owner of a barn like this have a son who's a colonel in the war? His uncle has been lying, and his aunts have never seen the place.

Jane goes bravely up to the counter, with the expression of someone who thinks nothing of buying pepper and mustard. He follows her slowly, searching in vain for something, perhaps the picture of a camel, to add a tiny exotic touch to this merchant's house where everything seems buried in an endless sleep. When

153

he reaches the counter nothing has happened, nothing is happening, no one moves.

"Where is he? Why don't you call him?"

Pierrot stands on tiptoe and with stupefaction discovers his uncle in the latter's true form, in which he must always have hidden away in this place – not proud, and with good reason!

"A flea in the bee on the sea!"

That's what he'd like to shout one last time, for he's finding out it was never a magic spell but a piece of foolishness invented by a poor little snot-nosed bastard with nothing but words to play with, for his uncle is no more than a fat man in his shirtsleeves, wearing a green eyeshade, a very ordinary man among all the others, and everything else has crumbled along with his imaginary prestige, and Pierrot must swallow once and for all this last disappointment of which he has had an inkling ever since he was let out, like lightning glimpses of a serpent in the tall grass, and now it's out on the naked rocks with nowhere to hide.

There are five or six uncles behind the counter, all the same in their wide sleeves, their big account books, their pens and inkwells, all leaning over under the low-hung lamps, forgotten for decades in their classroom, bleaching away without ever hearing the recess bell. Speaking to him would be like taking down an old picture that hasn't been touched for so long that everything around it would appear too grey, too darkened, darker and dustier than the store itself.

"It's no use, they don't even see a person," he says in a voice that he has trouble controlling.

"What's wrong with you? You're so scared your voice is shaking," says Jane, who can have no idea of what's going through his head. Finally it is she who calls out, in a playful tone that tosses a burnoose over his uncle's shoulders:

"Monsieur Abdoula, please!"

And her voice comes like an improbable sunbeam that could send them all hiding under their desks for fear they'd see the cobwebs woven from wall to wall and from floor to ceiling in this classroom from which they forgot to escape.

They all look up at the same time, shoving the eyeshades up a little into their white hair, their pens poised, their eyes frightened. His uncle sees him, though he's partly blinded by the low lamp with the shade the same colour as his eyeshade, and very slowly he gets to his feet, making a faint sign to the others who go back to scratching at their papers. He comes toward them, his jowls trembling slightly, astonished to be called to stand up in front of the class.

"Hello! We were going by and thought we'd say hello."

"Which one is Monsieur Abdoula?" asks Jane with her most serious air. "I'd like to smell the spices and see the Arab boss."

Uncle Nap doesn't laugh, but he's not angry either. He's twisting a pencil between his short, fat fingers, his eyes fixed on the counter.

"Monsieur Abdoula's been dead a long time. There's only Monsieur Sirois left now. Well, my little man, you should have told me you were coming. I'm busy now, I can't..."

"What about the spices?" asks Jane.

"The salesman hasn't come by yet," he replies, consulting his watch.

There's a pause. You can almost hear the pens scratching on the page of the big books. Uncle Nap clears his throat a little and speaks in a friendly voice to Jane, as if he were meeting her on the apartment stairs:

"And how's school going, eh?"

Jane comes down from the clouds.

"School? What school? I'm on holidays now."

She hoists herself stiff-armed on the counter to see behind it, looking for the non-existent camels and Arabs and long knives.

"I asked because school is the most important thing," Uncle Nap says to his pencil.

Then he reaches under the counter for a wallet from which he extracts a dollar and holds it out to Pierrot.

"You didn't have any lunch. The little girl likely didn't either. Go and have a bite."

"Oh, thank you, Monsieur Abdoula!" cries Jane, skipping toward the street door.

His uncle maintains his Saharan calm to warn him in the same friendly tone:

"You mustn't do those acrobatics on the balcony. Accidents happen. And tell people when you're not coming for lunch."

To avoid hurting this uncle who has so come down in the world, who has grown humble and kind, perhaps because he's embarrassed at being discovered in this shop, the back room of the dreams of an educated man, Pierrot takes the dollar and tries in vain to find the right tone to let Uncle Nap know he understands,

155

and that it really doesn't make any difference, but he comes out with a wretched:

"Good-day, Uncle Napoléon, and thank you."

And he hurries off to catch up with Jane who, immobile near the display window, is still trying to smell the perfumes of Arabia imprisoned in the great glass jars that are so well corked.

"I thought I got a sniff of cinnamon. Your uncle's like a nice big dog that doesn't know what to do with his feet. How can you get into a fight with him?"

"People are never the same. I don't understand it. It's as if they changed faces and clothes depending where they are. Hey, you can eat lunch all over again."

"I'd love a cinnamon candy right now. But we're going to look at the ships."

In Saint Paul Street the sidewalks have disappeared, there's nothing but a throng of people melting together in the sunlight. Trucks, horses, sailors everywhere, men in overalls carrying big hooks over their shoulders, and all the flies, the only creatures that can move freely. Jane dives into the crowd, her head down, using her elbows among all those legs. He follows behind, so worried about losing sight of her red mane as she ducks and reappears like a squirrel in this human forest that he keeps bumping into wagon wheels or legs that are just as hard, and even a horse's chest which, he observes with astonishment, is covered with some strong-smelling oil. He catches up at the corner of a little street that goes down toward the river and seems to be barred at the end by a high chain-link fence.

"D'you know, I thought how we could get out of the clearing and not lose a hair."

"You did? I'd like to know!"

"Balibou changes us into Indians."

"Girls always find the easiest way."

"How many girls do you know, my sir just in from the crows' castle!"

"I know Thérèse."

"She's not a girl any more. She works."

"Well, I'm sorry, but Balibou can only change himself, not other people. And when he changes he has to have time to say 'Balibouzoofluegluepew!' Just try it, you'll see how long it takes."

"Balibouzoo...gluepew..."

"See? If he had to wait for you he'd have an arrow in him while he was still a cat, and it's only when he's a cat they can hurt him. That's why he changes. I'll help you. It means: All of Balibou in the zoo like a flue full of glue in the pew. After his name you just keep the ew's."

"You made that up just now!"

"If I had I couldn't say it so fast."

They're running into legs and backs again, pressing against each other, even jumping up and down with shouts and men's laughter, all seeming to want to see or touch the same thing.

"My turn!"

"It's my turn!"

"They're all trying to go through the wall. People are a little crazy today. Let's have a look from the truck."

He climbs up first and what he sees roots him to the spot. He can barely murmur:

"Don't look, Jane, I don't want you to."

There's a girl, thin and dark haired, her skin as white as if she'd never seen the sun, with the front of her dress unbuttoned showing her small breasts, their tips almost black, and men's hands all over her, and they're slipping coins in her pants. She is pressed so hard against the wall that her arms are crossed and she can't move, and some of the men suck at her like babies. Jane is beside him now and he steps in front of her to stop her seeing, but she grips his shoulders and jumps behind him.

"Why can't I look? The truck was my idea."

She bites his arm, but he feels nothing, and finally he lets her look, too, shocked by what he sees, not understanding at first, then convinced by degrees that for the first time in his life he is seeing madmen. The joking, the grimaces, the brutality of their gestures stupefy him. He thinks of pictures in books, so obviously meant to scare you that they made him laugh, and they had faces, mouths and eyes like this.

"What are they doing to her? They're going to kill her!" screams Jane, covering her eyes.

Pierrot jumps down from the truck at the same moment that a young man in suit and tie runs across the street and begins kicking behinds and ripping at shirt collars so violently that he tears them open.

"You gang of pigs, let her alone!"

But he howls and rains blows in vain, he can't make an impression on this human cluster pushing ever harder against the wall. In a rage, Pierrot also hits into the heap, but it's as if he were attacking the wall itself. But he goes down on all fours and crawls among their legs. He is kicked and trampled but he persists until he can see the girl's naked feet, and coins rolling on the sidewalk, but there is a kind of ebb and the feet of the crowd are turned the other way, he hears shouts and blows and suddenly there's an empty space between himself and the girl and he stands up and starts hitting again but they pay no attention to him and through a gap in the crowd he sees the raging young man taking fisticuffs and kicks, in the face, in the stomach, on the legs, and blood running on the street, then the whole body crumpling and its head subsiding gently to the street, as if it were let down by a thread, then a great iron hook that falls beside it, and the madmen dispersing slowly with vague glances at the crushed form, then someone says:

"Christ, there was a kid."

And someone gives him a blow that hurls him against the girl crumpled against the wall, and his hand, outstretched to save himself, lands on the small, punished breast, and that disgusts him and he leaves her, and goes to the man knocked out on the pavement.

He kneels in the blood, and hears Jane's voice as he raises the man's head to help him breathe.

"Why are you getting mixed up in this, Plush? People are crazy. We have to get the police. What about her?"

He moves the man's head, and he opens his eyes only to shut them as quickly again. The skin of his face is torn, but it seems to be his chest that hurts the most, for he is holding his ribs with the flat of his hands and has trouble breathing.

"Tell her to go and hide, if she's not hurt."

But the girl comes toward them, pulling the coins out from her underpants, counting them silently, and suddenly she pushes Jane away and spits in the young man's face, kicking him at the same time. Jane, all trembling, her face redder than her hair, pushes her back with all her strength, and she falls, stretched out on the man, and Pierrot sees her breasts as she falls, as for a moment they seem to grow heavier. The head escapes from his hands and the man gets up, rolling the girl onto the street. The man is still staggering. He wipes the blood from his face with one hand and watches the girl buttoning her dress, growling like a dog or the vestry-nun, but she is so afraid of dropping her coins that she can't arrange her dress, and the man stoops down, takes her hand, and forces her to drop her pennies in the street.

Then he shakes out his jacket, smooths back his hair as if he had just finished shaving, and says:

"It'd make you sick. She's deaf and dumb! And they let her do it because it's the only way she's found to make a bit of money. Now, you kids, get the hell out of here, and fast!"

And he crosses the street to go his way, but comes back at once.

"I'm sorry, bonhomme, I know you wanted to help me. Don't ever try it again. You'll get yourself killed."

And this time he goes on his way. They see him go into a store called "JOS LAFORCE, BOIS ET CHARBON."

The girl has picked up her coins and put them back in her pants. Shaking her fist at them, she disappears in an alleyway, grumbling away like the vestry-nun.

Jane kisses him hard, her arms around his chest, and he hears a soft rapid beating that makes his own heart go faster, and her fine hair tickles his face.

"Promise me you won't do that any more, that you'll mind your business the way he said. It's not like your castle here, Pierrot, they're not all children."

He caresses her hair without really thinking about what he's doing, and Jane's heart beats more gently against his chest.

"Nobody told me there were so many crazy people in the city. We just had the Chinese boy, and he was quiet as a lamb."

"You've never told me about your Chinese boy or any of the others, except Big Justin that you gave an ugly face to."

She lets him go, and he is upset to see blood on her fine white dress, now the colour of a dust rag.

"You wanted cinnamon candies."

"I don't know where to find them here. There's a store beside Mama Pouf's."

"It's not on the way."

"Of course it's on our way. Beside Mama Pouf's place, I told you."

"It's not on the way if we run away together for life."

She comes back to him, takes his hand and confesses, her mouth in a tiny pout:

"I don't think we're big enough for all the scary things."

"You're nothing but a liar. I'll never believe anything you promise."

"Anyway, tell me what happens when we get out of the clearing."

"We don't get out of it, because we don't run away."

She makes a little laughing grimace and takes a deep breath, so that the dark gold of her eyes grows very serious. Her hand tightens on his:

"I think I love you. And that's true. More than I ever loved anybody. Even more than Mama, you know, when I'm sure I love her."

"How long is that going to be true?"

"Forever. Cross my heart and spit! If I lie, may I be changed into a frog."

"Or a flea? A flea in the bee on the sea...Take care, Balibou can hear you!"

"And I'll be stuck in the clearing with you the rest of my life, if you don't go on with the story."

They walk on without speaking toward the high chain-link fence, but just before it there's another cross street, very narrow, called de la Friponne. And in the distance they see, as if protruding from a hole, the orange smoke-stacks of a big white ship.

"If it weren't for money I don't think people would know when they stop being children."

"Why do you say that? I've always had some spending money."

"Because your mama's never there."

"That's true. She always says it's for eating."

"It's money that makes people grow up."

"How do you know that, anyway?"

"Because you have to be either strong or bad to make money. If I didn't know Mama Pouf and your Uncle Henri, strong and bad would be the same thing."

"He's not my uncle. I can't call him papa for I have one already. Everybody calls him uncle."

"It must be funny to know you're not a child any more. As if a wall fell down and you can't ever get behind it again."

"I need a cinnamon candy so bad it hurts. That's your fault."

Now there's nothing between them and the ship, between them and the river.

13

"Do you call this fair? When the sun rose they came to bow down
before you, a girl like you, a conceited fibber, peeing in your pants
and crying all night just because White Wolf was trying to keep
you warm with his brand-new fur which is a lot cleaner than your
dirty dress, and you thought the fire flies were red eyes. And because of all that I didn't get a wink, and I was too tired to outsmart
the Indians."

"It's not true, when I'm too scared I always go to sleep. I can
prove it: I always sleep when there's a thunderstorm."

"Don't you want to know why they bowed before you?"

"Because you wanted them to, Pierrot."

"Me! I wanted a fair judgement! I wanted them to pull out your
hair one by one and throw you into the crow's moat."

"Sometimes they chase us. But sometimes it's as if we belonged
on the ship and they play with us."

"Come on! If you're turning it into a ship I don't need to go on
with the story."

They're lying in the sun on the grassy embankment where the
wire fence runs along, watching the white ship with the orange
smoke-stacks. There's a big hole near the front, so big that trucks

can disappear through it, and that makes it dip deeper in the water and you can hear the sound of the hull against the concrete. The three storeys above deck, all painted white, seem empty, but there are a lot of men on the dock pushing crates on funny barrows with two iron wheels, from the great shed to the big black hole in the ship. There's a smell of tar and something sour, like rotten soap, that doesn't go with the white ship and the river.

"I had to do something in the crows' moat, so I thought of the ship."

"Now I'll tell you. They came to worship you just because of your dirty old hair. First we saw their feathers sticking up above the grass. White Wolf stood up on all fours and growled a bit. Then the feathers retreated, but when the sun rose higher they started coming again."

"Why because of my hair? And what about the feathers? Were they chickens?"

"Did you ever see chickens with blue and yellow feathers this long?"

"You didn't say they were blue."

"Can't you see, it was the Indians crawling toward us. They always do that when it's people they don't know. Then, all at once, we saw them. Hundreds of them, all on their bellies, with their hands above their head as if they were praying. And the chief said, 'Goddess with red hair and a white wolf, at last you have had mercy on us and come down to free us from the white man. May all the lands of the Saulteux be as honey beneath your feet and all the trees be covered with flowers.' And then with a terrible noise that came back from the mountains they shouted three times, 'Pow Wow! Pow Wow! Pow Wow!' – and you were so frightened you jumped into my arms crying like a baby, and White Wolf licked you to show them that you really were the red-headed Goddess."

A train is backing slowly along the rails that separate them from the ship, and a man, hanging out from the last car, waves a lantern as if it were night-time. It stops just in front of them, at the place where there's a car with the doors open on both sides, so that they can still see one smoke-stack and part of the three white decks.

She yawns deeply, sits up and tries in vain to spit.

"I feel sick. It must be the tar smell. You still didn't say why they thought I was a goddess. And I won't even ask you how you understood what they said, for you're going to get mad again."

"It's not the tar, it's because you eat too much, but just wait, you'll see, you won't be hungry any more. For the old chiefs had never seen a woman with red hair, so they invented a goddess like that, and they'd always prayed to her but never seen her. And they'd never seen a white wolf."

"And what about you?"

"Me?"

"You have blond hair, don't you?"

"Gee, you're stupid. They'd been fighting with white men for years, and they'd seen thousands with blond hair. But because I was with you, you were my protection. Isn't that unfair?"

"But why shouldn't I protect you?"

"Because I'm only Plush, with big boots, and I don't know anything, for I just got out of the crows' castle, and you only need me when you're hungry. And how could a silly girl protect anybody?"

"Well, I'm not as scared of the savages as you are."

"All right, you can stay with them. Get along by yourself. I feel like walking."

He gets up, walks to the last car of the train, looks for a long time at the tower without a castle in the middle of the island beyond the ship, and the big green bridge built wrong-side-up which goes down into the island, and in the distant blue haze, the grey shadows of two ships making headway so slowly that you have to shut your eyes for at least two minutes to see that they've moved.

When he starts back he feels a twinge at his heart to see her in the same place, all alone, so tiny, her white dress against the green of the grass and the red of the freight cars. He starts to run.

"If I'm silly why do you come back?"

There's a small tear, or perhaps it's only the sun blinding him, in the corner of her eye. But she goes on as if he had never left her:

"Papapouf. That would be a nice name for my Uncle Henri, for he's so little, Papapouf!"

Her hair, pulled back on both sides, leaves her face so thin that he can see the veins moving in both her temples.

"I think he'd laugh."

"With him you can't tell if he'd like it for he's always laughing. When the Indians finished shouting what happened?"

He lies down again in the grass, covers his eyes with his hands against the sun, and invents very quickly, for he's afraid she'll get bored. He knows she's very tired already.

"They bring a bed made of flowers and feathers, with two long

163

sticks at the side, and they put you on it and carry you to their village. They have such nice, red smiles that you're not scared any more, and I come after riding on White Wolf, with the children patting him. The chief's house is a big locomotive that they pulled to their village, but it was so long ago that trees are growing through it and there are pretty windows made of ermine skin all along the big black barrel."

"What's ermine?" asks Jane, yawning politely.

"It's like your hair, but white and soft as snow. But then the trouble starts, for their medicine man, who's like their priest and didn't know anything about all this, looks you over very carefully, but when he tries to touch your hair White Wolf bites him on the wrist, not hard, just enough to stop him. That's when he starts his Indian tricks. First he says the Goddess can only be fed with the blood of a baby freshly killed each day."

"I don't want to be the Red Goddess any more!"

"That's just what he hoped you'd say. A goddess can't wish she wasn't one. So he says, 'If she's really a goddess she will not be able to break her own image.' The Indians don't have mirrors, just water, and if they threw you on your reflection you'd have to float, but you can't, and the medicine man knows it. So they take you to the deepest place in the lake, they make you look at yourself in the water, then they throw you in."

"No! I don't want to!"

"You haven't time to say it, for you fall in the water. But Balibou had time to say the magic word with all the 'ew' sounds and he's there before you disguised as a block of ice that no one can see, and you don't go through your own image. When the medicine man turns back furious to the tribe – they're all on their bellies worshipping you again – there's White Wolf back in his place. Then he says: 'Our fathers never said that the Red Goddess had a white wolf. If he really comes from the heaven of the Great Manitou we should be able to shoot a thousand arrows in him without killing him.'"

"I don't want that!"

"That's what you said, but Balibou explains to you that they can only hurt him when he's in cat form. So one of the warriors, shutting his eyes for fear, shoots an arrow, and blood flows. The others, seeing the blood, shoot their arrows, and soon there's such a river of blood that it catches the medicine man and dumps him in the lake to drown. White Wolf laughs with all his teeth and

164

never moves a hair. And again they're on their bellies worshipping you."

"Show me how they worship me," she says, standing up and holding her head as high as she can. He sees the sunlight reddened in her hair, and he'd like nothing better than to worship her but doesn't know how, and he's afraid she'll never come down to her normal height again.

The train rolls slowly back where it came from, the same man still waving his lantern in broad daylight, and they can see the whole ship again. In front of the big black hole there is now a handsome blue car. A man in uniform with gold buttons and holding a cap in his hand is holding the car door open, but there's no one in the car, nor anywhere around.

"I'll show you later. We didn't get far. If you're tired we can sleep in the Indian village."

"Oh, no! Get us out of there and we'll go to Mama Pouf's."

"Right. Well, I whisper to you what to say and you repeat it to them: 'Never again will the white man make war on you, and as a token of my promise, I leave you three hairs from my head which you must always keep. But you must never again have a medicine man. I must go now to bring peace to your brothers in the North. You must hitch a hundred deer to our caboose, and may your women be full of honey!'"

In the hollow of his hand she places three golden threads so fine that they seem almost blond in the sunlight, and he can barely see or feel them between his fingers. He folds them carefully inside his handkerchief.

"If you do that at every stop you're going to be bald at the end of the trip."

"Where are we going now?"

"At this very moment they're taking us to the caboose and hitching up the hundred deer in teams, and they'll take us through the whole forest to the land of the Great Cold. And Balibou changes into a little green bear."

"Why? There's no such thing as a green bear."

"Doesn't matter. Now we're asleep behind the deer and they're running so fast their hoofs don't touch the ground. So you'll have to wait till tomorrow, my little Red Goddess."

"And how do you worship me, cheater?"

"I'm not an Indian, so it doesn't look so nice."

"That doesn't matter. Show me."

He goes back to the pavement of the dock, gets down on his belly and advances toward her, only elbows and knees touching the ground, his two hands joined and raised above his head, shouting in his deepest voice: "Pow Wow! Pow Wow! Pow Wow!"

Jane bursts out laughing, but her laugh turns into a kind of gurgle that sounds false, as if someone else were listening. And he discovers a tall shadow that reaches his own head from the top of the embankment. As he is not in a state of adoration bordering on ecstasy he turns to see who is casting the shadow. He hears Jane explaining in a faintly embarrassed voice:

"We're playing round the world."

Pierrot jumps to his feet, rubbing his eyes in the sunlight, unable to master a feeling at the pit of his stomach that almost hurts and makes his legs go weak.

"Going round the world like an Indian stalking! That'll take you a few lifetimes," says a fine, deep voice that comes not from a throat but from the back of a head which seems unreal, for the artist really tried and didn't miss a single line, and the hair, in a brush cut, half-and-half black and grey, is just the right length all over.

"We're not in a hurry," says Jane, who hasn't recovered her normal voice.

Except for his white shirt, the man is all in blue: his tie, his suit and his shoes. He stands out against the white of the ship with a contrast that adds to the strangeness of his presence in this place with its smells of tar and rotten soap.

It's not the embarrassment of being caught crawling at Jane's feet that gives him the feeling in his stomach and the wobbly legs, but all that incredible blue, the perfection and absence of volume of that head, as if it were in a picture, and the fine voice that rises from behind the picture, and the faintly bluish smoke that smells like confidence, rising like incense from the cigar between his fingers. In the stranger's blue gaze he feels that he has been recognized, but feels at the same time separated from him by a veil that blurs everything, the same kind of frontier that always exists between the illustration in a book and the eye itself.

"But you can crawl faster than that," the voice behind him explains. "You were really swimming. Look, if you want to crawl..."

"Oh, we're really sleeping in a caboose drawn by a hundred deer. You don't know the story," interrupts Jane, who has recovered her usual poise.

But the man, seeming not to hear, is down on his stomach.

"You're not going to drag your nice suit in that dirt!"

"You have to push with your forearms and your thighs."

"Oh, your suit's going to be a nice mess! And you didn't need to show us, that wasn't what we were playing."

The man crawls so quickly, cigar in mouth, that Jane retreats to the fence.

"If you go on your knees and elbows you can hit a sharp pebble, and that makes you shout, and then you might as well be standing up."

The deep voice is chewing its cigar and the blue smoke no longer rises but is wafted off in the direction of the ship.

"Why was he crawling, then?" asks the man, getting up.

"He was worshipping me," replies Jane, impatiently. "And I don't want you to."

"And if I want to worship you anyway, little Red Goddess, what are you going to do about it?"

"How did you know I was a Red Goddess?"

"Because I know everything, and anyway you can see it a mile away."

Now Pierrot goes head first at the veil that separates him from the stranger, for the latter had got into the story without being told what came before. He says slowly, hammering the words:

"A flea in the bee on the sea...."

"See the bee on the fleas," the man carries on as if this were the most natural conversation possible.

Pierrot had held his breath, sure that he wouldn't ask any questions, but on the man's reply he sees that it's only because he's used to playing and knows a lot of fine tricks.

"That wasn't the answer," he says coldly.

"I know. I just wanted to find out if you're serious and if we belong to the same tribe. Seas of bees in the fleas. Or even better: easway eesbay easflay. But that's for the higher-ups. "

"I come from the castle of the crows. Why didn't Saint Agnes take the place of Pigfoot?"

"I've left it all behind: the castles, the palaces, even the kingdom. The crows are in charge everyplace now. It's like going around the world, it's harder now, for it turns the wrong way."

"Like the bridge?"

"You mean you noticed it was upside-down? Well, I'm upside-down too. I'll never be serious again."

"What about the other children in the castle?"

"The walls will fall and there won't be any castle. Just big spider webs where the crows will get caught."

"Are you....are you the Blue Man?"

"I give up. No more disguises."

Jane, who hasn't said a word, but looked on with cold, wide-open eyes, interrupts authoritatively:

"He's a liar. I can prove it. What's the name of the cat with the stubby tail that is now a little green bear?"

The man takes a last puff on his cigar and throws it far away, looking seriously at Jane. At last he replies:

"It's a secret between the two of you. I couldn't know that."

"See!" Jane triumphs, putting on her high-heeled voice. "And I'll have you know, sir, that the Blue Man is an aviator. As you might know, I can recognize the uniform."

Pierrot could scalp her, he's so angry at her pretentious interference in a game she doesn't know, just when it was maybe going to stop being a game. He says angrily:

"Who ever told you the Blue Man and the pilot were the same? Girls don't understand anything. I told you I'd never seen either one."

"There may be more than one Blue Man who leaves everything behind and decides not to be serious because serious things are a lie, and maybe they're not all pilots. Maybe the more crows there are, the more Blue Men there are. And maybe the world will start to turn the other way. Who knows? And if all men went over to the blue side and went away there'd be nobody left on earth. The only important thing left would be the water, for it's always been blue."

He never smiles, talking to them with the same thoughtful gravity as if they had been grown-ups, or he had been a child. And you can't put him on one side or the other. He's like no one else, and you don't even feel like asking him what he'd be like if he weren't all blue. And when he plays, it's as if it were very important.

Jane is walking along beside the fence, letting her fingers slip into the holes of the wire mesh, her face sulky and her eyes on her shoes. Then she drops to the grass and shouts at him:

"I suppose you never talked about your father, either, or said the Blue Man would come back to the castle to chase out the crows! Walls can take a hundred years to fall down! So why doesn't he come and help you?"

"Because there's something lost, for everybody, and they can't find it. Can't you see he's all alone, just like anybody else?"

"Are we alone?"

"That's not the same. The proof is, they won't let us love each other. We have to hide, like you said. That's not normal."

"We have to stop doing things in secret, that's the truth," says the man who has also sat down on the grass. "Especially the things that give pleasure. Love is like trying to swallow the sea. That's why people forbid children to love, for children don't know yet that the sea is too big for their thirst. It's better to stop them before they drown trying."

Crack, crack, crack, go Jane's fingers.

"That's not the point. I'd just like to eat him up, and the only reason I don't is, he wouldn't be there any more. That's how simple and crazy love is."

"Don't you see it's the same thing as trying to drink the sea? If he disappeared would you be ready to drink the sea to find him?"

"I don't know. Never saw the sea. They say it's too salty."

"That's just why it's salty, and breathes as if it were alive."

"Pierrot, when do we get to the sea?"

"Never. We started the wrong way. We'll only see Panama where there's a street to let it through from one side to the other."

"Did you hear what he said? The sea breathes? He lies like the rest of the grown-ups. I suppose the river has lungs!"

The man talks on with his wise voice and seems untroubled by Jane's aggressive tone. She is standing at the top of the bank and the sun is shining through her little ear, thin as silk, and so red that it casts a coloured glow on the naked, white skin behind it.

"A day's sail from here the river starts breathing too, for it's getting near the sea, and its water grows salty. That's why I'm leaving on this ship, tonight."

"The beautiful car and the man with the cap, do they belong to you?"

"A man can belong to no one. And I'm giving him the car, for I won't need it now, and anyway it's too serious."

"If the man isn't yours, why does he stand there like a horse that can't get out of the shafts?"

"Because he's not a child, and he doesn't know yet that I've given up my disguise."

"You're too dirty for your car now. He's all shined up with his golden buttons. Well, good-day. We have to get back to Mama Pouf's."

She turns her back on him quickly and goes off in the direction of the ship, her legs pressed together and her bottom wiggling.

"I think I should get her on board. She can go to the toilet there," says the man, rising.

And he follows her without brushing off his clothes, stained with oil, tar and earth. His blue suit is perfectly clean behind.

Pierrot wants to show him that the game is over, and that he wasn't fooled for a minute.

"The kingdom and the castles and all that, that was just a joke. But how come you're so rich if you don't work?"

"Oh, I was serious for a long time."

"Were you somebody important, a boss or a manager of I don't know what?"

"I was worse. I was in the justice business."

They've caught up with Jane who puts on her ladylike airs, even though she's almost doubled over:

"Justice? That makes as much sense as if you said you were in the sunlight business. Did you make legs grow back on cripples?"

The man takes off his tie and whirls it in the air, as the Rat does with his chain.

"No. You're the Goddess, and I adore you too, even if you don't want me to. Come along, I'll show you the ship."

Jane's eyes light up for a second, but grow distant again at once.

"I can't. I have to go, fast."

"So come on board. That's why."

"I don't know what you mean," says Jane, barely opening her mouth and clenching her teeth, her voice reduced to a trickle.

"I don't either," says the man, "but come along." His voice is irresistible.

He takes them astern where there's a clean, white gangway. In the doorway is a man in a black coat with gilt buttons and a white cap on his head. He salutes their friend.

"Just a visit," he says.

"At your service," says the man in the cap.

They enter an immense room full of fat leather armchairs, with a round window taking up a whole wall, and he brings Jane to a narrow door.

"It's in there," he says, bowing.

Her eyes are no longer golden but the colour of burning coals.

"I didn't ask for anything."

"And I'm not giving anything."

But she goes in anyway, after a shrug and a look that make him responsible for the whole humiliating business.

Pierrot goes straight to the big window and sees a swimming pool filled with motionless green water, still as a mirror's surface, surrounded by lounge chairs and parasols; and down the river under the bridge, the shape of a bluish ship, much bigger than this one, pulled by little red tugboats.

"That's an ocean steamer, but it only takes soldiers now. It can go right across the ocean."

"How long does it take?"

"Ten days, maybe more. It depends on the submarines."

Jane is back already, her voice delighted, excited, as if they were actually sailing, marvelling:

"It looks like water that's just been washed! I'd love to swim in it."

The man pats her hair, very lightly, and she doesn't bridle, and Pierrot feels no resentment.

"I told them to make it that colour because of your hair," says the man, in a voice with a little smile in it for the first time.

"Now I know you're a liar. You'd say anything at all. And you're pretty serious for a man who stopped being serious."

"What? Me serious! I know, I'll go for a swim with my suit on to get it clean."

"Not in the pool, that would be too serious. And the water's too clean."

"What about the river?"

Jane shivers with pleasure at the idea, opens the door leading to the deck where the pool is and runs straight to the prow of the ship to look down at the river. The man is taking off his jacket.

"It's full of all kinds of orange peels and stuff and it's black, but there aren't any fish. And it's high! Really high!"

He takes off his shoes as well, and rolls up his shirtsleeves.

"And the water goes fast. Look at the paper floating, Pierrot. Can you swim?" she asks the man.

"No. That would be too serious. I'm not coming back and it'll all be your fault."

"Would you go right to the sea? I never saw anybody swim here. On the island on the other side I often went in. They've put sand, and fences in the water to keep you in."

Now his socks are off, and his pants rolled up, Jane is suddenly terrified:

"No, I don't want you to. The pool will do. They can wash the water again."

"Now who's too serious? Am I still a liar? Look me in the eye for just one minute to give me your Red Goddess power!"

Jane runs to one of the lounge chairs and curls up in it, shivering in the hot sun. He comes to her and looks in her eyes from very, very close. Jane grows gradually quieter, fascinated or caught again in her own love of provocation, then he leaves her, runs to the railing, and they hear the splash as he hits the water, so far away it becomes unreal.

"You're as crazy as a woman," Pierrot declares.

"He's big enough to know what he's doing. Pierrot, he has blue eyes and there's something like frozen tears in them."

They lean over the side and see him lying on his back, floating away, waving to them. Men on the dock and on the ship are shouting.

"He makes me feel cold," Jane says. "You didn't really think he was the Blue Man you made up?"

"I didn't make him up. There are things you feel, but you don't know."

He's approaching the ship with long strokes, his head in the water, but his progress is very slow, as if he were being pulled back.

"He's quite a guy, just the same!"

"He's some sort of crazy guy, too," Jane decides, her voice thoughtful. "It's as if he was playing to lose. Like the Rat. And nobody knows why."

"Just the same, he's somebody. Jumping in the water just to please you. He must be crazy."

"See, you said it yourself!"

"That's not what I said. I wish I had a father like him."

"And yours? If he's an aviator he must be as nice as mine."

"But aviators are in the sky. What's that castle on the island?"

They can see it better from the ship, rising out of a clump of trees, on top of a small hill.

"It's only a tower. There never was a castle. It's not as tall as it looks. I'll go there with you. There are picnic tables. Papapouf tells all kinds of stories about the tower that aren't true, and every time he has to lie because he can't remember what he said the last time."

Somebody lets down a rope ladder near them and they see the

handsome black and grey head appear, dripping with greyish water. He jumps to the deck and shakes his head to get the water out of his ears.

"You're a good swimmer, but let us know next time," says the man with the ladder.

"Well, it's there," the man says with relief.

"What? The bee or the flea?" asks Jane, showing no admiration.

"My submarine. I told it to pick me up here, but it came three days early."

"Maybe it's his brother. He's a submarine captain in the war."

"Certainly not. Mine's just a little submarine, a two-seater. Do you want to come with me?"

"With you? Never. But you could lend it to us. We were going to run away forever."

"Funny, so was I. Too bad there are only two seats. One of us won't get away. Where is forever? Tell me about it."

"I want to go out. You're dirtier than before and you smell of oil."

He takes his shoes, socks, tie and jacket and they go back to the white gangway.

"Did they enjoy their visit?" asks the gangway man.

"So much they pushed me into the oil tank. Next time I want it empty."

"At your service," replies the man with a polite smile.

He throws his clothing into the car through the door the golden-button man always holds open.

"Why do you throw them in there?" asks Jane.

"I can throw them in the river if you like."

"You just gave him the car. It's not yours any more."

"Not till eight o'clock tonight."

"Why not? That's cheating!"

"That's when the ship leaves. I have to pick up someone before then."

"What about us?" Jane insists.

"We'll get you back to your castle. No question about it. But what about the caboose and the hundred deer?"

"That's not the same. It's right there and we're sleeping. And our castle is Mama Pouf's place."

He opens the rear door for them, sits down beside them, and says to the chauffeur, in his beautiful deep voice but very softly:

"To Mama Pouf's."

The car reverses, then drives alongside the ship. For the first time Pierrot notices the name in gilt letters on the prow: TADOUSSAC.

"Is that an Indian name?"

"You know their language better than I do. It's the name of the place I'm going, just where you go into the sea, two days from here."

"We won't be seeing you," says Jane. "We're already in the country of the Great Cold, far past Indian country."

"Well, the country of the Great Cold will be my last stop, on the way back."

"In your submarine?"

He pulls on his socks and shoes without answering.

And they go to Mama Pouf's place in the blue car of the Man In Blue.

14

"I think I understand. This one's the Man In Blue, not the Blue Man."

They're just coming out of Pelletier's grocery store. Jane is sucking on a cinnamon candy, but she's out of sorts and he had to coax her to take it, and she pretends it's a new kind, not as cold as the ones he used to have, and she'll accept it just to please him, but it's making her sick to her stomach. She is, however, already on her second candy, in less time than it took to give the Rat's box to the grocer and explain about Siffleux, but Pierrot shouldn't have done that, for Monsieur Pelletier got angry and told him to shut his trap. For he hadn't forgotten the box, though Siffleux made a very strange face when he saw the blue car. Pierrot had remembered the box at the very last minute, and the thought of the Rat's expression as he drove his horse into the night's belly made such an impression on him, and the Rat had been so happy before, with a childish joy that made Skiff and Banana look old though they were much younger than he was, that he would have felt bad at making the Rat feel bad, and had asked if they could drive around by the market.

"I'd like to eat it to please you, I just can't. I wonder if it's really cinnamon?"

And she throws away the one she'd been sucking on, but carefully hangs on to the little brown bag that contains at least ten more.

"But I don't know what you think you understand. What's the difference if he's blue or in blue? I think he's playing at not being serious, and it's easy for him because he's got too much money. Rich people can act as crazy as they like."

175

"He's not crazy. You said yourself he had ice tears deep in his eyes."

"That's what I mean, though. There's something broken in him. Did you ever see eyes that were dry like that?"

"Yes. Pigfoot's. The crow that used to kick us, in the castle. And Aunt Maria's aren't wet, they just leak, like something sick."

"I stay sitting every evening till my feet go to sleep. And I still don't see the difference."

"It's hard to explain. It's like us, we could say 'papa' like everybody else but we can't say it for our papas are too busy with the war in the world to pay any attention to us. The Blue Man was like that too. But this one, you'd think he had nobody to care for. He's all alone."

She stops short in the middle of the street, in front of the passage that leads to Mama Pouf's garden, and bursts out with a temper that pinches her nostrils and makes her tremble from head to toe.

"I can say papa, and what's more I do say it, for I spent the whole day with him before he left and he writes all the time and I have his picture in my room and he's a lot handsomer than your crazy man. You've never even seen him, how can you tell the difference?"

To calm her he says in his humblest voice:

"Maybe because yours is an *anglais*. That's bound to be different. And you call him 'daddy' – I can't do that."

"Because *daddy* is more than papa, if you want to know."

"Don't you love me any more?"

"What! You believed it again, poor Plush! They believe every time, even when you've fooled them once."

"This time you said 'Cross my heart and spit.' You only love me when you're alone with me. I should have gone as far away as I could and left you there."

"And who'd have got lost 'cause he doesn't know anyplace, not even the Mountain!"

"That's easy. All the streets go the same way, and my feet don't get sore and I can go all day without eating."

She sticks out her tongue, then runs alone into the garden.

Suddenly he feels as if he were in overalls and ankle boots again, a stranger in the place, and imagines that a door has closed at the entry to the passage. He walks as far as Visitation Street to calm this new panic, wondering if people often get tired of each other this way, even when they love each other, their anger flaring up with the desire to hurt.

He returns slowly, stands for a moment in the shadow of the passage staring at the sunlit scene at its other opening. When he goes in the garden is deserted. He wanders around, observing the shutters that are closed over the photo of a soldier where a mother and a votive lamp keep their vigil. He tries to see the flame through the cracks between the dark green slats, favourite colour of the neighbourhood. Lilac blossoms have been raining down everywhere.

"Don't go there! It's forbidden!"

He jumps, and looks for the voice. It's one of the twins lying on the back of the wooden giraffe, so passive and motionless he could have passed within inches without seeing him.

"It's the cemetery!"

He looks down at his feet. In the midst of a few blue flowers, laid on a little cross of sticks, he sees the giraffe's head which has been cut off behind the ears, its mouth still gaping.

"The head's been dead for over a year. We put blue flowers around so nobody would walk on it."

"Why just the head?" he asks, for something to say.

"The neck was too long. It would have looked like a giraffe in two pieces, when it's really only dead."

"Oh! How did it die?"

"It was eating flowers all the time. We wanted to shorten its neck so it couldn't reach them. And papa says it's dead now, for giraffes have long necks to make room for the heart."

"Oh, I see," he says. "I'm sorry."

"We have to tell everybody that comes, for you can't see the cross for flowers. No harm done."

He makes it as far as the lounge chair and drops into it. He wonders if he shouldn't leave. He's not invited, and nobody comes out of the house to say hello. Maybe they're eating already.

The door of the verandah opens suddenly and Jane appears, holding Meeow at arms' length. The baby is howling, its arms and legs struggling in the air. She lays it on its stomach on his knees, and starts back to the house shouting:

"Mama Pouf is sick. Look after him for a while. It's her legs. We're making supper."

And she disappears into the house as if the soup were boiling over. He's never touched a baby in his life. He watches it paddling furiously on his knees, howling ever louder. There's a big yellow stain on its behind, and it's sprung a leak in front and that's running down Pierrot's pants. He spreads his knees to let it down on the crossed canvas of the chair, but it gets one arm in a hole and screams as he never imagined a baby could. If it howls like this perhaps he should take it in his arms, even if no one ever showed him how, or he might just see a leg fall into the grass and wriggle away on its own. He succeeds in freeing the arm from the hole in the chair, hurrying so that the whole neighbourhood doesn't run to see him torturing the baby, and lifts him up by the armpits to dandle him a bit and get the howling stopped. It's funny looking into his eyes from so close, they're blue as night and so big there's scarcely any white, and tears come out that aren't shaped like tears, a flood that runs in all directions. What astonishes him most is the expressionless fixity of these eyes, as if he didn't know he was crying or as if there were another child inside looking on with cool curiosity. And he feels so firm, much harder than he would have thought, so much alive that the thought goes through his mind that a baby can't die, even if it wanted to. His little brother must have fallen in fire or water. But he never knew about that.

He lays him in the crook of his arm the way Mama Pouf does and the baby at once begins sucking vigorously at his sweater, which makes him horribly embarrassed, but there's no crying for a few seconds and that makes up for the yellow stain now spreading on his chest.

"Poor Pierrot, he's going to eat you up! He doesn't know you're a little boy and dry as can be!"

Mama Pouf comes toward him with the rapid, decisive step that is hers when she has succeeded in getting to her feet.

"They told you I was sick, those little rascals. I was only having a sleep. I get lazy feeding him all the time."

She takes Meeow and, without looking at what she's doing, pulls off his diaper, drops it in the grass, and puts on a clean one.

"The lilacs are shedding already. It's been too hot."

Pierrot has risen to give her his place and now he's looking desperately for a spot where the baring of Mama Pouf's breast can be spared him. She reassures him at once:

"Stay, stay here and keep me company. They're making such a fuss with their supper, you'll only be in the road. Pouf!"

She plumps into the chair, unbuttoning her dress. The breast with its big, blue veins is rolling gently in Meeow's mouth, and he puffs like a puppy that's been playing for hours. The smell from the rubber factory is already settling into the garden. The twin seems to be asleep on the decapitated giraffe.

"By the way, Aunt Rose brought your boots in today. Henri's started cleaning them up. He says he's going to dye them brown, they'll look a lot better. Your Aunt thought you were here. You've been seeing some sights today, I hear. The squirrel started telling me. It seems..."

She's interrupted by an infernal noise under the passage and the diabolical silhouette of the Rat appears, his head triumphally higher than ever, on a black motorcycle which he steers among the flowers and the various monuments of wood, letting his long legs drag on the ground. Meeow barely reacts. Mama Pouf exclaims, in a voice that is full of tragic helplessness:

"Oh, no! Not that one, not tonight!"

On the giraffe the twin sits up like a jack-in-the-box but can't turn fast enough to shine his admiration on all the Rat's manoeuvres. In the doorway of his workshop the shoemaker shouts, shaking his fist, but nothing can be heard. Jane comes out of the house first, then Thérèse and the other twin. Mama Pouf repeats:

"Not him, not tonight. Poor little guy, his ass is on fire and he wants to blow up the world!"

The Rat finally stops his machine beside the long table and boasts in his most insolent tone:

"Who can catch the Rat now, eh? Squirrel, do you want to hear your goddam English song on this? Isn't this a fine black horse? And it can gallop down a street as well."

He turns one of the handlebars full open and the roar of the motor makes them stop their ears. Then he shuts it off, crosses his arms contentedly, his yellow boots spread wide and resting on the ground.

"Ever hear music like that?"

"Where did you steal it?" asks Jane, pretending to be haughty but very impressed just the same.

"From a cop, who else? I traded it in for the guitar, and got enough into the bargain to keep it running ten years."

"Rat, you've got to leave right now," implores Mama Pouf, trying in vain to hide her breast.

"Not before the kids get a ride. Coming, squirrel?"

She barely hesitates, just long enough so you can see she'd like to, then says with contempt:

"I suppose you think you're better looking on that horse. I liked the guitar better."

Now Skiff and Banana appear out of nowhere, each carrying a tire on one arm, their eyes dull, waiting for orders. The twins have already jumped onto the back saddle and are chorusing, "Voom, voom!"

"There's a cop down at the store," says Skiff, who then begins to whistle as if he weren't there.

"Where do we put them?" asks Banana.

"Get out of here, fast!"

It's Papapouf, a hammer in his hand, almost succeeding in getting angry and asserting himself.

"Well, the cops have a right to fresh air if they want it. The tires are for you, Monsieur Lafontaine. A present from the Rat: transport and import."

"Get them back where they came from. You're leaving nothing here."

He's waving the hammer around his head so fast you'd expect him to take off like a rocket. But he's really angry, and Mama Pouf is really worried, and the little garden, bathed in the smell of rubber, is suddenly electrified by the threat of a storm, and Pierrot feels the tension in his wrists and wishes he were elsewhere, especially as Jane keeps ignoring him, except for a quick look that was so cold he loses his appetite and would rather go back to the ship right away, for they'd promised the Man In Blue they'd be there when he left.

"Look, here's a dynamo for the Buick! You won't get another one before the war ends, and it's paid for, fair and square."

The shoemaker has a little more trouble turning down the dynamo. He casts a sad eye at his fine brown car, shining away there, before starting to brandish his hammer again.

"I said nothing, do you hear? Get out, and get out now!"

He shoves the twins down from the saddle without ceremony.

"Go play giraffe, you two. It's bed for you, right after supper."

"It's not as if we hadn't other takers," Skiff sings softly with his absent-minded air.

"We can trade them for a streetcar and have enough in the bargain to pay for the wires," adds Banana, as if he weren't sure of having said the right thing.

Flabbergasted, Papapouf and his hammer freeze as he stares incredulously at them.

180

"Shut up," orders the Rat.

"Yes, boss," Banana stammers.

"Who are those two galoots?" asks Papapouf.

"My partners and bodyguards. Just like lambs."

"Well, you're going to need them. But not around here. Let that sort of stuff happen someplace else!"

"My lord, Henri, don't get them worked up!" Mama Pouf sighs.

"It's no time to fool around. Paul and Isabelle are coming any minute. And Paul swore you wouldn't touch a girl after he left. I'm telling you, Rat, play dead for three days at least. After that, we'll see."

By now Papapouf's voice has grown peaceful again, almost supplicating. But the Rat bursts out with a laugh like a water tap spitting air.

"Yeah? What if he was the one that had trouble walking afterwards, eh? I've seen him. That's something to be proud about. Not even a soldier. He's an MP, for chrissakes! He'll not go over to fight but to knock off our chums from behind. A military cop, with a gun and a stick! Aren't you ashamed, Monsieur Lafontaine? I thought there were enough *anglais* for jobs like that. He's going over there to shoot them in the back, d'you hear?"

"You know what I think about the war. Don't worry. But he's almost got the right to kill you. An MP after dark, he can just about make his own law. So disappear for a while. I don't want any of that business."

The Rat laughs again in his nasty way, but there's sweat on his white forehead.

"A guy with no more than that left in his glass..."

And again he makes the gesture with his thumb and index finger:

"...he's going to drink it all. He can't even afford to be scared any more. Your MP forgets he's in my part of town. If he wants to come looking for me after dark, he's the one who's going to lose a few parts. And we'll make him eat them to give him some guts."

"Gaston, not in front of the kids," Mama Pouf interrupts, her voice soft and kind. "Poor little fellow, it's true you haven't much left in your glass, but don't pour it all out at once. Paul has the law and the army behind him. You – you're just a little rat!"

"Gaston, don't make trouble for them. Not for them."

Pierrot can't help getting his own imploring word in, for he is even more sensitive than the others to the mounting tension in the garden, where there's nothing left to breathe but burnt rubber, perhaps because he's the outsider.

The Rat turns to him, suddenly calm:

"Thanks for taking care of the box. If I'm going now it's to please you. Not for that MP son-of-a-bitch."

"Of course," says Mama Pouf quickly. "And we're very grateful."

The Rat starts up his motorbike again, enjoys another turn around the garden, stops to let Skiff get on behind him, and disappears out the passage without a good-bye. Banana is left with a tire on each arm. In his long raincoat he looks like a tall post for playing quoits. He stands there for a while, smiling into space. Then he sets the tires on the ground and starts rolling them out toward the street like two hoops, but one gets away and the twins come to his aid as far as the old truck that almost blocks the entry.

"Come on in the house, Mama, the air's too bad out here."

The shoemaker offers his meagre shoulder, and Mama Pouf, holding Meeow in one hand, grasps him with the other and raises herself very slowly, as if to give the milk time to run back down inside her legs. But again, once on her feet, she is astoundingly agile.

"Pouf! Maybe they won't come and we'll have a nice quiet evening after all. Poor Henri, you did get into a state!"

"Who, me? Why, I was just taking a little exercise to get up an appetite."

"It was me made the dinner," Jane lies brazenly.

"What! Then I need some more exercise!"

They go inside. Jane gets so much attention that Papapouf hasn't even seen Pierrot and nobody's invited him to dinner. Watching the twins play king of the castle on the giraffe, he wonders if he wouldn't be better to go and see the Chinaman a few doors down, sewing snow-white linen in the dark, and wait there until after the meal. But Jane comes over to him playfully, a pink apron over the white dress that's been gathering dust all day, her voice catching immediately at his heart, and her hair triumphing easily over the lilacs, which are moulting.

"Poor Plush, everybody's forgotten about you! But I had to help. For once Mama Pouf was sleeping, and Thérèse is always dreaming. You know, she doesn't work at the baby hospital any more. You should look at her knees, she has water in them from scrubbing floors."

She sits down beside him, wiggling her behind to make room on the canvas chair, which still smells of curdled milk.

"Push over a bit. My legs are tired."

She is pressed against him, the whole length of her body, and in her look as well he discovers a still light, a second being who is much more serious, so withdrawn that it is untouched by the air, as new and blind as at her birth, unknown, perhaps, to herself, to which you cannot talk. Like the cold stare of Meeow, concealed just deep enough to let through the little girl who knows she's being looked at.

Carefully she smooths out her pink apron, over to where it falls on his leg, and from somewhere pulls out the little bag of cinnamon candy. She puts one in her mouth and after a moment of deep reflection confides:

"This one's much better. They must be mixed, or maybe I was tired. Here, try it."

And it's not the candy she offers, but her tongue with the taste on it, at once hot and cold on his lips, so strangely alive it seems barely to be a part of her.

"It's good, isn't it!"

"I can't tell. You tickle too much."

Her tongue, her double gaze, the warmth of her naked leg against his trousers, and her voice more sugared and spiced than any cinnamon, throw him into a state of uncomfortable ecstasy. Then she puts her tiny, cool arm around his neck.

"I wasn't going to. But we'll go. It doesn't work here, because of Isabelle. Maybe the Man In Blue isn't a cheat. We'll see..."

And the sun gradually goes out in the little garden, for a cloud of rubber smoke is passing.

15

"Put that thing away. I don't want to see that in my house, ever!"

For the second time tonight Papapouf gives way to an anger you wouldn't think he could harbour. And it's even worse than that, for his hand, holding the knife, is trembling all on its own, and he'd shouted so loud that everybody jumped, even Isabelle, who since she arrived had taken refuge in a kind of frozen sadness where nothing bothered her. You can see she's been crying a lot, for she has big bags under her eyes where the powder doesn't stick, for he actually saw a pink flake of it fall on the white table-cloth.

Now on that white table-cloth there's this bluish object, gathered up within itself like a beast that could spring any minute, ugly like those naked, slimy things you discover beneath a stone.

"It's terrific!" cries one of the twins, getting up to admire it from close up, and touch it.

But the shoemaker has time to slap his hand with the knife, and he starts to cry.

"Henri, you hurt him!" Mama Pouf reproaches her husband, stretching out one of her great arms to gather him in beside Meeow who's sleeping in the other.

"Don't worry. It won't go off by itself," says Paul, who has a clipped way of talking, almost without opening his mouth or moving a feature of his face or that large squared head with its dark hair clipped short.

"If it won't go off by itself you can take it off, back where it came from, from the devil himself!" shouts Papapouf, standing up, trembling all over.

"Come on, I can't sit on it."

"All right, out in the street and shit on it. As if I had a gangster at my table."

Then, shaking the point of his knife at the twins, scattering its reflected light in all directions, he scolds:

"That thing was invented by all the cowardice in the world! And cowardice isn't terrific!"

"You're not going to insult the army in front of the kids!" Paul exclaims indignantly.

"Army or MP or whatever you are, that's what I think. And if you don't agree, there's the door."

A silence follows, nothing happens, except that Isabelle finally raises her head and looks at Paul with a kind of helpless contempt, then says in a voice as peremptory as his own:

"You heard what Papa said, Paul."

It's Gérard's turn to take his nose out of his plate, from which he always eats in silence. His voice, too, is shaken by anger:

"Go and put it in the delivery truck and let's hear no more about it, for God's sake! What do you need to cart that thing around for?"

Paul is not quite as tall or broad as Gérard, but he's tougher, and his gestures are powerful and abrupt. Under his battle dress with its wide, white arm band there are pulleys controlling well-oiled steel muscles. He gets up, takes the revolver from the white tablecloth and, to show how harmless it is, grasps it by the barrel.

His large khaki silhouette dominates them all, as astonishing as if it had just appeared, more foreign in contrast to Isabelle's lilac dress than the Rat's black scarecrow jacket.

"A military policeman's always on duty," he replies, parroting a lesson learned.

"Well, you're a visitor here. Leave your duty outside," orders the shoemaker, who has calmed down a little and begun to eat.

The MP is standing alone on high, contemplating the weapon with an expression of wounded pride. He leaves the kitchen.

Her elbows solidly on the table, her little pointed face turned toward the shoemaker, Jane bursts out in her shrillest tone:

"Papa....pouf!"

The shoemaker pretends to choke on his food, then laughs with the rest.

"You're not my Uncle Henri any more. You're Papapouf now," Jane goes on, very proud of herself. "I even told Pierrot already."

The twin slips out from under his mother's arm and goes back to his place at the table, with the expression of one determined to live down his disgrace.

"Well, Isabelle, eat up, now. Poor chicken, it's not easy to be a woman. If it wasn't for this damned war..."

"Mama! Not before the children!" Papapouf's laugh is cut short.

"You never understood a thing, you. You've done enough pushing around for one night. Now shut up. If it wasn't for this damn war you wouldn't be in such a hurry, you could enjoy being young. When I think people are afraid of the war factories closing! They shouldn't ever have opened."

"And I'd be shoemaker for all those barefoot people!"

"If you like the war so much you didn't need to go through your little act," concludes Mama Pouf.

"I hope he leaves, I hope he gets on his boat..."

Isabelle is thinking out loud the anger and chagrin the rest can only guess, even if they know that Paul has come back to take her for three days as if she were a dog he'd left in their house.

"I don't want you to fix up my boots, Papapouf."

He murmurs the new nickname, uncertain if he has the right to use it.

"They'll be so fine you won't even know them."

"I don't want them. They're no good any more. And they're not even mine, they belong to the castle."

"They're going to be so fine I'll paint the black one brown that's over the door. And I'll call my shoe 'La Bottine à Pierrot.' And you'll always feel at home here."

"If he's Marcel's brother he should feel at home here anyway. But it's not a bad idea, you've finally had a good one in that ugly shoemaker's head of yours," Mama Pouf admits.

"His name has been Plush for hours now. Ever since we went around the world together. We almost went away for life."

He can't understand her stupid way of blabbing such secret things, things that were true if only for a few minutes. What has been true for one single moment isn't a game any more, and can't be allowed beyond the two of them without dying.

"It's lucky you've got a few lives left, little mouse," says Mama Pouf, with an uneasy glance at Paul who has returned to his place beside Isabelle.

"We're going back to see the ships tonight. D'you want to come, Thérèse?"

What could poor Thérèse, who seems so dead tired, have to do with them and the Man In Blue? Girls are really like sparrows, everything is equally important to them, or unimportant, as long as they can flit around all the time from one place to another looking for sunlight in every puddle.

"I'm afraid not," replies the voice that's like the inside of white bread. "My knees hurt too much. I feel as if I had balloons around them."

"Balloons don't hurt. Gérard, will you take us there?"

"If you're ready in two minutes and come back by streetcar."

Then there's silence again, with a vague threat hanging in it, perhaps from Isabelle's swollen eyes, her rapid breathing visible under the stretched lilac of her breasts, her refusal to eat; perhaps from the solid, stolid, khaki block breathing her air beside her. It's the same twin who touches off the explosion.

In an innocent voice, looking up at the ceiling, he asks:

"I hear the MPs shoot our soldiers in the back so they'll shoot forward. Is there one MP for every soldier?"

Papapouf glances at him, amused and uneasy at once. The other twin chimes in at once:

"It's a funny idea, having policemen in a battle. Like if we hired guys to make us fight against the Irish kids, and the Irish kids didn't want to hurt us but the others would knock us out from behind. Why are you an MP?"

Paul goes on eating as if he hadn't heard.

Mama Pouf says quickly:

"You two, you're finished eating. Go play outside."

"Well, it's a fair question."

"If he can't answer it, who can?"

The twins are on the war-path, and wait, gaping, decided to settle their point.

"Mama told you to go play outside. Now, go!" Papapouf orders. He has no desire to be amused.

"Are you the one who told them stuff like that?" asks Paul coldly.

No one answers. He shoves his plate away brutally and grabs Isabelle's arm.

"Come on. We're having our coffee in a restaurant."

Isabelle struggles to free her arm.

"I'll go if I want to. If I don't..."

Gérard too stands up, wiping his mouth, and speaks in a voice no one has heard from him, impatient and commanding:

"She'll go or stay if she pleases. Do you hear, Paul? When you're invited here you don't leave the table."

"For Christ's sake! An MP is supposed to stop soldiers from fighting with each other. You could tell them that."

"And you need a revolver to do it?" asks Isabelle contemptuously.

"D'you think drunken privates fight with gloves on? And what about civilians? We protect them too."

"I guess you're going to protect some civilians tonight, is that it?" asks Papapouf gently.

The MP flops onto his chair again and goes at a piece of cake as if it were the enemy, almost gnashing his teeth.

The twins burst out laughing simultaneously and go out into the garden.

Isabelle, from the depths of a great weariness, with a kind of resignation, announces in a voice full of hesitations:

"I...have to get to bed...early. Have to work at seven tomorrow."

Paul continues to take out his rage on the cake.

From the doorway Gérard says:

"Are you kids coming?"

At once Jane's hand, a little cold, is in his, and he's in a hurry to be alone with her, he's yearning to see the ship, and the Man In Blue, and get back to the game in which she can be so genuine, so confiding, and so afraid that she goes to sleep on his shoulder and leaves him guardian of all the gold in the world.

"Maybe it's true he has a two-seater submarine. Is it always night under water?" she asks, curling her cinnamon fingers in his.

"Don't be too late, now, children. That's no place to stay after dark."

Mama Pouf manages easily to hug them both with one arm, and she gives them a smack as wet as a cat's tongue. In his sleep Meeow is puffing like a bushwhacker, as if he were rowing in a sea of milk.

"I do believe tonight's the full moon," says Papapouf, leaving the table.

"I'd love to come with you. It's so long since I watched the ships sail out."

Isabelle's voice comes from very far away, far beyond the bursting lilac of her dress. She too gets up, and Pierrot notices she has no perfume on.

Paul is eating cake, his eyes hard and steel blue, like his gun.

189

16

"Have you got enough money to take the streetcar home?" asks Gérard as he drops them off at the entry to the docks, but he drives off without waiting for an answer, for there are too many cars behind him. He's always in a hurry anyway, and he hunches over the wheel as he rushes back to work.

The ship is already lit up like a Christmas tree in daylight, for the sun is just beginning to go down at the other end of the river. The bridges are bathed in a pink earthlight that makes the air so featherlike that Jane's hand in his is gentle as a sleeping bird.

Even the heavy carcass of the green bridge, hurled toward the island, seems to float, and you can see sunlight flashing in the headlights of the cars coming in from the country.

Cars are lined up in front of the big hole at the ship's front and go in one by one, with a long wait between. All around, there are men and women dressed like foreigners and speaking English, very loudly, in voices that come through their nose. In vain they search for the blue car. In spite of the heat some of the women, many of them young, are wearing furs and walk with their heads thrown back a little as if they were afraid the animals might escape from their shoulders. Or maybe it's because of their high heels on the rough pavement.

"They're mostly Americans," Jane explains. "They're the only ones that can afford it."

"Where does it go?"

"I don't know. They call it the 'Saguenay Cruise.' It's never the same boat. And I never understood why they all take their cars along."

"So they won't cry. A car that isn't moving gets unhappy."

"Papapouf's car doesn't cry."

"Stupid, I was just talking."

"Idiot, I was just talking."

"It doesn't cry, for it's sick and they look after it."

"It can't get bored. They're always doing something to it."

"What if he doesn't come."

"We came to see the boat. Perhaps he never was there at all."

"We made him up?"

"And they hung him out to dry because he was too wet."

"Maybe he's going to swim here. He said he had to get somebody. That could only mean his submarine."

"Oh? Then why did he say he couldn't give his car away until eight o'clock?"

"Then it must be a woman."

"Why? That would make him serious, like anybody else. Maybe he went to get his Balibou."

"Or a fox with an American lady around its neck. A redhead!"

"I'm never coming to see the ships with you again. You're too silly."

She leaves him, running across to the white gangway, where she leans on her elbows and stares at all the passengers as they go up.

He joins her there, a little to one side, where he can see better. The white yachting caps and the uniforms with gold buttons fascinate him. He waits for her to turn back to him, but she slips between the cables and the passengers' legs to turn around on the other side and stick out her tongue at him. He is reassured.

He is the first to see the Man In Blue, as dry and neat as if he had never crawled on the grass or jumped in the river. He's walking quickly without looking around, and holding his arm is a young woman, blonde and pale, very lovely, wearing a tight dress, salmon pink, which would suit no one else, a bouquet in her hand, her head proud, but you can see that she too has been crying, not that her eyes are swollen like Isabelle's, on the contrary, they're back under the surface and the front is just wet enough that it can't be hidden by her powder. The pink sunlight on her dress seems to pass through her, as it does through Jane's ear, and the flowers, which are white and sad smelling, take on the colour of her skin.

He can't stop looking, for she's certainly the prettiest, proudest, saddest thing he's ever seen in his life, and she was surely invented to go with the icy tears of the Man In Blue. But suddenly Jane is beside him, pushing him in the stomach and begging:

"Come away. Come on! I told you he was a cheater."

He resists her, and even rubs her ears a bit, thinking she's playing, and he doesn't feel like it.

"Because he's serious, with a beautiful lady? Let's wait for him to see us, at least."

But to his astonishment Jane isn't fooling, she's not even pretending to be angry, she's choking with panic and pushing him harder, with her whole body, butting him in the stomach with her head, and he hears, out of the whirling red cloud of her hair:

"A beautiful lady! An ugly, stuck-up pig! It's my sister, Pierrot. Emily! Now will you come?"

"You're talking nonsense. If it was your sister you wouldn't be scared of her. All right, then, she's ugly as my Aunt Maria. Now are you satisfied?"

"I haven't seen her since the other house, but it's her all right. I swear it. And the cheater who knew everything, that was because he recognized me. Come on, Pierrot."

Too late. The crowd has grown behind them and pushes them back toward the gangway, and the man in blue sees them and pushes his way through to them, and the lovely proud sad lady makes an impatient gesture to free her arm, and the flowers fall, and Pierrot picks them up with hands that never seemed so heavy, and holds them out to her, blowing on them to wake them up.

"At last!" the man says simply, lifting his arms, as if he'd done nothing but wait in line for hours just to get where they were. And he smiles so slowly it's as if he were cutting it in stone. He adds:

"I didn't think I'd see you. I couldn't have left without saying goodbye to my little Indians."

The lie is too obvious, and Jane is wiggling so hard trying to find room behind his body to hide a frightened squirrel that he can't afford to go on being intimidated by the lady, who doesn't even deign to take her flowers. The bouquet, close up, smells faintly of honey. Then he says, much louder than he had intended:

"You're worse than serious. You're a liar."

The man can't give up the smile he had achieved with so much effort. He takes the flowers and gives them to the lady, who holds them head down, at arm's length, for their perfume is falling out like powder, and they no longer are coloured like her skin pierced by sunlight but are as wilted as her eyes.

"Tell him, Emily. We've been looking for you for the last half hour. And she's angry because she's tired, and I told her about you, and we even brought a friend for you."

He begs his companion to corroborate in such a sad voice that the lie becomes almost true, and the lady looks at them at last, speaking nonchalantly, but in a voice whose music is dangerously similar to Jane's, and affects his stomach in exactly the same way.

"He bought you a green teddy bear, I can't imagine why."

It is Emily, with that mellow voice, but the gold-dust has gone leaving only this pale honey-coloured hair. As at the shoemaker's, he feels an electric shock, especially in his wrists, that might turn everything topsy-turvy and shatter his images yet again. The man's deep voice has lost its power and no longer comes from the back of his head, superimposed on life, but from his throat, a little hoarsely:

"You're Jane's sister," Pierrot hears himself saying, from far away.

"Jane's sister?" she asks, and she too is far away.

"Her sister!" exclaims the man in blue, suddenly stunned. "We never leave anything behind," he murmurs again, there in the pink earthlight of the sun.

The motors of the ship rumble softly beneath the black water. For a moment there's nothing but the passengers going step by step up the gangway, pushing them back a little and rubbing at the upside-down flowers. Then two blows on a whistle, very short, which fail to tear the veil between the man in blue and himself, but give Jane her battle signal:

"Hello anyway, Emily. I didn't come on purpose."

She stands on Pierrot's feet to gain dignity, and express – more in looks than words – the aggressive indifference of disappointed love. Their two voices are alike even to their way of going up very high to seem distant and cold, but in Emily's case it also seems to mean that she's been shaken badly, for she suddenly begins to show signs of the most abject panic. The man in blue, for his part, is absorbed in an interior revelation that blinds him to everything else.

"She's not well," he says suddenly, and drags her swiftly off toward the uniforms with gold buttons who are checking people's papers.

"Do you see how stuck-up she is? As if she'd never been my sister. She's been mean like that for years and years."

"Look, she really is sick. She's pale, even her eyes."

"She's cheap, you mean. And the other one's a fine cheat, too, going after her. My sister! The cheapest thing in the world."

But the man comes back at once, a tiny green plush teddy bear in his hands.

"Are you going to hate me?" he says to Jane in his new, pitiful voice. "I really didn't know. It's terrible how you can't ever know, and how paths can cross in the most deserted forest."

He holds out the bear.

"It's for the ice floes."

There he went again. How did he know about the ice floes?

"We don't want it. The one we made up was nicer."

The ship's whistle sounds again, longer this time, and the hundreds of little lamps grow brighter. No one else is left on the gangway.

"I'll take it, Balibou belongs to me. If you don't like it he'll change into a squirrel."

She leaves them brusquely, without a word, and runs to the grass slope.

"Thank you," says the man. "It would have been a very bad sign for me if you hadn't taken it. I was really worried."

"So was the lady," Pierrot replies, putting on the voice and expression of a disinterested observer.

"We're leaving now. I just have time to tell you that on Saturday at a quarter past twelve the sun will disappear and the birds will stop singing. That will be a sign that we'll see each other the following day, right here. If it doesn't happen, if the birds sing and the sun shines, that will mean that the white flowers are not dead."

He has to go, for they're pulling the gang-plank away and slipping the cables, and he knows Pierrot will ask no questions but has understood what was incomprehensible.

The rumbling of the motors grows louder, and the ship, very slowly, leaves the dock, like a feast enclosed within itself, forbidden, and as it slides away little darts of light grow longer on the dark water. He looks in vain for the form of the man in blue among the shadows standing and waving.

He looks at the bear. It has golden eyes. Two tiny buttons.

The TADOUSSAC picks up speed into the dark, toward the sombre mass of the bridge. On the island the tip of the tower still catches the last embers of sunlight.

Jane is doubled up, her head between her knees, a tiny colourless shape excluded from the feast. He hides the bear in his pocket so as not to re-awaken her anger, and goes to sit down beside her, waiting patiently for her to come to life.

When she finally raises her head, she has no eyes for the big patch of light floating off beneath the bridge. To know she had been crying you'd have to touch her cheek, but that would be like putting your fingers in her heart. She simply says, with a voice more drowned than water itself:

"I'm cold."

He takes her chilled hand and helps her up, but she jumps and shouts in a joyous voice:

"Look! Papapouf was right!"

In front of them, licking at the silhouette of the tower, an enormous, reddened moon rises from the river to announce a more silent celebration.

Jane jumps up and down, clapping her hands, then kisses him and starts dancing around him, singing:

"Mon ami Pierrot, Prête-moi du feu...."

"The moon's a redhead," he says, astonished.

He had never seen a moon like that. He's not even sure he's ever seen the moon before, or perhaps only as a bluish whiteness on the snow, the colour of cold.

Then she's quiet again, takes his arm and makes him come along to the very edge of the dock, with long steps, lifting her legs high. She leans out over the reddish light on the water and says:

"That was a nice night to leave on a ship."

And she leads him back to the street, shivering a little. As soon as they leave the dock they're back in the humid heat and the stale smell of their village.

"You know, I always wished Emily had stayed with me. There are days when I really wish I had a big sister."

And she starts in on a cinnamon candy, frowning to herself, resisting the weight of her hair which, all at once, seems too much.

196

17

He'd like to go to bed now, to sleep, giving himself up to the slow unrolling of the pictures of the day, but his uncle is reading his paper in the den, preventing him from using the green sofa until later in the evening when he'll go to smoke his pipe in his room. In the parlour, Eugénie has some ladies in. They sit very straight in their chairs and all talk at once, with laughs and cluckings that swell and fade in waves, and silences that give them time to clear their throats or change a pose. Then away they go again as if somebody had scored and they were starting a new game. The only thing left is Aunt Rose, and the kitchen.

As he comes in she quickly closes a long, flat cardboard box, a trace of embarrassment or shame in her eyes. He had time to see that the box contained his blue-striped shirt and his overalls, well washed and ironed.

"Why are you keeping that?"

"You don't throw away clothing," she answers, in her usual grumpy voice.

"It's not even clothing. What good is it?"

"You never know. Look at your pants, little man. Where on earth have you been all day?"

"I went down to see the boats sailing away."

"And you went to bother your uncle with that fresh little trollop."

"Don't you dare talk..."

Because he's so tired, and he has a feeling she'll start shouting, he backs away a bit and starts again:

197

"I don't want you to talk about her like that. She's nice and she has nobody to play with."

"Nice! Like her mother, I suppose!"

He doesn't answer, and Aunt Rose sits down across from him, her face tired, the wart on her nose quite red. She sighs several times and sits there with her mouth slightly open, waiting for words that don't come out or swallowing the shrill conversation in the parlour. He gives up watching her and drops his head on his arms on the metal table, and the sounds fade away as he slides toward sleep. Then he jumps as if someone had pinched him. He can barely open his eyes. Aunt Rose is shaking his shoulder and talking close to his face, so loudly he expects his uncle and the lady visitors to come running.

"Don't you pretend to sleep. You heard what I said!"

"Heard what?"

"The police came tonight. Starting off just like your brother."

"I think I was asleep for a minute. What about the police?"

"I don't know. They spoke to your uncle."

"Well, I don't know why any more than you do. Why don't you go out with the others? I'm sleepy."

"Those are her friends. They work at the same place. Your uncle said we'd have to keep an eye on you, and he was going to see the director."

"The director? Director of what?"

"The home where you'll learn a trade. That's why I took your boots to be fixed."

"Mama Pouf told me. Why did you do that? Do you want me to leave?"

Aunt Rose does her best to sound friendly, and talks to him as if he were a child.

"I don't want that. No. You're younger than Marcel was, we could manage if we were used to handling boys. But your uncle is so tired, and your aunt is sick. I know your mother would never forgive me for letting you go. She suffered too much, she'd want to be proud of you! I told her we'd see you got an education. It could be done, you were still so little..."

He's wide awake now, he feels as if he's swallowing snow, and anger surges inside him against his aunt's attempt to be gentle. His voice doesn't reveal his anger, but his gaze is icy:

"Why are you talking about my mother? She's not suffering, she's dead."

198

"There, a person never knows how to handle a boy. They don't feel things as we do. I was just trying to show you in a roundabout way that I wanted to do right by you because of your mother."

"But you don't like me," he interrupts coldly.

Again Aunt Rose's eyes darken, but she goes on trying to speak to him in a way she thinks appropriate in conversing with a little boy.

"You know, your brother gave us so much trouble! The image of his father. It's so hard to keep on thinking well of people."

"Why didn't you get married?"

"Listen, you, that's the kind of question children don't ask. You're just trying to hurt my feelings for nothing. I looked at your mother's picture this afternoon, and I promised her I'd do my best. But you have to help."

She speaks as gently as it's possible for her to do. She can't, after all, change her voice or her face.

"Look. That's her."

"Who?"

"Look, will you? It's your mother. We had a print made for her funeral. It was your father's idea."

He drops his head on the cold metal and says, from as far away as he can get:

"I don't like you to talk about my father. And I won't look, because it isn't her. She's in my head, and she belongs to me. That's worse than asking you why you aren't married."

A long silence follows. She probably thinks he's crying, for she goes on, trying even harder to be kind:

"She's beautiful. A real saint in heaven. You're too little to understand. Why should I explain? When you've worked twenty years at Dominion Rubber and you have to work ten hours a day to buy your clothes and help with the house and then take our mother's place because Maria's sick and your uncle's alone and your mother..."

Again he rises through his sleep to look at her through the thick glass that separates them:

"Never mind her! Don't mention her again. She belongs to me!"

Despite the thick glass something gets through to him, a shadow on a white cardboard with a lacy edge, showing between his aunt's reddened fingers, and a certain perfume, the hem of a dress where he tries to hide because people are shouting, he's not alone with her, and every time he's there something breaks out above him

199

and he feels smaller than usual and burrows around in the folds of her dress.

"She was the youngest, but she'd have been better off working in the factory like the rest of us. We were all girls, but we never had a chance to be real girls. But she wanted children so much."

She smooths away at a stubborn fold in a tablecloth that isn't there. He feels that she has indeed come as close as she can, and even that she's never been that close to a man, that she's reached her own limit, and probably got hurt every time she came near it before, and that's why she stays away among her pots and pans, in silence, for she's not married and she could have been a mother but didn't even have that to offer. But she can't tell him about it. And what good would it do? There are so many walls to be jumped over, and he too has already learned to empty himself to protect against rejection. Though he's not ready to promise to kill Jane off, to enter on the submission to solitude expected of him, he makes a small step forward through his emptiness to say:

"If you'd had kids of your own you'd have been different."

She takes one short, chilled look at this most ordinary of dreams, then catches herself at once:

"Before the children come there have to be men. And men..."

To cure her of men and deliver her from an infirmity he had perhaps ascribed to her too soon, he tries quickly to fill this silence into which she had dumped the race of men:

"You could have been a mother, too."

He smiles at her with all the generosity he can muster, and she makes an involuntary face to ward off the sudden gust of warmth. Then she gets up, the funeral photo in her hand, unable to absent herself longer from her usual grim self. She has to pause to give respite to her back, for it obeys her only with a certain delay. As she goes into her room she issues an order:

"You won't run around with her any more. Maybe your uncle was just asking questions. Maybe..."

He doesn't answer, for it would only be a lie, and the threat is so far in the future. Somebody in the parlour is playing the piano. He goes to see.

It's Aunt Eugénie. The same fat bottom on the bench and a similar book of notes in front of her. How come she's playing? He doesn't understand. She works at a trade, she makes collars, how can she penetrate the mysteries of educated Uncle Nap? But she doesn't play for herself. She plays for the others, laughing, never repeating a phrase, with the pride of a child accomplishing something difficult. He goes closer and sees PERVENCHE printed at the top of the sheet. Without stopping she informs the others:

"It's the boy. He's more like his mother."

Every night she changes and puts on makeup and does her hair for a party that never happens, for she never goes farther than the church and always sees the same friends. He knows she never wanted to have children and she's very close to thinking and wishing she had a different life and if it weren't for Aunt Maria she'd always be in good humour, all by herself, without looking back or forward.

When she stops she turns around and admits with a smile that can only provoke polite protest:

"I usually play it better, but it's been such a long time..."

It's not the same music as his uncle's, though he couldn't say why. It's like chattering, and it doesn't get to your nerves so much.

"But you didn't stumble once!"

"That takes you back, that piece does."

Are they all old maids, too? Probably, for they work with her, and dress the same and pretend all together that they're having a good time as if they were young girls about to turn into ladies who can get on very well without a man.

"Good Lord, has he heard everything you've been telling us?"

"About the bathroom? And even if he did, he wouldn't understand."

"All the same! When she sighs, and says to him, 'Now go cover up and wait till we're in bed!'"

"Well, let's ask him, now he's here."

They have a great laugh, as if they were going to play a fine trick on him.

"What do you hear in the bathroom, through the window over the roof?" asks Aunt Eugénie, certain he'll give an answer that will make them all laugh again.

"The doctor beating his wife," he says, to make them happy.

And at least three of them come out with the same exclamation:

"He calls that beating his wife, the poor kid!"

Through the window of the light-well, always open, the aunts listen to the play of the young doctor and his wife making love below, for they're newly-weds, and you can't imagine the things they invent, and there's really no way to quiet a man, even one as distinguished as the doctor.

The laughs and voices die away in a new void of silence, which seems to make them anxious, for they all start fidgeting at the same time, and Aunt Eugénie announces with beatific false modesty:

"I'll try the other piece. It's harder."

This time she makes her attack with a very serious face, wagging her shoulders slightly like Uncle Nap. On the sheet he reads: MENUET A L'ANTIQUE, and goes back to the empty kitchen.

His blood runs so slowly, and his whole body is so heavy, that he has no time to summon a glint of gold in the darkness of his mind before he goes to sleep.

18

The door opens so suddenly that he can't find the facecloth in the water and has to cover himself with his hands.

Aunt Maria comes in the bathroom and looks him over from head to foot with her eyes in which the blue seems to have run.

"Will you get out of here!" she says finally, choking with a raging cough.

"Go out yourself. I was here first."

Indignant at being caught in this defenceless state, he'd love to hurl the soap right at her face. She pretends to be looking for something in the wall cupboard, then looks at him again, murmuring:

"Little pig! You could have bolted the door!"

He's used to the evil-mindedness of the crows, something that had no name and was worse than a slap for it was real and not real at the same time, like when Pigfoot made Justin take off his clothes and looked at him for a long time before going at him furiously with her hardwood board, but they all knew how to stick together against that. Aunt Maria's worse, and he can't move, alone with her like this. She was the one who told him never to turn the bolt, for it didn't work properly, and he could lock himself in. She probably hung around behind the door, for he didn't hear her coming, so he was ready for the worst. But he feels tied hand and foot by this stare that pretends not to stare, while scorching him with its intensity.

It's the first time he's been naked in the water. In the other place they'd been put through the ceremony of a collective bath from time to time, and everyone hated it, though it gave them a chance to act up. They had to put on ragged trunks and wait, two by two, in a line in front of a tub so high you climbed up a little step-ladder to get in, still by two's, and the only real humiliation was that moment, when you had to face each other in the tub and watch a crow scrubbing the other one, revolted by the dirty scum of the water already used by predecessors. Maybe there had been two tubs, he didn't remember.

But alone and naked with Maria, there's nothing to act up about. All he can do is insult her as grossly as possible so that she'll go out at once. So he shouts at the top of his voice (for the door is open):

"Aunt Rose, come and see the dirty old woman!"

He gets a slap that sends him spinning, but she goes out and slams the door. He dresses without drying himself.

And rushes into the bedroom where Aunt Maria is lying in misery on her bed, a handkerchief over her mouth. He raises his hand to return her blow, for there is no doubt in his mind that he has to bring her to terms once and for all, and any means is fair. But his hand stops in mid-air for it seems she's not pretending but really crying and sobbing, and she seems to be ashamed, wringing her hands and breathing with a sound of rustling paper, like the Rat. She still manages to shout:

"Out of my room, you little wretch!"

He'd like nothing better, but he's no longer sure if it's not himself who's unnatural, because of coming from the other place, if he's not the one suffering from some infirmity, consisting precisely of having spent too long in the chateau, hurting people out of ignorance, for he's just discovering them and his ignorant gaze is a torture to them because he abolishes their whole lives which have given them their faces, their gaze, their gestures, and along he comes being surprised at things that surprise no one else, asking questions no one asks, throwing stones because there's nothing else to do when you're faced with a wall. Aunt Rose is no longer quite the same, now, for she's given him to understand that perhaps you have to accept, that there's no other reality but what you see, except that what you see, strangely enough, has to be there, for what could have been is not, and there's nothing you can do about it.

And so he lowers his arm and murmurs, biting his lip:

"I'm sorry. I was...I was..."

He can't find a word to allude to the nameless thing without giving it a name.

"Little monster! A man! Dirty, just like a man, that's why I never married."

"I'm not dirty," he protests. "I'm not used to bathrooms, it's not the same."

His aunt seizes him by his two wrists and talks without stopping, though she's still crying and coughing and sobbing:

"It starts with little kids like you. They want to see, they want to know. And it's like that forever after. It's dirty, not just like hands or feet, but in their heads. Like dogs! You've watched dogs, haven't you! I could never have touched a man or let him touch me. Nor wash his shitty underwear. And you come saying you're sorry! You're just like the others."

"Have you always been afraid like that?" he asks, in his detached observer tone.

"Six months from now I may be able to tell you why," she says, cherishing her mystery.

"Being afraid makes people mean. Like dogs, the way you said."

"We know what it is, loving men. Dirty dogs."

"Why in six months? If I knew you were afraid today..."

"You'll know by then. And it's not fear, it's..."

"And what about all the other women that are married and have children?"

"They put up with it. Like your mother..."

At this word he knows he was wrong to listen to her, that what she says is a lie, and that it's a kind of sickness in her head, and she's as much like the crows as he had thought at first. Coldly, he asks:

"Why did you come in the bathroom?"

"Because you'd been there too long, and there was something I needed."

"That's not true. And what you say about men, that's all in your head, and it's probably you and not them."

"You snot-nosed little devil! Get out! You can't even respect a woman's tears."

She sits up, waving her arms in a blue rage, and spits in his face.

He wipes it off with a corner of her sheet, calmly.

"I'm not scared of you, you know. Nor your sickness. What about Uncle Nap? If he didn't get married, did he think the same thing about women?"

205

He goes out on the balcony to listen to the rain which has been falling since morning, a heavy, steady rain that will never stop. Over at Jane's place, nothing but silence and absence.

If only she would appear he'd run away with her, for always. He'd teach her that you don't have to go through all this ugliness, and what they'll discover together can only be better, all they need is to be alone, the two of them, and always able to see each other without even touching, and so invent their days, for others always lie and have invented in their own heads the thing they call their life. Even the rain is real only if it prevents you from seeing someone. Otherwise it's nothing. And Jane will never be afraid, for he'll always be there. And he'll always be as patient as he needs to be, waiting for her to get over being angry, for anger is like hunger, it always goes away in the end.

19

A long while after lunch something finally happens. Time suddenly stops falling slower than the rain, and he cocks his ear at once, ready to dash outside. It comes from the alleyway, a voice that sings as if at vespers, taking up the same phrase time after time, starting very high and sliding downward, leaving just silence enough to draw a breath. The psalm is very close now, in front of the high melting poplars of the old people's home across the way. He rushes out on the back gallery. It's a vegetable peddler, crouching under an old umbrella with missing ribs, drifting along his route as if borne against his will down the streaming gutter, calling his wares in a voice that waits for no reply. His horse is so wet that its hair hangs in pointed tufts all along its belly and on its fetlocks.

"Hey! Monsieur!" Pierrot shouts with all his might.

The man sticks his neck out from under the umbrella, looks up at him incredulously.

The door of the green porch next door opens a crack, and a voice that hasn't eaten for days calls him in a whisper:

"Come in! Come quick, Pierrot!"

"Why are you shouting like that?" asks his aunt, who doesn't dare set foot in the wet gallery.

"It's the vegetable man."

"I don't want anything, and it's no weather for running down in the alley."

"Doesn't matter. I feel like wet carrots."

And he dashes into the green porch, which smells of wet sawdust and sunless dust, but where the warmest light of Arabia, Jane herself, is to be found, pale in her dressing gown and pink pyjamas over which, resplendent, falls her loosened hair which he never thought could grow so long in a single night.

"Come back here this minute," storms his aunt, who still doesn't venture out.

A little mouth, burning like a wasp's sting on his lips, hot hands on his neck, the smell of hair everywhere in his face.

"Come in, quick. I just washed my hair."

He enters a room which corresponds to his uncle's den, but is unfurnished except for a few cushions on the floor, dozens of dolls, several decapitated or armless, picture books scattered everywhere, empty chocolate boxes, a big mirror on the wall and wide white muslin curtains on the window.

"My grandmother went out a long time ago, and she made me wash my hair so I couldn't go out. This is my playroom."

"It's the same as my uncle's den. That's where I sleep. But it seems bigger. That's because it's yours."

"See all the paint spots I made on the carpet? I told Mama I'd go on making them if she didn't stay with me sometimes."

She makes a face as she contemplates the mess, and the spots which look as if they'd fallen from the ceiling, there are so many of them, all about the same size but in different colours.

"When there's no more room I'm going to start on the good blue carpet in the parlour, and they'll all be red so you can see them. Imagine! She tells me I'm not allowed in the front room. As if it stopped being my home out there."

The kitchen is the same, too, but the table is varnished wood, the chairs have wicker seats and the windows look out on the next house instead of on the street.

"I've been looking over at your place for more than an hour. I even managed to get a shutter open. See, this one. But you, you didn't even look this way."

"I was helping Aunt Rose wax the floors. I knew you wouldn't be allowed out in this rain."

"So that's the smell! Floorwax! Grandmother told me I mustn't get dressed, there was no point in it."

Being there with her, and because – even counting the polishing – he'd never spent such a long day, he realizes the incredible loneliness of Jane in this apartment, which around her seems ten times as big as his aunts' place. He asks:

"What do you do when you're by yourself?"

"The same as when Grandmother's here. All she does is listen to the radio and eat chocolates. The only time she speaks is to say don't. It's more fun alone. She doesn't even know my dolls' names, and she saw them all come into the world."

He looks at her in wonderment, but ill at ease for he's never been alone with her in a house. He sits down, gets up, goes to the window, comes back. It intimidates him even more to see her dressed as if for bed, her hair so long it makes her face still smaller, and he feels as if he were spying on a Jane who's alone in her room and forbidden to his eyes.

"I haven't any games for boys," she says, disgruntled. "And I don't have games for more than one to play. When Mama plays with me she pretends something's wrong with her and she doesn't pay attention."

It's the same soothing voice, and she's just as natural as outside, but something's missing, they're not really together, and it's not games he misses but someplace to go and just walk together. Without realizing it they manage to avoid each other and when one gets up the other sits down. He looks around toward the dining-room and parlour, but she quickly says:

"No, we can't go there. That belongs to Mama and the gentlemen that come home with her in the evening. It's cold and not nice there. There's nothing but the balcony..."

She doesn't end her sentence, but opens the door to her bedroom.

"I'm mostly in here. Not that I sleep all the time!"

Her laugh, just the same as it is when they're outside or at Mama Pouf's, relaxes him a little.

"This is my cave. It's the only place where I can talk to myself. Sometimes I go for hours without talking, then I talk to myself, fast, fast, just to hear myself."

There's a bed that's far too big for her, a little desk in natural wood with books, scribblers and ink bottles. And a long, white dresser covered with girl things and in the middle a large photo that doesn't smile at all, a man who must be tall and blond, with a young face so smooth and empty it looks sandpapered. Even the smart peaked Air Force cap looks as if it had been drawn in after the photo was made.

"That's Daddy," she says, very proudly, with a strong English accent. "He really is handsome and nice, isn't he? He's often the one I talk to, and I'm sure he hears me, for when I look at him a long time, especially at night, his eyes move. But I don't remember what his voice was like."

Her mouth turns down at the thought of that voice she no longer hears, then she springs up again, laughing:

"I tried to draw a green bear, but the green was all I got right. Come here, I'll show you."

In her playroom she searches among the scribblers and books scattered on the carpet, spills the water jar for her paints, then finally with a comical little shrug holds up a large sheet of paper on which a big green balloon is waiting to take form, as if it had not been quite blown up.

"Is he running very fast?" asks Pierrot.

"Why?"

"Because, you can't see his head or his legs."

"I left holes for his eyes, but the paint ran."

From his pocket he takes the teddy bear of the man in blue, sets it up, and tries to correct the balloon. She lies on her stomach and watches.

"There aren't many things sticking out from a bear," he explains. "Bits of ears, a little tail and four cucumbers."

"She said yesterday it was all settled, I was going to a convent because I always had to have my own way. And she'd found a house near where we lived before, and it wasn't far from the convent."

"She's only trying to scare you. Don't worry," he said, wetting the paintbrush in his mouth.

"I wanted to tell her about Emily, but she was with the same man and he was kissing her, and she said, 'Not in front of her, please!' – but she didn't mean it. You know, I've decided I don't love her any more, for I only bother her all the time, and I told her she wasn't to have visitors every night."

"All right, we're going to run away. I decided we should, anyway."

"You draw pretty well, but you should have started fresh. His colour will run in the snow. Afterwards she was crying out, with terrible sighs, as if the man was beating her."

"You must have dreamed it. She doesn't look as if she'd let anybody beat her."

She picks up a doll with its eyes torn out and an enormous black moustache, and protests angrily:

"I did not dream it. And it's not the first time. It happens with the others, too. She cries so loud sometimes you'd think she can't breathe."

"Then she's the one that's dreaming. That happens, you know."

210

"I asked her about it and she got mad right away and said what goes on at night is no business of little girls. So I put out the doll's eyes for it was a Russian doll and I hated it. Then I gave it a moustache and threw it at the wall. I even burn her with a match sometimes."

He sets the bear up to dry by the wall, and sticks his fingers in the empty sockets of the doll's eyes.

"Is the doll the nasty man now?" he asks.

"Yes. She's Olga, and now I call her Mister Pig."

"I'll paint her a pair of pants with holes in. Then she won't look like a girl any more."

"Pig is English for *cochon*. What'll we do when we get to the country of the Great Cold?"

She leans over him to see how he draws black lines down the doll's legs.

"Leave the burn marks, so they'll go on hurting."

"He's going to be so ugly nobody will ever come to see your Mama any more. Well now, it was Balibou in the shape of a green polar bear who went to sit on the ice floe. The deer pulled the caboose backwards onto the ice and disappeared."

He can see nothing but her hair, which falls in a curtain around his head, and it's hard to think of ice floes in all that chestnut red, but he doesn't move for it's as if the rain had stopped, and he can smell the flowers of the soap in her hair.

"What's an ice floe?"

"Countries floating on the ocean at the North Pole. Should I give him a beard, too?"

"Yes, and pimples all over. How can a country float?"

"Blue pimples. That's worse. People that don't know any better think they're just blocks of ice as big as the United States and nothing on them. But they're wrong for they don't have a green bear."

She stands up suddenly, shakes her head to get her hair behind and pretends to shiver.

"It's too cold. Tell me in bed. It's easier to believe when you're lying down."

He picks up the man in blue's teddy bear.

"Do you know what he said when you were mad because your sister was beautiful and sick?"

She passes him a pillow, and lies down with her hair fanned out.

"I have no sister. What did he say?"

211

"He said tomorrow, at a quarter after twelve, the sun's going to disappear and the birds will stop singing."

"Not rain again! Mama says I have to go out in the country with her all day!"

"No, I think he meant there wouldn't be a sun but not because of clouds. And that would mean we're going to see him on Sunday. And if that didn't happen the white flowers wouldn't be dead."

"He's crazy, and he's a liar and a cheat. And what's he doing with my sister?"

"What sister?"

"Plush, you make me sick. I'll scream. Now: Balibou on the ice floe, is he waiting for it to snow?"

"You didn't let me tell you that those floating countries are very, very hollow, and what you see is just the roof. And a country as big as that floating around in the water can be dangerous. That's why they always have a little white bear on top."

"So why is Balibou green?"

"When he turns green it means there's danger and they open the door – they call it a porthole – and they get him inside fast, and then the country dives deeper into the water to go beneath boats or other countries and so on."

"Who opens the door?"

"The people in the ice floe."

"Oh. Living in the block of ice. But they must have a bear already, so Balibou would be one too many."

"No! Don't you see, when Balibou arrives the other bear is white, but he's green, so they open up and we go in."

She curls up close to him, slipping a hot hand under his sweater. He's so busy with his story that he barely notices.

"Why do we want to go into the ice? Hold me tight, I'm cold. You've got funny ideas about going around the world, you have."

"We want to go in because the ice floe is on its way to the North Pole and you have to go there to get to the South Pole."

"Your skin isn't like a boy's. It's smooth."

"If you don't stay quiet we'll be stuck on top of the ice floe and freeze."

But she goes on caressing him under his sweater, and now he can't fail to notice it because she's taken his hand and put it beneath her pink pyjama top which is as soft as her skin, and he'd rather she didn't do all that stuff, for her little hand tickles but her skin under the pyjama makes him want to shiver though he's not cold. So he rushes back to the story.

"There's a long escalator like the one in the store where I went with Aunt Rose, and it's so deep it gets us right down to the warm part of the ice floe. The sun shines through the ice and inside it's as bright and nice as when you play with the sun on a looking-glass, but everything's green, the streets, the houses and the people too."

"Well! Now I'm getting hot! Why is everything green, especially the people?"

She takes off her dressing-gown, pulls up his sweater and places her lips against his naked skin, and he has to talk through her hair and observes his hand, as if it belonged to someone else, on the peach-coloured skin below her pyjama top.

"Because wherever there's life there's green. Especially in ice. And all the people there are children. I mean, they never grow up, but they're not dwarfs or little people like in the stories. They stay children for a hundred years and then they grow up in five minutes and die. There's no money or work or school but machines everywhere for getting green food and everybody does what he likes all the time. They don't have to talk for they can read each other's minds, and that's good, for they know what's what all the time and nobody can lie, but nobody wants to anyway, for they can do what they like, and there aren't any policemen for they can see through each other and they know they're good and don't want to hurt anybody."

She lies on her back and undoes her pyjama top, sighing:

"Don't you think I'm pretty? Do they never have any children, if they're always children themselves?"

"You're pretty, but you're so little I'd need another word. Little mouse..."

She bursts out laughing and repeats:

"Little mouse! Now, tell me about their children."

"Of course they have children, or it wouldn't be a country."

"How do they get them?"

"Well, I don't know. That's their secret."

"Do you know how we make children?"

"Yes."

"How?"

"They go to the hospital."

"Wrong! The man has to put his seed into the woman. Mama told me."

She laughs again from under his sweater. Then, suddenly serious, she asks:

"Have you never seen a girl?"

"Dozens of them. I can't even count them. And I see you."

"That's not what I mean."

She sits up, kisses him on the mouth, stroking his ear, and he has such an urge to rush outside that he doesn't dare move a finger.

"It's hot here," he says.

"You should be hot," she murmurs in his ear in a voice as smooth as silk.

And he sees that she has taken her pyjamas completely off, that the gold of her hair has never been so soft, for its light glimmers on her small belly and her long thighs that make him so hungry he begins to tremble.

"I mean, did you ever see a girl this way? How I am, I mean. See?"

And she takes his head and bends it so that he can see between her thighs when she spreads them.

"That's where you have to put the seed. Did you see?"

He hadn't seen for he'd shut his eyes, and his stomach is burning so that he'd like to crawl naked on the ice floe.

"It's nice," he says. "There's nothing there."

She takes his hand, which is no longer his, for he has no control over it, and lays it down there where there's nothing, and her voice, trembling slightly, begins to hurt him.

"You have to see with your fingers. The little hole for the seed. Look."

It's as if he was playing at putting his finger in her ear, but an ear like a sponge, soft and slightly wet, and warm. She twists a little, and still has the strange voice that hurts him, a hurt that runs faster than his blood and he can't stop it and doesn't want to. And Jane's little hand presses softly against his blood at the place where it never beat so hard, and he's so afraid she might take her hand away that his blood stops, and she slides beneath him, and his heart is beating against the sponge and an unknown force inside him, which was never him before but now grips every part of him and pushes him outside himself, makes him sink into the voice of Jane's stomach, and she groans:

"Push, push..."

But suddenly his blood ebbs, and the sponge resists.

214

"You're not grown-up enough yet," Jane says in her usual voice, slowly stroking his back. She too is quieter now, appeased, almost like a grown-up herself.

"That's where the seed comes from. But you're not ready. It's like me, I don't have any breasts yet. And what happens to the green child people in the ice floe?"

It had all happened so quickly, like a secret that had grown naturally between them because they loved each other, like love itself which had only been a word until now, though heavy with a mystery that he had always felt without knowing its nature. For lovers are always struck by love unexpectedly, that it's not until he looks again at her little face with its lovely but irregular features, now framed again in pink, that he realizes something just happened that will force him to think about it for a long time, and everything has changed, forever. Discovering her, he discovers himself, and he looks at the wall as he says:

"I love you, Jane."

"I love you too, Pierrot. For life."

He kisses her gravely on the forehead like a knight who has been admitted to the mystery. And he picks up the story:

"Well, your red hair goes and gets us into trouble again."

"It's not red, it's auburn!"

"The green children don't know the difference. In that country full of ice the thing they're most afraid of is fire. And when they see your hair in a colour they've never seen before, they forbid us to walk around their city, and shut us up in their coldest room."

"I suppose the colour of your hair doesn't bother them for it's always been green."

"Mine looks more like sunlight when you see it through ice. It doesn't scare them so much. But they're not bad, you see, and they can read in our minds that we love each other, they shut us up together in a place where there are movies and electric cars and pretty green dolls. But Balibou's in a bad way. They can read in his head that he's only a cat, and a dirty one at that with a stumpy tail, and they think he's a liar because he disguises himself, and they'll never know where they're at with him. So they make him go up the long escalator again and chase him out in the snow, where he turns snow white. But the older ones – and don't forget, their faces are just like ours – they get together to study the question. In their whole history, and they've been going on longer than we have, they never had to judge anyone. The thing is, when it stops snow-

215

ing Balibou will turn green again and the other bear cub that's their guide won't be able to pilot them because of the mix up. They take three days thinking about it, for they see in our heads that we like Balibou, and then they decide to shut him up in the caboose and give him nothing to eat."

"Oh, no!"

"And they tell you they have to, for they eat nothing but green food and it turns you green, and that would only make Balibou's problem worse."

"Do we turn green too?"

"Sure! The very next day your hair turns green, and they let us out for a walk in town, and it's nicer than under the biggest trees or the swimming pool on the boat."

"I don't want green hair."

"You don't need to say it. They can read it in your head. They tell you, as soon as you've left their country and eat some raw fish your hair will turn red again."

"I hate raw fish."

"You won't hate it when you're out on the snow again and your hair is all green."

"Why do you make up such horrible stories? I'm always the one who has a bad time."

"I'm green, too!"

He makes the teddy bear cub jump around on her pink pyjamas.

"Just like him. With blue eyes. Don't I look handsome?"

"It's not the same for you. You get me into all sorts of scrapes," she says, with an odd laugh that makes her seem strange to him all of a sudden. "I need a drink of milk right away. You scared me."

She gets off the bed by crawling on all fours toward the foot. He can see the outline of her body under the thin stuff of her pyjamas, and now that he's stopped telling his story and doesn't have to make his head run around inventing crazy things, he has time to think more coolly of what happened before, so coolly that what happened before suddenly sends a chill up his spine. He tries once again to tell himself that he's come from too far away to understand things immediately, and that everything he'd imagined in the other place came out of books or what he had experienced inside those walls, and he must make himself wait a long time before even thinking about reacting in a new way, or reacting at all.

Jane comes back with two glasses of milk, some cookies and a chocolate bar. Seeing her like this, walking clumsily because she's trying to carry too many things, her face pale and her features drawn, her nostrils pinched, her hair unkempt, as if she'd been running makes her seem still more like a stranger to him. He can't understand how he could have wished for a moment that she might enter into him, become himself, so that the two of them would have one head, one heart, that the russet-gold cloud might be forever inside him, hidden from all others. Now he discovers that she's different from the girl he saw the first time, the one who made him happy at once by making a face at him; and he discovers that he'd never since seen anything in her but that one picture, as if she'd been without a body – which would explain why he didn't like to see her eat. And what he feels now, thinking about what just happened (where somebody else, not he, someone unknown to him, wanted to devour Jane) reminds him too much of Jane eating. He's lost the squirrel, whose essence was so light and delicate, and found himself with the Jane who eats, whose head is too small for her body; and he himself has known for the first time, a terrible hunger of which he is faintly ashamed without knowing why, and it's a bit like anger for it flamed up so quickly, but it was an anger that brought relief, as eating does. Maybe that meant not being a child any more. Maybe Jane already wasn't a child when she made the face at him over the bannister, maybe she'd fooled him a little without meaning to.

For the first time he looks at Jane, too, with his detached gaze of someone from far away, and isn't quite sure about her, as he isn't sure about the others, and it's not the same as being afraid he won't see her tomorrow.

"Well, you could take a glass instead of staring as if you'd seen a ghost. Pssst! Hey! It's me!"

And she spills half of one glass while holding the other out to him. He takes a mouthful and puts the glass on the long dresser where the aviator's handsome face is constantly emptied into the evening grey of the bedroom wrapped in rain. She gulps down a biscuit, then unwraps the chocolate bar and puts it in his mouth for a bite.

"Why won't they let us eat snow? It's white, at least,"

"Because they only live off green things. I told you."

"What's wrong, Plush? Why do you talk as if I'd disappointed you?"

She's eating the chocolate with one hand, fingers in her mouth, and running the other through his hair.

"Sunlight through the ice, that was what you said. It's true. You're not like other poeple. You've got ice in your eyes sometimes."

"That's all silly stuff. I just say anything at all."

She lies down, her head in the hollow of his shoulder, licking her fingers.

"No, there's something real in the stories you tell. Go on."

She yawns, a long yawn, with chocolate on her nose.

"I'm sleepy, but never mind. I'll listen. What about the green children's babies?"

He'd like to leave her now, and be alone, think about her without seeing her, for she prevents him from thinking about her. And he doesn't like her asking that question again, for it's not the same question now, as if the most important thing was no more than a piece of chocolate, for example.

"That's easy to guess. Because they're green. They plant them in the ground, like grass."

She's swept away on the waves of her deep, regular breathing, one hand (slightly sticky) under his sweater, the other lost in the russet that no longer shines.

He goes on for a while, as if saying a rosary:

"After a week there's an earthquake on the ice floe, for it just hit the North Pole, and the Pole is a country of ice mountains on the earth. You're green as a cabbage and not very pretty, for you ate a lot more green than I did. They make us go up the high escalator and just before they open the porthole they make us drink a little bottle of stuff that makes us forget we were ever on an ice floe. And the last green child we see grows big as a man in a minute and dies. And they grind him to powder before our eyes and put him in the bottle we just drank from. And Balibou brings you a big frozen fish."

He lies down beside her and gives in, like her, to his breathing which soon has him turning, turning. He lays one arm over her pink pyjamas and his hand touches cookie crumbs.

"And that makes you even greener, for you feel sick to your ..."

* * *

The light, suddenly switched on, hurts his eyes, and the voice hurts too, dry, shrill, more piercing than if it were loud:

"Well, I declare! A young man in my daughter's bed. And she's in pyjamas!"

Through the hurt of his eyes he sees a tall, blonde woman and, behind her with his arm around her waist, a man laughing, murmuring:

"They're only children. Don't make such a fuss!"

"Children, my dear! When it's gone this far they aren't children any more. If you please!"

"Hello, Mama" says Jane, squinting. She accidentally touches Pierrot and gives a frightened start as if they hadn't just spent hours together.

"Now, you be quiet. And you're not to get up. As for you, sir – I suppose you're the little neighbour boy – you can go back to your virtuous aunts. I'm going to have a pretty story to tell them!"

He has regained his submarine point of view, and he finds her a very interesting lady, who talks with fine words and pronounces them carefully and puts her anger together calmly, the way you draw a picture, without losing her temper. The man still smiling behind her speaks again in a thick voice as if his mouth were full of cotton:

"I don't know, I think they look just fine together. It's even rather...touching."

"Please go and wait for me in the front room. If you please. This is a family affair." She's having less success at hiding her anger.

The laughing man withdraws, tripping over his own feet, bowing and clowning:

"Madame, Arthur awaits you in the salon. To the salon. . . Arthur!"

He disappears into the shadows, doubled up with laughter.

"Mama, I never want to see him again, that man! I'm going to run away," Jane screams, filled with panic and anger at once. She turns to Pierrot and kisses him on the mouth in her rage.

"And don't you try to tell me anything. All the men can touch you, and you never kiss me once."

"Jane, we don't talk about family in front of strangers. And I'm the one who does the bringing-up, not you," says the lady, very coldly.

He gets up, never taking his eyes from hers, far away behind his iceberg.

"The door is there, monsieur, and don't let me see you again!"

He stoops down to Jane and kisses her in turn, but he kisses a storm.

"I don't like you any more, Mama! I hate you, forever!"

He bows, as the man had done, and says very politely – and it's she who lowers her eyes, but with such dignity you'd think she was closing them on a hurt that was too noble for him to see:

"Goodbye, madame. She and I are going away for life. We've reached the North Pole already. The ice floe is very beautiful."

Sitting up in bed, Jane is shadow-boxing. She stops just long enough to protest:

"I didn't even hear the end."

Then she stands up on the bed, where she's almost as tall as her mother:

"You and your parachutes! That's just an excuse not to have any time for me. What's more, I saw Emily yesterday and I won't tell you about it. Go on out to the parlour. Go and let him beat you."

As he opens the door to the back porch he can still hear her shouting:

"This is my room. Just go. Go and let him beat you, you like that better than kissing me!"

How could she talk that way to such a beautiful, well-dressed lady, who calls him "monsieur," pursing up her mouth very haughtily, as dignified as Saint Sabine unwilling to speak of her sufferings caused by visions?

And why doesn't Jane come out and walk in the dark with him, just like that?

20

Beautiful trees, such as he's never seen, tall, isolated, very dark green on immense stretches of well-kept grass. There's even a colonnade and two heavy, black iron gates. This could be the real park of the chateau, if the Blue Man had finally taken time off from the affairs of the world to set them free from their prisoners' smocks and let them pass through to the other side of their view that was flat as pictures in a book.

There is a long walk, perfectly straight, that leads to a round pillar in pink stone surmounted by a greenish gentleman who surveys the crowd approaching in its Sunday best, a quiet, almost silent crowd which after the pillar disperses in all directions along narrow paths bordered with clipped grass and wreaths or crosses or bouquets of flowers so numerous that they crush each other.

In front of him walk the three aunts, equally spaced, wearing hats with little black veils, except Eugénie, who has a blue one. Maria's thick legs form a roll above her new shoes. Rose, straight as a ramrod, letting her purse hang down like a pail of water, marches with a firm step as if it all belonged to her, and Eugénie, who trots oddly because one side of her ass is always slightly late, bobs her head, her small veil waving, and reminds him of a pigeon cooing.

"This is the anniversary," Rose had announced in a tone that allowed of no comment.

And it's like a feast, this beautiful setting in which he feels like a visitor, where nothing can exist but calm and relaxation. Birds, invisible and with unfamiliar songs, accompany the promenade with a sound like the bubbling of fountains. He is wearing for the first time his good navy-blue suit with short pants, which disguises him as a little gentleman not allowed to run on the grass. His polished shoes with their hard soles are punishing his feet and he has some trouble walking like a boy who's used to the family pleasures of a stroll in the park.

At the feet of the man on the pedestal there's a consultation.

"It's that way," states Eugénie, pointing down the middle path.

"You always say that and we always have to come all the way back," says Aunt Maria, whose face is pink and almost pleasant under her black veil.

"It all depends where you start," Aunt Rose pronounces. Even when her voice isn't loud, it's grumpy.

The crowd splits around them and flows in equal streams down the three paths.

"We'll start with our own, we don't know the other so well," Maria decides.

"It's not far away anyhow," says Eugénie, and starts off down the middle way.

Maria and Rose take the path to the right, and Eugénie resigns herself to joining them, trudging across the grass, grumbling:

"It's always the same. They'll have to come back."

And the procession is on its way again. They pass alongside little cellars that back into grassy banks, with doors of big iron bars. He peeks inside one, but Rose drags him away and as she adjusts his bow tie (which is strangling him) she lets him know:

"We don't look in. It's not polite."

Then there are no more trees, but suddenly, as far as you can see, vertical stones close side by side, with posies of flowers tossed helter-skelter as if by a gardener too busy to watch where they fell. Chiseled into the stones are names, numbers and even Latin words.

It's his first cemetery, and he doesn't find it a sad place, in fact it's a lot more fun than Lagauchetière Street, and it doesn't make you think for a minute about the phrase "six feet under" and what that evokes. He finds, in fact, that they've done it with a good deal of imagination, and children could play there quite nicely. There's not a dead man in sight.

He stops at a stone that's taller than the others and counts the names. Thirteen, with their dates. He reckons that with their stone so close to all the others, only names can be buried there. There's no room.

Finally, the aunts have discovered something. Eugénie, who's the most alert by a long shot, announces, quite pleased with herself:

"Here are the Larochelles. It's just over there."

She almost sounded as if she'd been going to say, "Just three doors down." The stone is a squared pillar, with a cross on top like an X. There are no flowers, and the neighbours seem to have encroached a little on its land, edging closer. The aunts kneel and simultaneously pull out their rosaries, and Maria is the one who says her beads aloud, with long pauses which the others observe as well. When she has finished, she bursts into sobs, and people look at her with discreet sympathy, for everybody knows that. . .She stays a long time thus, her eyes riveted to the earth, yellowed in the middle of its space.

Pierrot gets up because his bare knees hurt, and looks up, where he sees something quite different. He begins to tremble, and he has to open and close his eyes several times to be sure it's not an effect of light on his mind. The sky has turned dark blue, there's not a cloud to be seen, and the sun is being devoured by a shadow which now covers it almost entirely. Just a little fringe is left.

He listens, and it seems that the birds' voices are stilled, one after the other, and it's really night in the cemetery, and all is so quiet that suddenly he can hear Maria's wet breathing. She has stopped crying. And the sun throws out in all directions little arms of flame which try to fight their way out under the devouring shadow. And when all is dark, Maria lies down on the grave and kisses the earth, sobbing so hard that people looking up at the sky glance down to where she lies. He sees, too, three stones farther along, a thin young woman with a stomach so enormous that she has to lean back to keep her balance, with a child holding each hand. She too begins to sob, and his own eyes begin to burn, for it's the first time he's seen a pregnant woman, and there's no papa there, and the sun is shaking off its shadow, and all the birds start singing loudly, and a squirrel darts like lightning between her legs and obliges the pregnant woman to step back so quickly that one child falls and she herself has to grasp a gravestone, and saves herself by leaning on it, her feet in a floral wreath.

"That's Alma's daughter," Eugénie tells them. "Her husband got drowned in the port. I thought she'd had the baby. There was some kind of eclipse, did you see that?"

Maria is on her feet, and because of her veil you can see the tears only when they drip from her chin. The two others take her arms. They have to look for a long time before finding the other place, which isn't with "theirs." Finally, it turns out to be a very small stone, rounded on top.

He wonders if it's only people from their own neighbourhood who die, or if they bury together only people that know each other so they can find them more easily, so that perhaps the whole city that's still unknown to him is here in different parts, divided in the same way, with the same families in the same places.

"Four years today," sighs Rose. "I still can't believe it. The youngest of us all! Come here, manikin, this is it."

"And the baby we never saw again!" adds Eugénie.

He looks, hastily, and sees nothing but a name – his name all right – cut in the stone like the others, but he doesn't try to see any more for the name seems as strange to him as his own face in a mirror, for he refuses to find the slightest connection between the stone and that which no longer stirs in the deepest place of his memory. He has always refused, and always will, to go back through time to find the source of all cold, but there is a kind of smile in his memory which has always been with him, though at a distance, a presence like the sky which is always there even if you don't look up, and an absence, too, which time has not healed, but which, because it can't be healed, he has also masked behind his block of ice.

This time it's Eugénie who says the rosary aloud, very fast, her small blue veil wagging.

There are signs that reach him just the same, and the snow-white forehead is there, and the perfume, or certain words, like when Saint Tomato made them peel vegetables or pick up washing in the laundry, or the contact of his own hand when he sleeps, but the signs disappear at once, for you can't keep them there. And this stone, with his own name on it, is so foreign to him that it never occurs to him that she might be there, or the baby.

The rosary ended, the three of them look at him without pity, waiting for something that doesn't happen.

"A real saint! What she had to put up with, and never a complaint!" says Aunt Rose.

From behind her black veil Aunt Maria is staring at him so fiercely that he can see her chin tremble. Then she burst out:

"And you don't even shed a tear. The first time you see her again!"

Suddenly he does cry, and he hadn't felt the tears coming, but they're tears of rage, against the aunts, the way they've arranged it all, the way they're old and still alive, dragging him there as if he were guilty, or should take the guilt for somebody else, and making a saint of her when they never talked about anybody without tearing them to pieces.

"There, you see, he does have a heart," says Aunt Rose, taking his side.

"She's not your mother. I don't want to see you again. Nor her either. Not with you!"

And he escapes, running like a madman, bumping into people, seized with panic in this graveyard as big as a city with its streets going in all directions and people in his road everywhere with their sad faces and watery eyes or shocked expressions, and stones that can't talk despite all the names cut into them, and cut flowers that also smell of death and give it a further presence here.

Today there was just one death, and that was Balibou, who had lived only in his head.

Uncle Nap had gone out right after lunch, in such good humour that he sang, "J'ai trouvé mon père égorgé dans son sang. . ." Just that one phrase about a father with his throat cut, but adding such jolly "dum-diddle-dums" that you knew he'd never get past that pool of blood. They'd told him that Uncle Nap disappeared every Saturday and came back very late, and nobody knew where he went. He always said he was going to a movie, and nobody, it seemed, had ever asked him how many films he saw the whole day long.

Then Pierrot had put on his new suit and waited on the back porch like a good boy, near the shutters which were closed upon Jane's absence, for his aunts to dress and take him to the party.

And he'd seen Balibou – with his whole tail, it was true, but the right colour and the same skinny alley-cat body. A little girl of four or five was throwing it down from the second storey of the next house. Each time the cat took a little longer to get to his feet and shake his spine to recover his spirits and wait for the child to come down and get him for another dive.

After the fourth time he'd decided that was enough, and the cat might never get up again, for Balibou in his normal shape as a pussy cat had a right to only nine lives like any other. Pierrot ran down the back stairs four at a time, glad of the chance to get a little dust on his new suit, and picked up the cat which was writhing and trembling interminably. But as soon as he had taken it in his arms and petted it Balibou had leapt for his face, spitting with rage, claws bared, and left his marks on one cheek, as if it were Pierrot who'd been torturing him.

If a cat could spit in his face like that, a cat he wanted to save from torture, Balibou must indeed be dead and nobody in the world knew him now.

He had taken some blood with his left hand from his wounded cheek and made a cross on the back of his right hand, singing in a voice that was full of the hurt of this senseless death:

"Dominus vobiscum!"

The little girl had watched him, laughing, her eyes joyous in the sunlight, then had picked up her pet by the scruff of its neck, the cat mewing with contentment, and climbed the stairs again to start her cat-and-mouse game all over.

Now he's running through the park with its invisible dead, through the sober-faced strollers looking for their own names on the stones, not because he's a little monster who doesn't cry when he sees his mother's earth for the first time, but because Balibou can never play a part in another of his stories, and there are no parks for cats to sleep in, and he understands that Jane by giving up her mystery to him, is herself the poorer for it, is less unique and less alone, for there can hardly be much difference between different girls' bodies, and perhaps a girl you know all about has fewer secrets than a boy; and he understands, too, but in the way you can understand letters without reading a whole word, that the mountain of unknown marvels has subsided noticeably, and in the depths of himself lurks someone he never knew who can be stronger than himself and take up all his room and make him do things he knows nothing about, and he's not sure if this is love, and he's not sure if Jane didn't invent it all because she likes to eat, not only with her mouth but with her whole body. He runs in the cemetery because life has got too far beyond him, and he's no longer sure what makes grown-ups freeze in the same role to the end of their days or what prevents them from having a different face every day, like children, and that in the light outdoors much darkness is concealed.

When he ran out to the balcony after breakfast the beautiful, cold, blonde lady was already sitting in the green car and Jane barely had time to stick her head out and throw him a kiss before being pulled roughly back inside. He had heard the lady speak very loudly, but couldn't understand the words. The man, dressed up like an American in red pants and a flowered shirt, made a funny gesture to him, a fist with the thumb up, before sliding behind the wheel and taking off fast, as if the beautiful lady had her toe on his foot.

He's still running. Wondering why at times Jane is afraid of nobody and even dares things he wouldn't dare himself, while at other times she's timid as a rabbit, and always does what she's told. Why is she going off now with that man when she said she'd rather run away forever than see him again? She'd only have had to wait for him at Mama Pouf's or in the park or in front of any restaurant. He'd have found her. Anywhere.

He's running, as well, through the white flowers that died because the birds stopped singing, in the shadow of the man in blue who made the sun go out, as he had promised, running toward the meeting he had also promised, where he was to reveal to Pierrot something very important that he's been waiting for a long time, for otherwise he wouldn't have given him such powerful signs that everyone could see to tell him he'd be at their meeting place. But what did he mean by the death of the white flowers?

He runs to the heavy black iron gates, and can't understand how, if he ran so fast, he can be confronted now by the veils of the three aunts, who are surely the deadest things in this park that would be so marvellous if it were kept for children.

"I've never been so ashamed of a relative," says Aunt Rose's bitter voice.

"She was your mother, your very own mother," Aunt Eugénie's trailing voice is scandalized.

"Little blasphemer!" says Aunt Maria, very briefly, but with a concentrated hatred he can almost touch. Aunt Maria, who kisses the earth to make the sun disappear.

The whole family climbs into the streetcar, silent, motionless where they sit, eyes closed upon their happiness, amid strangers as happy as they, speaking English.

21

"Eat your meat."

"No!"

"You don't even know what it is," Aunt Rose insists.

"Calf's liver! I suppose monsieur had too much of good things like that where he came from," Aunt Maria begins, softly. She seems to have something up her sleeve, for, not eating anything herself, she's staring at him without a pause, less than a foot away, her face redder and puffier than ever resting on her two fists.

"Calf's liver isn't good, and I don't want any."

He puts his plate in front of Maria.

"Here, you can have it. It's good for what you have."

But it's Rose who slaps him, holding back a little at the last moment, and this prevents him from retaliating violently.

In Uncle Nap's absence they're really going to let themselves go, he's sure of that. Ever since they came back they've left him alone on the balcony and followed Aunt Rose around as she prepared this little surprise for him, some kind of meat he's never eaten.

In his early days at the other place he used to vomit his soup, and Pigfoot made him eat it again until she herself couldn't stand the smell and then she'd beat him until her stomach settled. With that kind of training behind him the aunts haven't a chance to win, and a little slap from Aunt Rose is no worse than Saint Tomato giving him a dig in the ribs when she didn't like the way he peeled her vegetables.

Eugénie, who for once is not Maria's target, has not said a word.

Rose picks up his plate and sets it back in front of him, with the order:

"Eat that, or go to bed and stay there."

He pushes it toward Maria again, saying innocently:

"No. I think I'd rather have a beer."

He's surprised them with this, for there's a long silence and a kind of white flame in the air before anything happens. Again it's Rose who grabs him by the shoulders and tries to make him get up, but it's easy to keep his seat on the chair. Eugénie, unsure of herself, comes to help, but she puts no more into it than if she were playing the piano.

"Very well!" they say, together, going back to their places, as if they were waiting for the second round.

Maria takes over, and hits below the belt right away.

"Never mind. You can do what you like now."

"I want a glass of beer."

"In two days, on Tuesday to be exact, you'll go to the Brothers, and they certainly know how to tame heartless little wild beasts like you."

The thought of Jane tightens his throat at once, more unique, more precious, more gently mysterious than ever. Without her he won't be able to breathe.

"Maria!" Aunt Rose's indignation rides on her grumpy voice. "Napoléon said not to tell him. He was to do that himself."

Aunt Rose, the one who promised the lace-edged photo that she'd do everything so she could be proud of her last son, and he was little enough to get a good start, Aunt Rose doesn't come to his rescue, all she can do is try to make the others share her shame. But she's the real killer, for what she just said confirms the worst.

In his head he makes the Rat's gesture, with thumb and first finger, to measure how much he has "left to drink." And he has a terrible thirst for Jane, in his whole body, he'd dash off anywhere to find her, wait for her all night on the porch, break doors and windows, anything but go to a place where there was no more Jane. But Maria drives it home:

"What can Napoléon tell him? Pack your bags, that's all. He can't say any more than that. There's never been a place for you here. You take after your father's side."

Aunt Rose's hand touches his arm with a trace of compassion:

"I did what I could, manikin. But you got off to a bad start, right from the beginning. Out with the Rat, the very first day."

"The Rat's better than you are. It's not fair, nothing's fair, that's all. And I'm not a manikin. What is that anyway?"

"It means a little man. Just an expression," Aunt Rose replies, withdrawing her hand and her compassion. "The Rat was convicted of armed robbery. And that's what would happen to you if we let you go on."

"Better than we are?" exclaims Aunt Maria, somehow delighted. "He had you smuggling American cigarettes, and he never even told you!"

"That's why the police came to see your uncle. The box you took to Pelletier's store. The Rat's into frigidaires and car parts and even penicillin...."

"Your brother was the Rat's friend and he did time in jail, too."

"That was a mistake!" he shouts, getting up and leaning on the window.

Everything they say makes Jane more and more impossible, and the Rat helped too, for he'd made a fool of him.

"Eugénie, you've no right to say that. It was over a pair of shoes, and out West at that, and in the depression..."

"He was a bum, like the Rat, and like his father," hisses Maria who has turned so that she can continue staring at him with her runny eyes, her flaming cheeks still embedded between her fists.

"Good heavens," coos Eugénie, "who can live down his own blood? Between the two of them they killed your mother."

"Eugénie!" Rose interrupts again. "Watch what you say! They made her suffer, but that's all."

He's trembling slightly, his head against the pane, his fists clenched, torn between a desire to run away, anywhere, forever, and a confused wish to hear everything to the end, once and for all. And Maria helps him out:

"He was a drunk, and he drove your mother to begging, and he'd rather go to the whorehouse than work, and he beat her, yes, he beat her, and right in front of you! Because she had to hide her bit of money to feed you with and he wanted to get it out of her. He'd go away for weeks with some female and when he came back he was worse than an animal, dirty, foul smelling and sleeping for days on end. That's the good blood you have in your veins. And Marcel's another one. And small as you are, you're on the same track."

231

He's not crying, but he has trouble getting into his submarine because his body's trembling, and the ice is melting and getting inside him, worse than Pigfoot's vomited soup. He can't leave the window.

"We had to take your mother in here to protect her," says Eugénie, who likes calf's liver, and takes some more.

Behind what's left of the ice, eyes dry but squinting now, he asks Aunt Rose for help, to keep her promise to the photograph:

"Aunt Rose, all that's not true, is it? It's because she's full of beer, isn't it?"

But Rose, her head bent down, looks intently at her hairy fingers tapping on the tablecloth, and when she speaks her voice seems to come from under the table:

"My God, how she cried, that woman, when she was hiding! When she'd be at our place he'd come in the middle of the night and call her, howling like a dog till he went to sleep in the yard downstairs. And it took all of us together to keep her from going down to him and washing him like a baby. We couldn't even call the police, for he had his rights over her. That's what Napoléon used to say."

"We had to wait for your mother's death and for him to go off God knows where before we dared to show ourselves in the neighbourhood, we were so ashamed," Maria triumphs again, and she even starts nibbling on a little piece of meat, never taking her eyes off him, noting that his icy protection has melted away, that he'll never again have his untouchable detached-observer look, that he's just a child who can't always find the strength to armour himself against the mysteries of life.

Rose murmurs to her drumming fingers:

"She was a saint. She never complained. As for him, maybe he was sick, maybe he was possessed..."

"And you're just as big a disgrace to us, hanging around that redhead, and her already as big a slut as her mother!"

He no longer has the dizziness of the window behind him, nor the nausea that empties him of his whole existence, nor the nameless feeling that is like the word shame. What he feels is a pressure of violence that explodes at once, without his knowing, for he needs at least that outlet to keep from stifling under Maria's baleful gaze.

And he goes at her with all the rage she has instilled in him, hits her, first with only one hand, then with both, and she falls and he

232

kicks with his new shoes, and the two others are on top of him with all their weight but even on the floor he keeps striking, made even madder by the flabby flesh that gives under his fists, seeking desperately the resistance of a hard place that would hurt her more.

He stops only when he sees blood running on his hands. He slips out from under the weight of the others, stands up, still crackling with the white flame that has turned his life to ashes, and in the howling tempest that fills the kitchen spits out, cleaning himself of all the filth that is trying to stop his breath, and it's his own voice, one that he has never heard, which screams:

"Slut! Drunkard! Whorehouse! Dirty pig!"

He pushes the table to get away, and dishes crash in all directions, but they're paying attention only to Maria, who is groaning and hiccupping and wiping from her mouth drops of blood scarcely redder than her skin.

Before he leaps for the back porch door he recovers just enough presence of mind to see in Aunt Rose's eyes a reproach so desperate that it goes beyond reproach.

22

On St. Catherine Street, in front of a sidewalk display of fruits and vegetables, he looks at a pyramid of melons, wondering what they taste like, and whether they grow on trees, and he's hungry, but he has no money, and he knows he'd be sick at the first bite for he's cold and hot at once like when he had measles, and things he looks at suddenly lose their shapes and start to float uncertainly a little higher than where he saw them first.

Then somebody bumps into him and he bumps into the display, and a melon falls down. He picks it up, and sees a group of soldiers too wide for the sidewalk. The melon on his fingers doesn't taste good. He holds it out to the storekeeper, who seems unperturbed.

"Sorry," he says.

The storekeeper replies, in a funny accent that smells like onions:

"Arrmy. Too manny. Not good."

He's been walking a long time, for he's passed the big store and is back in front of the movie house near Visitation Street and his feet have never been so sore, but he doesn't want to stop. He has almost succeeded in thinking about nothing, not even about Jane, not even about time, which goes by to no purpose, and yet the street on both sides is full of little girls in their Sunday best with their papas and mamas, and everywhere there's a party atmosphere as if something nice were going to happen, but not yet. The little light bulbs of the movie house are lit. The sun is bright only on the rooftops. But his head is wearier than if he'd read three books without moving, and it's without thinking that he drifts toward the shoemaker's house, for the stream is flowing that way and he goes with it. He's barely turned into Lagauchetière when a ball hits his legs and somebody shouts:

"Hey, Pierrot! Catch!"

One of the twins had recognized him at once despite his disguise. He picks up the ball and throws it back, and the twin sends it his way again. Catching and throwing, he arrives at the entry passage. It's too dark there to go on playing, and the twin leans on the wall and says:

"Let's talk. Things are bad."

"What? You too?"

"What do you mean, you too? It's not me, it's Isabelle. I mean, it's the Rat. No, it's the MP."

"Has he left for the war?"

"I guess not. He may never go now. His mother's been here for an hour. She's crying all the time. I think she's going to sleep over."

"The MP's mother? You know her?"

"No, the Rat's mother. You never get anything straight."

"Why would she sleep here?"

"The Rat told her not to show her face at home, it was too 'hot'."

"Too hot?"

"You know, hot! If I have to explain everything ma's going to call me and you won't have time to find out. The MP's in hospital."

"Why?"

"Because he got it in his parts, you know, in his balls, and he'll never touch another girl, not even Isabelle, and she saw it all. And I'm glad."

"Did he fight?"

"Are you kidding? An MP? The Rat's a champ with that chain, as good as Tom Mix. The MP followed Isabelle. She'd gone to meet the Rat, and when the MP saw the Rat he ran and pushed Isabelle against the wall and waited with his gun. The Rat just came toward him as if he hadn't seen him, and at the last minute wham! – the chain flew off with that iron ball on it, faster than a bullet, and the Rat flopped on the ground. That Paul, he was shooting at thin air, but he got the chain and the ball between his legs, and he fell down as if the chain had gone right through."

"Why was Isabelle with him?"

"Are you just making out you don't understand? She thought he'd left long ago, but he was watching from the street corner."

"Yvan!" shouts Mama Pouf from the garden.

"Well, that's what happened. You'll hear about the rest. Isabelle came back running. She just looked back once, but she saw the Rat hitting him with the chain, right in the balls. Apparently he hasn't got any now. Papa called the police. And when they found the MP he had the revolver up his ass, inside his pants. They say he'll get better soon but he won't be a man any more."

"Yvan!"

This time it's close by, and Mama Pouf appears with her swift, gliding stride.

"Would you answer when I call you? Oh, it's you, Pierrot? Are you all alone? Then come on in, even if it isn't such a good time."

In the kitchen are Papapouf, sitting alone at the table and seeming to think hard about something, and the Rat's mother sleeping in a rocker. That's all.

"Papa, look at our fine visitor! This handsome Pierrot who's sad because he can't find his squirrel."

She gives him a chair, and the shoemaker smiles, but not easily, as if he had just awakened.

"Is the squirrel out running the woods? I finished your boots today. And I dyed the one on my shop the same colour! They're beautiful, you'll see."

"Pouf! Do you know the lady, Pierrot?" she asks, flopping into a chair. "She doesn't know where to turn, the poor old thing."

He's sorry now that he came in, because of all that happened, and the trouble they're taking to be friendly, but also because everything's coming back now, in his head, and the cold lump in his throat is choking him. He'd like to help them, but he needs them too, and it's not a good time, as she said. But they know, they knew those people, and they always understand and don't judge or condemn. And he'll never sleep again with those visions crowding his head.

"You mustn't stay too long, for the police came once and they may be back. And I'm anxious for I don't know where Isabelle is. But you don't know about it, of course..."

"Yvan told me. It's...it's..."

He can't find the right word, but Mama Pouf says, in a voice scarcely altered by fear:

"Terrible! She couldn't even let him alone for three days. Just three days! No. She's an innocent, and she's too young to know it drives men crazy and it isn't their fault."

She points to the ceiling, limply:

"He made them like that. When a girl doesn't know what a terrible force it is, that they can't control, she can cause awful things to happen. Even in the Bible. So what can we do, people like us?"

The shoemaker listens with a tired smile, glancing from time to time at the Rat's mother to see if she's still sleeping. Mama Pouf is off and running:

"And the poor Rat, now, he's just a child, he only did what he had to do to stay alive. In front of a revolver, now I ask you! But he'd better take to the woods. They'll be after him now. I think men would rather be dead than lose that."

"Shush, mama! He's only a child. Besides, she might hear."

"The twins understood, why not Pierrot?"

"You're talking too much. Just rest a bit, now."

Then, suddenly, it comes out, all by itself, for he knows he hasn't much time, the old lady could wake up, and he can't think of anything else to take their minds off their troubles:

"Did you know my parents? What were they like?"

"They loved each other very much, in their own way, and they knew it," Mama Pouf affirms at once, without hesitation. "What have your aunts been telling you? They did what they could to break it up. And it's always the same, they didn't know a man can have his head full of darkness and has enough trouble living with that, and needs a little sunlight every day like everybody else."

"Who was my father?"

The shoemaker pushed back his chair a little to come closer and be able to talk, but softly.

"He was a smart man, one of the smartest I ever knew, but he was a mystery. Because he understood more things than we did he wasn't, like us, and he. . .he turned rebellious, I think that's the word, and when he rebelled nobody understood him but your mother."

"But your aunts didn't want her to understand, and they wanted her to be unhappy. For them, a man was supposed to bring home money, and go to work and stay in a corner until he was spoken to. Like my poor Henri, here, working all day tied to my apron strings, can't even go out for a glass of beer by himself."

"Beer. And women. He drank, didn't he?"

"Maria, everybody knows she drinks. She ought to understand if a man wants to have a blowout once in a while, to get rid of what's too much for him. Come here a minute."

She puts her arm around him and speaks softly in his ear:

"Now you stop thinking about all that. You had good parents, just like anybody else. The only sad thing is she's not there to tell you herself how much they loved each other."

"They told me he beat her."

There's not a real hesitation, but he's watching her so closely to discover the slightest lie to please him, that he sees the little glimmer of surprise.

"They have him beating her now! What they don't think of! I suppose they saw him caressing her in front of them too!"

The shoemaker comes to her rescue with his quiet voice:

"It happened sometimes that he...rebelled in front of her too. But he never beat her. He had a way of getting mad like somebody who wants to knock his head against walls. He couldn't understand why people couldn't understand that he felt things more than they did."

"Don't think about all that, dear boy. I'll tell you, I'd rather be married to a man like he was than this wretch of a shoemaker who can't even defend his own daughter. All he had to do was tell Paul the truth, and not let him come back here. Now what am I talking about?"

She kisses him, as she gives her breast to Meeow, without thinking, for peace emanates from all parts of her, and she's there to give it to others.

"Look at him, now! What are people going to say about him when he's dead? That he never did any work harder than raising his little shoemaker's hammer, that he always had his head up a woman's skirt, and right under my nose, too, and if he was so thin it was because he ran around every night."

"What does 'whorehouse' mean?"

The shoemaker's smile makes her indignant, and she forgets about the old woman in the rocker and bursts out:

"Look here, dirty mind, if you answer that I'll send you to sleep with Père Eugène's cow, and she won't be proud about that. That's a word that only old maids understand, for they dream about it all the time."

She laughs, proud of the way she has acquitted herself, and Papapouf laughs even harder. But Pierrot doesn't trust this laughter, for it proves the answer wasn't a true one.

"And what's a slut?" he insists, in his most controlled voice. "They said Jane would get to be a slut like her mother."

"They told you that?" says Mama Pouf, scandalized, but stalling for time.

"It means a woman that has her own way of being happy, and they don't like it."

"Like Isabelle?"

The two are silent, looking at each other in a panic. And he's ashamed, without knowing why, at having asked a question that caused them pain. Quickly, he follows up and manages a laugh:

"I soon won't have to worry about being happy. I'm going Tuesday to another big house. Uncle Nap decided."

"Don't tell me! Not that!" exclaims Mama Pouf. "You had enough of that! It's a shame they left you there four years, till you were eight years old, like a little animal in a cage. You're going to stay here with us."

The shoemaker makes a hopeless gesture with both hands:

"We can't do it, Mama. He's his guardian. He'd send the police. You know very well they'd be ashamed to have him here. As long as he's there nobody knows and nobody thinks about it."

"Good God, they've even made sure nobody can look after an abandoned child! You can do more for a cat or a dog!"

He clenches his teeth over this forbidden happiness, this house with lilacs, with Thérèse, and Gérard and Meeow and the twins, this picture-book *chaumière* near Visitation Street that contains all the kindness in the world and Jane included, and he reassures them:

"Don't worry about it. I'm leaving before then. With Jane, for life."

"My poor dear boy! Like Marcel, and the police brought him back, and he was in three different reformatories, one of them was in Ontario, before he finally got away. But he was ten years older than you are. I'm going to try out an idea on your uncle. Maybe he can see reason."

"Why did my father leave?"

It's too late. This question too came out all by itself, and he's ashamed to see them so embarrassed.

"You know, when your mother died, it just killed him. That's not hard to understand."

"And they didn't give him time to get over it. They took advantage of his worst time to have you put away there," the shoemaker adds.

"Oh, my, oh my! Is that you, little boy?"

She's no sooner awake than she's crying.

"They've told you. Dear me! What's going to happen to him? What will they do to him?"

"We didn't tell him. He's too young," says the shoemaker, who talks to her as if she were a child.

"My, oh my! He took his gun and killed Lucifer, right in front of me. He said he wouldn't need the dog any more. Oh my! And I was to get out, it was going to be too dangerous for me. He only defended himself, but after what he did they're going to kill him for sure. Oh, my! They'll find where he is!"

"The Rat was in too big a hurry, for his glass is empty," says Pierrot, to show he understands.

"How was that, now?" The shoemaker is astounded at the expression. "The trouble is, he won't even get to drink to the bottom. They've already seen some MPs around the neighbourhood. Nobody knows if they're real or false."

"He's got Skiff and Banana with him, but my! They're good for nothing! And he refuses to leave town. I've got family in the country where nobody'd look for him."

A silence full of ghosts invades the warm kitchen. He looks at the others, who can't help him but fall back into their own worries, and he wonders how a happiness so quiet and small could be threatened so suddenly, and how this madness could get in where everything was so sensible and wise.

Without admitting it to himself, he'd hoped, in his fatigue and exhaustion, that he could spend the night here, for he can't bear to see his aunts and he's sure Jane will come as soon as she can. But he realizes that he has to go home, just because they're trying so hard to be kind, or else sleep in the covered stair-head.

Meeow starts crying somewhere in the house. Mama Pouf gets up, leaning with both hands on the table and sighing loudly. Papapouf hurries to help her.

"Pouf! Where can Isabelle be, dear Lord! Why doesn't she come? That's all I ask. Will you let me alone? I'm still younger than you, old man!"

As she leaves the kitchen she gives him a tender smile, with eyes that have no milk left.

"Sleep here if you like. There's room in the twins' bed," says the shoemaker, and goes back to his seat, moving his mouth and staring into emptiness, as if he were swallowing nails.

The clock on the wall says it's after ten.

"Thanks a lot, but I'm going back. I don't want to spend another day in their Sunday suit."

"Well, good-night, son. Why not, by the way? Tomorrow's Sunday."

He's back at Lagauchetière walking toward the bridge, for he has some questions to ask the Rat, and he'd like to see Isabelle and tell her Papa and Mama Pouf are sick with worry and all she has to do to cure them is turn up at home.

He takes off his shoes, ties them together, and slings them over his shoulders.

The street is deserted, but there are couples under the little roofs that cover the doorways, from each of which the same green paint is flaking off; silent couples that don't even see him passing.

23

Standing on a red chair in the kitchen she's hanging up the washing, and he sees only her legs on the chair, and she never came down from there until her stone forehead lay in the white satin. The same smell, cold and hot at the same time, as in the laundry-room. That was all.

He's beginning to understand that there are families bigger than single families, like tribes, and they know more about each other from one house to the next because they have the same place in life, and he himself belongs to the larger family to which the Rat also belongs, not because the Rat lives next door to the house Pierrot had forgotten, but because he was Marcel's friend and the Rat also is always doing surprising things and will never behave the way grown-ups are expected to behave because he's caught irrevocably in what the shoemaker calls a state of "revolt." And Pierrot understands that there's the tribe of those who refuse to give in, as most people do, to what's expected of them, expected because decided on by somebody or other, maybe another tribe with many more members, all wearing suits and ties, educated but not proud, going to work every day at the same place for twenty or thirty years and very convinced of the importance of the decapitated heads of kings disguised as ordinary heads on coins but with never a glance for a marble which can tint the sunlight with such lovely colours, and that tribe fills the streets with seriousness in the morning, with the sprinklers, and makes laws that prevent Mama Pouf from taking him in, but it opens empty chateaux where four hundred children wait in a walled, treeless park until they become little men who, like the Rat, will be caught in a forbidden land, trapped between play and earnest, between work and strange trucks that carry strange cargos. The children of that land – Skiff, Banana, himself and Marcel as well, and perhaps, more recently, the man in blue. . .and the one who had made the aunts so ashamed – they all belong to the larger family of the Rat. Papapouf is another family, still unique for Pierrot because he hasn't travelled far or long enough as yet. Jane is another special case. And there must be many other kinds that he hasn't had time to know.

This is why he's walking in his sock-feet toward the Rat's house, for the Rat is the only one likely to give the right answers without lying out of kindness or cruelty, and he'll quite normally use the words of Pierrot's tribe, and Pierrot will understand, for he was born among them even if he has forgotten everything. And he's ashamed not to know how things were in his home, as if he'd purposely spent all those years inventing an "elsewhere" where he had never been, a family of shadows that never existed except in his head where he himself had hidden away all that time to keep other things from getting in. And now it's so much harder going back four years and trying to start from there to find out who he really is, for there's no doorway he can begin at. Only the Rat, in his hay-filled courtyard beneath the bridge, in his horseless cart amid the scrap iron of those other days, knows everything and remembers, including the things you don't understand when you understand more than other people or when you're more intelligent than others and end up crying like an animal at night because people stole away the only woman who could accept this pain that made others so ashamed. But as he crosses the streetcar tracks before the bridge he suddenly sees (as in a flash of lightning so distant you're not really sure if it flicked its rope between the sky and earth) an arm raised, and a stick, and a face, barely visible, weeping and pale, and Marcel's bare back receiving the blows. He could day-dream any old thing at all, he's so tired, and words, even spoken with the sole purpose of hurting, end up by being pictures that make no sense, and there are always many more lying pictures than true ones. The trouble with the Rat is, he doesn't think about these things, and everything in his world seems so normal to him, he doesn't go looking for meanings. He lives the way he breathes, and others like him too, and he'd have to work at it like Pierrot if he wanted answers. It's easier for him to whirl his chain, and perhaps that explains who he is better than anything could, and there's no sense hoping he'll change for that wouldn't even

244

occur to him. It was only when Jane explained the words of the song, which she herself didn't understand, that the Rat seemed to understand the most important thing about himself. But that has nothing to do with what Pierrot is searching for.

He is past the Rat's entry passage and standing in front of the delapidated board fence and the oldest house in the suburb, such an old house that Pierrot is much too young to have known it. He shuts his eyes as tight as they'll go (for this way he often finds a forgotten word) and opens them again, but nothing moves in the darkness of his memory, and the last thing he remembers before the first rumble of boots in the long corridor is still his uncle's apartment, and he'll never know why.

High in the sky the moon passes through a cloud and sprinkles with salt the ancient stones and even the empty holes of the gable windows, and he sees that all the flowerpots have been left lying there as if the old woman were sick. And from the big dark opening beside the house comes an odour of manure and country – a world he can't imagine but which must be full of surprises, more so than the city where he knows only one cow and it's just been jailed by the police.

The idea strikes him that after what happened the Rat must be in hiding, and if Lucifer isn't there to bark the Rat can't wait in the darkened house for the MPs to come and see if he really has a chain with an iron ball on the end, and he's come for nothing and might as well go back to his uncle's apartment and try to sleep in the sawdust smell of the porch stairway. His feet are too sore to walk much farther, but he's never felt so wide awake, and his mind is running in all directions around something grey and enormous in which his aunts have punched holes through which he refuses to look, though his eyes have been drawn to them ever since he left the apartment.

Between the lamplit sidewalk and the tall hay of the courtyard, where a milky light trickles down, there is the passage blacker than night, but he is forced to stop in it just before the yard, for he hears Isabelle shouting aloud, first with short cries then in a long, wild wailing that he can feel in his stomach, not a sob, more like the choking cry of someone being strangled. Then there's the Rat, breathing quick and hard, too out of breath to go on strangling Isabelle who is still struggling, for he can hear thumping sounds, and all this coming from the buggy full of inner tubes. For a while he doesn't dare to move, for Isabelle's wailing cries, though they

245

hurt him so, are not quite like cries of pain, and he thinks perhaps they're just playing at hurting each other. But another cry rises up, more shrill and terrible than the last, for it's held and held until the last pinch of air is gone, and the Rat's grunting sounds like some filthy, malevolent satisfaction, and the thought of Mama and Papa Pouf's sad faces force him out into the moonlight, half in anger, half in anxiety, dizzy with fury at something crazier than he's ever seen, horrified by an event too monstrous to imagine.

First thing, he cuts his foot on a piece of old metal in the grass, but he feels nothing, and leaps into the buggy to hammer the Rat on the head with his shoes.

"Are you crazy, Rat? Have you gone crazy? Stop it!"

And he hammers and hammers away. The Rat isn't strangling Isabelle with his hands but with his whole body. He raises himself up then falls on her again with all his strength. He pays no attention to Pierrot's shoes hitting his soft body which seems not to feel the blows; but Isabelle has stopped crying out. To his immense surprise, it is she who pushes him back with a limp hand, saying in a tiny babyish voice:

"Go away, Pierrot."

The moon lights up her belly and her bare breasts, for her dress is pulled up to her neck.

"Go away!"

This time she shouts angrily, succeeding in raising her head slightly above the Rat's shoulder, and the Rat stops groaning like a sick dog and stretches out an arm, trying to push Pierrot to the floor of the buggy.

Astonished, he stops hitting and looks at his shoes. Then he sees that the Rat was inside Isabelle, between her legs, for now he straightens up, trembling like a leaf, his pants down, and that thing – like the wino's when he....Isabelle is trying to hide herself and the Rat with his shirt.

"You little bastard! What're you doing here?" he asks, puffing like a man about to die who has come from too far for anyone to follow. He looks like a rag that only a breeze can stiffen, and his eyes are glassy.

"Now scram, God damn it!"

He jumps down from the buggy without saying a word, his mouth full of a taste of blackened snow, and he runs, legless, lungless, never looking, his head so empty now that his heart hammers inside it louder than a drum, and he'll never manage to vomit all the misery freezing his mouth because of Isabelle, and the shame burning his whole body. Isabelle's wailing still tears at his stomach. He puts his hands over his ears and runs and runs to get away from this part of life that is not yet his, so strange and foreign that he might have been looking at a horse with no skin galloping by, all red and blue, with fat, white elastics in place of legs.

At the street with the car tracks he runs headlong into Skiff who grabs him by the shoulders. Banana comes from behind to pinion his arms.

"Where are you coming from like that?" asks Skiff in his stony voice.

"And where are you running to with your shoes over your shoulder?" Banana demands from behind him.

He stares, not understanding, wriggling to free himself.

"We're on the lookout now."

"Things can happen any minute, so you'd better tell us."

"Let me go!" he shouts as loud as he can.

"Is she still with him?" Skiff insists, his fingers digging deeper into his shoulders.

A streetcar stops opposite. People are getting out.

"Let me go!" he shouts, louder still.

This time, his struggle is successful and he's free, for the two had relaxed their hold a little as passengers approached. Pierrot rushes into the street as the streetcar starts up, and barely hears the furious clanging of its bell as the green metal brushes past him.

He arrives in front of the apartment at the same time as Uncle Nap, who is manipulating a bundle of keys big enough to open every door in the street, and he's singing, wagging his head comically, jerkily, as if he were a juggler pretending to balance his hat. Not too surprised, in excellent humour, he barely looks at the boy.

"It's you, is it? Where are you coming from at this time of day?"

"From Lafontaine's."

"Oh! That's all right, then. Fine people."

He opens the two doors and climbs slowly, still singing away with his boom-boom-boom. A man who's just performed a thousand good deeds. A real Father Christmas emerging from his last chimney. At the third landing he says with a giggle:

"Mustn't make a noise! They're asleep."

The iodine smell is stronger than when he plays the piano, and he seems in a mood to play that or anything else. Pierrot forces himself to speak in the same joking way, though his voice is quavering like Aunt Maria's. He asks his uncle with a smile that hurts his ears:

"I hear you're going to put me in another home on Tuesday."

Nap has the right key at last.

"Do your shoes hurt? Hey! You've cut your foot. You're leaving marks all over the place."

He opens the door and puts his finger to his lips.

"You're to put some alcohol on that."

"Am I going to another home?" he insists, still with the ear-stretching smile.

"It's a home for bigger boys," says his uncle in his Santa Claus voice which refuses to be taken by surprise.

Pierrot goes straight to the green sofa and lies down fully dressed, hugging close the dead child who formerly was frightened because he heard hundreds of small boots pounding on the metal roof.

Uncle Nap goes and comes between his room and the bath with his heavy step and his muted trumpet song.

"Nap...Nap..." Aunt Rose's voice calls from the kitchen.

His uncle comes back again.

"I have to talk to you. It's serious."

"Shhh!" says Uncle Nap. "The boy's sleeping."

24

They don't all go to the same mass, so it takes a long time. He had waited until his uncle had his breakfast, after everybody else, before getting up and drinking a glass of milk amid their silence. His uncle had barely looked at him, just enough to tell him that he knew. Rose made him a bread and jam just the same, letting one phrase slip out:

"Manikin....Oh, what's the use...."

He didn't eat his bread and jam but went to play outside, wearing his sweatshirt, his dirty pants and running shoes. For hours now the bells of the two churches had been ringing for all they were worth, and nobody could doubt that it was Sunday.

He has time to wander through all the streets in the neighbourhood, even along St. Catherine, almost deserted, to far beyond the big store, and back to the bridge, until he's almost sure lunch will be over and he'll be free to take refuge on the back gallery without too much risk of being stared at. They leave him alone there for at least an hour, during which he listens to the birds and watches the big trees of the old people's home door waving slowly in the warm breeze. In the alleyway, sparrows are picking at the week's accumulation of horse-buns.

Then Rose comes out to tell him they're going to a relative's house for the afternoon, an hour's streetcar ride away, and he'd better go play in the park, she's locking everything up. He replies that he'll go, but not just yet, and she can lock up anything she wants.

And he falls asleep, seeing Jane walking alone through a field of bees and flowers, for her mother and the gentleman had told her they were putting locks all over so as not to be disturbed, and he loses sight of her behind a curtain of red sunlight. He tries to swim up the curtain but he falls, falls, until he's in total blackness, and invisible slimy creatures light on him in heaps, and he stifles in a sponge-like silence with a thousand eyes.

It takes him a while to wake up and shake off all those creatures with their soft, slippery legs, fighting his way back to the blood-red curtain, to hear someone say:

"Pssst! Pierrot! Come quick. Down in the alley."

The little sunburned face sticks out through the partly opened door, and her tiny, freckled hand is making desperate signs.

"Hurry! They've gone to get stuff from the car."

He rushes over to her and hugs her so hard she protests:

"Hey! You're hurting. We can kiss each other downstairs. Quick."

He goes down behind her for the stairway is too narrow, and she's wearing a pale yellow dress, probably the colour of country fields, embroidered at the top with green thread, and he finds her so pretty and clean that he holds back so as not to raise dust near her. When she passes through the shaft of sunlight in the dirty entryway below, his heart almost stops at the russet gold, miracle of a second.

In the street she kisses him greedily, her mouth open, her lips moist with raspberries. More than ever before he sees her, after this absence, so lovely, luminous and fragile that his heart sinks at the thought she came back for him alone and that she can fade away as swiftly as the powdered gold of dusk. He's astonished to realize that her hand in his, light though it is, has more weight than a dream...."

"You took long enough to wake up!"

"I wasn't asleep, I was dead. If you hadn't come back till night..."

"Lucky, there were millions of mosquitoes there! That's why we came back early. Look at my arms."

A dozen times he caresses her thin arms but it's not the mosquito bites he feels with his finger tips, it's the far sunlight that has gilded her skin for so many hours. Her hair is pinned back again behind her head and the red of her ears makes the delicate skin of her neck even whiter, and he kisses her there, tasting invisible hairs.

"You were sleeping like a log. I'm never going with them again. They kept sending me away, and the only times Mama spoke to me was to say I was being bad. And they'd invited friends..."

"I'm going to the other home day after tomorrow. My uncle decided it with the director."

"Their friends did nothing but drink and pinch my bottom and touch Mama all over. The country's worse than the city, Pierrot."

"What about birds and flowers, weren't there animals?"

"I didn't see any. Just a lawn with their drinking chairs and a bed that smelled of old pee."

"I saw a squirrel. He almost made a lady fall down and she's going to have a baby."

"You didn't! Where was that?"

"In the cemetery. That's country, for me."

They've arrived at Visitation Street, and he notices proudly that even the women turn around to admire her, though at times there's a kind of anger in their looks as if they'd like to throw mud at her.

"What was that you said about a director?"

"They're shutting me up again, day after tomorrow. Is that all you care about it?"

She looks at him, despairing and powerless.

"That's terrible, Pierrot! That means we have to run away right now...or almost."

"Right, before they find out. Are you really sure you don't love your mother any more?"

"I hate her!" she shouts, tightening her hand on his. "Do you know what she said there, when she'd had so much to drink she was laughing all the time like a silly, and talking the same way they did, as if she had to look for her words with her fingers in the back of her throat! Do you know?"

"That you were coming away with me to the end of our lives?"

"I'm not joking, Plush. She said she'd had a letter more than three months ago saying Daddy was. . .wait till I remember the words...and she was laughing, eh?"

"I pounded Aunt Maria with my fists because she said rotten things about my father."

"Why don't you ever say papa?"

"Because..."

And he stops there, for even to himself alone in bed at night he's never said it.

"Reported missing over Germany. That's what it was. And that means he's dead and she was laughing, with strangers!"

"No, listen, mouse, there are parachutes, and your mother knows that better than anybody. The aviators fall down like big butterflies and then they hide. You'll hear from him again."

"Not me! She'll hear, and she won't tell me, because she thinks it's funny."

"OK, then, we leave. Tonight, to the end of our lives. And this time you promise with all your heart."

"Yes, Plush, with all my heart. And I'm not scared. Cross my heart and spit."

He stops on the sidewalk, looks gravely into her eyes through the tears welling in his own, for he finds her far too beautiful and fragile for all this to be true, and it's a nameless shame that they won't let the two of them stay with Mama Pouf, and it's the last time they'll ever play "running away," their last chance and he hasn't the right to ask her to come for she has a mama, and a mama – even as strange as hers is – pretty, speaking very well but cold as an old maid, always has a little love hidden away even if she doesn't show it all the time. He holds out his hand in a solemn gesture and says, trembling a little:

"If it's going to be true for life you have to bite me till I bleed."

"I can't bite you, Plush! I love you!"

"That's the very reason. And it'll be a proof that we're almost married, with our blood. You just scratch one of your bites, and put my blood on top of it and I'll put yours where you bit me. Go on, if you love me."

"I can't Pierrot. There must be another way."

"No. If you love me."

He puts his hand on her moist mouth and waits, shutting his eyes. He barely feels her teeth.

"You're not biting, you're kissing. Harder. It won't hurt."

She tries again, but barely leaves a tooth-mark. He gets angry:

"You're doing that on purpose. Imagine you're eating, greedy-guts."

That did it. Her squirrel-teeth bite him, and there's blood, and she licks it away.

"I'm sorry, Pierrot. It was your idea."

"It works better with a knife. But you wouldn't have dared."

"Your blood tasted good. It's like medicine."

"Will you stop that, vampire! There won't be any left to put in yours."

"Vampire yourself. What's a vampire?"

"I don't know. A kind of owl and it only eats blood. It's a night flyer, anyway. Now, it's my turn."

She holds out her arm, her eyes squeezed so tight that her forehead has almost disappeared.

"I'm not going to bite. Don't make such a face."

The mosquito bite immediately gives a drop of blood under pressure from his fingernail.

"That doesn't count. It didn't hurt."

He looks at the drop and realizes her hair was never red, nor her freckles either. He rubs her arm against his, but between them there's so little blood that he's not sure the marriage really took place.

She kisses him solemnly, sober and self-controlled as if she were at her first communion.

"When do we leave? Tomorrow?"

"Tonight. If we don't, they'll find out."

As he says "tonight" he's astonished to see how dark it's grown. The street lights are already on. He must have gone home much later after lunch than he had thought.

"Tonight?" says Jane, shivering a little. "I didn't bring anything. And where are we going to sleep?"

"We're not going to drag suitcases around so everybody will know. We'll sleep at our place."

"Our place? Where's that?"

"I have a house," he says mysteriously, and leaves it at that.

"You never told me!"

Her yellow dress is shaded darker now, and her reddened arms are coppery in the filtered orange light that still falls in the street.

"Have you finished your tortures? Have the Redskins made peace?"

It's Papapouf, who's been sitting quietly in his doorway, and now has a laugh at their expense.

"I see funny things going on in my street! But I won't tell anybody. I'll tell you why: I got married like that myself, once. And it wasn't to Mama Pouf. Not a word, now!"

"If you saw, it doesn't count any more. That's not nice, now we have to do it over again, and I won't be able to bite again, ever!"

"Come on! Squirrels are made for biting. You'll have to get used to it. We waited a long time for you, Pierrot. We had a picnic on St. Helen's Island. We thought you'd be along."

"Without me!" Jane protests.

"My poor mouse, you can't go to the rich man's countryside and the poor man's island at the same time. Everybody's sick, they've got sunstroke or too much ice cream or too much river water. Only the tough guys like me can take it."

Through the half-open door they hear Mama Pouf shout:

"Bring them in, have you no manners?"

Then her tall form blocks the doorway, making Papapouf even tinier.

"My lord, mouse, you're pretty today! It's almost sinful! If I had a daughter like you I'd lock her up so you couldn't talk to old bums like my husband."

"Aha! If Pierrot wasn't here she and I could go for a walk!"

He gets up, and standing below the steps, barely comes to Mama Pouf's knees. His face darkens, and he speaks to her alone, but they can hear:

"The MPs are all over on motorbikes. I never saw anything like it. And that little fool, he went by just the same like a black devil on his black bike. I think he's still living in the house. What's his old lady doing?"

"You know very well he'll never stop provoking them, or run away anywhere else on that fire-spitter of his. She's sleeping. Isabelle too. She was vomiting again."

"Well, come on in, children. Maybe we got too much sun, but it feels cold now. Did you eat yet?"

"Yes," says Pierrot, too quickly.

"Come in and have a bite anyway, little liar," says Mama Pouf. "And this one, she never eats. She won't be hungry."

Thérèse is dozing in the kitchen, her face sunburned, her eyes half open showing their whites.

"Thérèse, shut your eyes, you look terrible!" cries Jane.

She opens them slowly and smiles benevolently at them as if she were emerging from a dream full of angels and chocolates. Jane is already munching something at the table.

"We're going down to the ships," Pierrot announces. "Never mind making us things to eat."

"You're not going to take her down by the water to freeze in that thin dress. Little girls that eat all the time catch their death too easy. You know, you look like a butterfly tonight, mouse. You'd better take along the blanket on my chair in the garden."

"A butterfly! Come here, I want to see if the powder comes off!" jokes Papapouf, but his eyes aren't joking and he can't quite conceal his worried air. Even Mama Pouf has little flashes of anguish in her expression.

"I got a sunstroke and now my knees are swollen worse than ever," says Thérèse's white-bread voice, but she manages to get up, groaning a little, and beckons Jane to follow her to the bedroom.

"Gérard, you could take them down to the port, couldn't you?" asks Mama Pouf from the door that leads to the garden.

"The Buick almost started. He found a generator, but it'll take him a month to fix it."

Mama Pouf is putting things in a paper bag.

"This is what they got sick on. You can eat it down there. It's getting late. Don't forget the blanket."

Jane comes back alone, her expression that of one who has been let in on an astonishing mystery.

The shoemaker goes to the garden with them. As they climb into the panel truck, while Gérard wipes his oily hands on his pants, Papapouf gives Pierrot's shoulder a friendly shake:

"You've had a bad day, old fellow, all by yourself! We've been talking about it here, I'm going to speak to your uncle. Don't you worry."

And when Gérard has his noise going, Papapouf shakes a warning finger:

"And don't you try to go on board for your honeymoon! She still gets mad too easily! Wait a bit!"

Gérard piles in behind the wheel and drives without a smile, but he has a way of slowing down for lights that shows he doesn't mind.

25

"They've left already," Jane states, disappointed.

Its lights much brighter than the other evening, the water darker, a ship is going under the bridge, and a second, whose passengers are still waving, has just left the dock. Because of the long line of cars coming toward him Gérard had had to leave them in the narrow street.

With one hand Pierrot holds the old grey blanket rolled on his shoulder, in the other his picnic bag. Jane is skipping along in front of him, her little dress moving against the flow of the crowd leaving the dock.

Then she stops and waits for him, her mouth opening twice to say something but he isn't close enough to hear. Then as he catches up she says very quickly, as if she were throwing him a ball:

"Isabelle's going to have a baby!"

He walks on without answering, not knowing what to say, especially to her, and besides, she just spoiled his happiness without knowing, and this whole part of life (which seems to him the greatest part, and he can't look at it without backing off a little from its touching strangeness) is again too much for him.

"That's why Thérèse wanted to talk to me. It won't be an ordinary baby, and that upsets everybody, and when she's there they let on they don't know. Hey! I saw the eclipse!"

"The eclipse?" he says, glad of a change of subject.

"When the moon lies on top of the sun. I didn't notice about the birds, because everybody was talking loud and looking through films."

"What films?"

"They said it makes you blind if you look at it with your naked eye."

"Then I'll never see you again. I looked at the bursts of fire coming out."

"What a cheater he was! It was in all the papers before. And he told us as if he was the only one who knew, as if he could put the sun out himself."

"The white flowers are dead just the same," Pierrot says, to hide his disillusionment.

"I feel like talking to Emily tonight, since we're going away. Do you know why?"

"No. Because you're not as mean tonight?"

"Because now I understand why she left home."

"Why did she?"

"I can't explain it, I just know. But at least she could have come to see me sometimes."

The crowd has dispersed. The second ship is passing under the bridge now, leaving luminous trails much longer than itself. A few workmen are still busy around the big shed.

So everything was false about the man in blue. Another one that takes advantage of children by using the things grown-ups know. An eclipse! He'd even taken care of the fact that there might be clouds and nothing to be seen. It's always easy for them to get into children's games and pretend to pretend, for they've seen everything already and they're at least ten jumps ahead and always know how the game will end, and marvels to them are no more than a toy that's stupid after you've used it once, like all useless things. The man in blue tries on the disguise of wearing no disguise, and just for the two of them. Jane was right to have seen at once that it was cheating to go on the ship with her sister (or any other lady, it was all the same). And he realizes that, without knowing it, he had somehow imagined going away with him, and that could have been a real party, the thing he had been training himself to expect for so long. But now he doesn't want to see him again. He's been fooled once again, and that's normal.

"Let's go," he says. "The ships are gone."

He turns his back. Jane catches up with him.

"Oh no! Don't tell me we came for nothing! What about my sister?"

"He's a liar. I don't want to see him," he says soberly.

"You know, he didn't say he was going to make the eclipse himself. Pierrot, I'm hungry."

"Well, eat. I don't know what's in there. Everybody got sick."

He spreads the blanket on the grassy slope. They sit down with the bag between them.

"You're not going to get mad on our wedding day? I'm going to tell Papapouf that you're the one with the bad temper."

She unwraps a sandwich and starts eating, seeming to think hard at the same time. He fishes a cookie out of the bag.

Swallowing, she goes on:

"And anyway, he isn't even here. What about the submarine, is that true?"

"It must be. He's left already, hasn't he?"

Then they see him coming, they know his form and his way of walking though it's too far to see his face. He shouts to them:

"Am I not invited?"

"Where's Emily?" she asks.

He doesn't answer, but sits down in front of them on the damp grass. Still in blue, but unrecognizable, as if he'd aged a few years on board the ship, or come back swimming. Tieless, his suit rumpled and dirty, his hair standing up and, above all, the stubbly beard all over his face, a beard which in the half-dark looks blue as a revolver. His voice also is changed, or seemed so from farther off. Pierrot says at once, to bring it to a head:

"You're a liar. The eclipse was in the papers."

"The dead are in the papers too, and you don't see them."

The voice has changed, it too has grown a beard. It's a lot more than three days older, and doesn't come from the back of his head but from a foot in front of his mouth, and it talks all on its own.

"What have dead people to do with it?"

"They are the future. Like the sea which makes love impossible because you can't drink it dry. Newspapers are life that's dead already. Never read them."

"What about Emily?"

"Is that your Sunday beard?"

"If I don't want to disguise myself any more I have to let it grow."

"Are you going to tell me where Emily is?" asks Jane, getting aggressive.

The voice that speaks on its own, beyond his beard, takes up the question, mysteriously:

"Where is Emily? Only the water knows, and the white flowers are dead. She turned blue, did Emily, like the sky, like the sea. How to find her in all that blue? Emily is not the sea, to be drunk, that's all I know."

"All right, if you're going to talk in jokes we're leaving. It's getting dark anyway."

"That's a pretty dress. A butterfly dress."

"Mama Pouf said so first."

"But a day butterfly, not a moth. Your voice is the same as Emily's. And that hurts. A voice that touches more surely than a hand."

He may be a liar and a cheat, but tonight he has a way of playing that makes you furious: fascinating and frightening at once. What he said about Jane's voice, it's true, but Pierrot thought *he* was the only one to know it, and he feels robbed. He doesn't want to share that with the man.

"What happened to the caboose and the deer? Are you still in the country of the Great Cold? How's Balibou?"

"Balibou is dead," Pierrot says simply.

"So is Emily," he replies as simply.

Jane gets up, trying a nasty laugh:

"I suppose she's in the papers."

"Perhaps. They pick up everything that's dead."

"Come on, Pierrot, he's even crazier than last time. He scares me."

"I'm not scared. And he isn't crazy. He's just pretending to be somebody who goes around saying things you can't understand. That's all there is to it."

"Is your submarine here?"

"Waiting for me. I'll have a long wait if I try to find somebody for the other seat."

"Can you go to sea in it?"

"Yes, and it's hard finding anyone there."

"Because it's dark down below?"

"No. Because everything is born and everything dies. The sea is life, and how can you find somebody in life itself?"

Jane takes another sandwich, bites into it and spits out her mouthful on the grass beside him.

"The sea is death. The proof is, you drown in it. And ships sink. And nobody ever swam across. And your little submarine, all it has to do is run into a little shark this big, and..."

"Before, the sea was over all the earth, it was even frozen in

260

places, and yet life started and kept going. We were fish once."

"And you were a crocodile," Jane finishes him off, throwing away the rest of her sandwich. "Now I know why they all got sick. Mama Pouf put floorwax on the bread by mistake. Phhooo, I'm sick. Come here, Pierrot!"

Pierrot goes to her. He's sorry it's not daylight so he could see into the man's eyes. Here in the dusk they look like great empty holes, so empty you'd like to stick your fingers in them.

"When women feel sick, it's because they've lost their memory."

"What's that supposed to mean?" asks Jane, picking up her sandwich. "Have you got a memory? Here, eat this and you won't get sick. Anyway, it won't be you that'll put your finger down my throat so I can vomit!"

The man tastes the sandwich, gravely, then gently says:

"You've got to be hungry. Come, I want you to see my submarine. We're always hungry."

To calm her he says:

"Your sister not only has your voice, she has your stomach."

But it doesn't help at all when he adds:

"We're always hungry for what doesn't exist. And that's why women don't remember what disgusted them."

She throws the paper bag at his face, but he laughs, as he speaks, from somewhere in front of his face:

"But they were all children once. And that only the men know, the men who stole their childhood."

"Where's your submarine?" asks Jane, who has suddenly decided it's not worth taking a madman seriously, and that this one, despite the dark, is not dangerous. "Men. Women. What a way to talk! There's you, me, him, not one of us alike. Just as well, too!"

They're walking toward the water, past the big shed.

"You're right, Red Goddess. The submarines are all one-seaters, and you're always alone, and when you try to get a companion on board the whole thing sinks, it's too heavy."

"I wouldn't say that," Jane protests. "Pierrot and I are leaving on the same submarine, and there'll be nobody to keep us from being happy and loving each other. Sundays are bad for you, did you know?"

"Because you're still small, still children, and you have no memory."

"You're always talking about memory, memory. How long since you went to school?"

261

"I know. I'm not a child any longer, and I know that what's possible lies behind."

"At least tell me where Emily is. I have to see her."

"She stayed behind. In my memory. A girl at sea, a mother in the sea."

A somewhat deflated moon appears suddenly in a gap in the clouds and casts its slim, broken reflection on the water.

"The Rat isn't as crazy as this one, by a long shot," states Jane, leaning over the water. "You can't see a thing. Are you diving to the bottom?"

"I have to, it's anchored."

"I'm not worried. You can swim better than anybody."

He sits down with his legs dangling over the water.

"There. I've left everything behind now. Nothing left but the blue, but that's enormous."

"Don't you smoke cigars any more?" asks Pierrot.

"No smoking in submarines."

"Why did you want to see us again? We're not serious."

"Neither am I. That's why."

"Not true. I never saw anybody as serious as you. As if you were asking us for something we haven't got."

"You gave it to me. I thank you for that."

He gets up so that he can see more of the man's eyes, and finds nothing left but the tiny glint that Jane called frozen tears.

"Look in his eyes, Jane, and tell me if it's the same thing."

She leans down, hands behind her back, and examines him with glacial calm. Then she gives her verdict:

"Yes. But everything else is gone."

"Did you sleep long, or look at the eclipse for a long time?"

He allows this examination without embarrassment or impatience.

"Both. Why?"

"You look blind."

"Those are my submarine eyes," he says in a voice which now seems to come from the river itself.

He glances at the moon, then slowly takes off his wrist watch and holds it out to him.

"It's time now. You can keep this, it's an earth-watch, not for water."

The gold shines faintly in the moonlight, the numbers too, they're black and green at the same time.

"D'you want to give me a little push?"

"Why? You can dive."

"But I have to dive backwards to get right to the conning tower. And if I don't have a good start I won't make it. There's no springboard."

He stands up on the edge of the dock, his heels over the water, his arms over his head, a touch of moonlight in the depths of his wide-open eyes.

"Maybe I'll see you in the country of the Great Cold. One, two, three, go!"

Pierrot hadn't touched him. For a brief second they see his dark blue silhouette, straight as a ramrod, suspended over the river, which it breaks like a shattered mirror, almost without a sound and without making a ripple in the river. Then a feeble slapping of water against concrete. They wait for a long time in silence. Finally he says:

"You can't hear engines under water."

"I'm cold," says Jane.

"Come, we'll go to our place."

He's so sure that the man in blue is going alone to the sea that he knows (perhaps he no longer exists, perhaps he was Pierrot's unconscious invention) that he'll never see him again. And he's alone in the world with Jane, the only light in the darkness of his mind that he has not been obliged to imagine.

26

"There's another mouse. I can hear it scratching. There! Just behind us."

"It's only a frog."

"In the wall?"

"Down below, in the old lady's flowers. Frogs like flowers, everybody knows that."

"Did you ever see frogs in flowers? It's in the wall, I tell you."

"I never saw frogs in a wall either. And in summertime there are never mice in houses. Everybody knows that, too."

"And never more than two spiders."

"Just as I told you. And I killed those two. If there's more they chew each other up like old maids. Go to sleep. If you spend all your nights talking we'll really look like children with no home."

She is silent for a time, and he can hear quite clearly the gnawing in the woodwork, as well as slips and slides that end with a little thump. But he's so happy that he's willing, just to please her, to stay awake all night and eat the rodents so as not to make a noise when he kills them. He knows she's not asleep, for she breathes deeply a while then stops to listen, then draws a few quick breaths. She's wrapped in the grey blanket so as not to dirty her pale gold dress, and the blanket, above all, keeps out the things that crawl and creep in empty houses. Her head is resting on his legs, and he's sitting with his back to the plaster wall which crumbles every time he moves.

So he stops moving, for it sounds like hundreds of falling spiders, and his bottom starts going to sleep. The moonlight comes feebly through the attic window along with the mingled smells of flowers and manure, one flower especially that's almost like cinnamon but sweeter, and he doesn't know what it is, but it's surely a spice of some sort. In the shadows her pointed face shrinks still smaller, and her hair falls in waves like grass in a field.

"Plush. . ."

"Go to sleep or I'll put out the moon."

"What time is it?"

He's only too glad to shift his buttocks to get at the man's watch in his pocket. It takes a long time to see and read the pale green hands.

"After midnight. Think how you're going to look tomorrow if you don't sleep!"

"Put your hand on my skin, under my dress. Then I'll always know you're there."

"Stupid, you're lying on my legs. If I get up you'll know."

"Do you think the submarine was real?"

"If it wasn't he'd have come up. Nobody can stay more than five minutes under water."

"What if he drowned?"

"I like it better when you're scared of mice. A good swimmer can't drown if he tries."

"I was bad to him. Never saw such sad eyes. I think he played to lose so hard that he lost, and if there was no submarine he drowned himself. Do you ever think about your memory? I never do. What is it, anyway? Nobody asks."

"Memory! Well, uh. . .it's like you in my head, say. As long as I live you'll be my memory."

"You'll be mine, too. But he said women don't have a memory. Because his was Emily, and she wasn't there any longer."

She sits up suddenly and asks in a voice that comes from the depths of her stomach:

"It can't be true that Balibou's dead?"

"Of course not! I just didn't want to tell him the story."

"You had me scared," she said, lying down again.

"So it must have been the same for him. Because he didn't want to tell us about it, he said Emily was dead."

"Right. He didn't know how to play. You couldn't believe him. Now, sleep, stupid, or I'll tell your mother you're dead."

"You know, we drove past the convent. It's big and nice like a castle, beside the water, and there are trees and flowers."

"Good. That's where you're going to be after all."

"And our new house, I saw it. Not far from there. It's in a terrible place, at the end of a new street that isn't finished yet, and nobody around."

"I'm glad. Why don't you go there and get it over with. Let's not talk about it any more."

"Why are you so cross? I talk to forget I'm scared, and you get mad!"

"Because that's what you mean by leaving to go around the world with me. Telling me about the convent and the house, as if you were packing your bags. I can't tell you about the other home. I haven't seen it yet. Anyway, you swore you wouldn't be scared."

"It's not so much being scared, Pierrot. It's the first time I didn't sleep in a bed. I'll prove it."

She searches on his arm for the place where she'd bit him and keeps it for a long time against her lips. Then she drops it and sleeps for a while. He too shuts his eyes and feels a little wave of sleep that goes right to his toes. Then once more the "voice that touches more surely than a hand" is heard through the layered cloth of sleep.

"I don't hear the mice now. Do you think it's true that we were fish once?"

He doesn't reply, pretending to be asleep.

"Pierrot? Were we all fish before?"

"You woke me up. Fish? Of course. You have red eyes and scales on your arms."

"You can make jokes, I don't care. It makes me sleepy to think I'm a fish."

"Then why do you wake me up?"

"Because I want to be sure I'm the first one to fall asleep so I don't get scared."

"All right. I won't sleep. I'll wait for you."

"Leave your hand on my skin. Good-night, Pierrot."

He doesn't reply. He wonders why the man asked him to give a push. As if he'd been just a bit scared at the last moment to dive by himself. He wasn't crazy, but it was all hard to understand, including why he wanted to see them again. Maybe to give him his watch.

"Pierrot...tell me there's only half a night left?"

"It's going to rain. Are you satisfied!"

"I just wanted to know if you were sleeping. When the time comes do what I do. Imagine you're a fish. You'll go to sleep right away. Good-night."

"I'm a fish now."

"Just wait till I drop off."

And she sleeps at once. He can feel it from the weight of her head. And her hand that held his has fallen open.

Her deep, regular breathing, so confident that he wants to cry, slowly brings him closer to sleep. Through the window, in the milk-yellow moonlight, appears a wisp of something bluish, so thin, so reassuring, that he forgets not to sleep and drops off in turn, his hand catching one after the other Jane's warm, quick heartbeats, and he could go on for hours without ever having a handful.

In his other hand is the man's gold watch, which ticks much faster, like the tiny motor of an almost-invisible submarine in which there isn't room for a single thought, not even a blue one.

* * *

First it's the sound of hundreds of boots, far away, much farther than the endless corridor, perhaps tramping in snow, for if he didn't know it was boots tramping it might be nothing but rain on the roof, or the children turning all at once in their beds in the dormitory that's as long as rain on the roof. But they're boots, sure enough, for you can hear the heels. And instead of coming closer they march off down other corridors he doesn't know, and climb all over the house. Then there are long pauses, not ordered by any clacking of a rattle, and they go away again, as if the big house with the long corridors could elongate itself out into the fields of snow. And he's alone, abandoned by the old lady in the dark which in winter falls long before supper time.

Then they come, hundreds of them, all wrapped up in themselves but suddenly so angry that the boots resound as if the children had grown heavier than adults and were trying once and for all to break through the track in the corridor they'd worn thin over so many years. And now the rattles are clacking as they've never clacked, so long that everyone is caught in their jaws, and bones break and fall with a sound of metal on pavement and he hears screams of pain such as he's never heard, a laughing sob that makes him back away in terror, and the plaster at his back is running down like a barrel of salt and Jane's voice, screaming, reaches the bottom of his belly and opens it to the cold.

"Pierrot...Pierrot...Wake up! It's terrible! Can't you hear? It's the Rat's horse of death. In this house!"

"Just boots walking. You're not used to..."

She presses close to him with such violence that the wall gives way behind him and she's strangling him, her arms are so tight around his neck. Plaster is raining on their two heads.

"Wake up! It's coming up the stairs!"

She goes on screaming in his ear, her body trembling, her teeth chattering against his, she clings so tight. And he hears heavy footsteps in the house, movements of great animals rubbing their rumps against the walls, and outside the whole street is full of a madness of galloping, steel shoes trampling the night in all directions.

He too starts trembling with astonishment, holding Jane tight with all his strength to get her completely inside him so that she can withstand the noise and terror of the night. She burrows to get under his sweater, biting and scratching.

He grows a little more calm when he remembers what the Rat told him: people had kept horses in the shed, where he'd still seen some hay. But he can't understand them galloping in the dead of night as if there were a hundred of them filling the street, rushing off to come back again at once, as if someone had blocked both ends.

"They keep horses in the shed, you know," he says in a voice that has trouble getting out.

"Not right in the house!" Jane screams.

"It's right beside. A horse can't get through a house door."

"And what about the street! And everyplace! The Rat, in the night's belly, Pierrot!"

"I'm going to look."

"No! Don't move!"

She'd screamed so loudly her mother must have heard her six blocks away. The sound of his own voice had reassured him and restored his body to him.

He tries to loosen her arms and push her back so he can breathe, but she resists with a strength that astounds him, her muscles hard as steel.

"Horses. It's nothing but horses, and we're safe in the house. Let go, Jane, you're hurting."

"Talk, talk, go on talking."

"They must have let them out for a run at night when there's nobody around. And there must be people looking after them. You're not a little baby."

He strokes her hair, and it's full of dry powder that crumbles in his fingers, and he can feel her hot tears running under his sweater. She grows a little quieter, but loosens her grip only slightly.

"At least let me go and look. Then you won't be afraid."

There's no moonlight coming in the window, but he can see the reflection of the street lamp farther down, in front of the Rat's house. She takes a deep breath at last and turns him loose, saying in a pitiful voice:

"I was afraid, Pierrot, more than ever in my life."

"I know, mouse. We're not cowboys. You've got to be used to things like that."

"If you look I'm coming too. Don't leave me alone."

Downstairs in the yard a great shape is chewing at something, knocking over pots of flowers that die as quietly as a clod of earth falls apart. Farther down, toward the bridge, a horse with an enormous belly is scratching his head against a brick wall. They can hear the other horses without seeing them, at the other end, near the street with the tracks. One or two windows in the street are lit. Next door, at the Rat's house, they hear trampling and a clanking of scrap iron. Then the ruckus starts again, growing and coming toward them. Jane digs her fingernails in his arm. They come at a gallop, heavy, snorting, whinnying, jostling each other across the whole width of the street, including sidewalks. Their red manes shine under the streetlight.

"They're naked," murmurs Jane in a toneless voice.

"They're just as beautiful as the Molson horses," he adds to reassure her.

The horses pass below them with the same heavy gallop, a mass of heads with ears forward, nostrils raised to get air above the rumps of the leaders, jostling with legs and bodies, and continue under the bridge. The one rubbing his head doesn't move, but the one in the garden eating flowers bounds off to join the herd. Then there's a silence, hard breathing, and they hear men shouting at the bridge.

"That was more fun than the movies," Jane says admiringly, forgetting her fear because of the men's voices and because the horse that was climbing the stairs has left his flower bed.

"They must have got away from the livery stable. That's why they're naked. Do you want to go down and see?"

"Are you crazy, Plush? They might come back. Horses are big at night!"

"Nothing can happen. They're catching them with lassoos. That's the first movie I ever saw."

"But Pierrot, things like that never happen in our street."

"Here either, big goose! It's just to see if you really aren't afraid with me. But you are."

"You were too. You were shaking."

"Because you choked me. I never thought you were so strong. It's true you eat a lot."

"I'm hungry now, too, Plush. From being scared."

"I don't want to see you vomit after all this. We still have cookies. But only if you let me go and look."

"I'll come with you," she says, in a voice of utter despair.

Three cookies are left in Mama Pouf's bag. She takes them all and starts nibbling, almost leaning on his shoulders as they go down the narrow stairs.

In the courtyard the old woman will find nothing but mashed flowers and stems. The spice perfume that isn't cinnamon still smells strongest. Jane walks behind him, holding his waist, ready to beat a retreat at the slightest alarm.

Out in the street, he looks in the direction he couldn't see from the window, on their own side of the street. More voices are shouting down by the bridge, but he doesn't turn that way, for at the foot of the streetlamp lies the Rat's black motorbike, flat on the sidewalk, one wheel turned to the sky. Something's running out of it into the street. And fastened to the lamppost is the chain whose glimmer stretches a short distance toward Banana's raincoat, and the raincoat covers a long shape, folded in two, of which he can see no more than the feet.

Jane walks with tiny steps, putting her feet down as if she were walking on dynamite. She swallows a cookie at one gulp, and says, with her mouth full:

"It's the Rat's black horse. I was right."

He too advances slowly, his eyes fixed on another shining object that's unfamiliar to him. As they reach the lamppost the enormous horse is still on the sidewalk near the old lady's house, and he starts toward them, walking normally as if he were pulling a wagon, his head high, sniffing the breeze.

Windows are lighting up all along the street, and, farther along, men are coming out. Jane hides in a doorway and makes him stand in front of her. The horse stops in front of the passage leading to the Rat's house, where something is still poking around among the scrap iron, then turns and stops once more just under the street light, where he stretches his hind legs out until they almost touch the raincoat and urinates long and voluminously before going back into the passage.

"Pig!" says Jane, swallowing her last cookie.

Again her fear has disappeared.

Pierrot has already recognized the yellow boots sticking out from under the raincoat, but he refuses to see them until he knows what else is shining besides the chain.

He goes closer. The head with its long, black, girlish hair is bent

271

down on the chest, as if broken, and pink foam dribbles from its open mouth. The thing shining in his back is a long bayonet blade. Why Banana's raincoat?

"Don't touch! He's dead!" she cries suddenly behind him, then runs back to her refuge in the doorway.

The pool of piss mingles with what's running from the motorbike. Where the chain lies there's a big, dark stain. He lifts the raincoat at one corner. Torn pants. The other end of the chain passes between his legs over a gaping red wound. He pulls back suddenly, filled with nausea at seeing the thing lying in an open hand.

"I told you not to touch," Jane reproaches him gently.

But he can't answer for he's shaken by spasms of nausea, and vomits his heart out of an empty stomach. Each time it's as if he couldn't breathe normally again, and grows quiet. He doesn't move when the two horses emerge from the passage, one on each side of him, to take off toward the voices under the bridge.

"Why did you look?" asks Jane, pulling up her pretty dress to wipe his mouth. "It's crazy to get hurt for nothing."

He pushes her roughly away and stands alone, trembling, in the street. Then some people come, and they talk, standing around the raincoat.

"Come on," he orders.

And Jane comes back, looking at him with a world of wounded love.

"He wasn't a friend of yours."

Not until they're back in the house does he answer:

"He wasn't my friend. And he got what he deserved. But why are people such pigs? He was going to die anyway!"

She looks at him as if she'd never seen him before, and in his anger he sees that she's afraid of him, and that's even worse. He speaks softly to her as they climb the stairs:

"I'm sorry Jane. I wasn't mad at you! I shouldn't have taken you to the end of the world. The end of the world isn't such a great place. Even your mama and my aunts are better than this...."

He sits down against the wall again, and she lays her head on his legs. After a silence she asks, in the quiet voice that comes from her stomach:

"Did you never see one before? A dead man?"

"Why?"

"I often saw them. And people laughed and made jokes. It's awful for you to have never seen anything all that time and then come out and see everything all at once. We've had time to get used to it."

272

"Some things you don't get used to. The proof is, my father was a man in rebellion. Papapouf told me."

"What does rebellion mean?"

"I don't really know. Something like the Rat, I guess. When you know you've been robbed from the start. Then you hurt people...."

"That's not very nice."

"And it's when you understand more than other people about things you don't understand. Papapouf said that too. The man in blue must have been in rebellion."

"Rebellion isn't nice, and it doesn't do any good, either."

"What are you doing here, then? You're in rebellion against your mother."

"That's different. I love you. It's not the same thing at all."

"I don't know about that. I guess when you're in rebellion you do things that aren't nice. But you can do terrific things, too, like we do. If it weren't so nothing would change. By the way, I'm a liar. My father isn't an aviator. He's in rebellion."

"Why did he never come and get you? Is that the way rebellion changes things?"

"We can't understand everything. We're too little. Maybe later. Look at the Rat. A guy who can make music like him has some good things inside him that he wouldn't even know about if he didn't make music. What were those last words of the English song?"

"Do you think I remember that crazy stuff?"

He's angry again, and orders her roughly:

"Yes, you remember. Now tell me. Right away."

"He's quiet...and he doesn't move...I think. I'm not sure of the rest. Something like riding a black horse into the night's belly. You scared me again, Pierrot, as if you didn't love me."

He caresses her hair, and the rising sun shows up the white powder of the plaster in it.

"If I didn't love you I wouldn't get hurt or mad so much. The Rat was family to me in a way, but I can't explain that."

"Why not? I'm older than you!"

"I beg your pardon, I'm sure. You're going to be a fine mess when we go outside. Your hair full of plaster and your best dress full of my old house, and a big horse galloping around in your head."

"Funny, I'm sleepier now that it's light outside."

"Well, sleep now, then, or they'll see you're a lost child. And they won't take you home but to a big house like the one I'm going to."

"Will you shut up! It's our first day and you're talking about leaving me!"

"Sleep. I'll wait for you."

He stops talking, and it quiets him to see the daylight slowly lighting up her hair, and her skin where not a trace of their marriage remains, and her dress, so dirty now. Then he hears people going in and out of the Rat's house next door. And he can see Isabelle again, and his hands tremble because he'd like to kill the Rat all over gain. Then he feels sick again, but just the way you do when you spin around too long and it goes on after you stop.

"Jane."

"Yes."

"Are you asleep?"

"I think so."

"What you did with me...the...green babies, was that the first time?"

She grumbles a little, for she was half asleep, and replies from far inside:

"Wanting to? Of course! What do you think!"

"What do you mean, wanting to?"

It's the Pierrot he doesn't know, but who, he realizes, can sometimes take his place, asking these questions that surprise him and make him a little ashamed, like his old notebook about Saint Agnes, but Jane is here with her head on his knees, alive and warm, the only real warmth in his life that he can touch and breathe, as if he were a little man on his way in life, and he doesn't really know if it's shame he feels or what name he might give to the contraction in his stomach.

She half-opens one eye, and he sees more white than gold, and speaks as if it cost her a great effort:

"There was a dirty grown-up. I was very little. In the stairway to the alley..."

With all his strength he refuses to retreat behind his block of ice and take shelter there. He goes deeper into his fear as he says:

"And was he able to..."

"He hurt me a lot," she groans. "Mama even...the police..."

She turns her head to the wall to get the sun out of her eyes and breathes deeply against his stomach, her nostrils swelling and sinking like a bird's breast, and the sun, which is brightening as fast as the moon rises at night, sprinkles gold everywhere in the hair that he'd now like to push away and cover with plaster until it was white and then wet it to make it stick and never go away. His disgust is in his legs, as if it was the dirty grown-up lying on them, and he's in rebellion, and knows there's humiliation in rebellion, for you discover that the most precious thing isn't so precious because it existed before for others who had only to take it without feeling anything or trembling at the prodigious gift, the way you pick up a melon in the street, a thing, no more, and despite all his efforts and his long-established habits acquired perforce over so many years, the block of ice slips away from him, and he can't stay at a distance, and shame empties him and he weeps, stupidly, forgetting that from the first months in the big house he had made himself only one rule which he'd always obeyed: never to cry, because you can always find the ice and make yourself small inside, but now he can't for there's no room for anything inside him but the emptied look of the man in blue and his voice that spoke all by itself, separate from him, saying women don't have the memory of their disgust and you're always hungry for what you don't have. . .and he realizes, because he's drowning, that there never was a submarine, and the best swimmer, as Jane said, can't cross the ocean.

His tears are calm, frozen, silent, running down his cheeks, and he manages slowly to get his distance back, to relegate the green babies, Isabelle, and the Rat to the limbo where there is already a photo with a lacy frame and a house that's crumbling and has no memory and a face in rebellion with a raised arm striking the air.

A last frozen tear drops on Jane's eye, and she jumps up with a start, smiling like the sun, then sees him:

"Plush! You're crying!"

She kisses him, licks his tears away, suddenly tremendously alive and ready for any voyage. He smiles as quickly as he can, a smile that's had a sleepless night.

"Plush, my Plush, I don't want you to cry, not ever. You'll forget the Rat. We're going to say good morning to Mama Pouf and then we'll go up on the mountain or over to the island."

"Easy now, stupid. It's the sun in my eyes. I'm not used to waking up in the sun. I was sleeping. The plaster dust does it, too."

"Why don't we clean this place up? It could look nice! I like that little window in the roof."

He hugs her tightly as if he'd break her bones, and he's shaken by sobs, trembling with happiness that she's there and alive, so little in his arms, her skin so soft and warm, her voice happier than the water of fountains, her eyes made of moon and sunlight; and he bites her, licks her and tastes her with the greed of someone who has almost died of hunger. Her smile has washed his brain with a great rush of clear water and he leaps back to life, on her arm, in the fullness of her vitality, and he's the happiest little bastard in the world, and he almost threw away St. Agnes' pear!

"You're crazy, Plush! We need water and soap and brooms. Thérèse could help. And we'll pick up the old lady's flowers."

"And plant trees all over the bridge and dig a little creek for the frogs that climb in the walls at night."

He stands up and sparks the dust out of his pants, and she sneezes. Then he brushes the snow from her red grass that could do with a raking.

Through the window he sees Skiff and Banana crossing the streetcar tracks. Banana is carrying the guitar like a suitcase, and he's bigger and sloppier than ever in a pink sweater and green pants. There are people all over in the street, but the form under the raincoat has disappeared. Then his legs turn to lead and his joy leaves him abruptly.

"Jane," he says, "our trip is over. The police are here."

She runs to look, but isn't upset.

"Quick, we'll go out another way. You said there was an attic."

But he hasn't time to answer, for the first blue cap shows at the top of the stairs.

"What are you kids doing here?"

"This is our place," he says icily.

Two other policemen and a man dressed like an ordinary man follow the first one.

"He says it's his place."

"His place," says a policeman that he recognizes, "is at his uncle's, across from the church. Her too. She's Madame Power's daughter."

"Yeah?" laughs the man in ordinary clothes. "Madame Power's daughter, eh? What a hope!"

The policeman he knows is Eugène, the one who put him up on the big horse.

"You kept hanging around with the Rat, I hear. I warned you. Where were you last night?"

"Here. At our place," his icy voice replies.

"This hasn't been your place for quite a while! Ever since that bum of a dad of yours disappeared."

He leaps at him, but they have him pinned in a second, hands behind his back, pawing at nothing, humiliated in front of Jane.

276

She decides to take a high tone, in her high-heeled voice that makes them all laugh:

"It's more his place than yours. How dare you come in here without knocking?"

"We'll tell you that at the station, Red."

"I am Miss Power. My father is an aviator and he'll see to you when he comes back."

"OK, I'm knocking, Miss Power. Will you answer us now?" says the ordinary man, rapping on the wall from which a chunk of plaster falls on his shoes.

"Look at that! We can't let kids play in a dangerous old house like this. You were here all night?"

"Yes. We're running away for life. We're married now. So we can do what we like."

"We'll talk about that. Did you hear the horses?"

"Of course. We're not deaf."

"And before the horses?"

"We were asleep."

"And the horses scared her so bad we didn't see anything else," Pierrot hastens to add.

"Did you know the Rat?"

"Eugène just told you."

The ordinary man scratches his head, puzzled.

"You know Eugène, too?"

"We come from the same street. I ride horses with him. I'm not scared of horses."

"People said you were the first ones to go near the..."

He seems to be looking for the right word.

"...near the motorbike. The raincoat didn't belong to him?"

"I don't know."

"You didn't see anybody when you went out?"

"There were people everywhere, right down to the bridge."

"And you came back here right away?"

"Yes. Three o'clock is children's bedtime."

"How did you know what time it was?"

He takes out the watch and hands it over without speaking.

The ordinary man takes it and examines it closely.

"Where did you take this from?"

"Somebody gave it to me."

"Who? The Rat?"

"No. The man in blue. Before you ask, he left yesterday in his submarine."

"His submarine, eh? Well, I'll keep this for a while. You'll get it back. It belongs to an important gentleman. Something bad happened to him."

"We know. He was very sad," says Jane in an even more grown-up tone.

"Don't you have a sister called Emily, you?"

"Maybe you'd like her address! I never heard of her."

"We'll have time for a longer chat," says the ordinary man with a kind smile. "Eugène, since you know them, take them home and tell their parents to keep them available, it's a real pleasure to talk to these children."

They go as they came, saying no more. Eugène pushes the children toward the stairs and brings up the rear, whistling softly. Outside, the old lady, crouching in the sand, tries to put together new clods with her broken plants.

He gives Jane his hand, sure now that their voyage is over, that this is the last time he'll be walking with the squirrel. For they'll both be shut in the rest of the day, and tomorrow's Tuesday and there's only one way out: jump over the wall of the new big house, just as Marcel did so often, until he grew big enough to get sunk in the North Pole sea. But where will Jane be? How will he find her again?

Her mother opens the door first, her face haggard, her hair mussed, not as slim and pretty as usual in her big green dressing-gown full of cigarette burns. It's really strange to see this ice-cold woman crying like a child. She pulls Jane close to her and caresses her nervously, as if she'd really been afraid of losing her. Jane breaks away to give him a kiss, weeping like her mother, and she shouts in defiance of the whole world:

"For life, Pierrot! I swear it!"

The door of Uncle Nap's apartment is wide open, and Aunt Rose is contemplating the scene with her grumpiest face. He's astonished to hear Jane's mother say softly to him:

"You can come and see us anytime. I'll be staying home from now on."

Aunt Rose pushes him into the apartment without a word. His uncle barely lifts his fork to watch him go past. Eugénie turns her back to him.

He flops on the green sofa and goes to sleep at once in the irreparable grief of having discovered a mama in Jane's mother. He doesn't cry, but no mama has ever made him so sad.

27

The Russians are advancing faster than the Americans now. I don't understand the Germans, letting them through like that...."

His jowls hanging over his hard detachable collar, gazing into the distance out the window toward those far battlefields, Uncle Nap has issued his daily war bulletin after his last gulp of coffee. He removes his napkin from around his neck, wipes his mouth, gets up, moves his lips over words that only he can hear, and leaves to go to the bathroom.

Aunt Rose steals a moment to sit down. She too looks out the window and mouths words that remain unpronounced. Aunt Maria is still in bed. The doctor had come the day before and it's definite now, she's going this week to a big house, the hospital that scared the Rat so much he bought a gun which he finally used only for his dog.

When Pierrot awoke he found on his uncle's chair his old overalls and his prisoner's shirt, very clean and well pressed, and even softer now, with the pliable softness that comes of much wear. On the rug are his boots – their new brown colour almost as fine as that of the shiny Buick condemned to wait in the garden until the war's end, which Uncle Nap now believes will come much later than he had thought, and business is going better than before because the Americans are spending so much money.

It was so natural to find his old uniform again that he hadn't asked any questions. His feet, which have grown unaccustomed to the boots, hurt a little, especially at the ankles, but he knows he was born with feet meant for boots and he'll only have to run in them once to forget he hasn't worn them for seven weekday Sundays. He has noticed his new suit, his linen pants and his sweaters folded neatly in the same flat cardboard box on the dining-room table, but he felt nothing special about it because the great break came yesterday and mentally he has already left town, and is more withdrawn into himself than when he arrived. The ice barrier is solid before his eyes and once again he can look at everything with the perfect detachment of one who has seen nothing, with Meeow's new and impassive eyes.

Aunt Rose starts her tambourine on the oilcloth table cover, and her fingers, reddened and worn by so many Monday washes, actually make the metal of the table ring.

"I'm keeping your new clothes here, heaven knows what would happen to them in that place. But they're yours, and I'll keep them, and you can wear them any time you come back."

He doesn't answer. He's wondering if one couldn't cut off that great wart on her nose, on which she squanders so much powder. She sighs at his silence, and if there's any emotion stirring in her, that rough voice fails to express it.

"Poor little manikin. I'm sorry for you....But what can we do?"

Uncle Nap comes back, his felt hat on his head and an umbrella on his arm despite the bright sunshine outside. He lays a blue bank note on the buffet and, hurrying as if he were late for something, he says without turning back:

"That's for a little pocket money over there. Good-day now...."

And he's gone.

"You could have said thanks," says his aunt, reproachfully.

"I don't need money. I never will," he replies from inside his submarine.

"You'll have to ask Aunt Maria's pardon, too. She's got six months to live, and she's so frightened."

"I know. That's why she drinks beer."

"I don't know how it is at your age that you haven't got a little feeling for others. It doesn't cost anything to say you're sorry, and it can help somebody. We'll stop and see you at the home on the way to her hospital. It's not so far away."

"I'll tell you I'm sorry. Because you tried, and it's not your fault if you didn't understand very much."

"But there's nothing to understand, except you're a little wild animal! As the policeman said yesterday, 'The only thing they learn there is how to fight. Like dogs in a cage!' Marcel was worse. But you're so little!"

"As far as your promise goes..."

"What promise?"

"To the photo. You don't need to worry. I'll never make her ashamed of me."

"You did already."

"Well. I think I'll go play outside for a while."

"Don't run away. They've got your picture everyplace now."

"I'm not ready yet."

"Of course you're ready. You've nothing else to take along."

"I mean ready to run away."

He goes out without a glance at Jane's apartment door. It's true the police came to take their pictures yesterday, singly and together, and asked them a bunch of questions, almost all about the man in blue, as if he were the one who'd been nailed to the sidewalk with a long blade.

Before the church stands a dusty hearse which no one has time to wash between corpses. There's no one around, no bells ringing.

And so, he goes toward the church, for it's the only thing here that's a little like the other place, and you can think all alone even if there are hundreds of others around, for it's big and you're not allowed to talk.

But there aren't hundreds of people, just the few that he had liked. Gérard is there, in the front pew, twisting his cap as if he had somewhere else to go. Gérard looks over at him with a nice, embarrassed smile and a little wave of his cap. Then, not far in front, are Mama and Papa Pouf, Isabelle and Thérèse and, finally, right at the other end, closest to the black thing, the Rat's mother, all alone, and you can hear her coughing or sobbing even that far away. He turns around, for he's heard a movement behind him. Banana and Skiff standing in the shadows, come nearer to him, then stop as if there were an unseen boundary a few feet from Gérard's wide shoulders. He goes back toward them through this brief no-man's land, for they're holding their hands out. They say, in strange voices that are supposed to be serious and filled with emotion but only turn out funny:

"Our sympathy, Pierrot. He was very fond of you."

The word "fond," coming from them, sends a chill up his back, and he leaves them and crosses to the pew where the Rat's mother is kneeling. He kneels beside her. She wasn't coughing, she was crying, but saying her rosary at the same time, out loud, and it sounds a little like the psalms at vespers. He stays beside her for a while, wondering if she notices he's there, then he takes her arm, kisses the salt on her cheeks and whispers:

"I'll come and see you. We were friends."

She looks at him as if he were under ten feet of water, then astonishes him with a request:

"Tell me the way he used to say, 'Don't cry, old girl!' "

"Don't cry, old girl," he murmurs softly.

"Thank you, Pierrot."

He presses her arm again, glances blindly at the silent cherubs on the ceiling, then goes to sit down beside the Pouf family.

He'd never thought they might bury the Rat. Now that he's seen the cemetery he has no idea where they could put him. It's not his style.

He's rather pleased with himself, for he feels comfortable now within this new rift in time where nothing seems to touch him. Policemen are supposed to come with a car an hour from now to take him away. He doesn't have to listen for the Angelus or worry about the mood his uncle may be in or try to find out how you're supposed to act if you're an ordinary child in a city street. He doesn't have to think about the Chinese boy or whether he's lost his taste for ants, or about Balibou who's no more than a cat that's back in the bag, or the Blue Man who wasn't even a whiff of smoke, for smoke he never saw. And he doesn't have to worry what might happen, for it's happened already, nor about pictures, or books that certainly have hidden things in what seem to be harmless words and pages, but it's all lies, and you have to wait for life if you want to really find out. Nothing surprises him, for every time he looked at a star, which is the only thing so clean you can be sure it's untouchable, it was very cold. And the warmth you can touch always has something false about it and a little dirty, like everything living, and outside the chateau people act exactly as if they too were within walls, though these walls were hard to see and hurt more, for when you run into walls you're surprised when you don't know they're there.

"Don't turn around. Mama's behind us."

The little voice is touching the back of his neck with a cold breath. She kisses him, and he knows he has raspberry on one cheek. Then she puts her hand in his and stays a long time without moving, as if she were praying. Then he ends the story, also without moving, as if he were saying a rosary:

"Ten white bears pull the caboose past the North Pole. But as the man in blue said, the world is turning the wrong way now, so every step they take the world turns back just as much and the white bears go on like that to the end of time. And in the country of the Great Cold, you and I get bluer all the time. Amen!"

"Why did they dress you up like a prisoner again? It's as if I'd never known you!"

"It's so you can forget me. That's the point."

"Pierrot, it's too cold in here. Come for a walk in the sun with me, one last time."

He looks at her at last, sure of his strength, sure that he can leave her as the man in blue left the two of them, and that he won't have to ask her to give him a push. But minuscule tears, little crystals chipped from the ice floe, catch and hold the light of stars on her pale cheeks, and the gentle fire in her hair will never die for he can compare it with the sanctuary light and it's not at all the same thing, for gold doesn't waver in the air, it vibrates with such intensity that he has to turn away or the ice block before his eyes will threaten to melt.

"I can't. I have to say good-bye to Mama Pouf's family."

She turns around to see if her mother is listening:

"She says Emily will never come back. I think it was the thought of Emily made her start liking me."

"Emily doesn't need to come back. She's grown up already."

"This time I won't be caught. I've started collecting things I'll need. She'll never know where..."

"You don't even know where you'll be."

"No, but Mama Pouf told me she'd bring me to see you. She knows where."

But he can't go on talking to her like this, whispering, in a church, when he wants to fill himself with her until she takes up all the room there is, so that in the other place he'll lose her so slowly there'll be some left for years. He leaves the pew and sees Mama Pouf smile under the short veil that makes her head look like a big bell.

But at the door he sees that Jane didn't follow him, and it's Banana and Skiff who escort him out.

"We were hoping you'd come out, we're in a hurry," says Banana.

"We did all we could to help him. The horses, we did that. We let them out so everybody would come into the street and they'd have to leave the Rat alone."

"But we took too long, and we shouldn't have let out so many. Ten might have done it."

"And he wouldn't leave, either. I'm in my village, he said. He meant this neighbourhood, his hole in the ground."

"It was army guys did it. Those cowards, going on their boat to-morrow, we'll never find them again. A lovely war, eh! He took my raincoat because he was cold on his bike."

"He'd have been dead in two months anyway. He burned the candle at both ends, it never burned fast enough for him," says Skiff, handing him a letter.

"He asked us to give it to you when it was all over. He knew, eh? I'll tell you where for the guitar whenever you want it."

Jane arrives as they leave after raising their hands to their fore-heads in salute.

A Molson beer wagon passes with a rattling of barrels and clat-ter of hoofs, without slowing down. Then a second follows, slow-ing a little for the driver to shout at Skiff and Banana:

"Is that the Rat's Cadillac?"

He receives no answer and whips up his horses again.

"Mama kept me till I promised I wouldn't run away with you. As if we could. Maybe..."

She kisses his neck and runs her hands over his face, still crying.

"I love you, Pierrot. For life. We're married!"

"I'll come back and make your wedding slippers," he replies, thinking of the letter which he'd like to open.

"We didn't think of that! I can write you too!" she says, suddenly happy.

He moves away and opens the envelope. The letter is written in the blackest ink he's ever seen, and the writing is very elegant and careful. The Rat must have been able to draw well. He reads:

> I was the only one in the neighbourhood waiting for you, as I'd promised Marcel, for there weren't many families left from before. The others are immigrants, like your uncle.
>
> I'm sorry I didn't help you more. I hadn't time. When I knew they wanted to put gas in my lung I knew I was finished. Why should I get you mixed up in my crazy business?
>
> Especially I want to ask your pardon for the spectacle of life, which you shouldn't have seen. But Isabelle and I really love each other, and you'll understand later on. The only rea-son I would have liked to live was for her. I'm giving you my

guitar which Banana will guard for you, and Skiff and somebody else will guard him. It's the most beautiful thing I ever owned. I'm sure you can learn it. I ran into the *anglais* who taught me the song and I've copied it for you, because that's what it is to be a man, and I'm sure you'll learn English too, for the days of bums are over and you're going to get an education. So you'll learn the truth better than I did, if that's possible. I hope the squirrel will go on loving you, but if I were in your place I'd be worried. She's too beautiful, and she doesn't belong in our world. Goodbye, Pierrot. Marcel will tell you all the things we did.

The Rat

But after the words of the song he wrote his own name: Gaston.

He doesn't feel like asking Jane to read him the English words, and puts the letter back in the envelope.

"It was from the Rat," he tells her. "He knew he was going to die and he wrote to say he was sorry."

"I don't understand, but that was nice," says Jane.

The others are coming out of church. Gérard first, who murmurs, before hurrying away:

"We won't let you down, little guy."

Then Mama Pouf who, on the church steps, seems even bigger than usual.

"Henri spoke to your uncle," she informs him after a kiss. "But he got on his high horse and said he was the one responsible. But you're coming back for Christmas, and we're allowed to go and see you there. Here, I brought you a little present. It's some toffee I made especially for you. Don't open it up in front of this little greedy-guts. We'll be talking about you every day, eh mouse?"

He doesn't dare tell her that he hates toffee, and he's delighted at the thought he can give it to Jane, who looks suddenly lost. Her mother is standing discreetly aside.

"Well! I'm proud of our boots, that's good work!" says Papapouf laughing.

"Wretched man!" cries Mama Pouf. "How can you be proud of painting boots for prisoners!"

Then Isabelle kneels in front of him and kisses him, opening her great eyes, as big as Meeow's but moistened and milky. She hugs him very tight:

"I'm sorry, Pierrot, that I hurt you so much. But he and I were really in love. You couldn't know that. I was his life."

285

"I'm the one who should say I'm sorry," he answers, stumbling in his shame.

Then Thérèse, warm as the inside of a loaf and embarrassed at being there, looking for something to say:

"I promised to get thin if you'd get out quicker. But it's hard to do, and it's not fair. Jane eats all the time and she stays little."

"I promised too," says Jane. "We're going to help each other."

He goes off with her toward their apartment, for he can't stay icy in the midst of all this warmth and he's in a hurry to re-read word for word what the Rat had written, and he'd almost like Jane to translate the words of the song again for him now, but he's nowhere and everywhere, lost as he's never been, and is starting to feel as if he were the one being buried. His heart jumps fast inside him in his own absence, for the policemen are already there, waiting in their car.

"Not like that! Without any warning!" Jane is indignant.

He offers her Mama Pouf's package.

"You're going to look at this for two years and think about me, and if you haven't eaten it by then we'll get married again," he promises, laughing.

"I swear it. If only we'd slept at Mama Pouf's place..."

He climbs the stairs quickly.

"I'd have had to go just the same. We're going to be too little for a long time yet before we decide."

Aunt Rose is waiting for him in the open door, an envelope in her hand.

"Quick. This is your money from your uncle. You two will see each other at Christmas anyway."

She stands watching their last kiss, then pushes him away toward the stairs. She goes down with him to the landing and there she kisses him very quickly on the cheek, and he can feel the hairs on her face.

"I love you, Pierrot, I love you!...."

Jane shouts this to him until he's in the car.

And away he goes, between his two guards, toward other walls, away from this brief gift of life like a great sea on which he hasn't had time to watch a single wave approach. The streets he's barely come to know are distorted in the melted ice water in his eyes. Away toward other interminable days, to Justin, Nicolas and all the others who put their hearts on ice in order to wait for Christmases outside and other marvels which, though they don't know it yet, are strangely like the marvels inside, like the *later on* which even grown-ups still expect even when they've lost all reason to do so, and the real life and liberty that are as lacking outside as within the walls but suddenly are there in a voice that touches your stomach or a laugh as fresh as the sound of fountains, the miracle which really can happen, for he's known Jane, Jane who, by her very existence, stems all the injustice of the world (for there was the Rat, too).

When the car enters the walls he discovers again, for the first time since he left the other big house, a presence which has never had a precise form for him, not a movement, not a voice, but which has always been like music – there was no other word for it – a kind of music which has always kept him from despair and made him believe in the miracle of laughter and even in the lies of the Blue Man, a music to which he has never been able to give the name of tenderness, for he can't remember that, but which has survived the snow-white forehead, cold as stone, in the beautiful satin bed.

He goes alone into the house.

"You can come and see me Sundays," he says to them. "And you've got my picture if I ever get lost."

He hears no tramping of boots. The sunlight is the colour of a juicy pear, and birds are singing in the silence which takes the form of interminable corridors.

They had let him play in the park awhile, but there was a chain, whirling so fast he could see no more than a great disc of light. And the golden foam is extinguished by a forehead cold as snow.